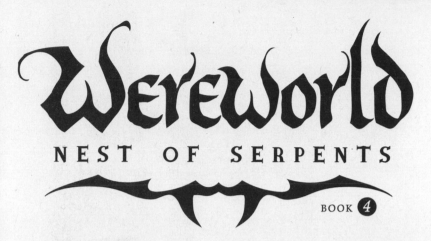

Wereworld

NEST OF SERPENTS

BOOK 4

CURTIS JOBLING

PUFFIN BOOKS

PUFFIN BOOKS
An imprint of Penguin Random House LLC
375 Hudson Street
New York, New York 10014

First published in the United Kingdom in 2013 by Puffin UK
First published in the United States of America by Viking,
an imprint of Penguin Young Readers Group, 2013
Published by Puffin Books, an imprint of Penguin Random House LLC, 2015

THE LIBRARY OF CONGRESS HAS CATALOGED THE VIKING EDITION AS FOLLOWS:
Jobling, Curtis.
Nest of serpents / by Curtis Jobling.
p. cm.— (Wereworld ; bk. 4)
Summary: "The war in Lyssia is thrown into an entirely new direction, transforming
Hector into Drew's most dangerous enemy yet."—Provided by publisher.
ISBN 978-0-670-78457-8 (hc)
[1. Werewolves—Fiction. 2. Adventure and adventurers—Fiction. 3. Fantasy.] I. Title.
PZ7.J5785Nes 2013   [Fic]—dc23   2012018608

Puffin Books ISBN 978-0-14-242193-2

Printed in the United States of America
Book design by Jim Hoover

1 3 5 7 9 10 8 6 4 2

Dedicated to the memory of
Tim Parry and Johnathan Ball

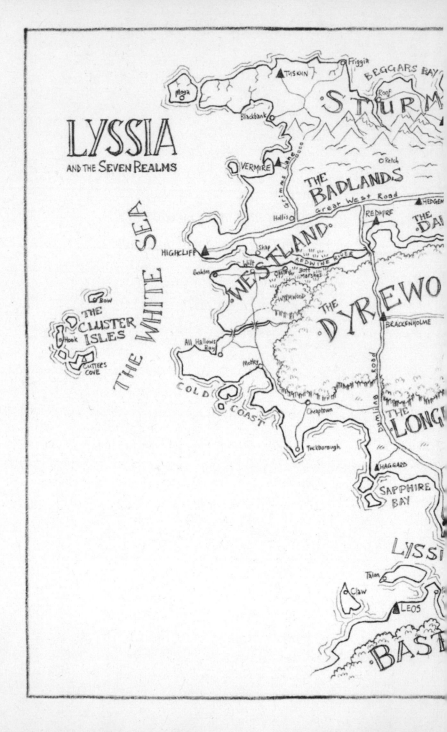

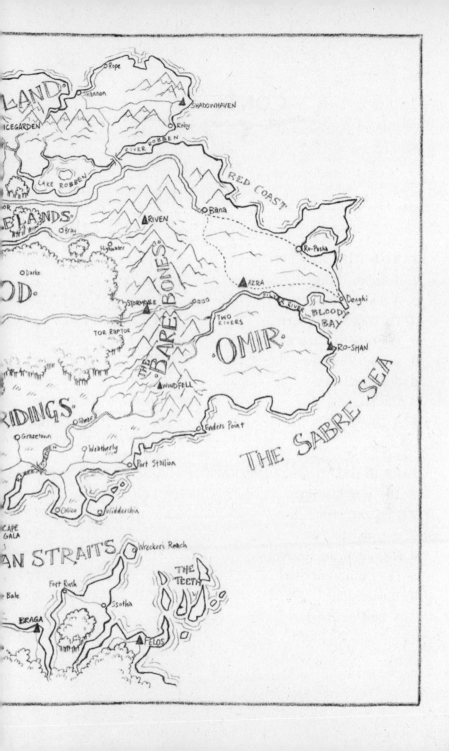

CONTENTS

CAST OF CHARACTERS

Wolflords

Drew Ferran, last of the Gray Wolves, rightful king of Westland

Wergar the Wolf, former king of Westland, Drew's biological father, deposed and killed by King Leopold

Queen Amelie, White Wolf, dowager queen of Westland, widow of Wergar and Leopold, mother of Drew and Lucas

Catlords and Human Allies

King Leopold the Lion, deceased tyrant king of Westland, father of Lucas, husband to Queen Amelie

Prince Lucas, deposed lion prince of Westland, son of King Leopold and Queen Amelie, Drew's half-brother

Lord Onyx, Pantherlord, the Beast of Bast

Lady Opal, Pantherlady, sister of Onyx

Field Marshal Tiaz, Tigerlord and commander of the Catlord army

Frost, albino Catlord army commander slain by Trent Ferran

Captain Stephan, nephew of Sheriff Muller

Sheriff Muller, Bandit-lord of the Badlands

Bearlords and Human Allies

Duke Bergan, Lord of Brackenholme, head of the Wolf's Council

Broghan, Bergan's oldest son, now dead

Whitley, Bergan's daughter and a member of the Greencloaks

Duke Henrik, White Bear, Lord of Icegarden, cousin of Bergan

Lady Greta, White Bear, magister, sister of Henrik

Baron Redfern, uncle of Bergan

Captain Reuben Fry, archer from Sturmland

Master Hogan, old scout, Whitley's mentor

Captain Harker, commander of the Watch

Captain Harlan, guard at Icegarden
Quist, senior Greencloak
Tristam, Greencloak
Machin, Greencloak

Foxlords
Lady Gretchen of Hedgemoor, former fiancée of Prince Lucas
Earl Gaston, deceased ruler of Hedgemoor, Gretchen's father
Duchess Rainier, residing ruler of Brackenholme, wife of Bergan,
    mother of Broghan and Whitley

The Ratking
Vorjavik, War Marshal for the Bastians
Vanmorten, Lord Chancellor for the Bastians
Vankaskan, dark magister to whom Hector was once apprenticed,
    killed by Drew
Vorhaas, twin of Vorjavik
Vex, youngest ratlord

Hawklords
Baron Gryffin, former leader of the Hawklords of Windfell, now
    deceased, father of Shah
Lady Shah, healer, daughter of Gryffin
Red Rufus, warrior from Windfell

Crowlords
Lord Rook, deceased leader of Crows of Riven
Count Croke, leader of the Crows of Riven
Lord Scree, son of Count Croke
Baron Skeer, ruler of Windfell
Lord Flint, messenger for Onyx

Eaglelords
Count Carsten, leader of the Hawklords, brother of Baron Baum
Baron Baum, leader of the Hawklords, brother of Count Carsten

Staglords and Human Allies
Duke Manfred of Stormdale, missing member of the Wolf's Council
Lord Reinhart, son of Manfred, acting leader of Stormdale
Lord Milo, son of Manfred, younger brother of Reinhart
Lady Mia, Duke Manfred's youngest child
Earl Mikkel, deceased brother of Manfred
Baron Hoffman, Lord Reinhardt's great-uncle
Magister Siegfried, advisor to Lord Reinhart

Sir Howard, knight serving Duke Manfred
Sir Palfrey, knight serving Duke Manfred

Boarlords and Human Allies
Baron Hector, ruler of Redmire and the Ugri, dark magister, former
  member of the Wolf's Council
Baron Huth, Hector's deceased father
Vincent-vile, the phantom of Hector's dead twin brother
Magister Wilhelm, healer of Stormdale, brother of Baron Huth

Ringlin, captain of the Boarguard, senior advisor, and Hector's
  henchman
Ibal, member of the Boarguard and Hector's henchman

Other Werelords
King Faisal, the Jackal King of Omir
Lord Conrad, Horselord leader of the defense in Cape Gala
Duke Brand, the Bull of Calico
Count Vega, the Sharklord, deposed Pirate Prince of the Cluster
  Isles, member of the Wolf's Council and Sea Marshal under
  Drew, presumed to be killed by Hector
Baron Bosa, Whalelord of Moga
Kraken Ghul, Squidlord and current ruler of the Cluster Isles
Baron Ewan, Ramlord of Haggard
Queen Slotha, Walrus Queen of Tuskun, killed by Hector
Vala, evil Wereserpent worshiped by the Wyldermen

Romari
Baba Soba, a wise woman of Romari
Stirga, sword-swallower
Yuzhnik, fire-eater and strongman
Baba Korga, a wise woman of the Romari
Rolff, Baba Korga's mute companion

Thieves' Guild
Bo Carver, Lord of thieves
Hitch, thief
Pick, young girl thief

Ugri
Creep, Ugri scout
Two Axes, Ugri warrior

Drew's Human Family
Trent Ferran, Drew's adopted brother, former member of the
    Lionguard
Mack Ferran, Drew's adoptive father, father of Trent, killed by the
    Lionguard
Tilly Ferran, Drew's adoptive mother, mother of Trent, killed by
    Vanmorten

Wyldermen
Blacktooth, Wylderman chieftain
Darkheart, Vala's most faithful disciple

PART I

THE CALM BEFORE

I

TAKE NO CHANCES

"DID YOU HIT him, master?"

The Lionguard scout lowered his bow, ignoring his apprentice. He stared out across the Longridings, squinting through the twilight at the fleeing Greencloak. Gradually, the rider began to slouch in his saddle as his mount slowed, weaving up a rocky incline. The bowman grinned as he saw the distant figure keel to one side, sliding from his steed and hitting the frozen earth in a crumpled heap.

"Have you ever known me to miss?" the scout finally replied, stowing his bow alongside the quiver on his saddle before clambering back onto his own horse.

His companion, a youth yet to see eighteen summers, grinned with delight. For one so young, he'd seen more than his fair share of bloodshed, having served his apprenticeship in the Lionguard scouts under his master's watchful eye. The boy wasn't shy about getting his blade wet: that would serve him well in the coming months as the Catlord armies mopped up the remnants of their enemies' ragtag force, scattered across the Seven Realms.

The scout had served in the army of Westland for three score years, his bow defending him against enemies of Wolf and Lion alike as they had fought for the throne. As a mortal man, he could never truly understand the noble therianthropes—their might, their majesty, and the old magicks—and it wasn't his place to question. His allegiances may have changed over time, but the role had remained the same: a life spent in servitude to the shape-shifting Werelords who ruled Lyssia.

"Let's see what we've bagged," said the scout as he spurred his horse on, his young protégé riding close behind as they raced across the barren slopes toward the fallen Greencloak.

Traveling apart from their comrades allowed the scout and his apprentice to move swiftly and stealthily across the Longridings, deep into hostile territory. Powerful as the Catlord army was in the south, the grasslands were still untamed, harboring the enemies of Prince Lucas the Lion throughout. Many of the Horselords had fled to Calico, hiding behind the coastal city's enormous seawalls, while others remained in the wilds. The Werestallions weren't the only danger to the Lion's forces in the Longridings: the traveling mortals known as the Romari had sworn fealty to the Werelord Drew Ferran, last of the Werewolves and the inspiration for this bloody civil war throughout the Seven Realms. The Romari were unpredictable and unconventional: they waged war through subterfuge and terrorism, striking the Catlord forces on their fringes, at their weakest points, before disappearing back into the grasslands. The scout and his charge had expected to run across the Romari; stumbling upon a Greencloak had been a surprise.

"What's a soldier of the Woodland Realm doing out in the Longridings, master?" called the youth from behind, his red cloak flapping in the stiff winter breeze.

"A straggler or deserter, perhaps," the man cried back. "Maybe he was left behind after the taking of Cape Gala."

"He could be a spy from Brackenholme!"

It was well known that the men of the Woodland Realm were aligned with the Wolf, which made this fool fair game in the eyes of the scout. They had encountered him by chance, the two Lionguard soldiers spying the lone rider as they had all crested hillocks in the grasslands; they were dangerously close and within hailing distance. While the Greencloak had spurred his horse away, the scout had leapt down with practiced ease, his bow quick to hand, and sent an arrow sailing on its way. He had taken only one shot: he rarely took more.

"Whoever he was, and wherever he was heading, his

message won't arrive." The man began to slow his mount as they neared the fallen woodlander, bringing their horses up the rock-strewn slope to where their enemy lay. "His war's over."

Twenty feet up the slope, the Greencloak lay motionless, facedown on the frozen earth, his horse nearby, its head bowed solemnly. A quarterstaff lay beside the body, hinting at the soldier's profession as a scout. The old tracker kept his eyes fixed on the fallen foe, although he could sense the movements of his companion beside him, keen to investigate. He heard the dry *shlick* of the young Redcloak's hunting knife sliding out of its leather sheath. The apprentice jumped down and began walking forward, shifting the dagger in his grasp as he approached the still woodlander. The thick green cloak covered the body like a death shroud, the hood obscuring the back of the man's head, only the scuffed brown leather of his boots visible, poking out from the hem of the long emerald cloth. A loud creak made the youth stop and turn. His master's bow was drawn and aimed at the body on the ground. With a sharp *twang* the arrow whistled into the body, joining the earlier one, buried deep in the Greencloak's back. The apprentice's eyes widened momentarily before he nodded.

"Best take no chances," said the scout as the young Redcloak covered the remaining distance to the body.

The apprentice kicked one of the fallen rider's legs, and the booted foot wobbled lifelessly. He looked back at his master and smiled. It was a brief moment of contentment, followed swiftly by a sensation of pure horror as the leg he'd just kicked lashed out, sweeping his own from under him and sending him crashing to the ground.

The scout's horse reared up, suddenly alarmed, as the felled Greencloak jumped into action. The old Lionguard let go of his weapon, the saddle quiver spilling its contents as bow and arrows clattered to the ground. The rider snatched at his reins in panic as the youth and the woodlander wrestled on the ground. The apprentice lashed out with his dagger, and his enemy raised a forearm to deflect the blade. In the split second before the weapon struck home, the Redcloak caught sight of his opponent's face. It wasn't a man at all, but a girl, her big brown eyes wide and fearful as she fought for her life. The hunting knife bit into her forearm, tearing flesh and scoring bone. The girl let loose a roar of pain.

The scout heard it, clear as a bell. The cry was deep, animalistic, primal. He'd heard it before, on the battlefield long ago, back in the time of the last Werewar. He'd switched sides, taking the Red at the first opportunity, and swearing fealty to King Leopold as the Lion seized Westland from Wergar the Wolf. The scout had been there when they'd brought Duke Bergan, the lord of Brackenholme, to his knees at the gates of Highcliff. That roar and this one were unmistakable. They were the roars of a Bearlord, and they chilled him to his core.

Whitley had struggled to imagine any greater agony than that of an arrow in the back. She hadn't had to wonder for long, with a second arrow joining the first as the Lionguard scouts approached her motionless form. Gritting her teeth, she thanked Brenn that the thick cloth of her cloak had hidden the telltale trembling of her shaking body. By chance, the arrows had missed her heart, thanks to her leather armor slowing the momentum of the shafts as they'd lanced through her torso. The injuries wouldn't prove fatal to a therian such as Whitley, but the pain was still immeasurable. She could feel blood pooling inside her breastplate, on the flesh of her belly, hot against her cold skin. The boot to her leg had told her it was time to act, her survival instinct kicking in as she brought the man to the ground in a tangle of limbs.

These two were dangerous, no doubt; scouts, just like her, searching for her friends. The Romari settlement, full of women, children, and old folk, wasn't a great distance away. If the Redcloaks searched the wider area, they were bound to come across her comrades. Whitley wasn't battling for her life only; she was fighting for the future of her friends. While the older Lionguard struggled to control his horse, the younger man came at her fast with his knife, the blade jabbing straight for Whitley's neck. With only a moment to react, she'd brought her arm up defensively. She could see the knife wasn't silver— the metal most potentially deadly to a therianthrope like her—

but it would still cause enormous damage if it struck her throat. The knife hit her arm, the steel ripping through muscle, blade squealing, scraping against bone like fingernails upon slate. The roar that escaped her throat was monstrous, a cry born of pain and fury that heralded the arrival of the beast.

She snatched the Redcloak's hand in hers, the blood pumping from her torn forearm as they wrestled for control of the knife. Her knuckles popped and cracked as her hand contorted, shifting in size and beginning to smother the Lionguard's. Whitley gritted her teeth, which were sharpening all the while, her gums slick with blood as the sweat beaded on her brow. The young soldier brought his other hand around, snatching at her transforming limb, trying to prize it loose as claws tore free from her flesh. His fingers splintered, crushed by her shifting hand as she ground them against the grip of his knife. He struck her across the face with his free hand, stunning her momentarily, loosening her grip enough to yank his maimed hand clear.

The hunting knife fell to the ground, and the Redcloak dived for it, snatching it up in his good hand and lunging at Whitley once more. The girl was already moving, though, reaching for her staff where it lay nearby, grabbing it by a steel-shod end and swinging it back at the young Lionguard. As he dived at her, the quarterstaff arced through the air, striking him cleanly across the temple and sending him spinning away.

The Redcloak went down hard, his head hitting the nearby rocks with an awful, wet cracking sound, his body instantly still.

Panting hard, Whitley struggled to her knees. *Where is the other one?* She couldn't allow him to escape: if he rejoined his companions he'd return with more men, more Redcloaks. All would be lost. Her eyes scoured the surrounding slopes frantically. She caught sight of a billowing crimson cloak as the Lionguard tried to put distance between himself and the injured Bearlady. Wincing, she scrambled down the incline to where the rider had dropped his weapons, every painful movement reminding her that arrows were still buried in her back. She picked up the bow, her hands already shifting back to human form, her fingers fumbling for a missile. A good bow, well made, almost as good as the ones the Woodland Watch carried back in Brackenholme. It would suffice until she finally returned to her home in the Dyrewood. Raising the weapon she nocked an arrow, picking out the rider as he raced desperately, and ultimately vainly, to safety.

The bowstring sang, and the whispered words escaped Whitley's lips before the arrow struck its target.

"Take no chances."

2
A SIMPLE PLAN

THE NIGHT WAS clear, with stars shining in the winter sky, illuminating the Barebones in all their war-torn glory. The first wave of Prince Lucas's forces had made the land around Stormdale their own. The hills had once been known as the Garden of Lyssia, rich in crops and cattle destined for the banquet halls of all the Seven Realms. Fires now dotted the snow-covered fields, and the ground had been trampled underfoot by the invading army as it camped around the walls of the ancient city.

Soldiers from Riven and Vermire made up the army, since the Crows and the Rats had combined forces as they pushed home the Catlord offensive. Highwater had already fallen behind them, those Staglords and mountain men who had defended it having retreated to their capital, Stormdale. It had been a rout, a resounding defeat for the allies of the Wolf. A Ratlord, War Marshal Vorjavik, led the second wave, drawing ever closer to Stormdale with the remaining mass of his army. Lord Scree, one of Count Croke's many Crowlord sons, had command over the light infantry that surrounded the city. It wouldn't be long before the bulk and muscle of the following army joined him.

A thousand men made up the pack that had chased the Staglords home to Stormdale. Scree walked among them, shaking hands and passing on words of praise and encouragement. *Not long now, lads. We'll be dining in Stormdale before the week's out. We'll take those antlers as trophies.* The men of Vermire and Riven were about the most mistrustful a pairing one could encounter in Lyssia, as Scree well knew. The Crow soldiers were already jealous of their better-equipped comrades from the west. The Vermirian archers even carried outlawed silver arrows, for the sole purpose of bringing down enemy Werelords. The precious metal, feared by therianthropes down the years, had found its way into the armory of the Catlords. Wounds inflicted by any other weapon were ineffectual against a Werelord, as their accelerated healing could magically repair all but the gravest of injuries. The kiss of silver, however, was permanent and often fatal.

Before leaving for Omir to lay siege to its capital, Azra, the Tigerlord Tiaz had predicted that an assault on Stormdale would be doomed, that the combined forces of Crows and Rats

12

lacked the discipline of the Bastian army. So the fact that they had worked together so successfully under Scree and Vorjavik's joint command gave the Crowlord tremendous satisfaction. Still, he needed to keep confidence high. He needed to keep the union strong until they finally crushed the Stags.

If Scree hadn't been preoccupied with building the morale of his troops, he might have noticed the dark shape that winged through the starry sky above, heading straight for the heart of Stormdale.

"Hold your fire!" cried the lookout from the Lady's Tower of Stormdale. "That's a Hawklord!"

Three arrows had already flown through the air from the Graycloak archers before they recognized that the therian attempting to land within the Staglord castle wasn't a Werecrow. In his talons, the great falconthrope carried a figure that hung limp in his grasp. As the red-feathered Werehawk beat his wings, the frosty air swirling with each stroke, the soldiers below cleared a space for him to land. The passenger suddenly came to life as he was dropped the remaining few feet, landing gracefully on the hard, snow-packed ground of the castle courtyard. He stood swiftly to his full height, dark green cloak flapping in the downdraft from the Hawklord's wings as his companion landed beside him.

The falconthrope was changing, rusty-colored feathers

receding beneath his skin, his avian beak, wings, and legs shifting to human features. He was an old bird, and his bald head bobbed as he shook the remaining features of the Hawk away, an angry scar carved down the left side of his face. In his hand he held a shortbow, an arrow nocked warily out of habit. The surrounding men of Stormdale remained equally suspicious, and a dozen arrows were trained on the two strangers who had arrived out of nowhere.

A handful of figures emerged from the doors to the keep, marching across the courtyard toward the visitors. A tall man in his middle years with a pronounced limp led the way, not letting the disability slow him down. He kicked up the snow as he strode forward, his stiff leg scuffing the icy ground as he approached. A gray cloak billowed at his back, the winter furs that trimmed it held tight around his throat. His long face was set in a frown as his hand rested on the pommel of a greatsword on his hip. He was followed closely by an elderly man who carried a staff of gnarled wood.

The tall Staglord spoke:

"Who are you, that you should arrive unannounced in my city at such a late hour?"

The stranger who had been carried into the castle stepped forward. He wore a studded leather breastplate that matched the shock of pitch-black hair that tumbled around his face. He raised his right hand to his chest, clenched in a fist, and knelt before the Staglord.

"My name is Drew Ferran, last of the Gray Wolves, rightful king of Westland, and I am here to offer assistance, my lord."

The assembled nobles took a shocked step back from Drew, while the Graycloak archers shared a look of astonishment.

"We were told you were *dead!*" said the Staglord, dropping to his knee, quickly followed by the rest of the men. Drew saw the therian wince as he knelt, the maimed leg making the movement painful.

"Far from it," said Drew, smiling from where he crouched. He rose, gesturing toward the Hawklord. "My companion is Red Rufus of Windfell."

"The Hawklords have returned?" asked the elderly man as he pulled himself up the length of his gnarled staff. The hope was unmistakable in his voice.

"They have, my lord," answered Drew. "Although I'm afraid they're presently engaged in Omir."

"Fighting the Jackal?" said another.

"Fighting *alongside* the Jackal," corrected Red Rufus. "Seems the Catlords aren't content with waging war in the west: they've sided with the Doglords, ain't they? Apparently this makes the Jackal our ally all of a sudden."

The Hawklord spat on the ground contemptuously.

"Some of the Hawklords have long memories," said Drew, eyeing Red Rufus disapprovingly. "It'll take time for them to realize that this war affects the whole of Lyssia. Until the battle for Azra is concluded—hopefully with our victory—we cannot count upon the help of the Hawks. Except for this one."

Red Rufus jutted out his scrawny chin defiantly.

The tall Staglord limped forward and took Drew's hand in his own, giving it a firm shake.

"I'm Reinhardt, son of Manfred, and you're a most welcome addition to our number. Come, walk with me to the keep."

Drew and Red Rufus both fell in with the nobles as the Graycloaks returned to the walls. A quick look around the fortress told Drew that the Stags of the Barebones had taken a beating. Many of the men were walking wounded, bandages visible beneath their cloaks, dressings binding their heads and limbs. The route the Hawklord had taken had given him and Drew a fine aerial view of the city's defenses. Although Stormdale was a city, it was tiny in comparison to the giant hubs of Highcliff, Cape Gala, even the island of Scoria. Stormdale bore more resemblance to Windfell, a fortified stronghold high in the mountains with a tiny town between the outer wall and the keep wall, crowded with civilian homes. The outer wall here had looked woefully undermanned as Drew had flown over, and having seen the growing army beyond the gates, he was filled with dread at the possibilities.

"How did you discover our plight?" asked Reinhardt as they strode into the keep, Red Rufus already deep in conversation with the staff-carrying elder at their back.

"A young Stag—Lord Milo—arrived at Windfell just after

the Hawklords had taken flight. He's your brother, correct?"

"He got there safely?" Reinhardt seemed both relieved and angry. "Foolish boy. I commanded him to stay put, but would he listen? He rode out of here as our forces returned to the city, the Rats and Crows right behind us. Said he needed to send out word, fetch help."

"He succeeded," said Drew. "Though only two answered the call."

Reinhardt clapped Drew's back and gave his shoulder a squeeze.

"I'm indebted to you already because you found my headstrong sibling in one piece."

"Not quite in one piece," said Drew. "It seems the enemy gave chase when he fled here, and their arrows found their mark. He arrived in Windfell alive, but only just. We left him recovering in capable hands."

Reinhardt scratched his jaw. "My brother lives while many of our Staglord brethren were slain in Highwater. This means some joy for my mother, regardless of the horror that surrounds us."

"What news of your father, Duke Manfred?" asked Drew as the group passed through a corridor that thrummed with activity. He noticed many serving staff within the halls, but alarmingly few soldiers.

"None has reached us. We received word that he was aboard the *Maelstrom* sailing from Highcliff when the city was attacked, but since then no word has arrived home. We pray to Brenn that he is safe."

"Your father was kind to me, Lord Reinhardt. He took me under his wing in Westland, showed me what it means to be a lord and a therianthrope. He's a wise man, and I share your prayers."

"I thank you, and offer you the same for your loved ones. Your mother, Queen Amelie, accompanied him on board Count Vega's ship, and Baron Hector, the Boarlord of Redmire."

Drew's heart soared with the news that so many of his friends and loved ones might still be alive. He'd almost given up hope of ever seeing them again, but word that they'd safely fled Highcliff when the Bastians and Doglords had attacked was music to his ears.

"To know they've escaped Highcliff is enough for me, my lord. Have faith. If your father was with Vega, Hector, and my mother, he was in good company."

The group entered a square hall within the heart of the keep—the throne room of Duke Manfred, Drew assumed. A tall arched window filled the eastern wall, a stag and an eagle straddling a mighty mountain in stained glass, lit presently by torchlight from the ramparts outside.

"Ah," said Red Rufus with a sigh. "Stags and Hawks, side by side: guardians of the Barebones. That was always the way, wasn't it? Before the Lion came calling . . ."

"It can be so again," said the elder with the staff. "I am

18

Magister Siegfried, and I speak for all the people of these mountains when I voice my relief that the Hawklords yet live."

The Werehawk grimaced.

Drew hoped that Red Rufus could hold his tongue. The falconthrope had made no secret of his displeasure at the actions of the old Werelords when King Wergar the Wolf, Drew's father, had been overthrown. While the Stags, the Bearlord, and the other Lords of the Seven Realms had bent their knee and sworn fealty to the conquering King Leopold the Lion, the Hawks had resisted, remaining loyal to the Wolf. As punishment, the new king had severed the wings of their leader, Baron Griffyn, and turned them all out of Windfell, exiling the Hawklords from their homeland and forbidding them from ever embracing their therian forms again, on punishment of death. The wounds were still raw for many of the Hawklords, even after all these years.

Drew spoke quickly before the Hawklord could insult their hosts.

"I notice that your walls seem undermanned, my lords. Where is your army?"

Reinhardt dipped his head as he sat on a table in the hall, the other therians gathering around him. The old magister cleared his throat to speak, allowing Reinhardt a moment to compose himself.

"Highwater was overrun after a siege that lasted for a month. The city had little time to prepare for the attack, as the Catlords timed their offensive to perfection, coordinating it with their attack upon Highcliff. Although Stormdale is our ancient capital, Highwater is—was—a strong city, built to be the cornerstone of the Staglords' land in the Barebones. It was from Highwater that we traded with our cousins in the west, as Earl Mikkel commanded control over the Redwine River and all who sailed up and down it from the mountains. Our military might was almost entirely stationed there, and the Graycloaks called it home. We thought we could withstand anything. . . ." The old man trailed off, his voice disappearing to a whisper.

"Magister Siegfried is right," said Reinhardt. "It wasn't so bad when we faced only the Rats and the Bastians. Then Count Croke sent the Crows to their aid. He'd been busy, too. Not only did a large contingent of foot soldiers arrive from Riven, but the old Crow also sent war machines that could be used to break our defenses and overpower the walls. He knew our stronghold better than any other Werelord; he'd looked down upon it for decades, hungering for control of Highwater and the Redwine. With the men and the siege engines came the Werecrows themselves, a score of his sons, adding another element to the battle: wings."

Red Rufus's laugh was grim. "The Crows know nothing of death from above. We Hawklords would've taught 'em a thing or two."

"If only you'd been there, my lord," said Reinhardt respectfully. "At least twenty of them took to the air, carrying their forces over our defenses, dropping their finest warriors into our midst as we struggled to hold the walls. The battle was fought on many fronts, and lost on every one."

Reinhardt rubbed his right thigh at the mention of the battle. Drew noticed.

"Is that where you sustained your injury?"

"A silver Vermirian arrow: they're well equipped, no doubt provisioned by the Catlords." Reinhardt gestured to Drew's missing left hand with a nod of the head. "You've been injured yourself, I see. Did the Lion take your paw?"

"That was self-inflicted," said Drew, shuddering as he recalled his escape from the Catlords of Bast and their allies in Cape Gala, when he had been forced to bite off his own hand to escape his chains. "It was lose the hand or lose my life."

"Did the old Crow show his face in the battle?" asked Red Rufus, redirecting the conversation back to their present predicament.

"No," said Siegfried. "Croke has remained in Riven throughout, leaving the dirty work to his sons. Why put himself in harm's way? He no doubt intends to march into Highwater and then Stormdale once the fighting's finished, to claim the Barebones for his own."

"He has one fewer son to worry about, if that's any consolation," said Drew. "Lord Rook had been whispering words of poison into King Faisal's ear in Azra for many months. It appears the Crows had their designs on Windfell also. He met his end at the Screaming Peak of Tor Raptor."

Reinhardt managed a strained smile. "Morsels of good news."

"It was at some cost," added Drew. "Before his death, he managed to kill Baron Griffyn on the mountain."

"Then who commands the Hawklords now?" asked Siegfried.

"Count Carsten and Baron Baum," said Red Rufus proudly. "The Eagles of the Barebones. If anyone can lead my people back to glory, it's the brothers."

Drew rapped his fingers on a table, considering the situation.

"What is it?" said Reinhardt.

"The army beyond your walls: which Werelord commands it?"

"Lord Scree, a Crow, but he's only holding the front line until the real force arrives. The war engines roll ever closer."

"And who leads them?"

"Lord Vorjavik, the Ratlord, War Marshal of Westland."

Drew blanched at the mention of the Wererats. He'd had run-ins with the so-called Rat King before—the five Ratlord brothers who gnawed at the crumbs the Lions threw their way. Drew had fought two of them, Vanmorten and Vankaskan, in single combat. The former he'd maimed, the latter he'd killed;

but both battles had been hard won. If Vorjavik was the real warrior of the family, he didn't relish the prospect of facing him in battle. *Perhaps it won't come to that?*

"I'd estimate that there are around a thousand soldiers out there," said Drew. "How many do you expect in the second wave?"

The Werelords looked at one another, their faces pale. They looked back at Drew.

"Many, many more," said Siegfried.

"And how many men do you number here in Stormdale?"

"Around eight hundred," replied Reinhardt.

"I saw the condition of some of your troops in the court-yard. How many are battle fit?"

Reinhardt didn't speak, his answer coming in the form of a sorry shake of the head.

Drew turned and walked over to Red Rufus, who was biting his nails anxiously, staring up at the stained-glass window.

"This ain't good at all, pup," whispered the scarred old Hawk quietly. "You might be able to hold the walls if your force was strong. This'll be a bloodbath."

Drew scratched his head, glancing over his shoulder to the weary noblemen. Only Reinhardt looked as though he was prepared for a fight: the rest looked ready for death.

"Tell me," said Drew. "The civilian population, how many do they number?"

"In Stormdale?" said Siegfried. "There are two thousand within our walls. They're peasant folk, farmers and the like. They're just old men, women, and children."

"Can they hold a bow? Can they wear a cloak?"

Reinhardt nodded, realizing where the young Wolflord was heading, but Siegfried shook his head disapprovingly.

"You cannot expect them to fight. They're simple humans," said the old magister.

Drew smiled, praying that his confidence was infectious.

"Simple humans?" he said. "In my experience, there's no such thing."

3

THE VAGABOND COURT

HOOVES CLATTERED ON the frozen earth, warning those ahead to stand aside. The crowd of Romari travelers parted as the three horses beat a path through their encampment. Tents and caravans made up the majority of the refugee camp, while the hardiest souls slept under the clear, cold sky. Only when the leading horse reached the fire pit that marked the camp's heart did the lone rider finally rein in, the two riderless mounts slowing to a halt close behind.

Whitley slid down out of Chancer's saddle, landing gracefully, while glancing around the small camp of Romaris and other assorted refugees. There were nearly two hundred gathered here; the exodus of people from the battle in Cape

Gala had left thousands fleeing the Bastians and Lionguard throughout the Longridings. They all shared the same questions: Why had the invaders come? How soon might their world return to normal? While the Horselords of Cape Gala had traveled to Calico in the south, seeking refuge in the city of Duke Brand the Bull, others had sought safety elsewhere. The Romari, a traditionally nomadic people, had returned to the road, and a handful of soldiers from the Woodland Watch, including Whitley, had joined them.

Chancer snorted at Whitley's touch as she patted him across the nose. Two stable boys stepped up, keen to take the horses from the young lady of Brackenholme. Whitley quickly unhitched the rope that had kept the mount of the Lionguard she'd slain tethered to Chancer, allowing one of the youths to lead them away. She ruffled Chancer's mane affectionately before handing the other stable hand the reins. The boy saluted Whitley as he departed, and the young woman nodded awkwardly back. She wasn't used to commanding this level of respect.

As the only daughter of Duke Bergan, the Bearlord of Brackenholme, Whitley was accustomed to the etiquette and various customs of court life and the fact that people looked to her for moral guidance. But since she had led the Woodland Watch's flight from Prince Lucas's attack in the Horselord city of Cape Gala, Whitley had taken on more responsibility, not just as a Werelady within their motley band, but as a soldier.

Captain Harker, commander of the Watch, had no doubts whatsoever about her abilities; he'd known her as a fledgling scout when she'd apprenticed with him in the wild Badlands. When Whitley's dear brother, Broghan, had been murdered in Cape Gala, the Greencloaks had followed Harker's example and looked to her as their new figure of authority. As Whitley was more accustomed to traveling solo or with a single partner in the Watch, she wasn't entirely comfortable with the notion of being a leader.

Unclasping her green riding cloak, she made her way to the fire's edge where her companions were gathered. A serving girl came to take it from her, and Whitley smiled politely, letting the girl know in no uncertain terms that she wouldn't be handing it over. She was one of the few remaining Greencloaks who had traveled south; the garment had survived her myriad scrapes and battles, and she wasn't about to be parted from it now.

"You'll be putting the girl out of work, cousin," said Lady Gretchen, rising from where she'd been seated. The Werefox had no qualms about letting the Romari work for her, no matter how menial the task.

"I'm not so infirm that I need someone to take my cloak, Gretchen," said the scout, embracing her red-haired friend. It never ceased to amaze Whitley how stunning the girl from Hedgemoor could appear, no matter her circumstances. Gretchen had been through a hellish ordeal, as bad as any of them, if not worse. Kidnapped by the unhinged Werelion Prince Lucas and tormented by the wicked Wererat Vankaskan, she'd endured horrors that might have sent a weaker spirit over the edge. Somehow, though, she had come up smiling. Stuck in the middle of the Longridings, hundreds of miles from the nearest bath and mirror, Gretchen still managed to look as though she were entertaining courtiers. Whitley glanced down at her own attire: filthy jerkin and riding boots pitted from the road. She didn't even want to *think* about the state of her hair.

"But this is court, Whitley. Everyone has their part to play."

"This is a field, Gretchen. Everyone shares the work."

"What a quaint view of the world, cousin," said the Werefox, dismissing the comment. "There is a natural order, Whitley, one which we must adhere to. I don't ask people to serve me for the fun of it. It is simply the way, and we all have our roles to fulfill, however tiresome. I, for example, have to shoulder the burden of nobility and the many responsibilities that come with it. Sharing the work?" Gretchen shook her head. "Drew Ferran has an awful lot to answer for, filling your head with such nonsense."

Whitley stared at the other girl for a moment, a heartbeat away from an irritated outburst. Common sense told her to hold her tongue, just as a traitorous smirk appeared at the corner of Gretchen's perfect lips.

"You jest, cousin." Whitley sighed, rolling her eyes at the Werefox's teasing sense of humor.

Gretchen laughed, kissing Whitley on the cheek and giggling just like her old self.

"It's so good to have you back. Come, sit down; get something to drink. You look exhausted."

The Romari had nicknamed Gretchen, Whitley, and their close companions the Vagabond Court. The so-called court consisted of an unusual bunch. The two Wereladies were the natural leaders, even if their age suggested otherwise. Captain Harker of Brackenholme's army had the final say on all military matters, while his companions, Quist and Tristam, kept a constant vigil around the camp. The old sword-swallower Stirga, formerly of the Romari circus, was the spokesperson for the Romari, with the fire-eater and strongman Yuzhnik at his side. Both performers had found a new calling in leading their people. The last member of the Vagabond Court was Baba Korga, the ancient wise woman and soothsayer who had shown such kindness to Whitley when she had feared all had been lost in the battle of Cape Gala. Her mute guardian, Rolff, was always at her side to do her bidding.

In addition to the Vagabond Court, their camp consisted of a couple of hundred Romari. Until a fortnight ago they had also traveled with the great and the good of the Longridings, the Horselords and their followers. Lord Conrad, the young

Werestallion who had led the defense against the Lionguard and the Bastians in Cape Gala, had tried to persuade Whitley and Gretchen to join the remaining Horselords in Calico, but the girls wouldn't be swayed. They preferred to take their chances in the north and travel to Whitley's native Brackenholme, as safe a refuge as any.

While most of the Romari nation had gathered somewhere in the northern Longridings, those who accompanied the Vagabond Court had sworn to escort the court through the grasslands. The Romari called themselves the People of the Wolf, seeing the Wolf as a sacred figure, and this troupe of Romari felt it an honor to escort Drew's dearest friends, Gretchen and Whitley, to the Woodland Realm. The ladies and their allies couldn't have asked for better traveling companions, as few in Lyssia knew the Dymling Road and its environs better than the Romari.

The whole Vagabond Court sat together now around a fire. Whitley picked up a pitcher of water, pouring herself a cup before settling beside the others. As she sat, she winced with the sting of her wounds from the Lionguard weapons.

"You look unwell, my lady. What ails you?" asked Baba Korga. The old woman sat close to the fire, Rolff at her shoulder.

Whitley had taken Chancer out into the grasslands on a four-day scouting mission, making sure the enemy hadn't followed their trail. The Romari were a cunning bunch, knowing unmarked roads through the Longridings. Avoiding the Dymling Road itself and traveling through the long grasses adjacent to it, they had picked a route that would bring them out at the Dyrewood's edge, close to the point where the old road entered it. Whitley had encountered two Lionguard scouts two days previously, and the skirmish had taken its toll on her; taking another's life wasn't getting any easier. Though her therian healing had begun to repair her wounds, she had remained dogged by physical discomfort while her mind repeatedly replayed the grim events, tormenting her.

"You may have noticed that I returned with more horses than I left with," Whitley replied to all around the fire.

"It wasn't lost on me," said Harker. "I was about to ask. Redcloaks?"

"A pair of them, scouts I believe."

"Only two?" asked Gretchen, obviously concerned by the possibility that the Lionguard might discover their whereabouts.

"Just the two, and they're enjoying the long sleep now. They thought it'd be a good idea to use me as a whetstone and a pincushion. Don't worry, I'll be fine; the blood of my ancestors has seen to my recovery."

"Therianthrope or not, I'll take a look at those wounds later," muttered Harker, his paternal side shining through as usual. "And the larger Lionguard force?"

"No sign," Whitley answered, "although the fires still burn across the Longridings. It appears they've concentrated their efforts on hunting the Horselords. No doubt they've moved on to Calico by now. I only hope Duke Brand's defenses can hold them at bay."

"Calico's a mighty city," said Harker. "The moat alone would be impassable for any army, let alone her enormous walls. The Horselords are in a safe place."

"It appears our plan has worked thus far," said Stirga. "The sooner we are beneath the boughs of the Dyrewood, the better. The nights in the Longridings have been unkind to us." He shivered involuntarily.

Whitley looked up from her cup. "Unkind? Has it struck again?"

"A girl went missing last night; seven years old," replied the sword-swallower.

"How many is that now?"

"A dozen since we left Cape Gala."

"Twelve too many," said Gretchen sadly.

The attacks had started when the Horselords still accompanied them, upon departing their sacked city. Everyone knew that the Longridings were home to many large predators, including bears and wolves. Whatever the beast was that had been creeping into their camp to abduct the youngsters, it had clearly followed the Romari since they'd parted with the Horselords. Four children had been taken in the previous two weeks, stolen from their beds while their families slept, with not a trace left behind.

"The monster strikes swiftly and silently," said Stirga,

poking the fire with his rapier and sending tiny sparks up into the air.

"But didn't we post more guards along the camp perimeter?"

"We did," said Stirga. "But it still got through. People are nervous, children aren't sleeping. Tomorrow can't come soon enough for many."

"Then let us pray that it doesn't follow us into the Dyrewood," said Whitley solemnly. Each of the other members of the Vagabond Court nodded their agreement, muttering prayers to their various gods as they did so.

"One more night in the grasslands and then we'll be in the woods," said Harker. "If the beast fancies its chances against the Dyrewood, it's in for a shock; there are creatures in the haunted forest that could eat it for breakfast."

Whitley placed her cup on the ground and rose.

"Where is the family of the abducted child?"

"To the north of the camp," said Stirga.

"I would have words with them," said Whitley, bowing to the others before setting off.

She was quickly followed by Gretchen, who caught up with her friend and linked arms.

"What do you hope we'll find in Brackenholme?" asked the Werefox.

"At the very least my mother; at best my father, Drew, and Hector as well."

Gretchen was silent for a moment. "What do you think happened to him?"

Of the three men Whitley had mentioned, she knew full well which one Gretchen meant.

"You heard what that boy from Cape Gala said. He witnessed him being carried away from the High Stable in the talons of a Hawklord."

"But the Hawks are gone," argued Gretchen. "The few who lived were banished by King Leopold when Wergar was killed. Baron Skeer rules over Windfell in the Lion's name, and he's the last of them. There's more chance of a dragon having spirited Drew away."

Whitley shrugged. "Perhaps it was Skeer who took him? Maybe it was a Crowlord and the boy was mistaken. Either way our friend has fallen off the map of Lyssia."

Gretchen sighed. "I only hope Lucas didn't capture him. Wherever he is, I pray he's safe."

The young Bearlady wasn't as hopeful as her friend, but she wouldn't voice her fears. Whitley had seen Drew when they'd stormed into the court of High Stable. He was teetering, his left hand missing, awash with blood as he staggered out of sight onto the balcony.

Whitley stopped walking to give Gretchen a hug. "Let us pray all our loved ones are well, dear cousin."

For all the Fox's charms and sharp tongue, Whitley knew a side of Gretchen that few had ever seen. While Whitley had spent much time away from her father's court, learning the life of a scout, Gretchen had remained closeted away, enjoying a life of privilege and luxury. Beneath her tough and confident surface she was vulnerable. Destined for life as a queen from a young age, she had not discovered another world beyond the palace walls until Drew had exploded into her life. She'd been betrothed to Lucas, but through her friendship with Drew, she'd found the will to fight back against the Lions. Now, after all they'd been through, Whitley knew Gretchen could never imagine herself Lucas's queen. But if Drew—wherever in Lyssia he was—were king? Whitley preferred not to think about that.

A woman's quiet sobbing made the two Wereladies break from their embrace.

"Is that the mother?" whispered Whitley.

"This way," said Gretchen, nodding as she led the Lady of Brackenholme by the hand.

Three families had set up their small tents and bedrolls in a circle around a fire. The mother was instantly identifiable, a woman of middle years sitting cross-legged between two others who comforted her. She held a girl's shawl, the tiny flowers of yellow and blue embroidered into the cloth illuminated by the firelight.

Whitley wasn't sure what to say. She'd seen her father meet bereaved families in the past—the wives or parents of slain Greencloaks who had died serving the Bear of the Dyrewood. He had always known exactly what to say. But how did it feel

35

to lose someone yourself? *Your child.* Whitley thought of her brother, Broghan, and the last agonizing moments of his life. And she thought of the young lion, Prince Lucas, the golden-haired killer who had stolen Broghan from her world. She crouched down before the mother and reached across, placing her hands over the sobbing woman's knuckles as they gripped the blanket.

"I'm so very sorry for your loss."

The crying woman looked up, suddenly noticing that Whitley held her hand. The mother pulled one of her hands free and raised it to Whitley's face to trace the length of her cheek. It came away wet as it wiped away the tears.

Whitley stared into the fire. The flames roared back, bright, fierce, and yellow.

4

THE DEAD AND THE BURIED

HE STILL LIVED, *though his body was crushed. Only his mind still functioned; all else was ruined beyond repair. How long he had lain buried, he could not tell; time held no meaning anymore. He was a spirit, clinging to a broken bag of bones. There was a sudden movement as the rock and rubble shifted; a rescue? Someone took hold of his legs; he was aware of a ghostly sensation of tugging and pulling without any feeling. He was being jerked, his body drawn feet first from his tomb. The rescuers were frantic now, their grip rough, almost savage. Fresh pain shot through his body as his torso emerged into the piercing light. His whole being was alight with agony as he felt teeth and claws shredding his flesh, dismembering his cold corpse. As his head finally emerged from the earth, he caught sight of the lion's jaws, wide open and hungry, as they came down to close over his face.*

Bergan woke suddenly, his right arm coming up swiftly to fend off the lion's bite. He let out a cry, his body protesting, before collapsing, exhausted. The Bearlord could feel his ribs grating against one another beneath his skin, hunger gnawing at his insides. He brushed his fingers against his face; his cheeks were hollow and sunken, his beard thin and tattered. The blinding light was gone, replaced by a cold darkness that chilled him to his core. He squinted into the gloom, trying to make sense of where he was, the nightmare still all too vivid.

The Lord of Brackenholme was in a low-ceilinged cavern, his thick cloak providing little comfort against the rough rock he lay upon. The constant dripping of water reminded him how thirsty he was. He tried to roll over, to search for the water's source, but every movement was agony. He grimaced and collapsed, his memory slowly returning.

The last time he had been conscious, he'd been in the Garden of the Dead, Highcliff's cemetery for the nobility. The forces of the Wolf, routed by the invading Catlords, had fled through the tomb of the Dragonlords, one of the few secret escape routes out of the city. They'd been guided through the Garden of the Dead by Bo Carver, the Lord of the Thieves Guild, along with his band of miscreants. Bergan alone had remained behind, helping all others escape while he waited for King Leopold and his soldiers. The only way to stop the

Catlords from following had been to bring the tunnel down around him. With a few mighty swings of his battleaxe, the Lord of Brackenholme had felled the ancient pillars, the tomb collapsing and burying him beneath it. He'd given his life to save the innocent.

To be given it back was most unexpected.

"You're awake," said a voice in the darkness, alarming Bergan.

"Who is that?" he croaked. There was something familiar about the voice. The dim outline of a man emerged, holding something toward him.

"Reuben Fry, Your Grace. Here, take a drink."

The Bearlord was instantly relieved. The archer from Sturmland had been one of his closest confidants throughout the siege of Highcliff keep. "You're a loyal man," said the duke. Bergan allowed the captain to press the tin cup to his cracked lips; the water seemed a gift from Brenn to his dry throat.

"Where are we? How long have I been unconscious?" Bergan asked.

"We're in the catacombs, my lord, the tunnels that the Thieves Guild guided us to. There aren't many in our group— everyone was separated as they escaped the city. I only hope that some found their way out of this foul darkness."

He gave the Bearlord more water as he continued.

"You've been asleep for weeks. A month, maybe. It's hard to tell; we've no way to measure time down here. The torches, lanterns, and oil flasks we brought have all but run out."

"How have you survived?"

"Everything's rationed. We're lucky the thieves had the foresight to bring oil flasks with them; a little smeared over a torn cloak goes a surprisingly long way. Still, we're down to the last drops now."

Bergan shook his head, struggling to take it all in.

"A month, you say? And I've been asleep throughout?"

"You've dipped in and out of consciousness, Your Grace, but you've been fevered. We've had to fight you to get food down your gullet. You've been dragged and carried Brenn knows how far through this darkness. I'll fetch you something to eat. . . ."

Bergan grabbed the man's wrist as he rose to leave. By the dim light he could see how thin the captain was, his face almost skeletal in the gloom.

"How many do we number?"

"This is the rearguard, Your Grace. A handful of fighters, that's all that's left."

"Then I'll do without," said the Bearlord. "I'll not take food from their mouths."

"With respect, I'm not sure you realize how close to death you still are. You've not eaten properly for weeks and your body's exhausted itself repairing injuries. You're a shell, my lord. You must eat."

Bergan nodded reluctantly.

"Well, you've my gratitude for coming back for me, Fry. There aren't many who would've done that."

"It wasn't me who came back for you, my lord. I obeyed your orders and set off into the catacombs. It was only later I discovered you'd been rescued."

Bergan was about to press Fry further when raised voices echoed through the tunnels.

"What's going on?"

Fry moved to investigate, but Bergan kept hold of him. His grip was weakened but even in his malnourished state was still formidable.

"Sounds like another argument."

"Another?"

"I'll find out."

"Take me with you. I've slept too long."

As Fry helped Bergan to his feet, the Lord of Brackenholme felt light-headed and unsteady. Shooting pains raced up his legs, which had been unused for so long. He leaned hard on the Sturmlander, allowing the captain to take all his weight.

A faint glow illuminated parts of the cavern, but Bergan had trouble determining where it came from. Occasionally his head thumped against the rough stone of the low ceiling; he may have been half his former weight, but he was still a giant of a man. As they passed a low pool, Bergan's eyes slowly adjusted to the surroundings. Firelight began to flicker ahead, reflected off the smooth walls of the tunnels. Bergan let his hand trace the rock, surprised at how unnaturally polished it was in places.

The firelight glowed brighter as the voices grew louder. By the time they could see the guttering torch flame an argument was in full swing. Eight men stood in a group, cursing and jostling one another. They looked weary; a madness gripping them all like a disease. None had noticed Fry and the Bearlord emerging from the darkness.

"He's a liar, I say!" said the man holding the torch, the oldest of the group, gap-toothed and wiry. Bergan didn't recognize him; the only familiar figures in the crowd were Sir Howard and Sir Palfrey, Duke Manfred's knights from Stormdale, who had stayed close to Bergan as they'd escaped from Highcliff.

"I'm a man of honor, Hitch," replied Palfrey. "I'm telling you the truth. I know what I saw!"

"You're a liar and a thief," said Hitch, spitting at the ground in front of the two noble humans. "I never took no food from the pack. It's him what took it, I'd bet my life on it. Speakin' proper don't make you honest, fancy man—"

"This is insanity," said Howard, pointing to a smaller figure in the group. "Your girl there, Pick, saw everything! Tell them, child; go on!"

The girl named Pick seemed to shrink as all eyes landed on her. *She's but a child*, thought Bergan. Hitch gave the girl a hard glare, which wasn't lost on the knights of Stormdale. She looked away.

"I saw nothin'."

"That old swine's intimidating her," said Howard, pointing at Hitch, who grinned menacingly.

"Gentlemen," said Bergan, but his voice cracked; the usual power was missing. Nobody heard him as the argument grew to a crescendo. The Bearlord cleared his throat just as Palfrey made a grab for the girl.

"Tell the truth, child!" Palfrey shouted, but it was too late as the stand-off boiled over into chaos.

Hitch's knife came out of nowhere, flying through the air and jabbing Palfrey in the ribs. The knight acted instinctively, lashing his arm out and catching Hitch in the face with a crunching blow from his elbow as he fell. The girl, Pick, caught him as he tumbled, as three of the other men suddenly launched a flurry of punches and kicks at Howard. Within seconds knives were drawn as the men turned on one another.

"Stop!" cried Bergan, his voice still weak, but the fight continued. Fry let the Bearlord lean against the tunnel wall before unsheathing his longsword and reaching into the melee to pull two of the men off Howard. Bergan caught sight of Hitch, his nose and grinning mouth bloodied, dagger in hand, as he reached down to wrestle Palfrey from Pick.

"What in Brenn's name is going on here?"

The yell echoed down the corridor, halting the scrap momentarily. From the tunnel beyond the crowd of bodies, Bo Carver emerged. The Lord of Thieves had a face like thunder as he stared the men down, bald head shining in the torchlight, the serpent tattoo that snaked around the right side of his face twitching as if ready to strike. Another of the thieves stood at his side, the two returning from a scouting foray.

"Seems we've had us a disagreement with your noble friends, my lord," said Hitch, standing and pulling the injured Palfrey with him.

"Put him down," gasped Howard from under a scrum of bodies.

Hitch held his knife close to Palfrey's throat. "Not likely."

"You heard the man, Hitch," said Carver. "Release him."

"Called me a liar they did, my lord. Said I was a thief, didn't they?"

"You *are* a thief, Hitch," said Carver, rolling his eyes. "Let the knight go and this goes no further."

The scrawny man dug the blade into the flat of Palfrey's jaw line. "Reckon I'm done takin' orders from you too, *my lord*."

"Now isn't the time for mutiny, Hitch," said Carver, stepping forward. His hand hovered over the row of knives at his hip, fingertips brushing the handles.

"Don't be getting any ideas. It ain't just me who's done followin' your lead; ain't that right, lads?"

The men muttered and nodded, disengaging with Howard and grouping together. Hitch and the others faced Carver defiantly; even the fellow who had moments earlier been scouting with the Lord of Thieves now stood with his comrades.

"See," said Hitch. "You ain't got our respect anymore. You've gone too soft in the company of these royals. So I'll make this easy for you." Hitch smacked his lips, running a tongue over his gap-toothed smile. "We'll be taking the food. What's left of it."

Carver snatched a knife from his belt and strode forward.

Hitch pressed his blade hard against Palfrey's throat. "I'm warning you! Back off or there'll be blood spilled."

One of the turncoats stepped forward and grabbed the provisions pack. By the firelight Bergan could see something shifting within the bag, the canvas rippling with whatever creatures they'd foraged from the cave. Another man took up the only coil of rope, a couple of remaining unlit torches, and the last of the oil flasks.

"What does this achieve?" asked Bergan, at last loud enough to be heard. They all turned to face him. A couple of the deserters looked away, unable to hold the gaze of the Lord of Brackenholme. Hitch had no such problem.

"The food goes further. The fuel goes further. That'll get us out of here."

"You don't know where you're going," said Carver.

"And you do?" said Hitch. "We been following you for weeks, goin' around in circles no doubt. We should've stayed with the civilians; I bet they're out of here now, not stuck dragging some crippled Werelord around!"

"And us?" said Bergan. "What becomes of us?"

"Ain't my concern, Your Grace, is it?"

One of the men tossed them a torch brand, the thin shaft of timber clattering onto the tunnel floor.

"Can't say fairer than that," muttered the man.

"Very noble," agreed Hitch. "See, we can be civilized like you folk when needs be. Wouldn't be leaving you alone in the dark. Plus, you can keep your weapons. Brenn knows what you'll bump into down here!"

The group edged their way toward the tunnel that Carver had emerged from. Hitch dragged Palfrey with him, using the bleeding knight as a shield. Carver stared as they passed him by.

"I promise, if we meet again," said the Lord of Thieves coldly, "you die."

"Revenge should be the last thing on your mind." Hitch chuckled. "Might want to start thinking about where your next meal's coming from."

With that Hitch let go of Palfrey, letting him crumple to the floor. The thieves dashed off down the tunnel, quickly putting distance between them. Carver and Howard rushed to Palfrey, working hastily to staunch the blood flow at his hip. Pick had remained and watched them nervously. Fry returned to the duke, who now slumped against the wall, in danger of passing out. His body cried out for rest again, but that was impossible.

"From bad to worse," said Fry, helping Bergan rise.

"Was it Palfrey and Howard?" asked the Bearlord, grimacing as he rose. "Must I thank Duke Manfred's knights for coming to my assistance and saving my life?"

"No, my lord; they were with me. We came back to help as soon as we heard he'd rescued you."

"He?"

"Dug you out of the rubble with his bare hands, he did. You should've been dead," said Fry, just as Carver looked up from tending to the wounded knight. The duke and the Lord of Thieves stared at one another.

"It's Carver you need to thank."

5

To Build an Army

AT A GLANCE, the mass of Graycloaks that filled the castle courtyard seemed impressive. Lord Reinhardt's great-uncle, Baron Hoffman, and the knights of Stormdale led them through their drills, the army having swelled overnight from eight hundred to nearly two thousand. Closer inspection of the new recruits, however, revealed some startling facts. Old men made up the majority of the militia, aged folk who should have been sitting by their hearths rather than swinging staffs and swords. These were men of the fields, farmers who had spent their lives hefting spades and pitchforks, not wielding weapons in battle.

Beside them stood the women of Stormdale, shoulder to shoulder with their fathers, pushing their bodies to the limit as the captains and knights watched, barking instructions. And then there were the youngsters, not yet old enough to steer a plow, let alone use a bow. All had stepped up to throw in their lot; none would let their city fall without a fight.

Drew stood on the ramparts of the Lady's Tower, watching the crowd work through the exercises Red Rufus had prepared for them. The old Hawklord had been schooling a large contingent of the militia in archery. Thirty straw targets had been set up against the northern wall, and the most promising bowmen and women were now under Red Rufus's wing. But too few arrows found their target and too many lay on the snow-packed ground at their feet.

Drew looked up to see that Lord Reinhardt had joined him, and the Staglord's eyes were fixed on the crowd below.

"Are we doing the right thing?" he asked.

"What do you mean?"

Reinhardt swept his hand toward the scene below. "Asking women, children, and old men to fight for us? What chance do they stand if the enemy should breach our defenses?"

"Better than if they hadn't stood up at all," replied Drew. "These people have willingly taken up arms, Reinhardt. None of them has been forced into taking the Gray. Looking at the army that gathers each hour beyond your walls, the choice is quite simple. Fight or die. If we do not defend Stormdale with every able hand, we may as well open the gates to the Rats and Crows now."

"I just fear I'm putting a great many lives in danger."

"You're doing no such thing—the moment the Catlord set his soldiers on Highwater you were in peril. And with respect, it's not our decision or mistake to make. The people of Stormdale make their sacrifice willingly."

Lord Reinhardt leaned against the crenulated stones on the tower's edge. "I'm under no illusions as to the challenge we face, Wolflord. And I'm aware of the limitations of my people."

Drew looked away from the crowd toward the Staglord.

"Limitations? These people may surprise you, my lord. In my experience, people will do extraordinary things if their lives depend upon it, be they therian or human."

If Reinhardt had planned to challenge Drew further on his people's ability, he thought better of it. Instead, the two turned to look out to the west where the enemy forces grew. There were maybe two thousand gathered now; battle-hardened warriors, men who had spilled blood in the names of the Rats and the Crows. Colorful banners could be seen dotting the encampment, highlighting the different factions that had traveled from Riven and Vermire to put the Staglords to the sword. While the largest portion of Vorjavik's army was gathered directly to the west, with the Dyrewood at its back, the tents and fires circled the city, leaving the occupants of Stormdale no escape route.

There was no sign of the Lionguard or any Bastians among their number. Drew suspected that Onyx, the Pantherlord known as the Beast of Bast, had set them to work elsewhere. The most feared therian in the known worlds, Onyx had brought his powerful Bastian forces to join his Werelion kin in their campaign against the Wolf's claim to the throne. There were many Werelords leading diverse armies against Drew's allies, but Onyx was at the head of them all.

"Did you send word to Brackenholme?" asked Drew, looking beyond the enemy camp toward the dark green forest that covered the horizon.

"Scouts were sent to Brackenholme and the other Bear city of Darke-in-the-Dyrewood, but whether anyone comes to our aid is another matter. With Bergan reportedly slain in the battle of Highcliff and Broghan murdered in Cape Gala, I should imagine the Bearlords have enough to worry about. No, I'm not expecting our friends from the Woodland Realm to help us on this occasion."

With thoughts of Brackenholme, Drew found himself wondering about Whitley and Gretchen. The last he'd seen of them had been just before he'd been swept away from High Stable in the talons of Lady Shah the Hawk. How he wished he could see them now, or at the very least could know they were safe from the violence that poisoned Lyssia. He hoped they were together and could find allies. He wondered, too, where his other dear friend, Hector, might be in this war-torn land. *Hector's out there, somewhere, too. I may be needed here, but my old friend won't let them down. He'll go looking for them, I know it.*

"Don't lose hope, my lord," said Drew. "Help is out there. Help shall come."

"You'd best get praying to Brenn it does," said a voice from the stairwell behind them. "Half of 'em are as likely to put out their own eye as find a Rat or Crow with their accursed arrows."

Red Rufus hopped up the last few steps to join them on the tower top, not even out of breath after the steep climb. He might have been as old as any therian Drew had met, but the Hawklord was still as nimble as a young falcon.

"The training isn't going well?" asked Reinhardt worriedly.

"What can you really expect 'em to learn in one day? They know which part of the bow to pull—that's about it as far as I can tell. It'll be a miracle if they don't sever their fingers before they've even loosed 'em off!"

Drew sighed at the Hawk's resigned demeanor.

"Surely you should be filling them with confidence, not beating it out of them?"

"Oh, don't get me wrong. I've said what I'm supposed to, built 'em up and all that. They all think they're world beaters now, ready to take on old Onyx himself should the Werepanther turn up on the doorstep. But I wouldn't put too much faith in 'em, cub. They're too green; they ain't warriors."

Drew was undeterred. "Every one of them has a part to play in the battle that lies ahead," he said.

"And that battle draws near," said Reinhardt, turning on

52

his stiff leg. "I'm going to address them. See if my words can help lift them a little more."

"Fill yer boots," said Red Rufus as the Staglord descended the staircase. "They need every morsel they can get!"

"Are you always this disheartening?" said Drew.

"Boy, this isn't some game we're playing here; it's life and death."

"I know that better than most," snapped Drew before he could stop himself.

Red Rufus nodded respectfully. "As do we all. But we're asking these people to do things they've never dreamed of in their worst nightmares. You really think they can take a man's life when push comes to shove?"

"They'll do what they must to defend their home. I don't doubt them for a moment. I only worry what the cost shall be."

"And what would you do, cub, when the bones are cast?"

Drew looked at the old Hawk as Red Rufus scratched at his throat, fresh snow falling around them. "Speak your mind, Red Rufus. Don't hold your tongue: it doesn't suit you."

The Hawk turned his face to Drew, the old scar creasing as his eyes narrowed. "I know you chewed your paw off. That must've taken some doing. But how far would you go to ensure the lives o' them people? How low would you stoop to win this war?"

"I don't follow," said Drew, his stomach cold at the thought of where Red Rufus's mind was taking them.

"Wars aren't always won by brave words, lad. Sometimes you gotta get yer hands dirty."

Red Rufus lifted his own, the filthy nails curling around as he balled his bony fingers into fists.

"Could you kill a defenseless foe if it saved the lives o' many?"

Drew paused, unable to answer the falconthrope's question. What was he suggesting?

Red Rufus looked back to the crowd below as they worked through their drills.

"That's where you and your old man differ, eh? Wergar wouldn't have thought twice about killin' anyone, no matter the situation, if it brought him the result he wanted."

Drew cast his mind back to his brief, peaceful time in Highcliff and the lessons he'd endured under Duke Manfred's watchful eye. The old Stag had taught him how to control his lycanthropy, and how to behave in the company of fellow therians. Manfred had also taught him how to fight, and of the rules of battle. *There's a time and a place for underhandedness,* the duke had told Drew so long ago. Never a lover of bloodshed even when fully embracing the Wolf, Drew had taken his message to heart.

"I'm not my father," said Drew. "There's another way. You advocate cold-blooded murder, Red Rufus? That's not who I am."

"If Onyx were here, now, unarmed before us, you wouldn't kill him?"

"I'd try to reason with him first. . . ."

Red Rufus stared over the ramparts as the snowfall grew heavier. "There's no reasoning with these folk, boy. They're killers. 'Tis the only language they understand, y'hear? Until you're prepared to take the life o' any of 'em—under *any* circumstances—then the hope you speak of so proudly? It's lost."

With that, Red Rufus turned, tugging his cloak around his shoulders before setting off down the stairs.

Drew stood alone on the tower top a while longer, queasy with fear and racked by doubt, the Hawklord's grim words ringing in his ears as the snow slowly blanketed Stormdale.

6

BLACKHAND

THE RAT CITY of Vermire rose high above the White Sea, ramshackle buildings clinging to the cruel cliffs and claiming the land as their own. Those homes closest to the seafront bore little resemblance to houses. They were a ragtag collection of huts and tarpaulins providing scant defense against the wind and waves. Above the shantytown stood the city, taverns and warehouses colliding with one another on the steep slopes, crowding out the smaller residences squeezed in between. The streets sang with the cries of the merry and murderous, the cobbles awash with beer, blood, and body parts. Higher still were the grand houses of the merchant classes, pirate captains and back-stabbing thief-lords who vied with one another for the attention of the Rat King. The Wererat brothers who ruled the land courted the wealthy of Vermire, playing them against one another. The mansions of these bickering sycophants were gathered around the base of the Ratlords' citadel, which rose like a monstrous black spire from the detritus below.

Hector, the lord of Redmire, looked down from the giant tower, the din of the city reaching the lofty balcony of his accommodation. As the newly appointed Lord Magister of Prince Lucas's court, the young Boarlord had been quick to pay Vermire a visit, the city being the final resting place of his old master, Vankaskan. Like Hector, the old Wererat had been a magister, learned in healing magicks, but also a practitioner of the dark arts. Hector's growing understanding of necromancy had served him well, and the young magister had leached a wealth of arcane knowledge from the skeletal remains of the dead Wererat.

Lord Vanmorten and his siblings, the surviving members of the Rat King, had been kind enough to afford Hector accommodation, even allowing the young magister's Boarguard to remain in his quarters. There were eight Boarguard in all, though that would change once the *Myrmidon*, the late Queen Slotha's warship, returned home to Tuskun from Highcliff without her leader. News of the Werewalrus's demise at Hector's hand would spread quickly. Her people—the Ugri, tribal inhabitants of the frozen tundra—had a new master now. Their warrior tradition of swearing fealty to any who defeated their leader was another piece in the jigsaw of the young magister's destiny: the fearsome Ugri were now his to command.

Hector glanced back to where his men sat, tossing bones and drinking. His cronies Ringlin and Ibal, his only true confidants, had wasted little time in getting to know their new Boarguard brethren, and the age-old pastime of gambling cemented their newfound friendship. Lean, rangy Ringlin laughed suddenly, clapping the back of Two Axes as short, fat Ibal scooped up the pot, giggling as he gathered his winnings. Two Axes was the chief of the Ugri who had first sworn the blood-oath to Hector, as he held the best grasp of the Western tongue. The giant warrior gave Ringlin a playful punch in the jaw, sending the rogue reeling and prompting a chorus of laughter from the other five Ugri.

All friends together, eh, brother?

Hector turned away from the scene, trying to ignore the whispers of the Vincent-vile, his dead brother's phantom that was never silent for long. The dark and bitter spirit was always close by, lurking behind the magister's shoulder, a constant reminder of the terrible part Hector had played in his brother's demise. As often happened when the subject of friendship found its way into Hector's ravaged mind, he thought of Drew.

The Boarlord had stood shoulder to shoulder with the young Wolflord, the two as close as any brothers could be, and his feelings for Drew were far stronger than any he'd ever had for Vincent. When Drew had emerged as the rightful king of Westland, Hector had been one of the first to swear fealty to his friend. Back then, he'd truly believed Drew would lead the Seven Realms of Lyssia into a bright new future, away from the dark days of King Leopold, the tyrannical old Lion.

Then the magister's world had slowly begun to fall apart. Hector's father had been slaughtered by the Lionguard; Drew had disappeared; Vincent had re-entered his life, first as a living menace and then as the evil, ever-present vile; and events had continued to spiral out of control until he found himself here. Through all he'd endured, every trial and heartache he'd faced and overcome, the one thing that had kept Hector grounded had been his friendship with the Wolf, forged in the Dyrewood what felt like eons ago, though it had actually been less than a year.

Unpalatable as the thought was, Hector occasionally wished his friend were dead, so Drew would be saved from witnessing the self-serving plotting of the Wolf's Council since his disappearance several months ago. But deep down, Hector hoped that he might be reunited with the young Wolflord one day. Drew was the one true friend he had left. Every other member of the Wolf's Council had betrayed Hector—Count Vega, Duke Bergan, Earl Mikkel, Duke Manfred—and of those friends-turned-enemies, only Manfred the Staglord yet lived.

Not for long, Hector. Not for long.

Hector smiled bitterly at the memory of Manfred. There would be a reckoning with the old duke. The Lord of Stormdale might think he was safe, hiding in the north, trying to sneak his way into the fortress of Icegarden, but no amount of Sturmish steel was going to keep the magister from having his vengeance. It was unpardonable that Manfred had abandoned him to the vicious Walrus Slotha. *And you thought you'd get away with it, Stag?* True, he'd once considered the duke a friend, but no more. The Wolf's Council had become redundant; there was no need for those old fools in the new order. The war was changing the map of Lyssia, and Hector intended to play his part in that. He would be rewarded for his new loyalty to the Lion, Prince Lucas, future king of Westland. He would take whatever he wanted.

A knock at the door caused Hector to turn.

"Get that."

Instantly the Boarguard ceased their merrymaking, rising as one and ready for action. The Ugri scout known as the Creep padded over to the door, his free hand close to his weapon belt as he grabbed the handle. They may all have been guests of the Rat King, but none of them trusted their hosts. As the Creep's fellow warriors fanned out around the room, he opened the door and stood back.

The hooded, robed figure of Vanmorten stood there, and dark-armored guards were gathered behind the Lord Chancellor.

"You seek Lord Blackhand?" asked the Creep, his voice rough as broken slate.

"You're sticking with this ridiculous new moniker then, Lord Magister?" Vanmorten chuckled.

Hector shrugged, pacing behind his line of guards.

"It's not my place to choose what the Ugri call me. I wouldn't mock them. Their naming rites predate anything your glorious city of Vermire considers a tradition, Lord Chancellor."

Although Vanmorten's face was obscured by the thick cowl he always wore to hide his disfigurement, Hector could sense that the Ratlord was annoyed by the comment. Hector made a halfhearted attempt to conceal a smile.

"Oh, please come in," said Hector. "What nonsense. This *is* your home, after all. . . ."

Vanmorten stepped into the room, followed swiftly by the Vermirian Guard. Ten palace soldiers entered Hector's state room, forming their own ring around the Wererat.

It's suddenly looking rather crowded in here, brother.

"To what do I owe the pleasure?" said Hector.

"We've had a Crow arrive."

The Boarlord's mouth went suddenly dry. The reputation of the Crowlords of Riven preceded them; they were cruel and petty avianthropes second only to the Wererats when it came to distrust. Hector's home realm of the Dalelands lay uncomfortably close to the Crow city of Riven, and he couldn't recall a time when his people hadn't feared their neighbors.

"You're still trusting messenger birds to carry information? There's a war on, my lord. Not the safest means of sending word from the front line, is it?"

"You misunderstand me, Lord Magister."

Vanmorten stood to one side as another man entered the chamber. He was a wiry fellow, only Hector's height, but he looked battle-hardened. His sharp nose was fixed in a permanent sneer, and his beady black eyes skewered all but Vanmorten with a suspicious look. A shock of black hair erupted above his pockmarked face, a widow's peak granting him a devilish look. He gave Hector a cursory glare before bobbing his head in a brief bow.

"Lord Flint of Riven," said the Crowlord.

Hector nodded and bowed. He'd heard enough about the Werecrows to know that, along with the Rats, they had been the eyes and ears of Leopold across Lyssia down the years. With the old king gone and a new one waiting to be crowned, the Crows had actively joined forces with the Catlords of Bast as they had come to Prince Lucas's aid, hoping to crush the Wolf and his allies. No doubt the Crows now served the young Lion just as they had his father before him. They would never enter a fight unless they stood to gain. For them to enter a fray meant they'd decided who the victor was going to be: the Crows of Riven backed only winners.

"It's good to have your kinsman Count Croke firmly on our side," said Hector. "The neutrality of your people is renowned. For the Crows to finally take flight you must have recognized the grave danger Lyssia is in."

Flint's eyes narrowed as he looked at Hector. He turned to Vanmorten.

"If the Boar has something to say, perhaps he'd better come out and say it!"

The Crow took a step forward, only for Vanmorten to take him by a bony shoulder.

"I'm sure the Baron of Redmire meant no offense, Flint."

The avianthrope backed down, shrugging Vanmorten's disfigured hand free.

"Why the visit, my lord?" asked Hector, lightening his voice to lift the threatening mood. "And what's so important that your message couldn't be relayed to the Lord Chancellor alone?"

You're a cocky one, brother. Do you fear no one anymore?

It was true. Since Hector had begun communing with the dead, developing his skills of dark magistry, he had turned from a gentle apothecary into one of the most powerful beings in Lyssia. His hunger for power had led him to terrible places, from the sinister White Isle in the Sturmish Sea to the pale skull of Vankaskan in the tomb of the Ratlords. Hector had a confidence about him that he'd never known before. Drew had put him on the path toward self-belief, and he'd become a changed man. He'd proven his power over life and death to Vincent, Vega, Slotha, and Lucas; with the dark magistry at his magick-blackened fingertips, there was little in life that scared him now.

"Two pieces of news," said the Crowlord, still glaring at Hector. "We hear that the island of Moga is in flames."

"Baron Bosa's stronghold?" said Hector, surprise clear in his voice.

"Is there another Moga?" said Flint sarcastically.

"Who in Lyssia would have attacked the Werewhale's island?" Vanmorten asked.

"Too soon to say for sure, but the dozen ships under the Kraken Ghul's command that controlled the port in Prince Lucas's name have been scuttled. Bastian frigates, Westlanders loyal to the Lion, privateers from the Cluster Isles; every ship burned, broken, and sent to the bottom of the harbor."

"How do you know this?" said Hector.

"News travels fast between the Crows," replied Flint. "The Baron himself is missing, as are many of the pirate vessels that called Moga their home. The city was torched, the garrison sacked, and all Ghul's men butchered. The Kraken's enraged, understandably, with his northern fleet in pieces. Whoever attacked left nothing to chance."

Has the Whale Bosa joined the party, brother? What might have prompted him to finally choose sides?

"Lord Onyx must be fearful for the safety of his armada now that such an attack has taken place. Is the Kraken investigating?"

"Indeed, Ghul has been given this task, but Onyx holds little faith in the incompetent Kraken," said Flint. "The attack on Moga took place during Ghul's watch—no doubt the Werepanther holds him accountable. The remainder of Onyx's fleet remains in southern waters, while the Bastian navy helps the army blockade Calico in the Longridings. The city harbors the fugitive Horselords; it's only a matter of time before its walls crumble."

"You underestimate the fortitude of the men of Calico," said Hector. "Duke Brand will not be easily broken."

"I suspect *you* underestimate the unwavering focus of the Catlords, Lord Magister," sneered Vanmorten. "Lord Onyx will not cease his campaign until all opposition is crushed. He had already called for reinforcements from his homelands, and more Werelords of Bast are coming to add might to his cause. Don't be surprised if Ghul is replaced as Lord of the Pirate Isles by one of Onyx's own."

"What other news?" asked Hector.

"Duke Manfred and Queen Amelie have been sighted in the Sturmish port of Roof. It appears Icegarden may offer them sanctuary: the White Bear has shown his true colors."

"As was always expected," added Vanmorten. "Duke Henrik was never going to turn them away. With a bit of luck, the frostbite of a Sturmish winter will be the death of that old Stag Manfred before they even reach Icegarden. What does this mean for Lucas?"

"Lord Onyx leads the prince's army toward Sturmland as we speak."

Hector cast his mind back to his childhood, when his father had recounted tales of Icegarden's splendor to the enthralled young Boar. The city was the ancestral home of the White Bears, built into the slopes of the Strakenberg, its mines the stuff of legend. The Daughters of Icegarden channeled the ancient mountain's magicks, Werebear magisters who worked alongside the mortal Sturmish smiths, enchanting weapons and armor for the greatest warriors of Lyssia. The stories told of a time long ago when the mythical Dragonlords ruled the Whitepeaks, hoarding their treasures deep inside the Strakenberg. Tales of the mythic Wyrmstaff had always captured Hector's imagination as a child; this powerful artifact had been left behind by the Dragons and was guarded by Icegarden's Bearsisters for all eternity. The staff's precise powers were unclear, although the scrolls Hector had scoured suggested at the very least it would magnify his magicks, whilst unlocking the ancient sorceries of the Dragonlords. If it existed, the Wyrmstaff was undoubtedly a dangerous relic of a time long gone, and the Bears were right to keep it hidden. Duke Henrik would die before revealing the mountain's secrets to his friends, let alone his enemies.

"The White Bear won't allow Onyx to march into Sturmland unopposed," said Hector. "He's no fool."

"That's debatable, Lord Magister," replied Flint. "His actions will prove how great a fool he is. Anyone who takes to the field, *willingly* meeting the Werepanther in battle . . . one has to question their sanity."

Hector's skin crawled as he imagined what Lord Onyx,

the Beast of Bast, might do to Duke Henrik should they clash upon the field. He had met Lady Opal, the Werepanther's sister, and she had been intimidating enough, counseling Prince Lucas, watching everything, missing nothing. Her brother's prowess in battle was reputed to be unmatched by any living Werelord. The Panther never carried a weapon into conflict; fully transformed, Onyx *was* the weapon, his bloody reputation built upon a great pile of slaughtered foes.

"I suspected Henrik's inactivity reflected a reluctance to pick a side," said Vanmorten, lifting a hand into his cowl to scratch at his ruined face. "We thought he'd lock himself away in Icegarden, hoping the war would pass by without him wetting his blade. It seems we were wrong."

"Then our hopes of capturing Manfred and rescuing the queen may be greatly reduced," said Hector. "A shame. I might have been able to reason with the White Bear. He might yet listen to me: he knew my father."

"Here's hoping he's unaware that you murdered Count Vega," said Vanmorten with a chuckle.

Hector's composure slipped a little as he glowered at the Wererat.

"We do what we must for the greater good, Lord Chancellor."

"Of course." Vanmorten nodded in mock agreement. "The greater good."

"If the Stag hunt is over, does this mean we're heading back to Highcliff?" chimed in Ringlin.

Vanmorten and Flint looked at the rogue in shock. Hector raised a hand to wave away their grievances before they could speak.

"Captain Ringlin may speak freely. He is, after all, the most senior officer of the Boarguard and my military adviser."

Vanmorten laughed.

"You make it sound like you have an *army*, Blackhand! There are eight of them—count them. What walls will you bring down with such a mighty force?"

Don't rise to it, brother.

"There are ways and means, Vanmorten," said Hector, waggling a black-gloved finger at the Ratlord.

"Well?" said Ringlin, still awaiting an answer. "My lords?" he quickly added, remembering his place.

Flint looked from the Boarguard back to Vanmorten.

"My orders from Lord Onyx were to instruct you to return to Highcliff immediately, Lord Chancellor Vanmorten. Let Prince Lucas know of Duke Henrik's impending treachery, and also the whereabouts of his mother, the queen. Lord Onyx suspects that this will galvanize the prince and encourage him to strike out at the Sturmish with all his might."

"This conflict shall be resolved before the last snow of winter falls," said Hector, clapping his hands together. "Mark my words, gentlemen."

Hector strode over to the desk in the corner of his stateroom, where a smart new leather medicine case awaited him. He opened a drawer, fishing out the black candle, weighing it in his gloved palm for a moment before stowing it in the base of the case. He proceeded to remove papers, scrolls, and other documents from the desk, purloined from the deceased Vankaskan's private library and many yet unread. There was a wealth of knowledge in the realm of dark magistry, and Hector had only scraped the surface.

"It will be good to get back to Highcliff," he called over his shoulder. "I can think of no better place to build my new life beside the future king."

Flint cackled, the laughter like stones falling into a gutter. Vanmorten joined the Crow, as if suddenly getting the joke.

"What amuses you?" asked Hector, his smile slipping.

"Lord Chancellor Vanmorten is to visit Prince Lucas. You, however, are not going to Highcliff, *my lord*," said Flint, his voice thick with glee. "You're going to the Badlands. Lord Onyx wants to meet you."

7

THE HANGING TREE

THE ROMARI, THE most ancient travelers of the Seven Realms, only gathered in great numbers for one of three events: a marriage that united any of the six old bloodlines; the death of a male zadka or a female baba; and, gravest of all, times of war.

A thousand of the nomads had made camp in the far north of the Longridings, pitching tents and drawing up their wagons along the edge of the border with the Dyrewood. Rumors persisted that two of the therian ladies who had escaped Cape Gala, Gretchen and Whitley, were in the company of a band of Romari, but this larger gathering had yet to encounter them. Grouping together in such large numbers afforded them some protection if they were to encounter any of the Lionguard or

70

Bastian warriors in the grasslands; any army would surely think twice before engaging such a force.

While the zadkas oversaw the day-to-day running of the camp, marshaling their people and scouting the surrounding hills, it was the babas who had the final say on all matters, both social and military. Six of the wise women had formed a council at the camp's heart, gathered around a large fire pit, each representing different branches of the old bloodlines. Any enemies captured were brought before the babas to be questioned. If found guilty, the foe was dealt with swiftly and dragged away to the Hanging Tree.

One such hapless soul now stood before them, his red cloak stained and torn. A guard took hold of the bag that had been secured around the prisoner's head and yanked it off, leaving the young man blinking at the blinding flames.

"Tell us, what were you were doing alone in the Longridings so far from your Catlord's battalion?" said one of the babas, her back to the fire, body shrouded in shadow.

"I'm a deserter," said the soldier. "I no longer serve the Catlords."

"Yet you still wear the Red."

"And a sergeant's insignia also!" said another.

"How long before your comrades arrive in your wake?"

Trent Ferran rolled his eyes, cursing his ill luck in having run into the Romari. He'd headed north since fleeing the camp of his former leader Lord Frost, putting distance between himself and his ex-comrades. Having slain the albino Catlord with his father's old Wolfshead blade, Trent expected his fellow Redcloaks to come after him and hunt him down for his betrayal. He'd ridden hard on his trusted horse, Storm, heading straight for the Dyrewood. There were few horses as fast as the outrider's, and the Redcloaks were too disorganized to give chase. Still, he felt sure he hadn't seen the last of them. Preoccupied with who might be following him, he'd been distracted from what lay ahead. When the Romari had ambushed him, casting nets and ropes over youth and horse, the two had gone down as if hit by catapults. Bound and hooded, he'd been marched through the grasslands into the heart of the Romari camp and brought before the Council of Babas.

"It's true, I *was* a sergeant with the Lionguard, but that life is behind me. I follow a different path now."

"Admirable," said the baba who had initially spoken. "Then you prove no threat to our people. I suppose we should just let you go?"

Trent glanced around the fire. In addition to the six wise women, men-at-arms and elders had gathered, standing at a respectful distance while the babas passed judgment on the outrider.

"He's scouting for them," said another baba. "Are your masters so fearful of us few—the Romari nation—that you've singled us out as a threat? Well, let them come, I say. They shall feel the full wrath of the People of the Wolf."

The zadkas and young warriors clapped their hands behind the babas, banging blades against shields and scabbards, voicing their support for the old woman's words.

"The 'People of the Wolf'? What does that mean?"

The first baba rose from where she sat, stepping closer to Trent. The farther she moved from the fire's shadows, the clearer her features were. Her face was weathered, reminding Trent of spoiled timber, rutted and worn with age. Her chin jutted out from below her shriveled gums, thin gray hair straggling down her face and curling like oily worms around her jaw. She blinked, and misty white orbs stared through the young man from the Cold Coast as her blind eyes rolled in their sockets.

"My name is Baba Soba, and I speak for all my people. We Romari live on the road, child. The trees are our walls, the sky is our roof, and the moon lights the way for our people. As the moon watches over us, so we watch over her children. We are the People of the Wolf, our lives inextricably tied to the great beast. Whoever attacks the Wolf attacks the Romari: when your masters attacked Drew Ferran, they waged war upon my kind."

Trent felt light-headed, her words commanding and mesmerizing him. He'd lost sight of all else around him as she spoke, and his eyes were focused on her puckered lips. His heart felt tight in his chest, and with a gasp he suddenly realized that he'd stopped breathing. He gulped at the air, the mention of his brother's name snatching him out of Baba Soba's bewitching thrall.

The baba smiled as Trent choked and coughed, bent double and panting as the air rushed back into his lungs. He looked up, eyes wide with fright at the power in her voice.

"Oh, you're a strong one," she said, surprised at Trent's recovery. "There are few who have the will to break an invocation."

"An invocation? What did you just do?" gasped Trent as the guards yanked him upright. "You're a witch?"

The menfolk shouted now, objecting to Trent's accusation. Baba Soba raised a bony hand to silence them.

"You may call me that, Westlander. I've been called worse. I'm simply a Romari who wants answers to questions. Tell me, what was it I said that revived you just then?"

Trent swallowed hard, his throat dry. *Do I tell them?* He felt he'd betrayed his brother enough in the many miserable months that had passed since he last saw him. *Has it really been a year since we were separated?* In that time Drew had been proclaimed rightful heir to the throne of Westland, sparking a war in which many Werelords had lost their lives, not least King Leopold, the Werelion. Could he believe that the Romari were loyal to his brother? *Can I believe these people* worship *the Wolf?*

"Speak up, child," said the baba. "I may be blind, but I hear very well. Must I summon your answer once more?"

"You mentioned Drew," said Trent quickly, desperate not to fall under her spell again.

"So," said the old woman, stroking a skeletal finger down her shriveled face. She stepped closer, a foot from Trent, smacking her lips as she asked her question. "Who is Drew Ferran to you, that the utterance of his name may break my charm?"

"He's my brother," said Trent. The words escaped involuntarily. The onlookers gasped; even Baba Soba stepped back with surprise.

"Brother, you say?" she cackled. "Child, I know a therianthrope when I meet one. . . ." She leaned in and sniffed at him, her big nostrils flaring as her face brushed his. Trent shivered, feeling cold to the core. "And you are no Werelord."

"My parents raised Drew. We grew up as twins. We may not be brothers by blood, but we're as close as any could be."

"So close that you took the Red?" said the baba.

Trent's stomach knotted as the old woman put the puzzle together. She stepped behind him, taking his bound hands in hers. He felt her chill fingers massage his palms, as if reading whatever secrets lay hidden beneath his skin. Trent grimaced as he felt something sharp jab into the flesh of his right hand when the baba clenched her hand over his. The warm blood flowed between their twined fingers for a moment, spreading into the old woman's palm, before she cast his hand away once more to shuffle over to her sisters.

"He lies!" said a zadka, growing tired of the interrogation.

"Hang him!" added another as the Romari men pushed their way forward, manhandling him away from the babas.

"I'm telling the truth!" cried Trent, but Baba Soba remained silent as the zadkas ordered him away.

The Romari were already stringing a rope in a nearby tree as the guards began to lead the young Redcloak away. He glanced over his shoulder as he was jostled through the travelers, hoping to catch sight of the soothsayer. He struggled helplessly against the guards' grip as the crowd parted to let them through to the Hanging Tree.

"I'm not the enemy!" he shouted.

Suddenly the noose was around his neck, the knot pulled tight. A barrel was rolled beneath the tree, and the guards lifted Trent to stand on the lid while they pulled the rope taut behind him. From over the heads of the gathered Romari men, he could see that Baba Soba had been joined by her five ancient sisters, the six in a huddle by the fire. The soothsayer held out her palm while her companions inspected it, casting eyes and fingers over the Redcloak's blood.

"Please!" Trent said tearfully, spluttering as he felt the barrel begin to move. One of the warriors gave the wooden cask a hard kick, and the rope yanked stiff in an instant as Trent found himself suspended in the air.

Trent lashed out, the noose tightening with each desperate kick. The Romari stood back, taking little pleasure in the execution of their enemy. They couldn't allow their whereabouts to reach their foes, and they weren't a force who took prisoners. Spittle flew from Trent's lips as he felt the darkness beginning to close in, his eyes bulging as he stared across at the babas, just at the moment when Soba threw her hands out toward the crowd.

"Stop!" bellowed the baba, her voice as loud as thunder.

The branch the rope was fastened to shattered suddenly, wood splintering as it came away from the tree. Trent collapsed, his legs buckling with the impact as he hit the cold, hard ground. He felt rough hands around his throat, as the Romari tugged the rope loose and rolled him over. Trent lay there wheezing as all six babas made their way across to him, the vengeful men parting to allow them through.

"The young man tells the truth," said one of the sisters.

"He *is* the brother of Drew Ferran," added the next.

"And he no longer fights for the Lion," said Baba Soba.

Trent struggled to speak, his throat raw from constriction. "I told you," he whispered. "I'm not your enemy."

"Where were you heading, child?" asked Soba, her blind eyes staring down to where he lay.

"To Brackenholme. My brother's friends—Lady Gretchen and Lady Whitley—they travel there and are in danger."

"Word reached us that the Wereladies you speak of travel with Romari," said a short zadka with a bushy beard.

"What kind of danger?" said another baba.

"I don't know. A friend of Drew's, Baron Ewan, said I had

to go to their aid; that they needed protecting. It's the least I could do for my brother." Trent lowered his eyes. "I am indebted to him."

Soba turned to her sisters, the babas muttering among one another while the men watched over Trent. The short zadka reached down and helped the young outrider to his feet. His grip was firm but forgiving.

"We can take no chances," he explained. "The Lionguard have never shown the Romari mercy, and with war spreading across Lyssia, we're more cautious than ever."

Trent nodded by way of an answer, turning back to the old women.

"We travel to Brackenholme," said Baba Soba, turning back to the Romari after discussing the news with her sisters. "Duke Bergan always showed our people great kindness. Any friend of the Wolf is a friend of ours. We would see these therian ladies protected."

"May I go on my way?" asked Trent hopefully.

"I'm afraid not, Master Ferran. Although you speak the truth when you tell us of your loyalty to your brother, the facts are cloudy. There's more that you haven't yet told us. Betrayal taints your blood."

Trent grimaced. *If I told them half the things I've done in the name of the Lion, they'd find another branch on that tree for me.*

"But I need to find Gretchen and Whitley. They're in danger!"

"Do they travel alone on the Dymling Road?" Soba sounded greatly concerned.

"No," said Trent. "They travel with another of your wise women: Baba Korga."

The menfolk began to protest, raising their voices in alarm as the babas turned to one another in disbelief.

"What is wrong?" said Trent.

"I don't know who the Wolf's friends travel with," said Baba Soba, her voice heavy with fear. "But it isn't Baba Korga."

"I know what I was told. Korga accompanies them to the Woodland Realm, offering them her protection."

"It can't be," said the soothsayer, her eyes reflecting the flames from the fire pit. "Baba Korga was killed in a Wyldermen attack months ago. Whoever 'protects' the Wereladies, it is not her." Her face was grave as Trent realized what she was saying. "Master Ferran, they travel with an imposter."

8

A DANGEROUS THING

FOR THE BRIEFEST moment, Whitley let her memory run away with itself. She was the young scout learning under the watchful gaze of Master Hogan once again, departing from Brackenholme with a head full of stories and a heart full of hope. Her father had reluctantly allowed her to serve her apprenticeship in the Woodland Watch, his words of encouragement about court life having constantly fallen on deaf ears.

She and Hogan had slipped out of the woodland city before dawn. The old scout had been given the task of hunting a strange beast that had been spotted along the southwestern edges of the forest. The mission had been potentially dangerous, as any foray into the Dyrewood was, but Hogan was too experienced to allow anything dreadful to befall the girl. The strange beast had turned out to be Drew Ferran, who had only recently discovered his lycanthropic powers and didn't yet know how to control them, and Whitley's life had never been the same since.

Now Whitley twisted in her saddle, looking back down the Dymling Road to where the small Romari caravan of wagons followed. She winced as she moved, feeling the flesh pull around the arrow wounds in her back. Thanks to her therian healing she was recovering swiftly, but the discomfort was a constant reminder of the grave danger the group was in. She'd taken the lead on Chancer, scouting ahead and keeping her eyes open for any peril that might await them. Though the old forest avenue was familiar to the Romari, none knew it quite as well as the folk of Brackenholme, especially the scouts of the Woodland Watch.

She turned back to the road ahead. Baba Korga's man, Rolff, was out of sight, as the wise woman had insisted that he should travel well ahead of the caravan on foot, without the noise of wagons or horses cloaking that of any would-be attackers. The mute Romari had been gone the whole day, under strict instructions to stay alert for any sign of Wyldermen. She hoped he would return safely when they made camp at nightfall.

Pulling Chancer off the road, Whitley allowed the caravan to catch up. Captain Harker rode alongside the lead wagon, and the experienced campaigner nodded somberly to her as they approached. It gave Whitley great comfort that the man on whom her father had leaned so heavily in all military matters was by her side. It was almost as if the Old Bear himself was present, and it broke Whitley's heart to think that she'd probably never see him again. News had reached them of Bergan's death in Highcliff, but the foolish dreamer inside the girl prayed he yet lived. As the daughter mourned her father, so the captain mourned his liege. His Greencloak companions, Tristam and Quist, rode at the back of the line.

Whitley waited for the middle wagons to pass by before falling in alongside the one that carried Gretchen and Baba Korga. With Rolff away scouting, Stirga and Yuzhnik had taken the reins, the sword-swallower and the fire-eater sharing the driver's bench up front.

"There's room for a small one up here," said Stirga, smiling.

"That's if you don't mind sitting between two old clowns," added Yuzhnik.

"I'm fine." Whitley smiled, patting Chancer's neck. "It feels good to be riding home, especially on this fine fellow."

The horse snorted, as if approving the compliment.

"How long until we make the city, my lady?" asked Stirga.

"A couple of days at most; I'd be there sooner if I rode on to warn them of our arrival."

"I wouldn't recommend anyone going on alone in these woods. I still say it's madness that the silent giant went on ahead."

"It's what his mistress told him to do," said Yuzhnik, his voice quiet.

There had been disagreements within the Vagabond Court regarding Rolff scouting far ahead of the group, but the old baba wouldn't be swayed; her mind was set on her man keeping a watchful eye over the Dyrewood.

"I'm sure he'll be fine. It'd be a fool, man or monster, who tangled with Rolff," said Whitley.

She waved to the two Romari and let Chancer slow once again, falling in behind the wagon, which was open at the rear, its canvas doors pinned back against the sides. Baba Korga and Gretchen sat within. The young Werefox's sleeves were rolled up, and she was busy skinning a rabbit. Badly.

"Good grief." Whitley laughed. "Are you doing some work at last?"

"Hold your tongue, Bearlady," said Gretchen in mock annoyance. "I decided it was about time I got my hands dirty."

Baba Korga watched as Gretchen tugged at the rabbit's skin, sawing at it with a tiny knife. The wise woman was smiling, clearly enjoying the noblewoman's struggle.

"Nobody should be so proud that they aren't afraid to get their hands bloody, my ladies. Each of us must eat to live."

"Quite right," said Gretchen, nodding enthusiastically as she lopped off another piece of fur-covered flesh. "And if you're just going to hang around there and poke fun at me, I'd suggest you trot off and make yourself useful. This is serious business, preparing dinner."

"Will there be enough to go around once you've hacked it to ribbons?" said Whitley, slapping her thigh.

Finally, Gretchen gave up her struggle to prepare the rabbit, joining Whitley in a bout of laughter. She raised her red-stained hands.

"I'm not really helping, am I? I just thought it would be good to show our friends that we're all in this together."

Despite the bitter cold, Whitley felt a warmth in her heart that had been missing for too long. Surrounded by violence for months, she'd forgotten what it felt like simply to be a girl enjoying a friend's company. Gretchen was proving a kindred spirit, a shoulder to lean on when times were so often dark.

Korga coughed suddenly, massaging her throat beneath her scarf with a liver-spotted hand. The old woman was clearly unwell, and the last place she should have been was on the road. She was covered in coats and blankets, layer upon layer protecting her from the cold. She'd spent much of their time while traveling resting within the dark confines of her caravan: this was a rare occasion when the girls could spend time with her.

"Are you all right, Baba?" asked Whitley as Gretchen washed her hands in a pail of water before drying them on her dress. Korga cleared her throat, waving Whitley's concerns away with a shriveled hand.

"I'm fine. Something I've eaten is disagreeing with me, that's all." She pulled one of the blankets closer. "You two have known each other for a long time?"

Gretchen and Whitley looked at one another, nodding.

"Since infancy," said the scout. "Gretchen would come and stay in my father's court occasionally while her father, Earl Gaston, resided in Highcliff. He was one of the Lion's advisers."

"Don't remind me," said Gretchen, still ashamed of what her father had endured under Leopold's reign. "I spent most of my childhood being shipped around Lyssia. If it wasn't Brackenholme, it was Stormdale or Redmire."

"Redmire?" said Korga. "The home of the Boarlords? So that's how you know your friend Hector you've spoken of?"

"Indeed," said Gretchen. "We all spent a great deal of time in one another's company while growing up. We're cousins in every sense of the word."

"So how is it that you know the Wolf?"

Whitley cut in, pleased to be able to tell her part in the story. She quickly recounted the circumstances of how she and Master Hogan had found a feral Drew in the Dyrewood, and their encounter with the Wyldermen as they made their way to Brackenholme along the Dymling Road.

"This very road?" asked the old woman. "It must bring back memories for you. Sounds like a frightening experience!"

"I wouldn't have changed it for the world."

The moment the words were out, Whitley blushed, as her

reply had come out a little more dreamily than she would have liked. Her response wasn't lost on Gretchen, whose arched eyebrow caught the baba's attention.

"And you, Lady Gretchen. You seem to know Drew equally well?"

"If not better," said Gretchen, instantly deflating the scout with a playful wink. "I was lodging with Baron Huth, the late Lord of Redmire, when Drew arrived." She proceeded to tell the tale of Drew's fight with the attacking Lionguard and their flight down the Redwine. Her near-death experience in the coils of Vala the Wereserpent, deep in the heart of the sinister Wyrmwood, had been chilling, and Gretchen was in no doubt that the monstrous snake would have devoured her had Drew not stepped in to rescue her. She recounted their journey to All Hallows Bay and subsequent abduction by Count Vega, who'd handed them over to the Lion before switching sides; there was little she left out.

Whitley knew the tale of Drew, Hector, and Gretchen; she spotted the parts of the adventure where the Fox had embellished the facts, but kept silent.

"Goodness," said the baba, her toothless smile making her ancient face scrunch up. "It sounds like Drew made quite an impression upon both of you. Does the Wolf know how you both feel about him?"

Whitley and Gretchen were looking at each other again, uncertainly.

"I don't know what you mean," said Gretchen, color rising in her cheeks.

"We're all just friends," added Whitley, eager to change the subject.

Whitley wasn't a fool. She knew full well how Gretchen felt about the young Wolflord. For all their differences and the fact that they came from conflicting worlds, a bond had grown between the Werefox and the boy from the Cold Coast. Gretchen had been betrothed to Prince Lucas for her entire life, and when her marriage to the Lion fell through, Drew had been there to comfort her. She'd never said as much to Whitley, but some things didn't need voicing. Gretchen's feelings were evident in her actions, the way her mood lightened whenever Drew's name was mentioned, and he appeared to thrive in her presence, too. There was something powerful between the Fox and the Wolf.

"My apologies," said Baba Korga. "If I've spoken out of turn, it wasn't my intention." She patted her hands over her leathery face. "From what I've heard—not just from yourselves—Drew sounds like a remarkable character. But a dangerous thing is love; I've seen many a friendship sundered by a broken heart over my long years."

Whitley smiled awkwardly, and Gretchen even managed a laugh, but each was suddenly numbed into silence. Whitley glanced at the sides of the caravan, then looked down the road as if suddenly seeing an excuse to be away.

"Excuse me," she said, her voice trembling slightly. "I'm needed at the front."

With that she was off, letting Chancer stretch his legs as she sped past the Romari caravans to the head of the line, resuming her position as scout. The horse slowed to a trot, shaking his mane, wishing to be running at full stride again. Whitley's memory took her elsewhere once more. It was the dead of night and she was on a bluff, overlooking the Longridings, Drew Ferran at her side, his arm around her. They looked into each other's eyes—and then, that sudden kiss, and her awkward reaction, fleeing into the night like a frightened animal. Little did she know it would be her last encounter with him.

She missed him terribly, and, as with her father, feared that she'd seen the last of him.

She had to be strong: her brothers in the Woodland Watch needed her, as did her people. With her father and brother having taken the long sleep, she was needed in Brackenholme. Dwelling on the past did no good, nor dreaming about what might have been. Whitley had to look to the future, and whatever dangers awaited her. Wiping a tear from her eye, she tried to concentrate on the Dymling Road.

PART II

DREAD AND DESPERATION

I

THE WAR MACHINE

THE FIRST OF Riven's siege towers had rumbled into the meadows around Stormdale late that evening, to the delight of the Catlords' army. A team of sixteen heavy horses had hauled the tower into the valley, four enormous wheels turning over, cutting up ice and snow as they drew inexorably closer to the city. More would surely follow in the coming days, but the sight of the first tower brought wild cheers from the men of Vermire and Riven. This was the first of many siege engines made to breach the Staglords' walls.

While the enemy encampment had settled for the evening, welcoming their allies around their fires, the people of Stormdale had watched miserably, seeing the stranglehold around their city tightening. It was late, and the night watch kept their focus fixed on their foes. There would be no attack this evening at such an hour, at least not from the Rats or Crows. Lord Reinhardt stood on the outer wall alongside Magister Siegfried, the old man leaning hard on his staff.

"Are you sure this is the right thing to do?" asked the old healer. "It's very risky."

"It's too late for second thoughts, friend," replied the Staglord. "He's already beyond the wall."

From their vantage point on the ramparts, Reinhardt and Siegfried caught the briefest glimpse of a dark shape dashing for the small copse of trees that stood nearest to the city walls. Stormdale was unlit, shrouded in darkness, as were her walls around their base. The only illumination came from the enemy campfires some distance away, the moon and stars obscured by a thick bank of clouds.

Drew crouched low in the sparse undergrowth that surrounded the trees. A small pack was slung over his shoulder, its contents wrapped in cloth to stop them from jostling together and making any noise. Moonbrand, the Sword of the Wolflords, remained sheathed on his hip, the weapon's apparent weightlessness providing little encumbrance. A stream bed snaked below him, winding its way past the trees before disappearing into the enemy camp, tantalizingly close to his target.

The Wolflord shook his head, wishing Red Rufus was still

with them. It had come as a huge surprise to Drew to discover that Red Rufus had flown away from Stormdale without a word of good-bye. He'd hoped the old bird would stay by his side; allies for Drew's cause were becoming few and far between in Lyssia, especially ones with military experience like Red Rufus. The Hawk had served as an aerial scout for Wergar decades ago, warning him when danger approached. To lose him on the eve of battle was a bitter blow to the Wolf and the Stags. Drew in particular had expected more from Red Rufus; the Hawk was the last person he'd expected to be a deserter.

The odds are grave though, thought Drew, taking a good look at the encampment from the ground for the first time. With thousands already gathered and more to come, what chance did the men and women of Stormdale have? If the Hawklord had remained, Drew's present task wouldn't be proving half as difficult. Red Rufus could have carried him into the heart of the enemy, flying him back out in no time at all. Instead Drew had resorted to going in on foot; this mission would be fatal should it go awry.

Dropping silently into the ditch, Drew set off alongside the stream bed, staying low. Soon he was running through the outskirts of the camp, careful to keep his bare, clawed feet away from the water's edge; a telltale splash would be sure to end his mission before it had begun. He couldn't do this without engaging with some of his therianthropic ability. Taking on a few of the Wolf's aspects, he became a stealthy hunter, his senses

94

heightened to aid his task. A low bridge spanned the stream ahead where it widened, joining one fallow meadow to the next, linking up the enemy's lines. He slowed as he approached and spotted a lone soldier standing in its center.

The man's back was turned, the warrior taking a moment to relieve himself in the stream. Drew hugged the dark wall of the ditch, shrouded by rocks and roots that hung from the frozen bank. The man finished his business, then turned to look back up the stream in Drew's direction. The Wolflord held his breath, careful not to exhale a telltale ball of mist. Then the soldier went on his way, heavy boots tramping across the bridge as he returned to camp.

Drew ran on, beneath the bridge, drawing closer to his target. The siege tower stood unguarded beside a huge tent, the machine safe behind enemy lines and out of range of Staglord attack. At least, so the Rats and Crows thought.

Climbing deftly up the bank, Drew crawled quickly across to the tent, pausing for a moment to lift the base of the canvas wall. A single guard sat in the center on a stool, a lantern at his feet lighting the contents of the tent arranged regimentally around him. Provisions stood stacked against one another— dozens of barrels crammed full of arrows, row upon row of spears and pikes.

This tent alone would supply Stormdale through any siege, thought Drew. He hoped it was their main store of weapons and not one of many. Ducking back from the foot of the tent, Drew clung to the shadows and scrambled toward the wooden tower.

It was just as he and Reinhardt had feared. The construct was perhaps four stories high, easily tall enough to reach the top of Stormdale's outer walls. Two sets of wide wooden steps ran around each other within its frame, allowing an attacking force to run both up and down the tower at the same time. Animal hide and wooden planking provided a shield along the entire front of the structure, protecting enemy soldiers from the bows of Stormdale's defenders. If the tower reached the walls with an army at its back, the results would be devastating. Drew had to work fast.

Climbing into the tower, he traversed the first set of steps to the first floor. Once there he unslung his pack, taking out five flasks of oil and unwrapping them. Removing the corks, he set about splashing the amber liquid from three flasks across the platform's deck. The fourth flask he threw across the hide wall, the oil soaking into the skin paneling and pouring down its length toward the base.

Drew held the last oil flask in his hand, formulating a fresh idea in that instant. He made his way down the slatted steps, the smell of oil now strong in the air. Hopping down from the structure, he rushed over and poured the oil across the munitions tent's rear wall, making as little noise as possible as he drenched the canvas. As the last drops fell, Drew quietly placed the flask on the ground and pulled out his three firesticks. Lighting anything with a flint and steel was hopeless for Drew with just one hand, but the ingenious Magister Siegfried had provided him with small, sulphurous-smelling sticks of kindling. Biting a stick between his jaws, he struck a shard of flint he'd been given down its length, and a spark briefly appeared, then spluttered out. He was about to strike a second time when he heard voices approaching.

"It's the Vermirians, ain't it?" said the first. "They've been takin' the lion's share from the field tent."

"They think because they work for the Lion that means they get first pick of everything. Greedy rats!"

Drew looked around—there was nowhere to hide, the booted footsteps were approaching fast and flickering torchlight glowed ever brighter around the side of the tent.

"Have you seen their gear?" asked the first. "Half of them have got silver-blessed weapons, and the rest are fully armored!"

"I'm just glad they're on our side," added his comrade.

"They may bring the silver, but we bring the siege engines. . . . " said the other as the two stepped around the back of the tent together.

The first soldier never completed his boast, as Drew's open hand caught him on the side of the head, sending him flying head-to-head into his companion with a sickening crunch. Only the first soldier fell, the second staggering blindly out of the way with his torch, wailing as he went.

"Brenn!" cursed Drew, leaping forward to silence the man. Before the young Wolf could reach him, the soldier had crashed into the side of the siege tower. The moment the torch's guttering flame licked the edge of the hide wall, the yellow fire raced up its length, half completing Drew's mission. The soldier's arm was now slick with the oil, and his wail became a shriek of terror as he dropped the torch to flap at his blazing arm.

Snatching up the flaming brand from the floor, Drew launched it into the side of the munitions tent before racing back toward the stream bed. He glanced back at the tent and tower, which were both alight, black smoke billowing into the frigid sky.

Drew hit the icy water in the bottom of the ditch with a splash. He pounded through the stream, back toward Stormdale. As he approached the low bridge, four black-cloaked archers appeared along its length, stopping their run as they saw his approach. They reached for their arrows, loading bows as he neared. Drew sped up, embracing the change fully now and unsheathing Moonbrand as he took to the air. The middle two bowmen were leveling their weapons just as the Werewolf leapt at them.

The first archer was run through cleanly by the sword, the glowing blade emerging from his back, shining momentarily before it was whipped free again. Drew's clawed foot sent the next man crashing into a third, the two tumbling from the bridge. Drew barged the dying bowman into the last of the black-cloaked men, but the archer sidestepped his companion, firing his bow wildly at close range to the Werewolf. The arrow cut into Drew's left shoulder, and the pain was instantaneous. A roar from the Wolf was enough to break the man's courage, and the archer jumped from the bridge to join his comrades in the ditch. Drew leapt back into the stream bed, running swiftly away from the melee as the call to arms went up in the camp. Soon he was clearing the copse of trees and dashing the final distance to the walls of Stormdale, where the gates were already opening to allow him in.

Drew staggered to a halt in the avenue beyond the gates, a crowd of townsfolk and soldiers giving him room while his body reverted to its human state. Reinhardt and his fellow Staglords raced down the gatehouse steps, and the limping nobleman was the first to approach the shifting Werewolf. Drew snarled, a trace of the beast remaining, as he reached for the arrow that was still buried in his shoulder.

"Be careful," said Magister Siegfried, the last to approach. "If that was a Vermirian arrow, the chances are it's silver. Come with me; I'll see to the wound."

As Drew stepped toward the old healer, a roaring, crashing sound beyond the walls was followed by a cheer from the Graycloaks who manned the parapets.

"It's the tower, my lord! It's fallen! Their camp is ablaze!"

Drew couldn't rejoice with the Graycloaks. His mind went

back to the soldier he'd left in the flames, his arm wreathed in fire, now likely burning to death. When he closed his eyes he could still see the slack face of the archer on the bridge, Moonbrand buried in his belly. The images made his stomach clench.

Like it or not, day by day he was following his legacy, shadowing the footsteps of his father, Wergar the Wolf. Each victory took him closer to being a king, every battle branding him a killer.

There could be no turning away from his destiny.

As Siegfried led Drew away, the men and women of Stormdale who were gathered in the street and along the walls began chanting triumphantly, using the dialect of the Barebones.

"Any sign of Red Rufus?" asked Drew.

"No," replied the magister sadly.

"Curse the coward," said Drew bitterly.

The chants of the crowd grew louder and louder as they spread throughout the streets and ramparts of Stormdale. Drew could sense the camaraderie and conviction behind them.

"You're a hero, Drew Ferran," said the old healer warmly. "That single act has given them hope."

"The battle's far from over, Siegfried."

"Allow them this moment. Let them enjoy victory; perhaps they'll get a taste for it."

Drew looked around as the chant continued to build. "What are they saying?" he asked as they continued on their way.

Siegfried walked steadfastly on, just a flicker of pride crossing the magister's weary face. "'The Wolf,'" he said. "'The Wolf is our savior.'"

2

INTO THE LIGHT

THE COLD WATER came up to their waists, chilling their aching bones to the marrow. Duke Bergan staggered on blindly, pushing the discomfort from his mind, his frail hand keeping a tight hold of Captain Fry's shoulder in front of him. His other arm was extended behind him, holding Pick by the collar of her soaking shirt. The only sources of light were the strange luminescent clumps of lichen they'd scraped from the walls, smeared across the blades of the daggers they held up before them. What caused the mosses to glow, nobody knew, but they were grateful beyond words for the faint illumination. Occasionally the briefest detail of rock could be seen as the tunnel ceiling sloped down ahead of them, threatening to submerge beneath the water before rising up beyond.

The knight of Stormdale, Sir Palfrey, had died during the night, and Bergan had taken the man's death hard. The knights had joined him in Highcliff's Garden of the Dead to fight by his side. For one to die in such dreadful circumstances, deep beneath the earth, far from home, weighed heavily on his mind. He shook his head, trying to stop his thoughts from returning to the cold body they'd left behind in the cavern. Instead, he looked ahead, squinting through the gloom.

Bo Carver and Sir Howard suddenly appeared in front of them, the glowing lichen illuminating them faintly in the dark. The tunnel ended behind them and the rock wall disappeared into the cold water all around them. Carver's barely visible face was dripping with water and set in a frown.

"We can go no farther without going under," said the Lord of Thieves.

"For what good?" asked Howard, exhausted by their ordeal and the loss of his friend. "We might drown before we reach air again! Do you even *know* if there's a tunnel there, Carver? We're lost, admit it!"

"The traitors came this way," said Bergan with a snort. "I may be weak and weary, but my nose doesn't fail me. The air's thick with their scent."

Carver turned to Howard. "Care to argue with a Bearlord, good knight?"

"How can you be sure they haven't drowned up there?" asked Fry, nodding to where the roof sloped beneath the water.

"We can't." Carver smiled.

Bergan passed Pick across to Fry, stepping past the Sturmlander and pushing between Carver and Howard. He placed his hands on the walls and took a few deep breaths.

"What are you doing?" asked Carver.

"Going for a swim."

"This is no time for jest, Your Grace."

"And I'm in no jesting mood. If you think I'm letting one of you risk your life for me, you're wrong. Besides which, who has the bigger lungs: a human or bear?"

"There's one problem," said Fry, as Pick rested her head against his shoulder. "If we all go through, the last torch brand will be soaked and useless."

Bergan stopped what he was doing and looked at the others.

"We cannot stay down here forever. Better to die trying to escape than curl up and lose the will to live."

They nodded, Pick's eyes wide with fear.

With great effort, Bergan allowed the Bear to emerge, his frame shifting as he threatened to fill the tunnel, the transformation exhausting the scraps of energy his body still had in reserve. The men stood back, keeping their distance as the Lord of Brackenholme's ursine side appeared. His bones cracked, joints broadening to take his great mass, as his huge muzzle broke through his skull.

"Wait here," growled the Werebear, before taking a gulp of air and diving under.

The submerged tunnel remained wide, with space for the therianthrope's body as he kicked down, following the descending ceiling. His enormous paws acted as paddles, propelling him swiftly through the cold water, beyond a point where the ceiling suddenly disappeared. With a gasp he emerged into air, and not the stale, dead atmosphere of the labyrinth, but a hint of something else: fresh air.

He shook his coat for a moment, standing in the shallows of the passage, before filling his lungs and diving back into the water-filled tunnel.

When he emerged on the other side, his companions all cheered with relief at his return.

The Bearlord clapped his paws together with childlike excitement. "You must go through!" he said, the joy evident in his voice. "Fresh air lies beyond! There's an exit from this miserable crypt!"

The men looked at one another for the briefest moment, before deciding who should go first. Howard shook off the remains of his armor, diving under and speeding on his way. Carver followed, with Fry in hot pursuit. Last to go through was Bergan, this time with Pick's shirt in his jaws, the big Bear spiriting them both swiftly through the freezing water and out the other side. Bergan spluttered, clearing his throat, as Pick trembled on the floor.

"Are you all right, child?" asked the Bearlord, his gruff voice softening. The girl nodded, although her body shook with shock.

Bergan allowed the Bear to recede, reaching back to loosen his cloak from his shrinking body. Soaking as it was, it was still another layer for Pick to wear. He lifted her from the ground, a bit of his old self returning as he found strength he'd thought lost. Carrying her in his arms, he looked down the tunnel, unable to see the others.

"Carver! Fry! Howard!" he called, taking the first steps up the incline. He was about to shout for them again when he heard the first scream.

Without hesitation Bergan began to run with Pick in his weary embrace. As he followed the tunnel upward, he noticed light reflecting off the smooth walls. The tunnel switched one way and then the other, climbing ever higher until suddenly dropping away at a frightening angle. Bergan's legs went from under him, the ax on his back striking the tunnel floor as he began a swift descent, Pick clutching his chest for dear life. The Bearlord picked up speed as he bounced down the tunnel, sliding out onto the floor in a crunching tangle of limbs.

The tunnel mouth opened into a large cavern. At the far side of the chamber, further hints of daylight bounced off the polished surfaces of another glassy-walled tunnel. Between the Bearlord and escape was a dark and dank scene of horror.

His three companions stood before him, their weapons drawn as they surveyed the grisly drama in the half light. Enormous worms writhed across the floor of the cavern, pale, blind, bulbous heads bobbing as they lurched toward the escapees. The creatures resembled giant earthworms, their translucent skin revealing innards that beat with white blood. They were as long as thirty feet and as tall as a hunting dog, their heads topped with circular rows of serrated teeth.

As Bergan surveyed the scene, it became evident that the treacherous thieves who had abandoned them had indeed come that way. Here and there the odd body part of Hitch and his gang could be seen, partly digested, suspended inside the worms' transparent intestines.

The Bearlord grimaced as he spied the half-eaten remains that littered the floor of the chamber. Six of the creatures squirmed across the cavern, winding their vile bodies among the numerous large stalagmites that rose from the ground, immediately drawn to the intruders' faint body heat.

"Move!" shouted Bergan, prompting his companions to action.

Carver was off instantly, cutting a path between the creatures, with Howard and Fry close behind. Bergan followed, clutching Pick. Carver's knives flashed as one of the creatures lurched at him, and he plunged both daggers into the beast's rolls of skin. The undulating flesh recoiled, sending Carver's arms and daggers flying back. Though the creature's milky blood oozed from the wounds, it showed no sign of stopping, snatching at the Lord of Thieves with its serrated maw.

Carver kicked at the head, the monster rolling away, allowing Howard and Fry to dash by. As Bergan tried to follow he found his path suddenly cut off, and another worm encircled them, so he and Carver were separated from their allies. More of the beasts were beginning to squirm out of the cavern walls around them. Bergan hefted his great ax from his back, swinging Pick around in its place, raising the half-moon blade as he tried to find a way through.

Carver lashed out repeatedly, his daggers making no impact upon the ribbed flesh of the creature as it looped itself around his legs and torso. It began to tighten its coils, the thief's arms trapped at his side as its terrible mouth opened wide, coming down over him. Bergan lashed out, the ax blade chopping clean through the creature's head, white blood fountaining from the decapitated body. The Bearlord tore the coils loose from the Thief-lord, as he and Carver looked for a way past the foul worms.

"The Bear, Your Grace; can you call upon it?" asked Carver.

"That last change took everything out of me," cried the Werelord, the ax now heavy in his grip. "I haven't the energy!"

As the worm in front of them reared up, Carver launched both his daggers into its open mouth, and the creature bucked back and writhed spasmodically. A gap had opened. Snatching the ax from the therian, the Lord of the Thieves pushed Bergan and Pick on, lashing out wildly when more of the creatures closed in at their heels.

Bergan ran hard, his lungs heaving with the exertion, Pick's hands throttling him as she clung on in terror. He heard his ax striking the ground behind him, the blade sending showers of sparks off the cavern floor with each blow. He prayed to Brenn that Carver was finding his mark with some of his swings.

Bergan collapsed alongside Howard and Fry at the base of the exit tunnel, where more light reflected down from above. Stalagmites were visible for maybe twenty or thirty feet up the slope, rising from the ground where the passage leveled out, but getting there would be impossible. With a heavy heart he noticed that the route had the same polished rock as those they'd come across earlier, but he was no longer sure this was caused by the passage of water.

"We'll never get out!" said Howard, his longsword slick with white blood. More of the creatures emerged from the cavern walls, finding their way to the cave floor.

Pick suddenly leapt off Bergan's back and jumped into the darkness in the direction of the creatures.

"No!" shouted the Bearlord, about to follow before he saw her rifling through the remains of one of the thieves. She scampered back, just as a worm lunged for her, Fry stepping forward and slashing at the beast. In her hands she held the long length of rope that the thieves had taken with them. Throwing it over her shoulder, she jumped up toward the exit tunnel.

"What are you doing?" said Fry, pulling Pick back for a moment.

Bergan tugged the Sturmlander's hand free. "Let her go."

Reluctantly the captain released his grip, and within moments the girl-thief was scampering up the slippery incline, finding handholds where nobody else would. Carver clattered into their backs, short of breath, Bergan's ax awash with gore.

"I could get used to an ax," the Thief-lord said with a hollow laugh, though his face was white with fear.

Pick was halfway up the tunnel now, slipping occasionally as she progressed, but nearing the slope's summit. She moved with catlike grace, no doubt learned from scaling buildings within Highcliff over her handful of years. Suddenly she reached the top and wound the rope round the largest stalagmite she could find before dropping the end back down the tunnel.

Bergan gave Fry a shove, sending the captain forward to snatch hold of the rope. Hand over hand he drew himself up the incline, soon joining Pick at the top. Next went Howard, handing his sword over to Bergan to help keep the creatures at bay.

"Thank you, Carver," said Bergan.

"For what?" panted Carver, hacking at the monsters.

"Coming back for me in the Garden of the Dead."

"You realize you're going next, don't you?" said Carver with a gasp, lunging forward with Bergan's ax.

"You know me: I like to be the last one out." The Bearlord grimaced, skewering a worm on the knight's sword. He gave the thief an elbow in his side. "On your way!"

Reluctantly, Carver swapped weapons with Bergan before clambering up the tunnel's length. Bergan roared at the creatures; not the bellow of a Werebear, but the scream of a man with nothing left to lose. One of the worms lurched at him, and the Werelord launched a fist into the side of its bulbous head, sending it snapping into its brethren.

"Climb!" shouted his companions, drawing the Bearlord from his battle.

The rope was waiting for him. Throwing the ax into the loop of leather on his back, he grabbed hold with tired hands and tried to climb. The rope slipped through his fingers, which were slippery with white blood, and his knees gave way as he almost tumbled to the floor. The mass of white worms rose behind him, squirming over one another in their attempt to reach him.

"Loop it about your arm!" called Carver. "Quick!"

Bergan's fingers fumbled with the rope, throwing it around his shoulder and forearm and holding it fast with his free hand. The men above heaved, hauling him up the tunnel a few yards. A worm appeared below him, opening its mouth speculatively and receiving the Bearlord's boot in its face for its trouble.

Another heave took him a yard higher, and soon the men were finding a rhythm, drawing Bergan away from danger. Or so they thought. The worms were climbing over one another now, filling the space below, four then five mouths snapping at the air as they allowed their muscles to undulate against one another, propelling them up the tunnel toward Bergan.

Howard reached down to the Bearlord, extending his hand toward him.

"Take my hand!" cried the knight.

"No!" shouted Bergan. "Get back, Howard!"

He kicked out again, as the circular mouths came ever closer and the stench of rotten flesh filled the air. Bergan was inches away from the top of the tunnel now as Howard lunged forward to grab hold of him. His hand connected, but his momentum took him too far, adding weight to the Bearlord's bulk. Fry and Carver struggled to keep hold of the rope, letting a few inches of the hemp run through their hands in response to the sudden additional load. Those two inches were all it took.

Howard's hand flailed in the space where Bergan had been a second before as the knight slipped forward. Pick tried to snatch at the man, but it was too late; he was already falling. Howard tumbled past Bergan and landed on the bed of worm heads, the monstrous mouths immediately closing on him. Pick screamed.

"Look away, child!" Fry wailed as he and Carver pulled Bergan up the remaining length of the tunnel.

Howard cried out in the worms' embrace as their teeth tore into him, his screams rising in pitch.

"Take the girl, Fry, and be quick about it," said Carver, pushing the Sturmlander and the sobbing child toward the

112

light. Bergan stood by Carver's side as the man pulled another knife from his belt. The Lord of Thieves looked at him.

"You don't need to see this," Carver said, raising the blade, ready to throw.

Carver was right. Bergan set off after the others without looking back, and Sir Howard's cries were cut short as the Thief-lord let his knife fly.

3

CUTTING THE NET

HAVING GROWN IN number over the previous weeks, the Romari forces were ready to move. Though they lacked the military knowledge and organization of other armies in the Seven Realms, they more than made up for this in spirit. Guerrilla warfare was their chosen method of combat, and once they had reached Brackenholme, they would take the fight to the Catlords.

With tents being folded away and wagons packed, the camp was a hive of activity. The solitary prisoner in their custody remained tied to the trunk of the Hanging Tree. Trent watched the Romari rushing about their business, each focused on his or her task and working quickly. He was impressed by their efficiency as the settlement vanished before his eyes.

They intended to take him to Brackenholme and deliver him to the Bearlords, where he could explain his tale firsthand. Trent had other plans: such a journey would take too long with the procession of wagons, and if Lady Gretchen and Lady Whitley *were* in danger, any delay could be deadly.

Behind the tree, the spare horses were tethered. Craning his neck, he could just see Storm's chestnut brown mane gleaming in the early-morning light. A short distance away, the fire that the babas had gathered around was burning low. Baba Soba's tent was still standing and would be one of the last to be dismantled. He'd seen them take his equipment in there and there was something he couldn't leave the camp without. A lone Romari warrior tipped a cauldron of water onto the embers, killing the smoking coals before kicking dirt over the pit.

Trent waited until the guard had moved on before shaking the cords loose around his wrists. The Romari had underestimated the young man's strength and experience, thinking that the ropes around the tree would be enough to hold him. But Trent had grown up on a Cold Coast farm. His hands were used to hard work, and ropes had played a key part in his duties. His apprenticeship in rope mastery had continued in the army, when as an outrider he was charged with looking after his mount. The bonds around his wrists had been a struggle to undo, but after two nights bound to the Hanging Tree he'd eventually worked them loose.

Squeezing the ropes from around his chest, he slid down

to the ground and scrambled around the fire pit toward the old woman's tent. Baba Soba had been the last to rise the previous day, only emerging around noon; he hoped this was routine for the soothsayer. The Romari would come to her last no doubt, only stirring her when they needed to be off. He pulled back the tent flap and ducked in.

The tent was small, no grander than any others in the camp. Even so, it had the soothsayer's marks all over it. The corpses of small creatures—rodents, sparrows, and frogs— hung from the fabric ceiling, their bodies desiccated. A chest lay open, all manner of strange paraphernalia cluttered within: pots, sticks, knives, animal skulls, lengths of fabric, and balls of twine. At the opposite end of the tent, Trent spied what he'd come looking for: the Wolfshead blade, still in its sheath, leaning against the head end of the cot. Within the bed, Baba Soba slept, oblivious to the noises outside as her people worked.

Nerves suddenly took hold of Trent, and the feeling he'd had the other night returned. He felt anxiety spreading now from his heart to his throat, threatening to choke him.

Just breathe, you fool! She's a blind old woman, and she's fast asleep. She can't hurt you!

He knew he was fooling himself. She might be old, but she was far from harmless. He'd heard rumors about the babas from his comrades in the Lionguard: that they were witches, dark magisters who could curse you in the blink of an eye. What she'd done when he'd been dragged before her had been no parlor trick. He was in no doubt that she had power over life and death.

Drew, thought Trent. *Drew needs me.*

As quickly as the fear had come, it was subsiding. Trent shook his head in disbelief. She was right about the words of magick: his brother's name warded off her enchantment. Drying his clammy hands on his trousers, he set off across the floor, treading lightly on the baba's colorful rug, toward the far side of the chamber. As he passed the cot, he glanced at the old woman covered in blankets and animal skins, lost beneath the pile of bedding.

Now at the bed's head, he reached a trembling hand out toward the sword, drawing closer to the shining Wolfshead pommel. Slowly his hand closed round the handle, the grip cold against his flesh.

In a flash, a skeletal hand shot out of the bedding, taking hold of his wrist. The grip was merciless, the touch like death itself. The covers fell away to reveal Baba Soba's face inches from Trent's, blind eyes wide and staring through the young outrider. Trent's heartbeat instantly accelerated, nausea assailing him, his vision blurring. He tugged, trying to pull free, but he was trapped fast like a rabbit in a snare.

"You love him?"

The soothsayer's words were quiet and gentle, though her

grip was violent and strong. Trent knew full well of whom she spoke.

"With all my heart."

The wise woman held on, considering his words. The scar on his palm ached from where she'd cut him when he was captured and read his blood with her sisters. She released his wrist suddenly, sending him sprawling onto the floor of the tent. Scrambling away, his back collided with the chest, causing the lid to slam down.

"Go," she whispered once, closing her eyes and drawing her hand beneath the blankets. She rolled over, turning her back on him.

Trent was crawling on all fours, the sword and scabbard dragging along the floor beside him as he made for the tent flap. He dipped his head through and looked around. The Romari who had covered the fire pit was returning from where the horses were tethered.

There was no time to delay. Though the baba had allowed him to go, it was *she* who was allowing him to steal away, not her people. If they captured him as he escaped, would she speak in his defense? He doubted it.

The Romari was almost at the tent when Trent leapt from the door, charging into him and shoving him out of the way. He let out a warning cry, loud enough to alert the whole encampment, but Trent was already running.

He was in among the horses, finding Storm in an instant.

She yanked at the tethering rope, delighted to see him. Unsheathing the Wolfshead blade, he swung it down, severing the rope in a fluid motion before reaching up to the horse's saddle. The startled whinnies of two neighboring horses alerted him that someone was fast approaching. He turned to see three Romari closing on him through the other horses.

Snatching at the reins, he hauled himself onto Storm's back just as the first man ran up, reaching for him with grasping hands. Trent lashed out with a boot, cracking the Romari across the jaw and sending him back. He kicked Storm's flanks hard, and the mare reacted instantly, breaking from the crowd of animals at a fast pace.

More of the Romari were running now, trying to intercept Trent as he tore out of the camp, but there was no stopping the former Lionguard. Bows were drawn and arrows flew, but Storm carried him clear of the Romari missiles. A few souls leapt onto their own horses, giving chase to the outrider, but soon gave up as he disappeared into the distance on one of the fastest horses that had ever ridden through the Longridings. Storm's hooves tore at the ground, kicking up clouds of frosty earth as Trent Ferran headed straight for the Dyrewood.

4

Help from the Heavens

STORMDALE'S NEWFOUND HOPE was short-lived. The scenes of celebration following the destruction of the siege tower the previous night had given way to panic along the city's walls. A dozen different war machines had arrived throughout the following day, and the army of Rats and Crows had wasted no time in placing them across the field. Four more towers had been transported from Riven, in addition to catapults. The towers stood by, as the bolt throwers and shot slingers moved into range. The second wave had arrived. By noon that day the enemy had launched their first onslaught.

Archers advanced behind mobile walls, launching volleys of arrows at the battlements, many finding their way into the city. For every ten that flew, one was wrapped in burning rags, a fiery projectile that occasionally found thatched rooftops within the crowded, cramped city. Those who hadn't joined the militia rushed about in teams, attempting to put out the fires before they'd truly begun, but that was only the start.

Heavy steel bolts fired from the ballistae crashed into the walls, sending broken masonry tumbling onto the Graycloaks and the city. Soon the catapults joined the fray, initially launching boulders over the defenses to devastating effect. Buildings crumbled as huge rocks smashed into them, destroying centuries-old homes in the blink of an eye. By late afternoon the Ratlord, Vorjavik, had given the signal to release flaming shots of pitch, and fireballs screamed through the darkening sky, adding to the chaos within the city.

All the while the Graycloaks on the wall rushed valiantly to and fro, desperately seeking targets with their arrows. Their own catapults were put to work, unleashing round after round of rocks back at the enemy, occasionally using parts of the shattered walls as ammunition. Although this tested the resolve of Vorjavik's army, it didn't break them; they could see firsthand the effect their attack had on Stormdale and took heart at the Staglords' misery.

The five transformed Crowlords who were present took to the skies, carrying out aerial attacks of their own across the rooftops. Led by Lord Scree, they were careful to remain out of bowshot, sweeping over the city and striking swiftly. Their attacks were more cruel than anything the force beyond the wall could muster, making the sky rain with steel shot as they launched handfuls of the tiny missiles down onto the defenders. Dropped from such great height, the metal balls acted like crossbow bolts, puncturing the Graycloaks' exposed skin, tearing holes through flesh and breaking bones. The only defense from such attacks was armor and shields, and too few of the defenders were equipped with them.

Drew watched from the ramparts, dark clouds masking the moon above, feeling utterly helpless. While he'd been useful the previous night, a one-handed warrior wasn't much help to anyone in a bow fight. Not for the first time that night, he cursed Red Rufus for deserting them. Their lack of aerial defenses had left Stormdale exposed; the Hawklord could have caused some mayhem above the city, launching attacks of his own upon the Werecrows.

By nightfall the city was in flames, with the siege towers rolling toward the walls. Those too young or infirm to fight had disappeared behind the keep walls, seeking shelter in the castle, while the gatehouse remained open should the defenders need to retreat. The Graycloaks and militia were in no hurry, though. They remained along the broken walkways, ready to engage the enemy, while archers led by Lord Reinhardt peppered a team of Riven soldiers who edged ever closer to the gates with a battering ram. So long as the bowmen could keep the ram back, the knights and the Graycloaks felt they could hold the wall. Now was Drew's time. He looked up at the dark heavens.

"Brenn help us," he whispered.

The first tower juddered to a halt, yards from the wall in front of the Wolflord. Magister Wilhelm had made a medium-sized round shield for him, with leather straps that were bound to the stump of his left arm and were supple enough to withstand any transformation. Drew raised it before him, holding Moonbrand aloft as he and the Graycloaks prepared for the attack. Drew was surprised to feel the sword humming in his grasp, the white steel of the enchanted Sturmish blade glowing brighter as the moon threatened to break out of the clouds overhead. It appeared that the sword had powers beyond those he had yet experienced.

The tower trembled in front of the wall, and the thundering sound of enemy boots rattled through the structure as the enemy raced to its summit. Drew looked at the men around him.

"None get through!" he shouted, his voice roaring over the noise of the battle.

The tower wall suddenly swung down on huge hinges, a planked walkway clattering onto the battlements. Men of Riven in their now-familiar leather armor rushed across, swords and spears stabbing and slashing as they charged at the defenders. Drew met them halfway, leaping onto the wooden bridge and immediately sending a handful tumbling from the rickety platform. Swords rained down on his shield as spears lunged in around it, feverishly trying to find their way to the young Wolflord.

But their weaponry was no match for Drew's. Moonbrand flew, tearing into limbs and torsos as the attackers poured forth. Those who got past the Werelord were met by the waiting Graycloaks, the defenders empowered to have one so brave—and seemingly fearless—as Drew beside them. Swords and shields clashed as the men of Stormdale held the invaders back, pushing against the tide and standing at Drew's side.

Drew could hear a commander in the tower, shouting at his men, urging them up the steps toward the combat. *How many do they number?* he wondered, stricken by sudden fear. A vicious flurry of blows enabled him to glance over the side of the walkway. A huge group of warriors were gathered below, the men of Riven reinforced by a large contingent of black-cloaked, chain-shirted Vermirian soldiers. The situation was hopeless, but Drew couldn't let the Graycloaks see how overwhelmed they were. He didn't want to think about how long it might be before they had to beat a retreat. There were twenty Graycloaks on the sundered wall around him, but there were more than ten times that many enemy soldiers racing up the tower.

A sword blow glanced off the top of his head, but Drew ducked at just the right moment to avoid being scalped. His head rang as he momentarily lost his balance. He'd held the beast back long enough. The leather-clad fighter who'd struck him launched a kick at Drew's side, sending him toppling close to the edge of the walkway. More of the Riven soldiers joined him, kicking out and stabbing down, trying to force the Graycloaks' leader with the shining white sword from the wooden bridge. They couldn't have known he was a therianthrope, but they soon found out.

For a moment, the invaders must have thought there was a wild dog on the platform with them, snapping at their ankles. When the jaws connected with bones, shattering limbs and severing feet, they realized their problem was far greater. The beast emerged among the mass of screaming soldiers, and even the Graycloaks pulled back as the Werewolf rose with a mighty howl. The moon chose that moment to finally emerge from the cloudy sky, and in an instant white flames raced the entire length of Moonbrand, blinding the frantic attackers. Drew brought the weapon around in a wide arc, the blade severing everything it touched: sword, shield, spear, and body.

Drew roared and jumped forward, bodies crunching beneath his clawed feet as the Werewolf sought fresh foes. He was within the tower top now, surrounded by panicked leather-clad warriors who stabbed vainly at the lycanthrope. The swords found their target, but the men of Riven were ill-equipped, their steel untreated by silver, unlike those of the Vermirian Guard. Moonbrand lit up the structure, making the siege engine's summit glow like a beacon. Drew forced the men back, and they toppled over one another as they fell down the steps onto their companions' raised weapons. Finding himself alone on the highest floor of the tower, Drew turned to the walkway and let the blade fly once more, emboldened by its power. Moonbrand cut through the wooden planking, and the platform tumbled away, falling to the ground far below.

With a graceful bound, Drew leapt the ten feet back across to the battlements, just in time to see a quick-thinking Graycloak launch a flaming cask of oil at the tower. The barrel exploded within, sending flaming oil pouring through the structure, racing over the crowded soldiers who were trapped beneath. The screams of the enemy filled the air as the tower went up in smoke.

With the point of attack repelled, Drew and the Graycloaks looked along the walls to where they were needed next. Overhead, the clouds found their way back across the moon, the flames snuffed from Moonbrand instantly. As Drew led the men along the parapets in the direction of the gatehouse, he could see that two of the enemy towers had connected with the walls on either side of it. Three Staglords stood toe to toe with the enemy, two repelling the invaders on the one farthest away, Reinhardt holding his own against the one nearest. Though the Stags had transformed, their antlers flashing, the enemy was beginning to learn its lesson.

A mixture of Vermirian and Riven soldiers poured from the structures, the silver of the better-equipped Rat soldiers adding bite to the assailants' attack. Drew raced beyond the Graycloaks, rushing to Reinhardt's side. While the steel and silver sought his flesh, Drew's survival instinct kicked in. The shield came up, blocking blows, and the white longsword parried every attack. Between each defensive move, he returned to the attack, cutting and biting at the enemy. The Graycloak who had thrown the flaming cask at the first tower called for his men to stand aside, raising another of the small barrels high over his head.

A Vermirian arrow sailed over Drew's head, catching the Graycloak clean through the throat, and the barrel spun into the air before crashing back down onto the battlement. Liquid fire erupted among the Graycloaks. Most of them dived clear of the deadly explosion, but some were caught in the middle of it. With chaos before and behind him, Drew could feel their grip on the fight slipping. The enemy surged forward, thrilled to see the Graycloaks falling from the walls.

Below, the gates began to splinter as the battering ram was finally utilized, the bowmen on the walls having been drawn into hand-to-hand combat with the invaders. The enemy army was crowding around the gatehouse now, hundreds deep, intent upon entering the city.

"It's no good!" Drew shouted to Reinhardt. "The walls are breached. We have to retreat!"

There was no argument from the battered Staglord, his antlers slick with blood. He raised a horn to his lips as Drew stood in front of him, drawing the enemy attacks. The sound echoed across the city, a solemn signal to all on the walls that they had to beat a path back to the keep.

Drew stood his ground for a few moments longer than the

Stag and the Graycloaks, allowing them time to race through the flames and down to the streets below. Across the other side of the gatehouse he could see that the rest of the defenders had disengaged from the enemy, and the troops from Vermire and Riven were spilling over the ramparts.

The Werewolf's yellow eyes returned to the tower where a large black shape emerged at the top of the steps, pink eyes glowing in the dark. The long, clawed foot of the Wererat Vorjavik, War Marshal of the Lion's army, stepped on to the walkway. Drew could wait no longer.

He turned and ran, just as the first Vermirian soldiers swarmed over the walls around him. He leapt into the air, a silver spear catching his hip a glancing blow as he launched himself back into the city. He cleared the street below in an immense bound and landed on the roof of one of the few buildings that wasn't burning. He bounced off the thatch, rolling and dropping to the cobbles below, but didn't wait, sprinting away as the gates exploded behind him. He heard Vorjavik's shout, his cry monstrous and guttural.

"Run, Wolf! You've nowhere to hide!"

Drew's lupine legs propelled him up the steep main avenue, the road obscured by blinding smoke. He ran into stragglers who had fled the outer walls, pushing them on, yelling encouragement as he urged them up to the gates. He remained at the rear, looking back all the while, waiting for the first enemy warriors to emerge from the choking cloud. As the last of the Graycloaks stumbled through the gates, Drew followed them in, the reinforced, steel-bound doors slamming shut behind him. Bars the size of tree trunks slotted into place and a portcullis slid down from the gatehouse, shuddering into the ground with a clang. Mechanisms sprang into life as heavy chains began to rattle, hauling the drawbridge skyward until it was flush with the gates.

The castle courtyard was crammed with panicked people, shouting and screaming. Drew howled, commanding the attention of everyone in Stormdale.

"Those who can't fight, get into the keep! See to the wounded! You know what you have to do! The rest, take to the walls!"

Reinhardt lay on the floor nearby, grimacing as Magister Wilhelm crouched over him, tending a savage wound in his gut.

"Silver?" asked Drew warily.

"Steel," said Reinhardt through bloodied teeth. "But it still hurts!"

Wilhelm finished binding the wound, tightening an herb-soaked bandage around the Staglord's torso. Drew helped Reinhardt to his feet, the black clouds from the burning city billowing over the walls and around them.

"This smoke will be the death of us," said Reinhardt. "We won't even see them coming!"

"Brenn be blessed!" shouted Wilhelm suddenly, as raindrops

pattered on his face. As the shower became a downpour, he added, "The heavens bring us gifts aplenty this evening!"

"Aplenty?" asked Drew, puzzled by the old healer's words.

Wilhelm pointed through the crowd to where a group of Graycloaks and the remaining five Staglords had gathered. Something had certainly captured their attention. Drew loped over, letting his body shift at last, gradually returning to its human state with each shortening stride. The Graycloaks stood to one side, letting him through, as the Staglords parted.

Red Rufus stood before them, the last of his rust-colored feathers retreating beneath his skin. At his feet crouched a bent and withered old man with his hands tied tightly behind his back, his head bare of hair and mottled with liver spots. He looked up at Drew, the act taking a degree of strength. His face was a mask of hatred, his lips turned down in displeasure.

"Now then, pup," said Red Rufus, stepping over to stand by Drew's side and clapping a hand upon the Wolflord's shoulder. "Let me introduce Croke."

"*Count* Croke? The Lord of Riven?"

Red Rufus smiled. "That's right, lad," he said, looking back to the crouching Lord of the Werecrows.

"Meet our bargaining chip."

5

THE UNFINISHED MEAL

STORM TROTTED GENTLY along the Dymling Road, all too aware of the threats surrounding them. Trent had initially ridden hard upon entering the Dyrewood, gradually slowing as the atmosphere of the haunted forest soaked through his bones like creeping death. If the old baba had set his nerves on edge, they were now stretched to breaking point. Both rider and horse felt it. The ancient forest was thick with the scent of predators—wolves, bears, and worse—but something else hung in the air: the sweet smell of decay.

Not long after departing the Romari encampment, the young outrider had seen the emerald expanse of the Dyrewood, stretching east and west as far as the eye could see. Following the forest edge he'd found the Dymling Road before noon, hitting the gloomy avenue at a fast pace, Storm's hooves hammering like thunder. The tree branches wove together overhead, giving the old road the appearance of a never-ending tunnel. It hadn't taken long for the Dyrewood to work its menacing magic, and the traveler's momentum faltered as the mood and forest darkened.

Trent had heard tales about the haunted woods throughout his childhood: his mother and father had warned their sons of the dangers within. Then he'd heard the stories about how Drew had survived in the wilderness and found them unbelievable. He was struggling to survive after only one night; what kind of resilience had Drew shown to make the forest his own, his home? How much had his brother changed? Would he even recognize him should they ever meet again?

That morning he'd heard strange cries. Trent knew these were more than the sounds of wild beasts. These were human: Wyldermen, the feral and fierce roving tribes that made the Dyrewood their home. Late that afternoon he'd caught sight of a pack of wild dogs, stalking him through the undergrowth, racing to get ahead of Storm and cut her off. Trent had spurred her on, outrunning the dogs before they had a chance to launch an attack. When night finally drew in, the promise of sleep seemed little more than a fanciful dream; the Dyrewood wouldn't let him rest.

Trent's breath steamed in the cold, freezing before his eyes into a white cloud. Storm's hooves crunched along the icy road, and the remains of a recent camp came into view ahead. Trent's fists were knotted into Storm's mane; he was warier than he'd been since entering the forest. The rotten stench was growing strong, curdling the stomachs of rider and mount. Storm snorted her disapproval, throwing her head back, eyes rolling, as Trent urged her on with knees to her flanks. The camp was a little way off the road, and judging by the churned-up earth, it been made by a large party of people..

He spied the telltale ruts carved into the ground by wagon or caravan wheels—*Romari, perhaps?* How far behind them was he? A couple of days? Having never traveled the Dymling Road before, Trent had no idea how far it was to Brackenholme. His only clue was that Gretchen and Whitley were accompanied by Romari. Or people pretending to be Romari, whatever that meant. . . .

The horse stepped gingerly through the abandoned campsite. Trent pulled her up, sliding off her back. One big fire had been buried, having clearly provided for a huge number of people. *A hundred? More?* Trent sniffed at the air, hand close to his mouth, following the foul odor. Storm remained where she stood, showing no desire to find its source. The scent took him away from the main part of the camp, deeper into the woods surrounding it. Twigs snapped ahead of him, causing him to halt immediately.

Yellow eyes appeared in the darkness, blinking out of nowhere. The two large amber pools of light, fixed straight

ahead, focused on Trent: the eyes of a predator. Trent's mouth
was dry; his heart beat wildly, the sweet, sickly smell washing
over him now. *Is the scent from the beast?* Tentatively, Trent went
for the Wolfshead blade on his hip. His hands closed around
the sword handle, sliding it from its sheath. It was halfway out
of the scabbard when the creature stepped forward into the
moonlight.

The gray wolf was the largest he'd ever seen, the tips of
its ears almost reaching Trent's chest. It calmly stopped a few
yards away from Trent, its eyes never blinking, fixed on him.
The Wolfshead blade rattled, half out of the scabbard. Trent's
grip was tight, but his arms trembled. The beast could take his
head off in one bite, but who was quicker? But the wolf showed
no sign of aggression; no baring of teeth, no low growls. It
watched Trent intently. He stared back, trying to read the
creature. Its eyes were mesmerizing, cool and confident. *Is that
you, Drew?* Trent stifled a fearful smirk at the notion, his pulse
strangely slowing in the presence of the predator. He let the
Wolfshead blade slide back into the sheath as the wolf stepped
away, even standing to one side to allow Trent by. The young
soldier stepped forward cautiously, coming within a yard of the
wolf as he walked past, close enough to touch its shaggy pelt.
Nearby, Storm whinnied nervously, but the wolf paid no heed.

Trent kept facing the gray beast, stepping through the
trees toward where it had emerged. The smell was dreadful
now, causing him to gag. Unable to hold the wolf's gaze any

longer, Trent retched, bile rising in his throat. He stumbled, his forearm across his face as he turned toward the source of the vile odor.

The child was wedged into the roots of a tree, curled in a fetal position, a strange bilious slime covering her. She was maybe seven years old, and the only clue to her gender was the tiny floral stitching visible on her stained smock. With horror Trent noticed that, below the slime, her flesh had been torn off in places. He dry-heaved again as he turned away, collapsing into a nearby tree. *What creature could do this?* The stories he'd heard of the Wyldermen bore no resemblance to this type of attack.

The wolf's head emerged between the trees beside him, bowed low, as if respectful of the dead girl. *Why is the wolf averse to feeding on these leftovers?* Trent wondered. The creature wouldn't go near the child, instead dropping onto its belly, huge jaws resting on its paws as a dog might lie before a fire.

Trent spent the next half hour digging a grave for the child, the Wolfshead blade acting as a terrible shovel. He hacked at the frozen soil, loosening it with the weapon before clawing at the chunks of hard earth with his bare hands, the wolf watching him all the while. When the pit was deep enough that he felt no scavenger could reach the contents, he tenderly lowered the child into the grave, praying to Brenn before pushing the earth back over her.

The young man returned to Storm, tethering her before

finding somewhere to lie down. His teeth chattered and chills seized him, bringing on coughing bouts that rattled his chest like stones in a barrel. He couldn't sleep for long. The creature that had killed the Romari child was no doubt stalking the travelers. Trent looked up, struggling to keep his eyes open as the big wolf lay down on the far side of the camp. Any anxiety he'd felt in its presence had all but gone. Its eyes were fixed on him, encouraging him to close his own, to rest, to sleep. Trent faded away, blacking out as the cold gripped him, disappearing into a world of dreams where he chased Drew through the forest.

Trent woke to the sound of Storm's gentle whinnies, hot snorts from the horse's nostrils hitting his face. The night was still cold, the moon still up, but he was no longer shivering. He clenched his hands, blood coursing through them, fingertips no longer numb. He sat upright, patting himself. His chest actually felt warm across the leather of his breastplate. His fingers touched the earth beside him, and the ground felt strangely cool, but not freezing. Trent picked at the stray, dark hairs that had appeared on his cloak and armor, thick and fibrous strands of fur. His head jerked up, looking around the clearing. There was no sign of the beast that might just have saved his life.

The wolf was gone.

6

HOMECOMING

FLANKED BY SIX branches of the Woodland Watch, the long Romari caravan entered Brackenholme to a chorus of cheers from its people. Whitley rode at the front of the procession alongside Captain Harker, smiles of unbridled joy beaming from their faces at returning home. Whitley sat straight in Chancer's saddle, every inch the Greencloak scout, while the crowds filled the streets, waving and rejoicing at the return of the Bearlady. Children sat on the shoulders of parents, and those who couldn't find space in the street hung from the upper-floor windows of the shops and houses that lined the road. Gifts were passed across to the Romari who had brought their own safely home, and the visitors were treated like conquering heroes as they traversed the city streets.

"She's a sight for sore eyes, isn't she?" said Harker, his jaw trembling with emotion as he looked over his city.

"Thank Brenn she's been spared the madness that's engulfed the rest of Lyssia," replied Whitley, waving to the crowd as the leading horses halted in the city's center.

A large fountain marked the intersection of the Dymling and Dyre Roads, the latter leading out of the city to Stormdale in the east. The Romari caravan pulled up around the fountain, still swamped by the men and women of Brackenholme bestowing their thanks upon them. Gretchen rode forward on a pony, sidesaddle like any noble lady *should*, Whitley noticed with a wry grin. Quist and Tristam accompanied her, riding on either side. Stirga and Yuzhnik walked behind them, soaking up the crowd's adulation for a moment, the big fire-eater clenching his fists over his head like a prizefighter for all to see. Whitley turned Chancer as the Romari stepped forward.

"My dear, sweet Stirga and Yuzhnik: I speak on behalf of both Gretchen and myself when I say we're indebted to you for the kindness and courage you've shown since we met in Cape Gala. If ever you've had enough of the open road, you can call Brackenholme your home."

Gretchen leaned down from her saddle, giving Yuzhnik a big kiss on the top of his bald head. The old fire-eater grinned, color rushing through his cheeks as if his face were aflame.

"I'd say that's unlikely," said Stirga, "though the offer's

138

well appreciated. Wherever the road takes us, you may always consider us your friends, my lady. It was a pleasure to serve you."

"If you'll allow us, my lady," added Yuzhnik, "the wee man and I would be honored to put on a show for your people this evening. The Vagabond Players' last performance ended in blood and thunder in High Stable—perhaps we can make this one end in tears of joy?"

"The honor is ours," replied Whitley, bowing in her saddle to the Romari men.

She and Gretchen rode past them toward Baba Korga's caravan, where the old woman now sat on the driver's bench beside Rolff, speaking quietly to the mute giant. Rolff's bravery in traveling ahead of the caravan to ensure no ambush awaited hadn't gone unnoticed by the therian girls. Korga stopped whispering as she noticed the Ladies of Brackenholme and Hedgemoor approaching, her toothless smile wide.

"Baba Korga," said Gretchen. "Words cannot describe the debt Whitley and I owe you and the Romari. I echo what Whitley told the others: the gates of our cities are open to your people. Always."

"You're too kind, my lady," said the soothsayer. She held out her bony hands, gesturing toward the vista of the city. "While we're here, we'll treat it as home." Korga waved her hands at the girls, shooing them away. "Run along now," she said, winking.

"One of you has a reunion with her mother to attend. Never keep a mother waiting!"

Whitley smiled, bowing again before turning Chancer around.

"Come, cousin," she said as Gretchen sidled up alongside her. "I'll race you to the Great Oak."

The horse and pony leapt into life, galloping away from the fountain and the crowd, down the Dyre Road toward the ancient tree at the city's heart, leaving the Greencloaks struggling to keep up and the Romari far behind.

Duchess Rainier stood in the throne room of Brackenholme Hall, surrounded by the ladies and gentlemen of the court, awaiting the arrival of her daughter as patiently as was possible. When the waiting became too much, she set off across the chamber, flinging the great doors open wide and rushing toward the balconies that encircled the lofty palace. Wide walkways ran between the enormous branches that spanned the Great Oak, leading toward armories, kitchens, laundries, and guest chambers. Rainier took none of these, instead heading straight toward the cage that was lifted skyward into the canopy, her court in tow. Barely containing her excitement, the duchess clasped her hands to her chest as the bamboo chamber finally rose to the decked landing of the ancient tree.

Whitley was first out of the cage, dashing the short

distance and embracing her mother, all decorum lost. Rainier kissed Whitley's head over and over, while the girl buried her face in the crook of her mother's neck. The courtiers watched in tearful silence, each of them smiling. Finally the two parted, clinging to one another's hands.

"My child," gasped Rainier. "Praise Brenn for returning you to our halls! I feared all was lost."

"Many are, Mother," said Whitley, her eyes moist. Her mother's face was wet with tears; clearly, news of Broghan's demise at the hands of Prince Lucas had found its way to Brackenholme.

Rainier shook her head. "You are home, my love, and that's all that matters now."

The duchess drew her in close again. Rainier noticed that Gretchen stood behind her daughter and pulled apart from Whitley briefly to allow the Werefox into the embrace. Harker watched from a respectful distance, the Greencape members of the City Watch already approaching to seek audience with him. Though they had all taken the green, their roles were very different, with the Greencapes watching over the city within the walls, while the Greencloaks patrolled the world beyond.

"Dear Gretchen," said Rainier, pulling away to look at her. "Look at how you've grown! And now you're back in our tree house when you were nearly sitting on a throne in Highcliff. The world has changed quickly."

Gretchen tried to laugh, but she was choked by emotion.

"My lady," she managed. "I can't imagine a palace in Lyssia more comforting than Brackenholme right now."

"Captain Harker," said Rainier, finally parting from the two girls. "I have you to thank for the safe return of my daughter and niece?"

"Your Grace," said Harker, bowing. "The Romari accompanied us up the Dymling Road. We are deeply in their debt."

"Then I would seek council with their elder to thank them in person for such service."

"I'll send word and call for the baba," replied Harker, his smile fading as he broached a difficult topic. "When I return, I would speak with you about Duke Bergan and Lord Broghan, my lady. Baron Redfern, the Duke's uncle, needs to be informed about what has occurred. Brackenholme is undermanned, with so many Greencloaks having accompanied the duke to Highcliff. The fortunes of the Seven Realms shift on a constant basis, and we need to prepare for what's to come."

"Agreed," said the duchess, her voice breaking. "We shall speak shortly. In the meantime, these ladies need refreshment, and clean clothes, too."

Whitley blushed at the idea that a change of clothes was her mother's chief concern. Dame Rainier's Werefox heritage was never more evident, and the parallels with Gretchen were all too clear to see. While the girl from Hedgemoor seemed delighted by the prospect of a bath and fresh dress, hugging her aunt tightly, Whitley's priorities lay elsewhere.

"If I have your leave, Mother, I would accompany Captain Harker and report to Master Hogan."

Rainier loosened her hold on Gretchen for a moment, regarding Whitley with fresh eyes.

"He didn't lie, did he?" said the Bearlord's wife.

"Who?" asked Whitley.

"Your father. In his last message from Highcliff, he mentioned how you'd blossomed. He said you were every inch a scout of the Woodland Watch."

Whitley's heart froze at the mention of him. "Any news?"

"Nothing firm, my love. The Lionguard boast that he was killed by Lucas in Highcliff, yet his body wasn't recovered. Those who fled the city say he got away, but again, no sightings. We can only pray he escaped. . . ."

Whitley swallowed her grief, forcing it into the pit of her stomach before the courtiers of Brackenholme. She didn't want to say what they all felt: that the more time passed by without him being found, the more likely the Lionguard's rumor was true. She steeled herself in front of her people. *Never show them you're weak, child*—that was what her father had always said. She swallowed the nausea that had risen in her throat.

"I'll return as soon as I've seen my master, Your Grace," she said, slipping back into the role of dutiful scout.

Rainier nodded reluctantly and dismissed her daughter from the throne room.

Harker and Whitley made quick time across the city once

they'd run the gauntlet of the well-wishing Greencapes and citizens who crowded the Great Oak's walkways. Everyone in Brackenholme wanted to see them and shake their hands. The anxiety of the guards and civilians was palpable to Whitley; she could sense the city was mourning the loss of Broghan and possibly Bergan. To have any of their own people return was something to celebrate. The two rode swiftly along the Dyre Road, back into the heart of the old town before taking the Dymling Road north to the Garrison Tree.

The giant tree was just as Whitley recalled, as misshapen and familiar as ever. With windows pockmarking the entire length of the twisting trunk, the Black Oak was part of the strongest memories of her childhood, visible from every corner of the city and likely to give children of all sizes nightmares. In sixteen years she'd never seen a leaf on its long black branches, even during the most glorious springs. While the Great Oak was a thing of beauty, boughs reaching for the heavens, the Black Oak that housed the garrison was its grotesque cousin, hiding from the light.

Guards wearing the garrison livery waited to meet them, trees cut from silvery cloth shining on their black leather breastplates. They led the horses away, Whitley pleased for Chancer that he'd finally have time to rest after their arduous adventure.

"Ho there, strangers!" came a voice, as the friendly face of

Machin emerged from the Garrison Tree gate. The last time Whitley had seen Machin had been at the battle for Cape Gala, when the woodlander had been sent back to Brackenholme to report on the slaughter of Broghan's branches at the hands of Lucas's Lionguard.

"You're alive!" cried Whitley, rushing forward to shake his hand. The man's ruddy cheeks were full of color, his return to the Woodland Realm and recuperation having clearly benefitted him.

"Sorry if that disappoints you, my lady," the Greencloak chuckled, saluting Harker. The captain embraced the man, patting him on the back.

"You seem well, Machin," said Harker, slapping the man's belly. "Hope you've left something in the galley for the rest of us."

Machin was flustered only briefly by Harker's mock reprimand.

"Come," he replied, smiling. "I'm sure they can rustle up something from the pantry for a couple of hardy Greencloaks fresh from the road, Captain!"

The three turned to the gateway into the Black Oak and stopped; Master Hogan stood there, his face stern and gray, bristly jaw jutting out like a flint dagger. The old scout arched an eyebrow as Whitley approached him, the young girl's steps hesitant after their months apart.

He's bound to disapprove of my exploits, scouting for Captain Harker when I haven't even officially been accepted into the brotherhood.

Hogan nodded his head, peering over Whitley's shoulder as she stood in front of him.

"See you've taken to carrying a quarterstaff, child, just like an *initiated* scout would."

"Yes, master," she said nervously. "You see, I—"

"Let's get you indoors out of the cold," he said, cutting her off with a wink. Machin and Harker smiled. "While we're at it, we can pay a visit to the quartermaster: see if he's got a scout's official green cloak in your size."

Whitley beamed as the old man put his arm around her shoulder and let the newest scout of the Woodland Watch into the Garrison Tree's yawning black gate.

7

A BIRD IN HAND

THE CELLAR BENEATH Stormdale Keep was a cold and miserable place. Puddles of icy water filled the arched chamber, and water rose from the ground and dripped through from above, gathering around the wall edges and soaking into the crumbling brickwork. The stench of damp was thick in the air, and a variety of colorful molds worked their way around the entirety of the curving ceiling. There were no windows, no shafts of light breaking the grim gloom—just a solitary torch spluttering in its sconce. It was the perfect place to interrogate a prisoner.

Count Croke sat bound by lengths of chain to a hard wooden chair. It was said that Croke was almost two hundred years old, and Drew had little trouble believing the claim. The

Crowlord was a shriveled husk of a man, his arms and legs wire thin, while his torso was misshapen and twisted. Lumps were visible beneath his tattered black robe, where gnarled muscles knotted over his bones, corrupted and deformed by disease and advancing years. Croke had spent a lifetime indulging in all manner of vile activities and was addicted to awful exotic medicines.

Brenn may have blessed the Werelords with longevity, mused Drew grimly, *but there is no accounting for the bodily abuses a therian will indulge in.*

"You can end this tonight, Croke," said Red Rufus, pacing behind the prisoner. "Call off your army, tell 'em to head home, and you can leave 'ere with your life."

The Crowlord laughed, a wet, wheezing sound that broke into a fit of hacking coughs. He craned his scrawny neck to look around at Red Rufus, launching a glob of bloody spit at him. That was all it took to enrage the falconthrope, and he backhanded the Crow across the face.

"Enough!" said Drew, the Hawklord's ways sitting uncomfortably with him. He knew there was no love lost between the birds of Riven and Windfell, and in Croke and Red Rufus he faced two therians who despised one another more than words could tell.

Lord Reinhardt placed a hand on Red Rufus's shoulder, pulling him away from the bound Crowlord as Drew stepped up to the prisoner.

"You would be wise not to anger Red Rufus, Croke. His temper matches his name."

"He's a worn-out old sparrow who's living in the past." The Crow chuckled through stained, crooked teeth. "The Hawklords' time is over. The Barebones belongs to my Crows, mark my words. You cannot halt the force beyond your walls any more than push water back up the Redwine!"

"We may not be able to, Croke, but *you* can," said Drew, crouching before the man to look into his rheumy eyes. "I implore you: speak to the Ratlord and your sons who gather outside. *Command* them to retreat. Spare the people of Stormdale the suffering that your force meted out in Highwater."

"And why should I do that for you, Wolf cub?"

"This city is no threat to you. The army's broken, routed after your recent victory. Stormdale merely houses injured soldiers, women and children, old men just like yourself."

The Crowlord cackled once more, choking on his laughter.

"There *are* no old men like *me*! I'm the oldest Werelord in all the Seven Realms. I've waited an eternity to see this day, when my enemies fall like skittles before me. At last I have a real army at my disposal, working alongside my brave men of Riven, and nothing will stand in our way. Certainly not the anguished, fear-soaked pleas of some whelp of Wergar, that's for sure!"

"Are you really so blinded by hate?"

"Hate? *Hate?*" spat the Crow, rocking in his chair, the

chains rattling as his face contorted into a spiteful grin. "Don't talk to me about hate, mongrel! Your father and all the Wolves before him looked down on my people for decades! You've sided with the Stags and Hawks time after time, never once listening to my petitions and complaints against the greedy, selfish scum who share my mountains!"

He jerked his head in the direction of Reinhardt and Red Rufus, yellow spittle dribbling down his lips.

"I'm listening now," said Drew.

Croke laughed once more, his awful cawing echoing around the chamber and making Reinhardt wince.

"You're listening *now*, are you? When a mighty army is camped at your gates, waiting to put you to the sword? Your father would never have begged his enemies for anything, yet here you are, rolling over like the submissive pup you are."

Croke kicked the puddles that gathered around his feet, sending a spray of icy water over Drew. The young Wolflord tried to ignore the insult, while Red Rufus snarled behind the prisoner.

"Let me wring 'is neck, my lord," said the Hawklord, grabbing the Crow by the jaw and twisting his liver-spotted face toward him. "How dare he speak to you this way!"

"Release him, Red Rufus," said Drew as the Hawklord's hand flexed against the Crowlord's fragile chin. "Let go of him!"

Red Rufus released his hold with a shove, sending Croke's head rocking forward as he continued to laugh.

"I'm not Wergar," said Drew quietly. "I beseech you, Count Croke: call off your troops."

"I want to hear you beg, Wolf," hissed the Crow.

Drew bit his lip, looking over Croke's shoulder at his companions. Reinhardt's face gave nothing away: this was Drew's decision to make, although it was his people who were besieged. Red Rufus glowered, shaking his head.

"Don't do it, lad," said the Hawk. "This blackbird's a trickster! He's playing with you!"

Drew looked back to the Crow, whose laughter had ceased. Croke's wide, expectant eyes were shot with blood. "You're kneeling, boy. You're already halfway there!"

"Leave Stormdale alone, I beg you," Drew whispered, his knees submerged in a chill pool of water.

"Louder!" shouted the Crow.

"I beg you!" Drew yelled, his voice stricken by heartfelt emotion.

Croke nodded slowly, transformed suddenly into a benign old man.

Is that what he wanted? Drew wondered. *All he really needed?*

A softer smile spread across the Crowlord's wizened features, his eyes half closing as he bobbed his head. Drew waited with bated breath, praying that his plea would be enough.

"Never," said Croke contentedly.

Drew staggered to his feet while Reinhardt struggled to

restrain a spluttering Red Rufus. Croke broke into another fit of laughter, his grating cackles descending into a further bout of coughing. Drew turned slowly and walked toward the stairwell that led out of the cellar. The sound of the battle echoed down the stone steps, as the siege of Stormdale continued above.

"Where are you going?" asked Red Rufus, pulling free of Reinhardt's grip and following Drew to the exit. "We can work this mangy bird over, pull out 'is feathers; *impress* upon 'im how vital it is he does what we demand!"

Before Drew could answer, Croke was chiming in again.

"I'd sooner die!" he screeched, stamping his feet up and down as his chair threatened to topple over.

"That can be arranged!" the Hawklord shouted back.

"I won't allow you to torture him, Red Rufus," said Drew, his anger rising. "I don't care what you've done in the past, and I don't want to hear another tale about what Wergar would've done."

"He's still our prisoner," said Reinhardt, and the Staglord glanced back at the bound Crow, who watched them intently. "Perhaps there's some way we can use him on the battlements? Show him to Vorjavik, see if that in itself is enough to make them retreat? It's worth a try, isn't it?"

"We'll do that," agreed Drew. "Whether the Crow likes it or not, we'll show him to his comrades; see if that changes their mind. Perhaps the threat of us killing one of their own will be enough to send them away."

It was Red Rufus's turn to laugh now.

"What's so funny?" said Reinhardt, his eyes narrowing.

"He said *'the threat'*—that's all it is, isn't it, lad? A hollow threat. You *really* wouldn't want to hurt a feather on that old bird's head?"

"Not if I can help it. Surely there's another way?" asked Drew.

"I've told ya before, pup; there are some things ya have to do in war that're unpleasant," said the Hawklord. He shook his head miserably. "There ain't no fairness in this game, Wolf: it's do—or die." Red Rufus trudged past him and set off up the staircase. "And right now, we're dying!"

PART III

TIDES OF TERROR

I

COLD COMFORT

THE BOARGUARD STOOD in a huddle, surrounded by the Catlord's soldiers. Tents were visible in every direction, a makeshift city of canvas and timber built by thousands of men in the shadow of the Whitepeaks. The ringing of smiths' hammers against steel was a constant reminder to every soldier: they were at war. Many were kitted out in the same livery, the Redcloaks of the Lionguard worn around the shoulders of Lyssian and Bastian alike. While the men of the Seven Realms could tolerate Sturmland's bitter cold, the Bastian warriors from the jungle were faring less well. Not so long ago they'd marched into the Longridings, wearing little more than breastplates and bracers, full of confidence and composure. Now in the far north, they were experiencing a Lyssian winter for the first time, and, judging by the miserable expressions on their faces, many did not like it.

Of the eight Boarguard soldiers, two remained in the center of the group, staying close to a steel drum of burning wood, while the other six, all Ugri warriors, remained unaffected by the cold. Ringlin and Ibal held their hands over the flames, willing the heat into their open palms. The journey from Vermire had been unpleasant, with the roads through the Badlands little more than rutted trails and quagmires. All the while the sleet had fallen, a steady drizzle of freezing rain that whipped at their flesh.

Bizarrely, Hector had seemed at ease in the conditions, not once complaining during their five-day ride. Leading the group had been Captain Stephan, the braggart young nephew of Sheriff Muller, the Lord of the Badlands. His ceaseless boasting and brainless bravado had done nothing to win over the company of those he escorted, instead earning new enemies from the Boarguard. Hector had taken no notice of the fool. The Baron had sat in the saddle of the black charger he'd purloined from the Ratlords, head down and cloak drawn about him, apparently deep in thought and sharing little conversation with his companions. The Crowlord Flint, Onyx's messenger bird, had accompanied them, making certain that they found their way to the Beast of Bast's camp. The young Baron had waited momentarily as the Crow entered the Werepanther's tent to report in to his commander-in-chief, leaving Hector with Stephan for a few more tiresome moments. Eventually, they had called him through.

Now Hector stood in the center of an immense red rug, his boots swallowed up in the luxurious pile around them. Braziers stood within the tent, the burning coals ensuring that the temperature in the tent bore no resemblance to that in the frozen world outside. Onyx didn't travel light: the grand interior was decked out with ephemera from his homeland, the stuffed heads and bleached skulls of strange beasts hanging from the canopied ceiling and walls. Chests, tables, and chairs of the finest wood had been positioned around the tent, pearl and gold inlays shining as the firelight caught their detail. A giant four-poster bed, larger than most of the tents Hector had seen in the camp, was visible in an antechamber, with two enormous black cats sleeping at its foot. Even with so much to catch his attention, Hector's eyes were drawn to the body facedown on the floor.

"Who was he?" asked the Boarlord.

"A scout from Sturmland," said Onyx, walking past the young magister. Hector felt his stomach roll at the sight of the Pantherlord, seven feet tall and seemingly as broad, his deep voice rumbling like a grinding portcullis. He wore a rich bearskin cloak, fastened around his throat by a thick gold chain, with the briefest glimpse of his enormous chest on show beneath its folds.

"How close did he get to your camp, my lord?"

"Close enough to make me think he wasn't alone, magister," replied the giant Catlord, rolling the body over with a huge bare foot. The corpse's eyes stared up at the ceiling, the exit wound from an arrow still gaping at his throat. His gray cloak was soaked in blood, and the pale leather breastplate beneath bore the outline of the white bear of Icegarden.

"Do you fear they've got word of your actual number back to Duke Henrik?"

"I fear nothing," said Onyx matter-of-factly, turning his attention to Hector. "I only wish we'd caught one alive so we could question him about the White Bear's capabilities. Sheriff Muller's Skirmishers are an undisciplined rabble; no doubt this scout's companions heard them coming from a mile off—if a single Bastian warrior had been among Muller's number, we might have a Sturmlander to interrogate now."

He seeks to question a prisoner? You may be able to help him with that, brother, whispered the Vincent-vile at Hector's shoulder, coiling around the magister's throat like a spectral polecat.

Lord Flint, the Crowlord, poured himself a goblet of wine at the rear of the chamber, the steady *glug* causing Hector to glance back at him. His shock of black hair rose around his crooked face, his eyes glaring straight at the Boar.

Nobody trusts you, said Vincent. *You might have traipsed all this way only to be executed! I told you not to come. . . .*

"So," said the Catlord eventually, "I've heard much about you. Tell me, boy: why switch sides now? Weeks ago you were a member of this Wolf's Council: why the change of heart?"

Hector held his breath for a moment, composing himself. He had to convince Onyx that he was now on his side. The answer he gave could make the difference between life and death.

"The Wolf's Council is meaningless—a collection of scared Werelords afraid to bend their knee before Lucas. We sided with the Wolf out of a sense of loyalty; I'd be lying if I said I didn't at one time consider Drew Ferran a friend. But he changed from the boy I first met. As time passed he revealed himself to be incapable of carrying out his duty as a nobleman; his heart conflicted with his head. When his country needed him, he dashed off as swiftly as he could, all for Lady Gretchen."

Hector knew this was a half truth. Although Drew had been uncomfortable with his newfound position of power, his decision to run away from his responsibilities hadn't been selfish. His reasoning had been sound, and the young Wolflord had fled Highcliff with Hector's blessing to chase after Gretchen, when the Fox had been abducted by Prince Lucas and his Lionguard. *If Drew had rescued Gretchen and brought her safely home, who knew what might have come to pass?* Only the end result had been grave for all, and now Hector needed to prove himself to Onyx. If that meant betraying the memory of his dear, departed friend, then so be it.

"Odd," said the Pantherlord. "I'd have thought you'd consider such loyalty between friends admirable. Is that not the kind of attitude you Lyssians respect, holding it dear above others?"

"Not when that attitude gets in the way of ruling a kingdom, my lord. It was a reckless, selfish act carried out by someone who cares nothing for the people of Lyssia. The sole remaining member of the Wolf's Council, Duke Manfred, has yet to learn that the Wolf is not the savior of the Seven Realms."

"The remaining member? You're confident Manfred is the only one who still lives?"

"Drew is lost; he has disappeared from the map, dead I suspect. Wasn't his severed hand found in Cape Gala? He's strong, but I can't imagine even he survived such an injury. I killed the Sharklord, Vega, myself—buried a silver arrow in his guts and tossed him off his own ship, so yes; I'm confident."

"And Duke Bergan?"

"Dead, I'm told, and buried beneath the rocks of Highcliff." Onyx chuckled.

This isn't good. . . .

"What's so funny?" asked Hector, his voice breaking nervously.

"Tell him," said Onyx, as Flint stepped forward.

"Bergan lives."

Hector's knees buckled slightly, causing his legs to wobble briefly before he straightened.

Onyx noticed, his eyes widening. "You seem surprised?"

"Aren't we all?" gasped Hector. "How can that be? The cliffs buried him: it was witnessed by the Lionguard, was it not?"

"It was," replied the Crow, supping from the goblet. "And yet he survived."

"How can you know for sure?"

Flint polished off the drink and slammed the cup onto a table.

"Our scouts have spotted him and a handful of companions making their way through the foothills of the Whitepeaks."

"Are you sure it's him?"

"He might have been crushed by a mountain, but it was him all right."

"What do you plan to do?" asked Hector, unsettled by the news of the Bearlord's survival. Bergan had been like an uncle to him throughout his childhood, a man he'd always strived to please but had disappointed as their relationship had broken apart. *Alive?*

Onyx clenched his fist. "I'll capture Bergan myself before he reaches Henrik's fortress. He's still some days away from the fortifications the White Bear has built in the mountains. The Duke of Sturmland has not been idle while war rages across Lyssia."

"Fortifications?" said Hector. "I thought Henrik had abstained from the business of selecting a new king and planned to make Sturmland an independent realm once again."

"Whatever his plans, he's prepared his people for war,"

said Onyx. "Wisely, I might add, because that's what's coming. However, there will be no separation from the Seven Realms. They will all swear fealty to the new king. They'll bow before a Catlord once more."

"We've come across unexpected resistance in the White-peaks and steely resolve from its inhabitants," added Flint. "I've flown over the land myself to see their work: their eyes are trained on the sky, searching for Crows. It's impressive. Walls of wood and ice have been erected along the southern edge of the mountain range, enclosing the White Bear's domain and providing his forces with additional protection. Even with our superior numbers we're struggling to enter from the Badlands."

"How do you propose to capture Bergan?" said Hector. "Clearly, he won't go down without a fight."

"He'll meet his match when I intercept his little band," Onyx replied with a sneer. "You Lyssian Werelords are no match for the therianthropes of Bast." He turned to Flint. "Ready fifty of our best light horsemen: we ride at once to capture this meddlesome Bear."

Flint bowed, clicking his heels, and turned to make for the exit.

"Wait!" said Hector, raising his gloved hands. "I have a better idea."

The Crow and the Panther both stared incredulously at the youth.

163

"*You* have a better idea than Lord Onyx?" said the Crowlord.

"Let the boy speak, Flint. There must be *some* reason why my sister Opal insisted we make a place for him on the Prince's council." Onyx looked at Hector. "Well? Spit this glorious idea out."

Good, Hector. You have their attention.

"Do not capture Bergan."

Flint broke into fits of laughter before Onyx raised a hand to silence him.

"There's got to be more to your grand scheme than that. Continue, magister."

"Let *me* meet him, with a couple of my men. If he's been lost in the wilderness, there's no chance word could have reached him yet of my business with Vega and Manfred. He'll trust me."

"And if he doesn't?" asked the Werepanther.

"Do you have any . . . *expendable* troops, roughnecks you can afford to lose? Not too many, of course, but enough to allow me and my men to prove our loyalty to the Bear."

Onyx looked at Flint.

"There's Muller's Skirmishers, my lord. We can send the sheriff's nephew, that idiot Stephan, to intercept them."

Onyx nodded. "Then what, Blackhand?"

"Once we've shown our worth, we accompany the duke for the remainder of his journey. I can get into Icegarden when no one else can. When I'm inside the White Bear's city, I can bring down its walls from within. I wouldn't just be delivering Duke

Bergan to you: you'd get Duke Henrik also, as well as any other Werelords who've sided against the Lion."

That's not all, dear brother, whispered the Vincent-vile. *There's more to your plan, is there not? Another reason why you want to visit the Strakenberg? The stories say the Wyrmstaff supposedly lies hidden in the White Bear's palace, guarded by the Daughters of Icegarden. Who knows what secrets you may unlock once you have the artifact in your grasp?*

Vincent wasn't wrong. His father had known that it was more than just a myth: the staff existed, a relic from the age of the Dragonlords, lost through time.

"There's only one problem with your plan, Lord Magister," said Flint. "You know *nothing* about the interior workings of Icegarden. The city's a fortress, carved out of the mighty Strakenberg. Henrik has kept Icegarden's secrets hidden from the outside realm for decades. Only the Sturmish know where its weaknesses lie."

"Only the Sturmish know the secrets of Icegarden?" asked Hector. "A Sturmlander like the one lying dead at our feet?"

Hector tugged off his gloves, folding them and tucking them into the strap of his belt. Onyx and Flint recoiled as their eyes landed on the withered left hand that the magister flexed before them. The flesh appeared mummified, stretching as Hector cracked his knuckles, threatening to split open with the strain.

"Have you finished with this scout's body, my lords?"

165

Onyx nodded slowly, his eyes fixed on the magister's black limb.

Hector opened his traveling case and began to remove an assortment of strange implements: thin metal spatulas, a glass jar of dark yellow powder, a black candle.

Very good, brother. You're not as hapless as you look. . . .

Hector ignored the vile's voice and continued as he withdrew what he needed. "You said you were unable to interrogate the prisoner?" he asked, smiling. "I can help you with that."

2

TRUE COLORS

THE DYMLING ROAD that cut through Brackenholme was empty but for a lone, barefoot figure swiftly making his way toward the southern gatehouse. Rolff hung close to the stoops that rose up from the street's edge, slipping between shadows as he passed the residences and businesses that lined the grand avenue. Baba Korga's bodyguard came to a halt when he reached the last building before the tall palisade wall. Crouching behind a rain barrel, he surveyed the scene ahead.

Two of the City Watch stood at the base of the sixty-foot-tall gatehouse, a tree trunk running from one tower to the other, barring the great doors shut. Rolff had been informed that the barring mechanisms were housed within the right-hand tower, the door to which was locked from within. But that was no matter to the hulking giant; he wasn't planning to enter from ground level. Reaching inside the fold of his dirty cloak, he withdrew his blowpipe and dipped his fingers into a small wooden box on his belt, delicately removing two darts. He checked the distance: perhaps forty feet. Dropping a dart into the chamber, he raised the blowpipe to his lips.

The first Greencape went down in a heap as the needle snapped into his throat before his companion could comprehend what was happening. The poison was fast-acting, and the man's heart was already shutting down as his friend reached down to help him. The next dart hit the remaining guard in the wrist of his outstretched hand, and the soldier's eyes widened. The last thing he saw was the Romari emerging from the darkness. He was dead by the time he collapsed onto his comrade.

Rolff wasted no time, dragging the corpses away from the gates and stowing them in the shadows beside the tower. Reaching into his cloak again he pulled out two long, serrated daggers, fashioned from the black flint found deep within the Dyrewood. Stepping up to the wall, he began to scale the logs, the knives providing purchase while his feet propelled him higher. Once at the tower's summit he craned his head over the crenellations.

Three more Greencapes stood before him, their backs turned as they looked out to the meadows and forest that loomed beyond the wall. A large brass bell was suspended from a scaffold in the center of the tower, an open staircase beside it disappearing below. Three pikes rested in their rack, close to hand but not close enough for the trio. Silently, Rolff hauled himself over the wooden parapet, bare feet landing gracefully on the decking. The blowpipe came out again, and three more darts were delicately removed from the box on his hip. One of the Greencapes was pointing into the darkness, his voice rising with concern. Rolff saw too that one by one the torches in the Watch Trees were being snuffed out, exactly as planned.

The first Greencape took a dart in the back of his neck, which sent him over the wall in a shaking death fit. Unfortunately for Rolff, his companions were already turning, rushing toward the bell tower and their pikes. The Romari giant dropped the blowpipe and whipped out his knives once more, leaping toward the nearest soldier, who headed for the alarm. He had lost the element of surprise, and the guard tore a dagger from his belt as his companion snatched a pike from the rack. Rolff threw the first knife, catching the Greencape in his weapon arm so he fumbled with his dagger. Before he could catch it the giant was on him, the second knife plunging into the man's leather breastplate in successive, deadly blows.

With his path to the bell still blocked by the Romari killer, the third Greencape shouted out loud, his voice booming along the palisade wall. Rolff cursed his ill luck, ripping his knives free as he faced the last guard. The Greencape lunged in with his pike, but the giant skidded forward beneath the swing, sliding along the floorboards and past the soldier's legs. The flint knives tore through the Greencape's hamstrings, causing him to fall crippled to the deck beside the Romari. The soldier screamed as Rolff rolled onto him, his great weight crushing the air from his lungs.

"Please!" cried the man. "I've a wife! A family!"

Rolff smiled, his face inches from his enemy's, lips peeling back to reveal the sharply filed teeth of a Wylderman.

"Family?" said Rolff, his rarely used voice grating like a bone-saw. "My family come!"

Baba Korga's henchman plunged his teeth into the soldier's throat, quickly turning the green cape red.

Gretchen stood on the balcony, looking out over Brackenholme. The hour was late, and, while the city slept, the Werefox found herself awake. It was good to have Whitley close by; the Bearlady slept in the neighboring bedchamber. Gretchen had scoffed at the notion of Whitley becoming a scout when she'd first heard of her cousin's desire, but seeing her in action, as capable as any man who donned the green, she found herself both envious and proud; envious of her cousin's liberation from the path most Wereladies took, and proud of her achievement.

The Werefox's quarters were more than comfortable, Duchess Rainier's attendants having hastily prepared the best state room her hall had to offer. All the accessories a princess required were present: the mirrored dressing table full of powders and perfumes, the bookcase provisioned with classics of literature, the wardrobe with countless beautiful gowns. Yet Gretchen felt strangely dissatisfied; the once self-absorbed Lady of Hedgemoor found herself thinking about her other friends, and where in Lyssia they might be.

Hopefully Hector was safe from harm. She'd been informed that a handful of Werelords, including the young Boar, had safely escaped Highcliff by ship when the Omiri Doglords and the Cats of Bast had attacked.

As for Drew, he was lost, Brenn knew where. Gretchen's heart faltered when she thought of what might have been. Prince Lucas had become a monster, a pale shadow of the young boy she'd been groomed to marry from a young age. At one time she had admired him, but after the way he'd treated her and Lyssia, she now reviled him. In Drew she had found someone who had revealed to her the wider realms of Lyssia and the struggles of those who lived there. Gretchen thought back to when she'd first encountered him, his gray eyes peering out from beneath an unruly mop of black hair, filthy from the road, desperately in need of a good wash. His lack of etiquette, his discomfort around nobility; all these traits flashed through her mind and made her smile. Until she remembered how *she'd* behaved: the spoiled princess who knew everything. How wrong she'd been.

"A copper for your thoughts?"

Gretchen looked up, shocked to find Whitley standing a

short distance away on her own balcony, leaning against the thick oak rail. Gretchen's cheeks flushed.

"I couldn't sleep. You?"

"I heard you pacing," answered Whitley, smiling. "For such a delicate flower your tread can be terribly heavy."

"Sorry. I'm having trouble . . . *adjusting*, now we've a roof over our heads."

"I know what you mean. Every time I returned from scouting I'd find—"

Whitley's words ended abruptly as she stood up straight by the banister, looking past Gretchen and out beyond the walls of Brackenholme.

"What's the matter?" asked the Foxlady, casting her eyes out into the Dyrewood.

"The lights," said Whitley, her face a mask of concern.

"Lights? I don't see any."

"That's just it. The guard towers in the treetops beyond the meadow: their torches burn throughout the night, as a means of signaling to the City Watch on the wall."

Whitley reached out, picking up her quarterstaff from where it rested against the banister. "The torches are out. All of them."

As Storm's hooves splashed through the puddles of the Dymling Road, Trent Ferran was one of the first to witness the signal torches vanishing from view. Through the dense woodland, the fires in the guard posts had marked his journey's end, confirming that his frightening ride through the Dyrewood was coming to a close. He'd spied more of them on his approach, spaced out evenly through the canopy atop the countless towering trees. When the initial torch blinked out he'd thought nothing of it, until more followed. One by one, they disappeared, quickly followed by the despairing cries of men.

When the figures began to appear through the trees, horse and rider both felt fear grip them. It was as if the forest had suddenly come alive, with scrambling masses of limbs and spears appearing out of the darkness, shaggy heads bobbing as a horde of Wyldermen charged in eerie silence through the bracken and mud. As some of the Wyldermen caught sight of the lone rider, they peeled away from the main mass and headed to intercept him.

"Hyah!" Trent shouted, spurring Storm on as Wyldermen swarmed around them. One of the wild men leapt into Storm's path, his skin daubed black with mud and etched with blue woad symbols. His ax came up as the horse charged him, its flight slowed when Storm's hooves kicked out, crushing his ribcage with a sharp *crack*. Then the two were away, charging along the Dymling Road and out from the cover of the trees.

The meadows might have been something to marvel at on a clear spring day—acres of open grassland in stark contrast to the woodland. But on a chill winter's night, with thousands of wild men running through them, they were the stuff of nightmares. The silence was broken by the cries of the Wyldermen, whoops and hollers that mimicked woodland animals: barking, snarling, and screeching as they ran ever closer to Brackenholme. Armed with spears and axes, clubs and daggers, shortbows and blowpipes, they had weaponry that was handmade yet deadly. Some wore headdresses, feathers fluttering as they surged toward Brackenholme, skulls and bones rattling around their throats.

The tall walls of the city rose up before Trent as he put distance between himself and the wild men. The gates ahead were closed, barring his entrance, and with rising dread he realized he was trapped in the meadows with the pursuing Wylderman horde.

"The gate!" he shouted as Storm pounded along the Dymling Road, disappearing into the shadows around the mighty gatehouse's base. The horse began to slip and slide through the clay, hooves plowing up muddy furrows as Trent reined her in. He guided Storm alongside the giant doors, hammering the timber with his fist.

"For Brenn's sake!" he cried, looking back into the meadows, the Wyldermen drawing ever closer. *"Open the gate!"*

In answer to his screams, the heavy mechanisms suddenly ground into life. Whatever barred the gates from within was suddenly hauled back, wood scraping against wood as the doors swung outward. Trent tugged at Storm's reins, and the horse whinnied nervously as she stepped clear of the enormous portal. Once the gap was wide enough, he urged his mount through.

"Shut the gates!" he called up to the guard tower. "I'm inside!"

He glanced back and saw with horror that the gates continued their slow, mechanical motion, inexorably widening.

"The gates!" Trent screamed at the top of his lungs. "You're under attack! Close them!"

It was at that moment that he caught sight of the pair of dead Greencapes lying in the shadows at the base of one of the towers. In the next instant the first wave of Wyldermen ran through the open gates and the bloody battle for Brackenholme began.

3

THE HUNGRY CHILD

THE BEAST OF BAST lounged in his chair, whispering into Lord Flint's ear as Hector performed before him. The body of the slain Sturmish scout lay spread-eagle on the frozen floor of the tent, the rugs and furniture having been cleared away to allow the young Boarlord room to work. Candles provided the only light in the Catlord's grand chamber, the greatest illumination coming from the burning black stick of wax that Hector clutched in his right hand. A brimstone circle surrounded the corpse, with arcane symbols etched through the yellow powder. It became clear to Hector that Onyx was a hard man to impress. The Panther paid the young magister little attention while he performed his rituals.

See how he talks while you work, brother? whispered the Vincent-vile. *He mocks you!*

There was no denying it: by conversing with the Crowlord while Hector carried out his necromancy, the Werepanther was showing great disrespect. Flint added to the uncomfortable atmosphere, sniggering along with the Bastian's banter, perhaps hoping the magister would make an error. Hector tried not to be distracted, whispering his incantations over and over, channeling the dark magick that would bring forth the answers he sought. No doubt Onyx was trying to unsettle and belittle him, to make him feel that he had to impress. Whether the Catlord's lack of interest in Hector's work was feigned or genuine, the Boarlord didn't care. The Beast of Bast would pay attention soon enough.

Hector tipped the spluttering black candle, allowing its dark liquid to pour into the palm of his withered left hand. The smell of smoldering flesh assailed his nostrils as he curled his knuckles into a ball, the molten wax oozing between his fingers and splattering the cold floor. He stopped chanting suddenly, striking the ground three times with his smoking mummified fist. The walls of the tent clapped, as a sudden gust of wind found its way through the chamber, extinguishing the candles instantly, all but the one that Hector still held in his grasp.

Onyx and Flint fell silent, and the Pantherlord sat upright in his wooden seat, craning his neck to see past the magister crouching at his feet. The Crowlord smacked his lips, his mouth suddenly parched as he followed the gaze of Onyx toward the flickering flame in Hector's hand.

"Rise, creature, and answer to your master's bidding," commanded Hector, allowing a chuckle to escape his throat.

That piqued their interest!

Gradually, the dead Sturmlander began to move. The movement started in the scout's feet, the toes of the man's boots trembling as a shudder ran through the corpse. Its fingers twitched, playing out an irregular rhythm as the limbs spasmed. Slowly, the body sat upright, as if pulled on invisible strings. Hector's black candle lit up the man's pale slack face, the cheeks already sagging, the poor fool having bled to death through the throat. The corpse's eyes flashed open in an instant, startling even Hector. But the magister quickly composed himself as he saw the familiar pale-blue fires burning within.

Behind, Hector heard the gasps of Onyx and Flint, and their affectation of nonchalance died as fast as the candle flames that had illuminated the tent. Now they were attentive, watching the magister as he rose from the ground. He opened his wax-drenched black hand and flexed his palm.

"Rise," repeated Hector. Again the corpse moved, drawn to its feet by Hector's will, standing unsteadily like a newborn lamb.

The dead Sturmlander's head turned one way and then the other, every movement clumsy, as it jerked unnaturally.

The blue eyes narrowed momentarily as it caught sight of the Vincent-vile, hissing as a cat might when facing a dog. Finally its gaze landed upon Hector. Its mouth swung open, tongue and teeth slick with dark blood that dribbled down its jaw, spattering its soiled cloak and armor.

"Where . . . am . . . I?" the corpse whispered, its voice rasping as the words found their way through its punctured throat.

Hector took a moment to examine the Sturmlander: a young man, not much older than the Boarlord. Somebody's son—perhaps even a husband—with his life ahead of him until the Skirmisher's arrow had found his neck. War was an ugly business, and he bore this soul no malice, regardless of which side the scout had fought for. Communing could be an enjoyable affair for the magister. There were some souls that he felt warranted his attention, those who had wronged Hector in their lives, like Vankaskan or Vega, but the dead northman was not one of those. He would ask what questions he needed of this broken body and send the poor spirit on its way.

"Do not fear," said Hector, managing a smile. "You're in no danger. I simply have some questions that I'd have you answer. Then you may depart and return to the long sleep."

"The long . . . sleep?" gasped the corpse, its burning blue eyes suddenly widening.

"Indeed," sighed the magister with a sad shrug of his shoulders. The corpse's jaw trembled, its lips wobbling as if it might burst into tears. Hector turned and looked back at Onyx, his look of sympathy replaced by a cold, confident glare. "You had questions, my lord?"

Onyx stepped forward, Flint close behind, the Panther cocking his head as he studied the corpse. It stared back, dipping its shoulder and mimicking his movements like a ghastly mirror. "Fascinating," said the Catlord, his deep voice unnervingly quiet.

Hector watched the three for a moment, Werelords and ghoul staring at one another, trying to keep his own pride hidden. By the flickering candlelight, he spied a sheen of sweat glistening on Flint's brow, the Crow unable to take his eyes off the grotesque risen scout.

They won't doubt you again, brother. The vile giggled.

"What would you have me ask him?" said Hector, leaning forward and whispering in Onyx's ear.

The Werepanther stirred from his trance, regaining the composure to direct his words back to the magister, his gaze still fixed on the corpse.

"How many were with him?"

Hector turned to the soldier, passing the question on. "How many accompanied you in your scouting party?"

The dead Sturmlander smacked his lips, his eyes returning to the magister. "Three more scouts. Hidden. Return to camp. Inform Duke Henrik."

Onyx snarled, his growl rising as he bared his teeth. Hector spied that the Catlord's canines were larger than they had been earlier and gnashed against one another in his broad, menacing mouth.

"Then the White Bear will have a fair idea of our number," said Flint.

"Don't you think I know that, Crow?" said the Panther, turning to glare at the black-haired avianthrope.

"Do you have more questions, my lord?" asked Hector.

"Indeed I do, magister," replied the Catlord as he proceeded to direct the young Boar's interrogation of the corpse.

Initial questions established the number and makeup of the Sturmish army, where on the Whitepeaks they were positioned, and what awaited the Bastian forces once they traveled farther into the mountains. The corpse revealed all it had known in life, spelling out the exact numbers of Duke Henrik's army and any weaknesses that existed in their defenses. There was nothing that could be exploited, simply fewer men in certain points through the mountains, as the White Bear had taken nothing for granted. The only promising morsel of information was the news that Henrik had brought virtually his entire army out of Icegarden, assembling them on the slopes of the Whitepeaks. Only a skeletal force remained in the city, with no defense of the Sturmish capital to the north. It was the missing piece to Hector's puzzle, confirming that his own plan was the correct course of action for their group.

"Don't you see?" said Hector, his eyes wild with promise. "This is perfect! With nobody guarding the city, once I get through their lines, there is nothing to stop me. The city is unguarded. It's mine for the taking!"

"*Ours* for the taking, Lord Blackhand," corrected Flint, a thick black eyebrow arching up his crooked face as he watched the excited Boarlord. Onyx ignored the two Werelords, his attention still captured by the shambling corpse within the circle of sulphurous powder, his face filled with dark wonder.

"Of course, my lord," said Hector, waving his withered hand in the air by way of an apology. "A slip of the tongue, that's all. Icegarden shall be *ours* once I enter its white walls."

"How exactly do you intend to bring down the walls from within, though? I could fly in myself and do the deed if it were a simple one-man job. There's still a force within the city—a garrison holding a fair-size troop of soldiers by all accounts. Plus there's a militia, according to our dead friend here. Your Boarguard number how many? Eight? Hardly an army, Lord Magister, is it?"

"Really, Lord Flint," said Hector, smiling. "You should let me worry about my Boarguard. You underestimate their ability—and their number—at your peril."

The Crowlord sneered, about to say something more before Onyx cut him off.

"Can this creature feel pain?" asked the Werepanther, his eyes narrowing as he studied the corpse.

Hector was taken aback by the unexpected question. "It has the ability to feel spiritual pain, my lord, but its physical form is just a shell. I think the body is beyond pain as you or I would understand it."

"Is it essentially harmless?"

"Far from it, sire. The risen dead are all dangerous. That said, communing with Children of the Blue Flame under these conditions, within the circle of brimstone, provides no danger to a magister." Hector's thoughts flew back to the Wyrmwood long ago, when he and Drew had faced the dead Wylderman shaman and the communing, his very first, had gone terribly, awfully wrong. Bile rose in his throat when he recalled the memory.

"We have the answers we need from this one, my lord," continued the magister, uncomfortable with the Catlord's fascination with the corpse. Hector's feelings about the Sturmlander hadn't changed: the man had been a simple soldier, caught up in a terrible conflict. He wasn't responsible for anything in the grand scheme of things. He was a pawn in the Werelords' grand game of chess, an insignificant innocent like so many humans. Hector took no pleasure from controlling one so simple.

"I have fought many beasts down the years, Blackhand," said the Werepanther. "But nothing as unnatural as one of these . . . *children*, as you call them."

"The Children of the Blue Flame aren't so different from normal humans. They need discipline, control; they need to know their place. As a magister, I can command them, as long as the brimstone and warding symbols are in place to keep their . . . *appetites* under control."

"And if the circle should be broken?" said Onyx, kicking the brimstone circle with his boot and sending a billowing amber cloud into the air. Instantly, the dead Sturmlander lurched forward, its expression switching from slack-jawed obedience to rabid hunger, its blue eyes burning with a fresher fire.

"No!" cried Hector as Flint stumbled back, away from the flailing corpse. The Boarlord threw his black hand forward, about to call the creature back, to prevent it from attacking the Catlord, but Onyx was fast.

The Werepanther was already moving, transforming in a single heartbeat. The magister's candle illuminated the dark giant who stood before him, and the sight of the shifted felinthrope made the stick of black wax shake in his hand. Onyx caught the dead Sturmlander around the jaw, holding him up in the air, the scout's legs kicking feebly at thin air. The Catlord's enormous hand cradled the corpse's skull as a normal man might hold a goblet. The ghoul's hands scraped at the surface of Onyx's shining muscled arm, the skin reflecting shades of purple by candlelight as the ravenous cadaver gnashed its jaws, desperate to taste Bastian flesh.

Hector wasn't alone in his discomfort: even the Vincent-vile was sickened by the Werepanther's antics. He felt the vile coiling around his throat, hugging his perspiring flesh, willing Hector to protect him from the Beast of Bast. *Do you fear the same fate, Vincent?* thought Hector, staring at Onyx with grim wonder as the monstrous Catlord brought the moaning corpse closer to his huge, feline face. *Here is a living therian who's unafraid of the dead, who finds a ghoul fascinating rather than fearful. What might he make of a vile, should he find a way to grasp one?* The Vincent-vile didn't answer.

The Werepanther lifted the dead Sturmlander higher toward the roof of the tent. Onyx shook the clawing, kicking body for a moment, its limbs jangling uncontrollably, then unleashed a bloodcurdling roar. Hector staggered backward, bumping into Flint, as the Catlord squeezed his mighty clawed hand into a fist. A sickening, wet *crunch* sounded a moment before the headless corpse tumbled to the floor, the fight gone from the Sturmlander's body once and for all.

Hector turned away from the Catlord as Flint disappeared through the canvas doors of the tent. He heard the Werecrow hail Captain Stephan, the commander of the Skirmishers, who was keen to be of use. *Little does the fool know of the true purpose of his mission.* Hector swept his vials, bottles, and belongings back into his case, his usual care thrown to the wind as his heart thundered in his chest. He glanced back.

Lord Onyx, the Beast of Bast, stood in the glow of Hector's candlelight. The young magister held the communing candle in his withered hand, gripping it in dark knuckles as he fought to control his nerves before the terrifying felinthrope.

"You have the information you need, Blackhand. You have your bait, your Boarguard, and your plan. So tell me . . ." The Werepanther leaned forward, stooping until his face was in line with the Boarlord's. "Why are you still here?"

4
ENDGAME

WHILE THE MOON threatened to break through the storm clouds overhead, rain and arrows showered down over Stormdale. War Marshal Vorjavik had likely expected the Stags' people to surrender, once their outer walls were breached. With the defenses in ruins and the city on fire, any other force crippled by injury and overwhelmed would have sought terms with the enemy and pleaded for clemency. Instead, the men and women of the Staglord's city fought back.

As Vorjavik and his Crowlord general, Scree, directed their forces against the walls—probing, prodding, searching for weaknesses—they were met every time with volleys of arrows, forcing them back, breaking their push for the citadel. The survivors weren't foolish; they knew the Ratlord would show no mercy. There were no terms Vorjavik would consider, not after the butchery he'd carried out in Highwater. But Stormdale would yield to nobody: its people would fight to the last.

The besieged Werelords kept their place on the battlements, standing shoulder to shoulder with their people. Reinhardt and the four remaining Staglords of the Barebones kept moving and talking, urging the defenders to stay strong and dig in deep. None of the Stags would leave the ramparts, putting the safety of the city's inhabitants before their own. Inside the walls, children scampered through the courtyard, reclaiming enemy arrows that had found their way into the keep and survived intact, handing them back to the defenders, whether they were steel or silver.

Lord Scree's siblings took to the air, riding the smoke and rain-filled sky, swooping over the castle. A Graycloak archer was positioned on every tower turret, watching the skies, his sole duty to seek out the Werecrows who attacked from above. The Hawklord, Red Rufus, joined them in the sky, chasing them away as they harried and mobbed him, but he couldn't be everywhere at once. When the Crowlords got too close, they found their wings clipped, but not before they had dealt out death and wreaked havoc on the defenses. Rocks and flasks of burning oil crashed down indiscriminately, shattering and exploding everywhere.

Drew stood on the summit of the Lady's Tower, high above the castle, looking down at the defenders on the walls. Magister

Wilhelm was at his side, the old man leaning hard on his staff, weary with worry and despair. Immediately beyond the castle's outer wall, the dark water of the moat shimmered, its surface broken by masonry, weapons, and bodies crashing down.

"My lord, the rubble at the city gates is clear now: look!" said Wilhelm.

Drew followed the magister's bony finger as it pointed toward Stormdale's main avenue. The collapsed walls of the gatehouse that Drew had defended the previous night had until now blocked the passage of Vorjavik's war machines. But the debris had been cleared away, and Drew's heart sank as the first of the enemy catapults was hauled into the city.

"I hope Reinhardt sees this," said Drew. "Those siege engines decimated the defenses of the city walls. What chance will the castle have? The sight of catapults trundling into the city could break our people's resolve. Their morale's already fragile. He needs to speak to inspire them!"

"Lord Reinhardt can inspire the most craven fool, but I fear you expect him to work miracles. They've fought valiantly, even as their loved ones have fallen around them," said the magister sadly. "These are farmers, bakers, and grocers; half-blind old men and terrified women. They're not warriors."

Drew knew how they felt. He may have been a therian-thrope, and a mighty one at that, but the boy in him was exhausted and as fearful as anyone in the castle. *Is this all my fault? This cursed war, all the death and destruction that's stricken Lyssia?* He tried to imagine what the father and mother who raised him, Mack and Tilly Ferran, might have done in this situation, faced by unimaginable odds. He tried to listen to his heart, searching for answers, but the only sound he heard was the battle's din.

"My lord," said Wilhelm, turning to Drew. "I fear we're approaching the endgame."

Drew nodded, stirred from his reverie by the old magister's words.

"The guards," Drew said. "Tell them to fetch Croke. Have them meet me on the wall."

By the time Drew arrived on the battlements, the first catapult was in position, launching its boulders at Stormdale's ancient castle. The screams of those who sheltered in the keep, too frail or young to fight, could be heard within. The defenders tried in vain to slow the progress of the trebuchet teams, but ranks of giant shields protected the engineers of Riven as they loaded their deadly missiles.

Every defensive position on the walls was under duress, as Vorjavik's army swarmed around the moat. The engineers hadn't been idle while the path for their war machines was cleared. The siege towers had been dismantled and transformed into makeshift platforms that could span the moat and reach the keep's outer walls. As the walkways reached out over the clogged water, the men of Riven hauled back on the attached ropes, raising them up as they pushed forward. The strongest remaining Graycloaks gathered on the battlements, clad in plate mail, waiting for the enemy to come. Finally the engineers let the ropes loose, and the end of each platform rattled down onto the ramparts. The warriors of Riven poured forward, racing up the wooden slopes, with the Vermirian elite guard close behind.

As the two forces engaged, Drew caught sight of Magister Wilhelm and four Graycloaks hurrying across the courtyard, the bound Lord of Riven in their grasp. Reinhardt snatched the Crow from them, dragging him up the steps of the gatehouse to where Drew awaited. The young Wolflord looked down the wall in each direction, his stomach heaving as he saw the greater number of enemy soldiers pushing the defenders back. Many fell into the moat, pushed off the walkways by their comrades or dropped by a well-placed arrow, but each time, another warrior stepped into his place. The surviving Staglords joined the fray at every point where the Crow's men spilled onto the battlements, but there were too many; the odds were stacked heavily against them. The Graycloaks were falling, the enemy was winning. *Time to roll the bones.*

"I have him!" cried Reinhardt, staggering up to Drew on his stiff leg, thrusting the gagged Crowlord forward. Croke's hate-filled eyes narrowed as he glared at Drew. The young Wolf took him by the shoulder, nodding his thanks to the Stag.

"You're sure about this?" asked Reinhardt.

"What choice do we have?"

With that, Drew stepped up onto the gray rock of the wall's edge, Lord Croke of Riven held around the throat in the crook of his left arm, Moonbrand brandished in his right.

"Vorjavik!" roared Drew at the assembled host from Riven and Vermire. "I've something you may want to see!"

The black-cloaked archers of Vermire gathered before the moat, cowls raised over their heads, training their bows and silver arrows on the Wolflord. Drew dug the enchanted white sword into the Crow's torso, until the blade edge threatened to separate cloth and flesh at any moment. He could hear Croke snarling, trying to work the gag free from his mouth. Drew brought his lips to the Crow's ear.

"Don't even *think* of changing, my lord," he whispered menacingly, hopeful the Crow believed every word he said. "It would be my pleasure to let Moonbrand find a way between your scrawny ribs."

The fighting ceased suddenly as the men of Riven disengaged with the Graycloaks at the sight of their master held captive by the Wolf. Lord Croke had been left behind in their mountain home, his long years and failing health making him unfit for travel. Yet now he stood before them, at the Wolflord's mercy. The Vermirian soldiers at their backs pushed forward, wanting to continue the assault regardless of whom was held hostage. Fights and scuffles broke out along the walkways as the Crows and the Rats traded blows, and a handful of former comrades tumbled from the bridges.

Good, thought Drew. *Let them fight each other!*

"Cease!" came the order from deep within the body of the attacking force, and the enemy ranks immediately halted their skirmish.

The black-armored figure of Vorjavik emerged from his personal guard below, wearing a long bearskin cloak. While Vankaskan had been sickly and Vanmorten rangy, the war marshal was a prize specimen of a therian warrior. His breastplate alone could have housed two men, his broad, stocky frame filling the steel to the full. A war mattock swung from his hip, the head of the hammer studded with bolts of shining silver.

"Well, well, well. It's been a while, boy!" snarled the Rat, gurgling with laughter. "We all thought you dead. If I couldn't see you with my own eyes I wouldn't have believed it: the Werewolf, coming to aid the Stags in their last days, wielding his old man's white sword. Wait until they hear about this back in Highcliff."

Drew thought back to the last time he'd seen Vorjavik, when he'd doused the Wererat's brother Vanmorten in Spyr Oil before setting him alight. The other members of the Rat King had watched through the flames, desperate to slay the son of Wergar in revenge.

The men on the nearest walkway parted as the Ratlord walked up its length. The elite warriors of Vermire accompanied him, with the Crowlord Scree a step behind, his head bobbing anxiously on seeing Drew's prisoner.

"Put my father down, Wolf!" Scree commanded. "He's a sickly old man: how *dare* you steal him from his deathbed!"

"Come no closer," called Drew, wary of the advancing Ratlord and his cronies. "This old Crow may not be far from his deathbed, but I can hasten his journey with one thrust of my blade!"

As Reinhardt and Wilhelm stood beside Drew, the war marshal of the Lion's army continued his march toward the top of the ramp.

"What are you doing, Vorjavik?" hissed Scree loudly, panic evident in his voice. "He has my father!"

"Don't underestimate what I'm capable of, Vorjavik!" shouted Drew, jabbing the blade deeper between the Crowlord's ribs. Croke choked, arching his gnarled back into his captor, muscles beginning to ripple beneath his thin robes. Drew was unsure how much longer he could hold onto Croke; there was danger of the feisty avianthrope changing at any moment, no longer fearful of the youth's threats. All eyes were on the Wolflord: Crows, Stags, the Rat, every soldier within his gaze.

More scuffles were breaking out beyond the walls. The differences between the Vermirians and the men of Riven were coming to a head as they were confronted by their lords bickering before them.

"He's not bluffing, Ratlord," said Scree, taking hold of the war marshal as Vorjavik threatened to step onto the battlements. Scree's brothers had taken to the air, swooping overhead, enraged by their father's predicament. Of Red Rufus, there was no sign.

The Ratlord turned, his face twisted in a look of contempt.

"Get your filthy talons off my shoulder, you foolish bird. *I* command these forces. Prince Lucas named *me* war marshal of his army, and that includes this ragtag rabble you've brought down from the mountains. What happens next is *my* decision." He prodded the Crow with a dirty fat finger. *"Know your place, Crow."*

Scree unhanded the Ratlord, his face draining of color as the war marshal stepped onto the wall top.

With a rip, the rope that had held Count Croke's arms to his sides tore free as the Werecrow's expanding chest pushed the hemp to breaking point. Drew kept a tight hold, letting the Wolf in, his own muscles growing as his chokehold on the Crow increased. A filthy black beak tore free from Croke's mouth, nose and jaw elongating as he sheared the gag in two. His withered wings broke free, flapping ineffectually as he struggled in the Wolf's embrace.

Croke's wheezing scream escaped from his constricted throat. "Kill them! Kill them all!"

Vorjavik and Scree stopped on the walls. The Vermirian Guard surrounded them, awaiting the war marshal's orders.

"But, Father," shouted Scree, "the Wolf! He'll kill you!"

Drew squeezed, trying to cut off Croke's airways, but the tyrant's voice still tore through.

"He won't do it! He hasn't the stomach!"

He's right, thought Drew, the blade's handle growing slick in his grasp as his sweating hand betrayed him. *I can't do this. I can't kill a man's father right in front of him, like my mother was murdered before my eyes. . . .*

"Are you sure?" Scree said, a caw of nervous laughter in his voice.

"This talk is getting us nowhere!" said Vorjavik, tiring of the stalemate. "You're a fool for getting yourself caught in the first place, Croke. Be it upon your own head if you're wrong, but this pup isn't going to stop me from taking Stormdale." He raised a clawed hand to the sky, the change beginning to grip the Wererat as he prepared to give the signal to attack.

The sharp twang of a shortbow came first, before the war marshal could sound the order. A hooded, black-cloaked Vermirian archer let loose his silver arrow from the muddy ground in front of the gatehouse, lowering his bow as the missile sailed straight in the air. Those who didn't see the archer's attack heard the arrow as it whistled through the bleak sky toward the top of the gatehouse. The warriors of Riven and

Vermire watched as the silver projectile found its target with a wet snap.

Lord Croke, the Werecrow of the Barebones, went limp in Drew's arm, the arrow buried deep within his heart. The silence was deafening for the briefest of moments, before the whole of Stormdale erupted to the sound of battle.

But this was not the battle that the weary defenders of Stormdale had expected just moments earlier. Drew lowered Croke's body to the ground as he watched the warriors of Riven charge into the Vermirian guard, comrades becoming enemies as they turned on one another. Magister Wilhelm turned to look at Drew, and the message from one to another was clear.

There is yet hope.

5

THE SHARPEST TEETH

THE SOUND OF feet pounding timber rattled around Brackenholme Hall. Greencapes ran along the walkways through the Great Oak's boughs, the ancient tree alive with panicked soldiers and courtiers. Whitley stood to one side as a branch of the court guard raced toward one of the caged lifts that would deliver them to the ground far below. The scout grabbed at their captain as they rushed by.

"Where are you going? We cannot leave Duchess Rainier undefended!"

"My lady," said the officer, recognizing the Bearlady beneath the green cloak of the Woodland Watch. "Four of our finest knights remain in the hall with your mother, under strict orders to let no one pass. Lady Gretchen is with her also, along with the rest of the court. With respect, I need to go below: the city's overrun with Wyldermen, and we need every able body down there protecting our people."

He was correct, of course. Whitley's interjection was a purely selfish one. The Great Oak was the safest place for her mother and Gretchen; so long as the lifts were defended, no force could invade Brackenholme Hall. The city's inhabitants were the ones most at risk, with the Garrison Tree short-handed ever since the majority of the Woodland Watch's Greencloaks had ridden west with her father on their ill-fated journey to Highcliff months previously. She let go of the man, bowing to him briefly.

"My apologies, Captain. Please, hurry on your way."

Whitley followed the men as they dashed into the cage, the door clattering shut as it began its descent. She leaned over the balcony to watch the lift disappear below and her heart froze. The buildings of Brackenholme burned, and tiny figures scuttled through the streets like ants. From this height and in such poor light it was impossible to differentiate invader from civilian as the ghastly scene played out far away from the branches of the Great Oak. But one thing was very clear. The city was overrun: the Wyldermen had taken it.

Storm snorted hard as she dipped her head, and Trent urged her to charge along the Dymling Road, into the heart of the madness and mayhem. Townsfolk ran screaming through the street, chased down by packs of berserk Wyldermen. Here and there a group of soldiers held the wild men back, the Woodland Watch fighting beside the city's Greencapes, but the pockets of resistance were few and far between. The attack had been perfectly executed by the invaders, who had caught the city asleep.

Trent had never heard of such numbers of Wyldermen gathering before. When he was growing up on the Cold Coast, there were occasional sightings along the edge of the Dyrewood, but the wild men were known to be tribal, living in small groups and fiercely defensive of individual territories. Trent could see differences between the Wyldermen now, the more he observed them. The blue woad or white chalk markings, the headdresses and choice of weapons: this was an army made up of many tribes, united in their attack on Brackenholme. Another Wylderman closed on him with an ax, a woman this time. He deflected her attack with a sharp kick that sent her reeling backward.

Trent looked ahead just as a longsword caught him square in the chest. Blind luck played its part, as only the flat of the blade struck him; he might otherwise have been cut in two. The force knocked him clean out of his saddle and down onto the road with a crunch, as Storm ran on into the smoke and was lost from sight. Trent rolled over as the sword hit the ground where he lay, scrambling clear as a Greencloak chopped down again.

"What are you doing? I'm on your side!" screamed Trent.

"You're Lionguard! You're with them!" shouted the soldier, switching his attack to a low swing now. Trent lifted the Wolfshead blade, parrying the blow before it connected with his stomach.

The red cloak! You fool, Trent! There it was, its hem trailing in the mud beneath him, a big, red target that marked him as an enemy. He'd needed it as protection against the winter weather when he'd escaped Lord Frost's encampment, but it was an error not to have removed it upon entering Brackenholme. He just hoped it wasn't going to be a grave one.

"I'm not with the Lionguard!" said Trent, scrambling clear of the next blow.

"Then you've a fool's taste in attire!" replied the man, raising his sword to strike.

Trent threw the Wolfshead blade, the sword flying from his hand. The Greencloak's eyes widened as it sailed toward him, point first, then disappeared past him.

"Missed!" snarled the soldier.

"No I didn't," said Trent.

The sound of a body hitting the ground behind him made the Greencloak glance over his shoulder. A Wylderman lay slumped in the mud, ax in hand, the Wolfshead blade rising out of his chest like a lance.

The soldier looked at the Wolf's head on the pommel, then back at Trent. "Red cloak aside, thank you." He reached out a hand, hauling the outrider to his feet. Trent looked around for Storm. He whistled shrilly, his signal for the mount to return.

"Your horse? That'll be long gone," said the man, as Trent withdrew his sword from the corpse. Judging by the insignia on the Greencloak's leather breastplate, he was a captain.

"Your gates were opened from within," said Trent, breathing hard. "You've a traitor in your city."

The Greencloak nodded grimly, absorbing the information.

"Come," he said. "We must regroup. The streets are no longer safe: our only hope is to get the survivors to the Great Trees."

"Great Trees?" Trent asked as they ran down the Dymling Road between the raging fires and banks of smoke.

"Never visited Brackenholme, then?" said the captain as they approached a dozen battered-looking defenders beside an enormous fountain. A handful of Romari stood among them, one big, bald brute with a corked wineskin dangling from his neck wielding an ax and torch. Beside him was a wiry old man who carried a bloodied rapier. The men in green immediately saluted Trent's companion, looking uneasily at the Redcloak outrider.

"What news?" asked the captain.

"We've got as many civilians into the Oaks as possible,

Captain Harker. Many have fled straight to the Garrison Tree, since the Black Oak holds a few hundred and is already full. Others have taken to the White Oak, where the clerics and healers are tending their wounds. In each case, the gates have been closed and will not be opened under any circumstances. The other two Oaks have their share of survivors, too. That just leaves the Great Oak, where Lady Gretchen and Lady Whitley remain alongside Duchess Rainier."

"Gretchen and Whitley," Trent said quickly, drawing more fierce looks from the Greencloaks with his informal references. "I was sent to warn them. They travel in the company of Baba Korga, at least a woman they *believe* is Baba Korga."

The Romari with the rapier chimed in. "What do you mean, *believe*? Baba Korga lodges in Brackenholme Hall presently, as a guest of the duchess."

"I met with a council of your wise women, sir. Korga's dead, slain some time ago by the Wyldermen." He turned to Harker. "Whoever's been traveling with the Wereladies . . . she's no baba."

Harker glanced at the wiry old man, as looks of grave concern passed between them.

"On no account is anyone to harm this man," said the captain, indicating Trent with a nod of his head. "He's with us. For the time being," he added with a glower.

Harker set off fast along another avenue that led away

from the Dymling Road toward the Great Oak. As the men ran, Trent fell in among them, his heart pounding as he joined his old enemies for the fight.

By the time they reached the foot of the Great Oak it was alive with fighting. A valiant crowd of Greencapes and Greencloaks held their position, desperately trying to protect the lifts that carried passengers to Brackenholme Hall. A mass of mud-covered Wyldermen swarmed over them, spears, axes, and knives raised as they bore down on the men of the Woodland Realm.

Harker led the charge, his longsword tearing into the backs of the Wyldermen as he took a straight route toward the lifts. His men followed quickly behind him, falling into an attack formation, driving an emerald wedge through the enemy. Soon the Greencloaks were toe to toe with the invaders, trading blows in a packed melee.

Trent felt a sudden surge as the Greencloaks pushed forward, steady steps taking them nearer to their comrades. The enemy's ranks broke momentarily, allowing Harker to drive through. A Greencloak went down in front of Trent, cutting off his path through the mob. He could feel himself being pulled away from Brackenholme's defenders, as if drawn out to the ocean by a deadly current.

The big Romari who'd accompanied them suddenly stepped into the space Trent had vacated, his giant ax scything out. Trent ducked as it tore through the Wyldermen around him, leaving severed hands and heads in its wake. The wiry Romari who stayed close to the ax man reached down, hauling Trent to his feet.

"Keep moving, lad," he said, pushing Trent between them.

The Wyldermen closed in behind them, swallowing their path like a great serpent devouring its prey. Trent lurched after the Romari, falling into the thinned ranks of Greencloaks who remained guarding the wicker lift above them. The bodies of slain Greencloaks and Wyldermen littered the floor around the base of the tree, providing a grisly obstacle course. The tree trunk was perhaps fifty feet across, with cracked bark rippling across its surface. Only thirty defenders remained now, including those Greencloaks and Romari who had survived the charge led by Harker: hundreds of wild men pushed home their advantage, tasting victory with every blow.

"Into the cage, Harker!" said the wiry Romari as he darted forward, rapier flashing.

"I won't leave anyone down here, Stirga!" shouted the captain, sending another Wylderman to the ground.

"The cage!" yelled Stirga, shoving Trent into the wicker lift. The outrider staggered in, quickly followed by half a dozen Greencloaks as the others drew back, retreating from the enemy. A horn hung from the roof of the cage, and the thickest rope Trent had ever seen was connected through the roof, disappearing into the darkness overhead.

Harker stepped back alongside Stirga as the Greencloaks

squeezed into the lift behind them. When no more could fit they clambered onto the roof, hauling one another to safety. Only the big Romari with the ax and torch still fought the Wyldermen, using the piles of corpses as a breakwater against the tide of evil.

As Harker and Stirga clambered onto the cage walls, the giant swung his ax through the crowd, briefly scattering his opponents. Snatching at the wineskin around his neck, he quickly uncorked it, throwing its contents over the dead bodies at his feet. He took a swift gulp from the spout before raising the torch to his mouth. A bright yellow fireball erupted, swirling over the heads of the Wyldermen, who cowered away from the inferno. Strapping his ax to his back, he tossed the torch onto the bodies, and with a loud *whoosh* they went up in flames.

Harker reached into the cage, snatching the horn and blowing with all his might. Trent trembled at the noise, and the lift immediately shuddered into life. The big Romari leapt as the cage started its ascent, leaving the flames and Wyldermen below him. Spears whistled through the air, rattling against the wall grilles, the odd one finding its way through the bars and hitting a target. Darts flew up, the deadly needles catching three of the lift's occupants and sending them slumping to the cage floor.

A Greencloak tumbled from the roof, a spear through his side, catching one of his comrades who clung to the outside. The two fell into the chaos below. Trent looked down, spotting the Romari giant holding on to the bars of the cage floor for dear life. He dropped to his knees, thrusting his arms through the bars and locking them around the man's wrists. If the Romari let go, he'd probably tear Trent's arms from their sockets. The bald ax-man stared up at the boy, his face contorting with the strain, the ground already far beneath him. Trent gripped tighter, fingers digging into the Romari's flesh.

"Just hold on," he said through gritted teeth. "Just hold on. . . ."

6

THE BEST OF ENEMIES

IN THE IMMEDIATE aftermath of Lord Croke's demise, the soldiers of the Rats and Crows launched into one another, their simmering resentment boiling over into all-out battle. In an instant, the Staglords' fortunes turned, that one rogue arrow splitting the enemy into two warring factions. The Graycloaks were momentarily astonished before seizing the initiative. Baron Hoffman, the oldest Staglord, led a charge into the enemies along the battlements, transforming with each swing of his greatsword. The handful of men who followed, knights of Stormdale and Highwater, rained sword blows down on the invaders, pushing them back down the siege engine bridge.

Not all the enemy were vanquished in the charge. Vorjavik, Scree, and a dozen of the Vermirian Guard had remained on the walls, having already advanced to where Croke had been slain. Scree lunged at the Ratlord, but the war marshal turned just in time to deflect the Crowlord's long silver dagger. The Ratlord barged into Scree, sending him spinning over the wall's edge, changing as he fell. With a sudden burst his cloak tore free, black wings arcing from his back as he plummeted, then swooped up to join his brothers overhead.

Vorjavik and his bodyguard found themselves where they wanted to be, deep within the castle's heart, but not in the unassailable position they had planned. As the Werecrows switched to their bows, the ramparts were peppered with silver-headed arrows while the Vermirians dashed for cover— straight down the wall's steps toward the keep. Their flight didn't go unnoticed.

"For Stormdale!" Reinhardt shouted, antlers emerging from his brow as he leapt down the gatehouse steps after the Vermirians. Drew directed the attacks of the bowmen skyward, while the Werecrows were distracted by the Blackcloaks who dashed across the courtyard. Two of the Crowlords tumbled, their bodies peppered with arrows. The steel-headed arrows wouldn't kill them, but the defenders in the courtyard held nothing back. The injured avianthropes squawked and screamed as old men, women, and wounded warriors attacked them with picks, swords, shovels, and staffs. None was silvered, but the relentless onslaught eventually took their lives.

Drew bounded down the steps, chasing Reinhardt and his

knights as they pursued Vorjavik and his men into the keep, the Grays and Blacks swiftly engaging one another. The Vermirians weren't standard foot soldiers, like those of Riven. These were Vorjavik's personal guard, each one a seasoned campaigner who had served Leopold down the years. Wearing the same black armor as their master, they wielded silver-blessed swords with ruthless efficiency. They were an enemy the Werelords couldn't take lightly, and one false step would most certainly lead to death.

With the throne room transformed into a battlefield, every Werelord in the chamber had shifted. The Staglord Reinhardt towered over all of them, his long, curved antlers stabbing at the Vermirians while his sword clanged off their breastplates. The Wererat Vorjavik was as big as Duke Bergan when changed, his oily, shaggy pelt invisible beneath the sheets of plate armor. His long pink tail whipped and lashed at the Graycloaks, yanking the legs out from under his enemies and flinging civilians into the melee. Drew couldn't get near; every time the Werewolf tried to maneuver around his opponents to reach their master, the Vermirian Guard would push him back, cutting him off and forcing him to defend himself.

Many of the townsfolk and servants who had sheltered in the throne room had managed to escape, finding antechambers to hide in or corridors that led away from the bloody brawl. One of the servants picked up a finely dressed young girl who wore a thin crown twined with snowdrops, holding her close to his chest as he turned and fled toward the Lady's Tower. Drew knew the child: Lady Mia, Duke Manfred's youngest daughter. To his horror he realized he wasn't the only therian who had spied the man's valiant deed. Vorjavik disengaged from the combat, turning on a large black-clawed foot to go after them. Spurred on by the sight of the Wererat giving chase, Drew fought with renewed fury, Moonbrand cutting through the Vermirians until he'd carved himself a path.

Drew found the servant's corpse on the stairs, a hole cleaved in his back from a mighty blow of the Ratlord's war mattock. Drew raced on, leaping up the stairwell, desperate to prevent Vorjavik from harming Lady Mia. He heard the roar of the Wererat ahead, in the highest chambers of the tower, accompanied by the sound of furniture being overturned and smashed open.

"Where are you, child?" the beast snarled, his voice echoing down the stairwell.

Drew paused to catch his breath on a small landing, where a narrow open window allowed the sounds of battle to enter the tower from the night beyond. The same question raced through his mind: *Where are you, Mia?* If Vorjavik had reached the tower top and missed her, then there was a chance she was nearby. Drew glanced into the alcove, catching sight of something unusual on the cold paved floor. A tiny white flower lay near the window's edge, its white petals trembling, the chill breeze threatening to carry it away at any moment: a snowdrop from

Mia's crown. Drew stepped into the alcove, craning his head out of the stone aperture. There was the terrified child, standing on the window ledge, a hundred feet from the ground, her back to the brickwork, fingers gripping the gray stone. The sight of the Werewolf's head emerging from the window startled her, making her lose her grip. Drew dropped Moonbrand on the stone sill behind him in the act of steadying her. The noise echoed through the alcove and stairwell, no doubt alerting the Wererat on the floor above.

Drew turned to the young girl who trembled at the window's edge, her eyes glistening with tears. He raised a finger to his black, lupine lips, insisting she remained silent.

"Come out, come out, wherever you are," said Vorjavik, his armor grating against the curved stone wall as he descended the stairs.

Drew knew why Vorjavik sought her so eagerly: if captured, she could be a hostage, the Ratlord's guarantee of passage out of Stormdale after the disastrous end to his siege. Drew composed himself, steadying his breathing as the footsteps came closer. Leaving Mia perched on the ledge, he crouched and picked up Moonbrand. The sword glowed for the briefest moment before Drew stowed it away, hiding the white blade inside his cloak, his back to the alcove.

"I'm not going to hurt you, little Doe," rasped the transformed Wererat.

As a long, clawed foot stepped into view on the staircase,

Moonbrand appeared in a flash from the folds of Drew's cloak. The sword struck the stone, severing the front half of the Wererat's foot. Vorjavik tumbled, screaming ferociously, his war mattock flying into the window's alcove. The hammerhead crashed into Drew's studded leather breastplate, sending him back toward the open window. The Rat filled the staircase, his maimed foot spouting blood as he righted himself.

Drew had to think quickly. Sheathing Moonbrand, the Werewolf stumbled out of the window and onto the ledge beside the child.

"Climb on," he growled. Mia clambered onto his back, grabbing the thick gray fur around his throat. Using his clawed feet he began to scale the wall, one hand snatching at the rough stones that provided holds. The Ratlord thrust his clawed hands through the window, snatching at the Wolf as he swung his trailing leg clear. Drew could hear Vorjavik's armor scraping against the window frame, preventing him from coming after them. There was a clatter of steel as the Rat shed his plate mail and emerged onto the ledge below them.

Mia screamed at the sight of the scrambling Wererat, digging her fingers ever tighter around Drew's throat.

"Don't look at him," said Drew, climbing higher, grabbing at the stones, using his left elbow for leverage. The climb to the tower top sapped his strength, and the crenellated edge was still twenty feet away. With each grasp and push he drew closer, the possibility of falling never far from his thoughts as the pitted gray stones crumbled beneath the weight of his lycanthrope body. Vorjavik was nearing them, unhindered by a burden on his back, although his chopped foot bled freely as he came closer. A shadow passed across the moon above, and Drew caught sight of Red Rufus battling against Scree and one of his brothers, Hawk and Crows spinning as they ripped into one another with talon and blade.

A clawed hand clamped onto Drew's right leg, tearing into his flesh as he neared the summit.

"You can't escape me!" gloated Vorjavik, sharp tongue flickering over his serrated teeth.

Suddenly, the Rat released his grip on Drew, striking his arm out against a furious black beak that stabbed at his neck. Fate had intervened, not for the first time that night. Having spied the Rat, Scree's brother left the fight against Red Rufus to swoop down and attack Vorjavik. The Werecrow's feet raked the Rat's exposed spine, talons clenching tight as they tore huge lumps of oily-haired flesh from Vorjavik's back.

Drew hurried on as the Rat snatched hold of the Crowlord's beak, using all his strength to swing it around and smash it into the wall. Again and again Vorjavik drove the Werecrow into the ancient brickwork, until he released his grip and the Birdlord fell lifeless from the tower.

Drew hauled his body over the tower top, and Mia dropped from his back to her feet. The Werewolf lay there for a moment, breathing hard, exhausted. A black, clawed hand emerged over the parapet, swiftly followed by another, spurring Drew back into action. He staggered back to his feet as the Wererat clambered across the battlements, his black pelt soaked in blood.

"Give me the girl," snarled a panting Vorjavik, as Mia hid behind Drew. "Hand her over and I'll let you live, Wolf."

"That's not going to happen," replied Drew. He ripped Moonbrand from its scabbard, the sword shining white, as Vorjavik unhitched his war mattock. A glance above revealed that the moon was hidden behind a bank of clouds, which obscured its light from the enchanted blade, though the sword shone with its own inner glow.

"You can't win this war, boy."

"Perhaps not," growled Drew. "But we've won this battle."

Below, beyond the castle walls, the twin armies of the Rats and the Crows had been routed. Each force hurried on its way through the ruined city, clashing with one another all the while, as Graycloak arrows hastened their flight. Vorjavik grimaced, spitting over the battlements.

"I ask for an army and they send me the Crows! Useless scum!"

"It was one of your arrows that sparked the violence, Rat. Perhaps it's your men of Vermire who are to blame for your failure? Your masters will be ... *displeased*, no doubt."

"I have no master!" screamed the wild-eyed Wererat, stepping forward on his ravaged foot. He looked unsteady as the blood loss from his wounds took its toll. "I'm Vorjavik of

Vermire! The Rat King Warrior! There shall never be another Ratlord like me!"

"Let's hope not," said Drew, as he lunged forward with Moonbrand.

The war mattock parried the sword to one side, and Vorjavik swung it back the other way to deflect the following blow. The Wererat's jaws snapped over the weapons, and the Werewolf met them with his own teeth. The therians bit at one another's faces, each trying to gouge his foe's flesh. Vorjavik brought a powerful knee up as he batted aside another sword thrust, catching Drew hard in the groin. Drew doubled over as the long handle of the Rat's mattock smashed him across the jaw. The Wolflord's huge frame hurtled back across the tower top toward Mia. He hit the crenellations with a bone-jarring crunch, Moonbrand clattering to the rooftop as he lurched dangerously over the edge.

Lady Mia grabbed at Drew, her feeble hands trying to pull him back. The Wererat backhanded her, sending her skidding across the tower, her head crashing into the parapet with a smack. Drew reached back, his fingers straining to hold onto the battlements, slowly dragging himself to safety. His head swam and his heart hammered as he struggled to catch his breath. He heard the sound of Moonbrand being scraped across the stone as Vorjavik lifted the sacred Sword of the Wolflords. Drew collapsed against the ramparts, lifting his head weakly as the Ratlord towered over him.

"It appears my campaign wasn't entirely in vain." Vorjavik laughed, raising the sword over his head. The blade was black, the glow gone while it was in the Wererat's grasp. "I shall return to Highcliff with the Wolf's execution fresh on my lips."

Vorjavik's pink eyes went suddenly wide with shock, his long snout trembling and needle-teeth rattling as he shook where he stood. Slowly, the tip of a greatsword emerged from his chest, inch by inch, his eyes looking down on it as he dropped Moonbrand with a *clang*. The Wererat's black head wobbled as blood bubbled from his lips, and the sword ripped free as he staggered toward the tower's edge. Reinhardt stood behind him, and the Staglord lifted the sword for one final swing.

"You return to the earth, Ratlord, with your blood fresh on my sword."

The greatsword flew, cleaving Vorjavik's head from his shoulders, and the decapitated body of the Wererat disappeared over the parapet into the night. Reinhardt went to his sister, picking up her limp body from the floor, cradling her in his arms. Drew could only watch. Even if he'd known what to say, he couldn't speak; the air had not yet returned to his battered lungs.

7
CONSTRICTED

THE CAGE JUDDERED to a halt thirty feet below the Great Oak's landing platform. The rope creaked and groaned under the strain of the overloaded lift, the bamboo frame swinging menacingly as the men cried out from within and around it. Those who clung to the exterior of the lift held on even tighter as the pendulous motion of the cage threatened to send them falling to their death. Trent grimaced, every muscle burning as he kept hold of the giant Romari who dangled beneath the barred floor. Above, the chilling screams of Greencapes could be heard, drifting down from Brackenholme Hall like dead leaves on the wind.

"The hall's under attack!" said Captain Harker, struggling to stand upright on the cage roof.

"How did they get up there?" asked one of the Greencloaks. "The lifts are the only means of reaching the hall, and this is the last to be drawn up!"

"The false baba must be behind it," said Harker as a green-caped palace guard fell past them, swallowed by the smoke below.

"Keep hold," hissed Trent through gritted teeth.

"I wasn't planning on letting go," said the Romari giant, veins bulging around his broad neck, eyes closed with concentration. Trent stared past him, looking down the length of the mighty tree trunk as it vanished into the darkness. He spied movement on the Great Oak's rough bark surface. Trent squinted; there was the movement again, here and there, dotting the tree's enormous frame: Wyldermen. The savages were scaling the oak, using knives, axes, and bare hands to climb.

"They're coming!" screamed Trent, making the cage swing more violently than before as the trapped Greencloaks panicked. The old Romari with the rapier jumped gracefully to his feet beside Harker, snatching up the thick rope with both hands.

"What are you doing, Stirga?" said the captain, as the old sword-swallower began to climb.

"I'm getting us moving again," he called back, scurrying up the rope with an agility that belied his age. "Don't go anywhere," he said sarcastically as he disappeared toward the platform, heading straight for the screams.

Duchess Rainier barred Whitley's way, four members of the Bearguard flanking her.

"Please, Mother; stand aside. I'm needed out there."

The duchess would not be swayed. She had waited too long to be reunited with her daughter to allow some foolish notion of duty to take the child from her again. Gretchen stood a short distance away, watching in silence, refusing to get involved in the family dispute.

"You're needed in *here*, Whitley," said Rainier, glowering. "I can't allow you to leave. I forbid it."

"You can't stand in my way. Please, let me pass." Whitley tried to barge past her mother, only for one of Rainier's most loyal soldiers to block her path.

"Stand *down*, sir," snarled Whitley, shifting her quarterstaff in her grip. The armored knight of the Bearguard stared back apologetically. Realizing that she would not be able to persuade him, she turned back to the duchess.

"Your Grace, I gave my word when I took the green, when I accepted this." She let the steel-shod end of the staff strike the hard floor of the throne room. "I am a scout of the Woodland Watch, and I am oath-bound to protect Brackenholme." She reached out with her other hand, squeezing her mother's hand tightly. "Please, Mother, stand aside. I won't leave you."

Rainier stared at her daughter, but it was clear that she could not dissuade her from her duty. Bergan's blood ran through her veins, of that there was no doubt. Reluctantly, the duchess stood to one side, the Bearguard moving with her, allowing the young therian lady to pass.

"Be careful!" her mother called after her, as Whitley disappeared through Brackenholme Hall's enormous double doors.

Running along the platforms and bridges that led away from the building, Whitley strapped the quarterstaff to her back and shifted her shortbow into her hands. The gray clouds that rolled up from the burning city obscured the walkways ahead, and her line of sight to the lifts was shrouded in choking smoke. She slowed as she spied the first bodies through the gloom.

Three Greencapes lay broken on the walkway, their limbs twisted, faces contorted into terrified death masks. She stumbled past them, her whole being cold with fear. Drawing back her bow, she edged farther along the platform, creeping ever nearer the lift deck, where she could hear the dying screams of the palace guards. Another Greencape lay ahead, his breastplate punctured by two fist-sized wounds a foot apart, one in his chest, one in his gut. The shortbow trembled in Whitley's grasp.

A great shape moved through the smoke, a long, undulating black mass, flashes of purple visible on its underbelly as it searched for fresh victims. She loosed an arrow, the missile whistling through the air to *thunk* ineffectually into the creature's body. It stopped moving, the silhouette of a huge, hooded head rising as it spied her. Giant green eyes appeared for the first time, widening as the stuff of nightmares fixed its glare upon Whitley.

It can't be, thought the Bearlady, recognizing the monster from Drew's description. She turned and ran, leaping over the corpses, heading straight for the hall with the beast at her back.

Whitley's fists hammered on the carved wooden doors, and the scout glanced back as she screamed, "Let me in!"

Bars clanked in their housings, whipped clear as the doors swung open. She collapsed into the arms of Gretchen, who looked out onto the smoke-filled walkway as the monster appeared.

"Brenn help us," whispered the Werefox, immediately recognizing the creature before her. "Shut the doors!" she shouted.

The Bearguard slammed the doors shut, driving the bars home on either side, reinforcing it without a moment to spare. The door shuddered as something enormous thundered into it with an earth-splitting roar, dislodging dust from the ceiling above.

"The windows!" cried Whitley. "Barricade every entrance! Quickly!"

The Bearguard dashed to every corner of the throne room, shuttering windows, upturning tables and bracing them against every portal, reinforcing them against the beast outside.

Gretchen and Whitley held on to each other, backing slowly away from the door, eyes fixed upon the entrance.

"Is that—?" began Gretchen before Whitley raised a hand to silence her.

A scraping sound could be heard through the doorway, as if a great weight strained against it. Whitley looked back toward the center of the throne room, where Duchess Rainier now stood, hands to her face, a knight at her side. Around them two dozen courtiers and servants huddled, whispering and sobbing as they stared at the doors.

The windows rattled as the enemy's great mass found purchase against the hall's wooden walls. The doors trembled, more dust billowing down as the building shuddered. The wooden doors bowed inward, timbers groaning as the monster squeezed against them, forcing its weight behind them. There was a snapping, splintering noise as the doors suddenly buckled, threatening to shatter.

"Do you think you are sssssssafe in there, ladiessssss?"

"It's Vala," gasped Gretchen, terrifying memories of the Wyrmwood flooding back, when the Wyldermen delivered her to the Wereserpent as a sacrificial offering.

Whitley took a step forward, and three knights of the Bearguard joined her. They may have been the best of Duke Bergan's warriors, but Gretchen could sense their terror.

"Leave this city, Vala!" cried Whitley, a fragile confidence in her voice. "Go back to your Wyrmwood or whatever stone you've slithered out from under. Remain here and we shall put you to the sword."

The Wereserpent hissed behind the door, the awful sound sending a wave of terror through the throne room. The noise was primal, striking a fearful chord in them all.

"Sssssssoooo, it'sssss the little Bear who sssspeakssss? Good, good . . . you've come a long way from the frightened rain-ssssoaked child we firsssssst met in Cape Gala."

Whitley turned to look at Gretchen.

"Cape Gala? What is she talking about?" asked Whitley. "You don't know me!" she shouted, facing the door once more.

"Don't know you?" cried the Wereserpent, her huge body bucking against the door, hammering the walls and windows. "I fed and clothed you. My Rolff even helped you find your friendsssssssss."

Whitley's legs gave way as she dropped onto one knee, a horrible realization dawning on her.

"Brenn forgive me," she said, to herself as much as the others. "*I* brought the monster here!"

"Monssssster?" cried Vala, her voice rising to a near scream. "Issssss that any way to ssssssspeak of a dear . . ." The door buckled again, struck from outside. "Old . . ." The timber cracked, no longer able to resist the constricting coils of the Wereserpent.

". . . Baba!"

The doors blew open, **showering** splintered timber across the throne room. A wooden **stake** caught a Bearguard in the chest, punching through his plate mail and catapulting him into the screaming courtiers. The two other knights with Whitley ran forward, swords and shields raised, as the giant snake slid into the hall. As roll upon roll of black-scaled skin rippled into the ancient chamber, Vala's monstrous head darted from side to side. She spat venom at the first warrior, the milky white spray catching him in the face, sending him screaming to his knees as his weapon and shield bounced off the ground. The other knight managed to carve a gash in the Wereserpent's side before her coils looped round him and tightened instantly, the knight's bones snapping like twigs.

Whitley snatched up one of the knights' swords and leapt forward, unleashing a battle cry as she brought the blade down on the Wereserpent's writhing flank. As a scout, she had been trained to fight with a quarterstaff, and the blade felt unwieldy in her hand. But now her city had fallen, her people were dying, and her mother was in mortal danger. The weapon bounced off Vala's black scales, juddering in Whitley's grasp before almost springing from her palm.

The Serpent coiled around her, making the girl spin on her heel, lashing out with the longsword once more. The enormous head darted forward, mouth open, a monstrous *hiss* escaping Vala's throat as her tongue rattled between her fangs. Whitley brought the sword around, both hands clasping the handle now for fear of losing hold. The flat of the blade caught the Wereserpent's jaw, knocking its head to one side, but not enough to stop it from wrapping its coils round the Bearlady.

The pain was instantaneous as the coils tightened, squeezing the air from Whitley's lungs. The sword fell to the floor with a clatter as the giant snake lifted the girl into the air. If she had had any mastery over the beast within, any knowledge of how to control her therianthropy, Whitley would have called upon it, channeled the Bear and fought back. She knew Gretchen could shift, but that was where she and her cousin differed. The Fox was fiery and aggressive, with a dark side that bubbled beneath the surface. Whitley was none of these things, an ursanthrope in name alone. She prayed to Brenn that the Bear might come to her rescue as Vala's coils slowly squeezed the life out of her.

Gretchen skidded to her knees beside the fallen Bearguard, trying to roll him clear of the Wereserpent's thrashing tail. The knight was gripped by convulsions as the white venom that smothered his face traveled through his nervous system. When his struggles suddenly ceased, he became a dead weight in her arms, the fight gone from his poisoned body. Gretchen rose as the Serpent wrapped Whitley within its coils.

One of the courtiers dashed past, sprinting for the splintered doorway, leaping over the fallen knight as he made a break for freedom. Vala's tail lashed out, catching him in the chest and sending him flying back into the crowd, splitting them as they ran screaming to every corner of the chamber. Gretchen rose, dancing clear of the deadly tail, searching for her friend among the Serpent's coils. Vala had a strong grip on Whitley now, and the girl's movements grew lethargic, her head lolling as the fight faded from her.

Gretchen looked back as the last Bearguard advanced, his weapon and shield before him.

"Stay with the duchess!" she cried as she maneuvered around the monster. It had been a long time since she had channeled her therian side, but now she called upon her inner Fox as she leapt gracefully, looking for an opportunity to strike. She could feel her teeth sharpening like needles against her lips, while her fingernails became razor-sharp claws.

"Sssssssoooo, the little Fox wantssssss to play?" hissed Vala, her big emerald eyes widening as she caught sight of Gretchen across the hall.

"Let her go!" growled Gretchen, dagger raised over her head, ready to throw. Beyond the walls she could hear the noise of battle in the treetop.

"It ssseemssss my ssssubjectssss have arrived! Thisss sssshall be their new home, thissss hall their temple! There'ssss a ready ssssupply of food to ssssate my appetite," she spat, her head darting toward the sobbing courtiers who cowered around the chamber.

"Curse you, Vala! I'll die before I let you harm any more of these people!"

"Oh no, ssssweet Lady Gretchen; you ssshall not die. Neither you nor the Bearladiessss ssshall be further harmed. At leassst, not until the Wolf arrivessss. That'ssss right, issssn't it? He'll come for you, won't he, jusssst assss my children come for me?"

"Drew could be dead for all I know," replied Gretchen, though in her heart she prayed he yet lived.

"Two pretty little Wereladiessss, both in love with the ssssame hound," hissed Vala.

"You said we wouldn't be harmed!" Gretchen gestured toward Whitley, hanging limp in Vala's coils. "If you've killed her, so help me Brenn, you'll be next!"

The Serpent shook the unconscious Bearlady. She tossed Whitley to one side, and her body rolled over the floorboards, limbs tangling lifelessly as she came to a halt before her sobbing mother.

"I have ssssspared her: sssshe merely sssssleepssss!" Vala rose, her hood broadening around her head as she towered over the terrified onlookers. The purple ribs of her underbelly glistened as she took an indulgent moment to boast victoriously, "Pray to your god all you like, child. It'ssss time you learned there issss only one true deity: Vala, the Sssssserpent Goddessssss!"

Gretchen sprang forward as the Wereserpent attacked.

8

SKIRMISH

REUBEN FRY STARED down at the three arrows in the snow at his feet, counting them once more as if they might magically have multiplied since his last glance. Three sorry arrows: that was his lot. He looked down the ice canyon ahead, catching sight of more of Sheriff Muller's men. Muller, the Bandit-lord, allied to Prince Lucas and the armies of the Catlords, had caught wind of Duke Bergan's miraculous survival and subsequent reappearance in the Badlands. Ambushed by at least thirty bandits, Captain Fry and his companions had been chased by Muller's Skirmishers into the narrow gorge, scrambling over ice as the enemy closed off any escape route. They were trapped.

When the four survivors from Highcliff had finally

emerged from the underworld, they'd found they were deep within Sheriff Muller's land, with the Whitepeaks agonizingly within reach. They had since been picking their way through the foothills of Sturmland, avoiding enemy scouting parties. The Lion had clearly sent his greatest force north toward Captain Fry's homeland; the myriad campfires of Prince Lucas's army twinkled across the Badlands as far as the eye could see. Bergan's only hope of survival had been to find a way to his cousin in Icegarden, Duke Henrik, but there seemed little chance of surviving this encounter in the frozen ravine, let alone reaching the Strakenberg. This canyon would probably be their tomb.

Fry looked down from his vantage point, a wide ledge of ice that jutted out from the gorge wall, spying Bergan, Carver, and Pick hugging the rocks below. The Bearlord was finding his strength again, his half-moon ax gripped menacingly in his hands. The Lord of Thieves, Carver, held a knife in each of his, with more in easy reach on his weapon belt, while Pick crouched behind him, a dagger shaking in the girl's trembling fist.

"Three arrows," Fry whispered to himself, plucking the first from the snow and nocking it in his bow. "Let's make them count."

Bergan let the breath steam gradually from his lips. The bandits might know that the four had fled into the gorge, and could no doubt see the sheer wall of ice a short distance away where the trail suddenly ended, but he wasn't about to go down without a fight. A traitorous cloud of exhaled air could reveal their position. There was no sense in making this easy for the enemy. If the bandits wanted them dead, he and his companions would take a few with them.

Fry, a crack shot with his bow, was fifteen feet above them, obscured from Muller's Skirmishers but visible to Bergan. The archer had been indispensable, managing to catch game— rabbits, pigeons, small deer—since escaping from the dread dark below ground. A campfire had been out of the question: they had eaten the meat raw, a grisly business but necessary to ensure that they weren't spotted by their enemy. Pick cowered behind Carver on the opposite side of the frozen ravine, her eyes watching the Bearlord, seeking reassurance. Bergan smiled, showing a jagged white scar within his bushy red beard. *You're right to feel afraid, child. . . .*

Bergan looked up, watching Fry draw back his bow, taking aim. The arrow's flight would be the signal to attack. The Sturmlander would fire when the enemy was within charging distance for Bergan and Carver. The space beyond their hiding place was a bare icy clearing between the gorge's white walls, which opened out from a narrower passage, wide enough to let through a handful of Skirmishers but no more. *Best to take them on our own terms*, reasoned Bergan, readying his ax.

The bowstring sang and Bergan leapt from the shadows,

Carver and Pick close behind. Five of the Skirmishers had entered the clearing, and one was already sprawled on the floor with a feathered arrow quivering in his chest. Although startled, the bandits were prepared, their swords and clubs raised as the Bearlord charged them. The first club took the full weight of the half-moon blade, rattling in the Skirmisher's hand as it bounced back and struck its owner on the skull. Bergan carried the glancing blow around, hacking a great gash into the belly of the next man. Another darted in with his shortsword, catching the Bearlord in the thigh before ripping it free. Before the bandit could strike again, one of Carver's throwing knives struck him in the neck, sending him to meet his friends on the cold ravine floor.

The last attacker avoided the men and went for Pick. His sword slashed forward as she stumbled to get clear. An arrow lanced down from above, hitting the top of the Skirmisher's bare head as he was dispatched with a gurgling grunt.

Carver leapt forward, plunging one knife into the concussed bandit before tearing his other free from the first he'd slain.

"Five down," he snarled as more rushed through the narrow passage.

Bergan decided he had preserved his energy for long enough; now was the time to channel the beast. His battered boots tore open, the rotten leather finally expiring as dark claws ripped free from huge, heavy feet. His ribs rattled momentarily with anticipation as his lungs expanded, the bones lengthening and thickening as his great barrel chest tripled in size. He shifted the ax into a huge, pawed hand, while the other remained free, enormous palm open, ready to strike. The Werebear's head shook, his beard transforming into a thick russet pelt as a broad, powerful muzzle tore free. His black nose snorted, lips bared and jaws open wide as he roared with all the fury he could conjure.

The Skirmishers slowed within the narrow passage, skidding across the ice into a heap as they thought twice about facing the Bearlord.

"Into them, you swine!" cried their leader from the rear.

Those at the back surged forward, pushing on the ones whose spirits were daunted by the sight of the Werebear. The bandits staggered into the icy clearing, weapons raised in defense against the monstrous ursanthrope. The first three who entered the frozen arena fell quickly, slaughtered by ax, tooth, and claw. Those who followed were grateful for their comrades' sacrifice, spreading around the icy walls and encircling the Bear.

Seven of the Skirmishers had swarmed through the gap while Bergan attacked their friends. Spear, ax, and sword stabbed and slashed at the Werelord. He struck out, felling one with each attack, but always another appeared in the dead man's place, their sheer weight of numbers tipping the tide in favor of Muller's men. Still their commander screamed, urging them on as they flooded into the ravine.

Carver busied himself with his knives, the blades flying from his wrists like steel lightning, but they soon ran out, and the Thief-lord valiantly used his remaining one to parry his enemies' blows. A sword tore across his shin, and Carver bounced off the wall behind him on one leg, with each bandit eager to deal the killing blow. The last of Fry's arrows ripped through the air, taking another Skirmisher in the throat, but still more poured through, clambering over their dead companions. Pick went over on one side as a blow from a club caught her temple. Her attacker stood over her, weapon raised. Fry landed on top of the man, jumping from above, sword in hand. The blade disappeared into the man's back, but another was on Fry immediately, his knife stabbing deeply through the archer's leather breastplate as the two fell.

Bergan's vision was clouding, as the red mist of battle was gradually replaced by a gray fog of exhaustion. A fully fit Werebear might have fought for hours against many foes, but his frail body and the weeks he'd spent beneath the earth had caught up with him. He swung his ax, but the bandits were dodging now, evading and flanking him, darting in when his back was turned. The swords and cudgels found their mark repeatedly. If he fell now, the enemy would finish him, silver weapons or not—he'd never leave this Brenn-forsaken canyon.

Is this the way Bergan, the Great Bear of Brackenholme, would die? Beneath a shower of clubs and rusty steel?

Though he was weakening, the sound of stones crashing

around him alerted him to a deadly rockfall. The Werebear staggered back toward the ravine wall, crushing one of his enemies with his broad back as jagged stones rained down. Then arrows flew, peppering the Skirmishers and whittling down their numbers with alarming speed. Bergan glanced up, and his weary eyes caught sight of men standing on top of the canyon, boulders raised and bows aimed at the Skirmishers. They were saved.

Hector stalked along the bottom of the ravine, Ringlin and Ibal on either side of him, as his Ugri warriors commenced their assault on Muller's men from the canyon top. Muller's nephew, Captain Stephan, stood at the entrance to a jagged tunnel whose white walls towered like a cathedral of ice, with three concerned-looking Skirmishers alongside him. They were backing nervously away from the dark pathway, as the screams of their comrades echoed down the frozen corridor like tormented spirits.

Stephan looked over his shoulder, spying Hector and speeding toward him.

"Blackhand," he said. "You're here, and not a moment too soon. Lord Flint said he'd be sending you along for the fight: I believe you have scores to settle with the Bear? Well, it appears he has help in there; my soldiers are taking a beating. You've brought your Boarguard, I hope?"

"I have indeed," said Hector as he stepped up to the bandit captain. His jeweled dagger shot out from the folds of his cloak, vanishing into Stephan's guts, the man's eyes ballooning in horror.

Ringlin and Ibal moved fast. The tall one's long knives slashed forward, striking one of the surprised Skirmishers in the chest, while the short, fat one scythed his sickle blade across the face of another. The third soldier started running, back toward the white passageway, stumbling to the frozen ground as a long knife hit him between the shoulder blades.

Stephan whispered as Hector held him in his embrace, slowly lowering him to the cold canyon floor.

"Why?" he gargled, his lips frothing red.

"Sleep knowing that your sacrifice was for the greater good, Captain," said Hector, cocking his head with morbid fascination as he watched the light fade in the man's eyes.

You're getting good at this, brother, whispered the Vincent-vile, curled invisibly around Hector's shoulders. *You won't need my help at all before long.*

"There's plenty more work for you yet, Vincent," Hector replied, gently settling Captain Stephan on the frozen rocks. He looked up as four figures shambled warily out of the tall gash in the ice, bloodied but alive. Ringlin and Ibal stepped away, bowing to Duke Bergan as the Bearlord limped into the light, Bo Carver and Reuben Fry supporting him beneath either arm. A girl staggered behind them, her hair matted with blood, feet stumbling gingerly across the uneven canyon floor.

Hector rose from the captain's body, smiling as Bergan caught sight of him.

"Can it be?" said the Bearlord, his bloodshot eyes watering as they fell on the Baron of Redmire. He pulled free of Carver and Fry, his arms wide as Hector rushed forward. The hug was heartfelt: Hector could still feel the awesome strength in Bergan's arms, weakened as he was, the Boarlord's ribs grating uncomfortably in the Bearlord's squeeze. Bergan held him at arm's length so he could better look at him.

"My boy," he exclaimed. "What a sight for sore eyes! How in the Seven Realms have you happened across us? Brenn must be watching over us!"

Captain Fry bowed respectfully at Bergan's side, while Carver stood on the other, nodding briefly at the Boarlord before turning his suspicious gaze on Ringlin and Ibal.

Does he know them, do you think, brother? The Lord of Thieves recognizes a reprobate when he sees one, I warrant. . . .

"Not Brenn, Your Grace," replied Hector. "Times are strange, events move apace throughout Lyssia, with unlikely alliances forming across the map." He pointed up to the ravine's top, where the handful of Ugri had gathered, their grisly work of slaying the Skirmishers completed.

"Meet the new members of my Boarguard. It was the Creep who spotted you, picking your way through the same foothills that we were traversing. He's my scout."

"Scout?" said Fry, as all four of Bergan's company looked up at the warriors. Fry squinted, his sharp vision never failing him. "They're Ugri. How on earth have they come to be in your service, my lord?" he asked as respectfully as he could.

He's a Sturmlander, this one, whispered Vincent. *He'll take some convincing; you're allied with his mortal enemy, after all.*

Hector ignored his brother's phantom, directing his answer back to Fry.

"Like I said, Captain; strange alliances. This band from Tuskun are renegades, not loyal to the late Queen Slotha."

"*Late* queen?" said Bergan.

"She was killed in Highcliff, apparently. We caught another of Muller's men a couple of days ago, and he spilled what he knew before he passed. Slotha had arrived in Westland seeking some kind of union with Prince Lucas. The Lion's new Lord Magister murdered her in cold blood," he added, unable to resist the temptation of embellishing his story. "Regardless of what one thinks of the Werewalrus Queen, it was a barbaric thing to do, especially under the flag of parley. The Catlords are to be feared, Your Grace."

"Who's this new magister the Prince has in his employ?" asked the Bearlord, his bushy brow furrowed.

"'Blackhand,' they call him," piped up Ringlin, interrupting the Werelords' discussion. Hector shot him a dark look. He felt his left hand clench inside its glove; he was desperate that it should remain concealed, and his knuckles cracked as the withered black flesh stretched beneath the leather.

"Excuse my man's lack of decorum, Your Grace," said Hector. "He forgets himself."

Bergan dismissed the apology with a wave of his hand.

"Your fellow there can speak freely, Hector: he and your Boarguard saved us. We're in your debt, my boy."

"I don't mean to harp on this, my lord," said Fry. "But the Ugri? How are they with you? As a Sturmlander who grew up in Roof, I know these people. They're not to be trusted."

"When the Catlords slaughtered the Tuskun Queen, Two Axes brought his men over to our side, seeking vengeance for their leader's murder."

"I'd be wary, is all, my lord," said Fry.

"Beggars can't be choosers, Captain; we take help where we find it. Lucas and the Catlords aren't content with Westland: they want to enslave the whole of Lyssia, from Cape Gala to Tuskun. These brave Northern warriors have sworn fealty to me, in return for my aid in protecting their homeland. What kind of man would I be if I turned my back on them?"

Bergan clapped Hector's back, the magister's passionate words clearly enough to convince him. "Wise words and a noble gesture, Hector. It seems you've done a lot of growing up since I last saw you. Your father would have been proud."

"How did you escape Highcliff and find yourself out here

in the wilds?" asked Carver, making no attempt at speaking to the Boarlord with even a trace of respect.

Vega's friend, whispered Vincent. *Cut from the same arrogant cloth, no doubt.*

"We fled on the *Maelstrom*," said Hector to Bergan, avoiding eye contact with the Lord of Thieves. "Queen Amelie was safely aboard, you'll be pleased to hear, as were Manfred and Vega."

"Why are you no longer with them?" asked Carver.

"We stopped for provisions in Moga, Baron Bosa's port. We encountered hostility there, and while my men and I were ashore," said Hector, indicating Ringlin and Ibal, "we were separated. They left without us."

"Great shame, my boy," said Bergan sadly.

"I bear them no ill will. They were in a terrible predicament. I wouldn't want to have been in their situation, faced with leaving a fellow Werelord and member of the Wolf's Council behind. They did what they had to."

Bergan embraced him once more.

"And you survived! Thank Brenn, Hector. Abandoned in Tuskun and yet still you've had the wits to get this far. Let us help you the rest of your way. To Icegarden, I presume?"

"That's where we're heading, Your Grace. I only pray that the Duke will answer our call for help."

"My cousin has little choice if he wants to survive this war," said Bergan, turning to all of them. "Come, we waste time;

we can talk as we travel. Onward, to the Strakenberg and the halls of the White Bear."

The Bearlord set off, his stride and spirit lifting after his reunion with Hector. Fry walked with him, while Carver waited, staring at Hector, his hand resting on Pick's shoulder at his side.

"After you, dear Baron," said the Thief-lord.

Hector set off with Ringlin and Ibal, the Ugri shadowing them above as they followed them down toward the canyon entrance.

He won't have you at his back, said the vile. *He's no fool, that one.*

Hector walked on without turning around, his eyes drilling into the Bearlord's back.

"He can walk where he likes," whispered Hector. "So long as we're heading toward Icegarden and Bergan trusts me, that's all that matters."

"Expertly played, my lord," said Ringlin quietly, assuming his liege was addressing him. "They'll welcome us with open arms, just as the old Bear did."

Hector nodded, patting Ringlin's shoulder. "Let's hope Duke Henrik's in a hospitable mood. He has a great many guests on their way to his halls."

9

THE GOOD REDCLOAK

TRENT DASHED UP the steps of Brackenholme Hall, bounding over the splintered timbers that littered the threshold. The war cries of the wild men echoed around him, a bloodthirsty chorus accompanying the defenders' screams.

The small Romari with the rapier—Stirga they had called him—was a fearless soul. His quick thinking at the lift had led him to climb to the platform above without a thought for his own safety. The cage had soon cranked back to life, just as the first Wylderman had begun to pass them, scaling the pitted bark of the oak. The butchered bodies of the palace guard had awaited them upon arrival, torn to pieces by a powerful foe. Trent had followed the trail of dead Greencapes toward the monstrous hissing sounds, across the bridges, between the branches, finally arriving at the Bearlord's hall.

Stepping through the debris, he felt his knees buckle as he caught sight of the beast within. A giant black serpent blocked his path, its shining coils undulating, writhing, its tail lashing out as it fought with one of the hall's defenders. The snake's body switched one way and then the other before Trent, rising up and down and from left to right as it weaved in front of the lone combatant. He glimpsed the figure that faced the monster, a young woman covered with wiry red fur, dancing around the beast as its great head lunged forward, trying to bite her. She was light on her feet, her clawed hands slashing through the dark scales along the snake's flanks. Seeing her vulpine form, Trent's worst fears were confirmed.

Gretchen sprang forward, catching hold of the Serpent's amethyst underside with her claws as she allowed gravity and momentum to carry her back to the floor. She left behind long, bloodied strips of torn skin with pale white muscle bulging from the wounds. Dark blood rose in the jagged gouges, spilling onto the floor as the Serpent recoiled, smashing its tail and wounded body into the walls on either side of the hall. The monster's great hooded head whipped down toward the panting Werefox, green eyes blazing with rage.

"The Bearladiessss will ssssuffice as hosssstagessss! You, Fox, have outlived your ussssefulnesssss! It hassss been too long ssssince I dined on therian flesssssssh!"

Before the monster could strike the Fox, Trent was running. Sprinting up a shattered timber that had once supported the hall's enormous doors, he launched himself through the air, the Wolfshead blade raised high as he landed astride the beast and plunged it deep into the snake's body. The Serpent recoiled from Gretchen, whirling through the air, its head flashing around until it faced the young Redcloak who had dared attack it.

"What meddlessssome inssssect issss thissss?" it hissed, as it bucked its body in the air.

To his horror, Trent realized he was attached to the monster by the Wolfshead blade, as the sword was buried deep in the creature's body. The more the beast shook him, the more strongly he gripped the sword, refusing to relinquish his hold as massive jaws snapped at the air around him.

"Vala!" shouted Gretchen, drawing the beast's attention as she leapt into the air.

As Vala turned back to her, the girl lashed out, her claws ripping the Serpent's right eye from its socket, blinding her and making the Serpent flail with renewed fury. Trent seized his moment, ripping the sword free, the blade emerging from the snake's body with a gout of black blood. He jumped clear of the monster, landing beside Gretchen and seizing her by the wrist.

"We need to escape, my lady!" he yelled over the wails of the Serpent, trying to haul the girl clear of the thrashing beast.

"I'll do no such thing, Redcloak," snarled Gretchen, tugging her wrist free of his grasp as Vala's tail rushed past, narrowly missing them. "I won't leave Whitley!"

Wyldermen now began to appear within the broken doors, spilling through the shattered entrance, blocking any escape from the hall. Sick with fear, Trent looked up just in time to catch sight of Vala's tail flying back toward them. He ducked, avoiding the blow, but Gretchen wasn't so lucky, and the Serpent smashed the Lady of Hedgemoor across the Great Hall. Trent watched the girl fly through the air and crash through a shuttered window, out into the night beyond.

He looked back at the monstrous snake as it rose before him, the right side of its face slick with black blood.

"Run, child! Save Gretchen!" shouted an older lady who knelt at the rear of the hall, cradling a brown-haired young woman in her arms.

Trent wasted no time, dashing toward the wall and diving out of the broken window the Werefox had flown through. The outrider tucked in his limbs as he went into a roll, tumbling out onto the walkway that circled the hall. Behind him, through the broken window, a monstrous roar shook the entire building. Shaking splinters and shards of glass from his pitted cloak, Trent looked up, surprised to find that he and the Werefox weren't alone outside the hall. Stirga knelt beside the girl's body, checking for signs of life, while Yuzhnik stood ready, waiting for advancing Wyldermen, as the ringing of stone on steel drifted through the smoke.

"Does she live?" Trent croaked, rising unsteadily.

"Barely," replied Stirga, bending to lift her.

"How do the Greencloaks fare?"

"Bad doesn't come close," muttered Yuzhnik, flicking blood from his ax. "The Wyldermen have overrun the tree."

"The hall," said Trent, nodding toward the window frame, its shutters hanging splintered on their hinges. "There are people in there, dying! Perhaps if we—"

"We need to leave," said Stirga. "If you re-enter that hall, you shall die alongside them."

"I can't leave without Whitley. I owe it to Drew and Baron Ewan, Brenn rest his soul."

"Your debt is half repaid, Lionguard," said Stirga, setting off along the walkway, away from the sound of combat. "Be glad you've saved one of the Wereladies this night!"

Trent watched Stirga disappear through the gray mists, Gretchen's thick red hair tumbling across his arm. Yuzhnik looked back as he followed the old sword-swallower.

"Stick around if you like, Redcloak, but I don't think these Wyldermen care much which Werelord you serve; if you ain't a wild man, you're a dead man."

Trent was spurred into action by the giant's words, combined with another bloodcurdling scream from the battle behind. Rushing after the Romari, he vanished into the smoke.

Duchess Rainier crouched on the floor, embracing the beaten body of Whitley. Vala snaked between the bodies of the injured courtiers, her scales reflecting the flickering torchlight, her monstrous right eye weeping dark blood. Scores of injuries laced her thick black body where her enemies had dealt her ferocious blows, but they were merely flesh wounds; it would take more than a pair of angry Wereladies and a stubborn Redcloak to bring the Wereserpent's long and wicked life to a close.

The Wyldermen continued to climb through the rubble at the threshold, hurdling the broken timbers as they spilled into the room like an army of ants. They rifled through the bodies, tearing jewels and trinkets from the still-warm corpses, baring their sharp, savage teeth at those who yet lived. The last knight of the Bearguard had stepped forward to repel the invaders, lashing out with sword and shield, but he was quickly overpowered by the mass of wild men. Vala rounded on the duchess, rising up before mother and daughter, hissing as she glared at Rainier with her one good eye.

"Ssssso, my lady. It comesss to thissss. You and your child, thosssse dearesssst to the Bearlord, bowing before me. Your husssband hassss tormented my people for many yearsss, assss hisss father and hisss father did before him." The Wereserpent brought her huge head down, her long pink tongue flickering in the face of the trembling Rainier. "I sssswear, your torment sssshall not be brief."

"Keep me, and me alone," said Rainier, finding her voice in the face of Vala's dark threat. "It was I who stood by my husband's side while the Wyldermen and the soldiers of Brackenholme fought over the Dyrewood. These people and Whitley are innocent of the crimes you believe have been committed against you. I beg you, Vala, do not harm my daughter further."

The Serpent laughed, purple coils rolling as she thrashed one way and then the other, bringing fresh cries of terror from the survivors.

"I *need* your daughter, Bearlady. I've lossst one of my hosssstagessss already tonight," Vala hissed, glaring at the broken window that Gretchen had flown through. "No, your daughter issss jussst the bait I need. I know full well what ssshe meansss to Drew Ferran. Ssshe told me sssso much while we traveled here, poor lovesssstruck child. Your daughter ssshall bring the Wolf knocking. . . ."

"Then spare the lives of these people!" cried Rainier. The Serpent lunged in close again, making the duchess fall back, Whitley's pale face close to her chest.

"Sssspare them? Thisss issss my new home, where I ssshall entertain my people. What kind of hossst would I be if I didn't have a well-sssstocked larder?"

248

"Where are we going?" asked Trent as he followed the Romari along the treetop bridges, away from the dwindling sounds of battle. Wooden structures loomed out of the canopy all around; staff quarters and guest chambers for visiting dignitaries most likely, reasoned Trent. Moving deeper through the boughs of the Great Oak, they had encountered only a handful of Wyldermen, dispatching them as swiftly as possible as they headed for the rear of the tree.

"To the laundry, of course!" called back Stirga, leaving Trent more perplexed than ever. His sword arm still throbbed from his initial encounter with Vala, and the choking smoke had left him disoriented. He stumbled after the Romari as they weaved through the giant branches.

"This way," Stirga cried, catching sight of a rope bridge. Wooden planks ran its length, vanishing into the pitch-black night.

The rope bridge swung as they dashed across, straining under the weight of the hurrying men, especially the heavy footfalls of Yuzhnik. The shouts of the Wyldermen were growing louder now: no doubt they'd found their slaughtered companions beside the hall, with no sign of green-cloaked casualties. They were being hunted.

Trent was the last to reach the other side of the bridge, in time to hear the enemy shouts from back the way they'd come.

Yuzhnik turned, but Trent pushed him on, withdrawing the Wolfshead blade from his scabbard.

"Don't stop!" he said, shoving the big man hard. "Keep going and get her out of here. I'll do what I can."

Yuzhnik looked at him hard for a moment, before nodding. "You're a good man, Redcloak." He turned and was gone.

Trent hacked at the first of the two rope handrails, the sword bouncing off the tough hemp. He could hear footsteps now, bare feet slapping against the planks as the Wyldermen dashed across. Cursing, he gripped his father's weapon in both hands, roaring as he brought it down. The steel cut a thick cleft in the rope. He chopped down again, and this time the sword cut clean through the rope. Cries went up in the darkness as the bridge swung, one scream fading toward the ground far below.

Shifting position, Trent struck at the other handrail, the blade biting deep into the hemp. He tugged at it, finding to his horror that it was snagged, the rope twisting and threatening to tear the sword from his grasp. He held tightly to the handle, just as a first volley of arrows bounced off the deck around him. One quivered in the wood at his feet, the shaft humming as its barbed flint head bit deep into the timber. *They're shooting blind, but all it takes is one lucky shot. . . .*

He braced his foot against the rope, screaming as he finally tore the blade free. He stepped up once more, catching sight of a steady stream of Wyldermen traversing the bridge, weapons gripped between their jaws, one hand over the other on the handrail, steadily getting closer. More arrows whined through the air, one hitting a wild man in the back and sending him cartwheeling off the bridge as others rained down around Trent. He spun on the spot as one struck him in the left shoulder, sending him to his knees. The initial pain was a knuckle punch, like the dead arms Drew and he had traded as young boys. The agony would come later, no doubt.

Trent stood, raising the Wolfshead blade in one hand and slashing down one last time. The hemp tore apart like a cobweb in a stiff breeze, sending the Wyldermen into a screaming panic on the bridge. Some tumbled from the walkway, clutching at the torn rope, snatching, missing, while others dropped to the planks fearfully. The bridge shook, and the wild men were still for a moment as they steadied themselves. Then they began to advance once more, crawling on their bellies, toes gripping the gaps in the planks, filthy hands hauling them nearer.

Trent ran.

"Stirga!" he cried. "Yuzhnik!"

"This way, boy!" came the call of the old sword-swallower as Trent stumbled through the open door of a thatched timber building. Huge barrels lined the walls of the longhouse, and the smell of soap and perfumes was thick in the air, almost as choking as the smoke outside.

"The bridge rails are cut, but they're still coming," he said. Staggering through the structure, he caught sight of the two men standing around a big wicker basket, bound around its edge by a thick net of rope. A winch was fixed to the wall on one side of it, and lengths of rope ran through the mechanism, while a large hatch stood open over the other, empty space beyond. The basket reminded Trent of the coracles the Cold Coast fishermen used, big enough for two men maybe.

Two men.

He looked up, and the Romari shared his look of concern.

"Get in," said Stirga. "I'll pass her to you."

"You get in," said Trent. "You can take her."

"The two of you stop bickering," said Yuzhnik, taking Gretchen in his arms. "*Both* of you get in, and I'll hand her across."

"But what about you?" said Stirga. "I'm not leaving you."

"Who are we fooling, Stirga? I'd probably break that thing if there was only *me* in it. Get in, you sprats. Take the girl."

Trent climbed in, but Stirga remained standing.

"I shall stay with you, Yuzhnik. I won't leave a fellow Romari to dance alone, especially one who's like a brother to me."

The giant passed the girl into Trent's arms, and the young man was unable to watch as the friends quarreled over who should stay or go.

"You have ballads to write and songs to sing, brother," said Yuzhnik, gripping Stirga's shoulder and giving him a firm squeeze. "Let me give you a tale to tell."

The two men embraced briefly, as the yells of Wyldermen went up at the front of the longhouse. Stirga clambered into the basket as Yuzhnik took hold of the wheel, winching it off the ground. He gave it a kick, sending it swinging over the hatch.

"Sing the songs for me, Stirga," bellowed Yuzhnik. "Make the ballads glorious, old friend!"

The giant's muscles rippled as he swiftly turned the wheel. The basket lurched into life, its descent painfully slow. Trent caught sight of the Wyldermen, flooding through the laundry as the basket disappeared through the hatch. One of the wild men had covered the distance already, leaping forward, knife raised, before Yuzhnik backhanded him with his forearm. With his other arm he kept yanking the wheel, the pulley screeching as the rope ran through it.

Both Trent and Stirga watched in horror as the Wyldermen poured over Yuzhnik, a mass of filthy arms and stabbing blades raining down. The winch stopped, the wheel abandoned, as the Romari fell beneath a pile of assailants. The basket swung wildly five feet below the longhouse, dangerously exposed. With a roar, the bloodied giant fought back, peeling the Wyldermen off like leeches. His ax scythed through them, scattering and dropping them where they stood. More came in their place, stepping over their fallen brethren, charging fearlessly toward the berserk Romari.

One of the Wyldermen appeared over the hatch, reaching across with his serrated flint knife, sawing at the rope that held the laundry basket. Trent tried to stand as the basket tipped precariously, threatening to dump the three of them out into the void. The Wolfshead blade was in one hand, his other gripping the rope as he rose. With great effort, his arm burning with the strain, Trent thrust upward, and the sword caught the wild man clean through the throat, his knife tumbling into the basket from his limp hand.

Yuzhnik was wrestling with another brute now, this one bigger than any he'd encountered. The Wylderman's long black hair hung across his face, but Stirga recognized him.

"Rolff!" he cried in horror, as the wild man laughed, revealing sharp, savage teeth. The black-haired warrior's knife plunged into Yuzhnik's thigh, dropping the Romari to the floor.

"There never was a Rolff," spat the tall tribesman, whipping his blade free, ready to strike again.

Yuzhnik jabbed upward with his ax, the steel head catching the Wylderman in the jaw and sending him back. Pulling himself to one knee, Yuzhnik looked at Trent and his friend.

"Your turn to hold on, Redcloak," he whispered as Trent wound his left arm around the rope.

Yuzhnik's ax hit the wheel mechanism, sparks flying as the cogs and brakes shattered and the basket suddenly plummeted with shocking speed. Darkness swallowed the giant's face as the basket and its fragile cargo hurtled toward the ground hundreds of feet below.

10

Dark Deeds

IT WOULD BE dawn soon. Drew sat stiff in the saddle of the white charger, the reins looped around the stump of his left arm, the stars fading in the sky above Stormdale. The horse had been a gift from Baron Hoffman, the oldest of the surviving Staglords. It was a small gesture of gratitude on Hoffman's part for the courage the young Wolflord had shown in the defense of the city.

The horse stood between the towers of the ruined gatehouse that marked the entrance into Stormdale. With the city still smoking at his back, Drew's attention was on the battlefield beyond. The routed enemy army was gone, the scene of their siege a wasteland of abandoned tents and war machines; campfires still burned, and equipment and weapons had been

255

left behind in their hasty retreat. Riderless horses wandered through the encampment, pulling at dumped backpacks and trying to worry their contents loose. The moans of the injured and dying drifted through the darkness, as the soldiers of Vermire and Riven cried out for aid. None was forthcoming, at least not presently; Magister Wilhelm and his healers were preoccupied with tending the wounded of Stormdale. If any enemy soldiers survived the night, there might be compassion in the morning. Drew turned Bravado around, the horse proving pleasingly responsive, and set off back up the main avenue, returning to the castle.

He passed squads of civilians led by Graycloaks, picking their way through the streets, meticulously searching through every building. The odd fugitive from Riven or the Vermirian Guard was found hiding, only to be captured and delivered to the keep for questioning. The knights of Stormdale had already gleaned a good deal of information from their prisoners: the greatest mass of the Catlords' forces was gathered in the Badlands and the Dalelands. Onyx himself was overseeing command while Field Marshal Tiaz, the Tigerlord, led the army in Omir. Drew hoped that the Hawklords had arrived in Azra in time to assist King Faisal against the staggering enemy force that surrounded his city in the East. He still imagined he might live to see his other friends who aided Faisal with his battle. Though it felt like ages since they'd been parted, Drew felt bound to them by their shared experiences in the gladiatorial arena of the Furnace on the volcanic island of Scoria and their united escape from that ghastly place.

As Drew passed through the gatehouse into the castle, he could see the now-familiar figure of Hoffman working alongside survivors, collecting the dead from where they'd fallen in the snow-encrusted courtyard. The white powder was stained dark with the blood of the fallen, men of Stormdale, Vermire, and Riven lying alongside one another. While the dead of the Barebones were placed tenderly onto a cart, to be transported to Brenn's Temple in the city, the enemy's bodies were thrown onto a great pyre. The blackest smoke billowed from the corpses of the Crowlords.

Hoffman passed orders on to the work party before staggering across to Drew, taking Bravado's reins from him. The Stag looked tired, as old as Magister Wilhelm, but he wasn't about to rest while there was work to be done.

"How did he handle?"

"Grand," said Drew, swinging down from the saddle. "He's quite a beast, isn't he?"

"I rode his father into battle many years ago alongside Wergar," Hoffman said, patting the white horse's nose. "He's from good stock, a long bloodline of warhorses. It'd be cruel to keep heaving my fat rump onto his back, regardless of his undoubted strength."

Drew smiled as he clapped the horse's flank. "Your generosity is appreciated, my lord, but entirely unnecessary."

"Tish!" said Hoffman gruffly. "You helped us win this battle, lad. Bravado is a drop in the ocean compared to what we owe you."

Drew blushed and bowed before departing to the keep. The throne room had been converted into a temporary house of healing, with cots filling the floor, injured soldiers and civilians being tended to by Magister Wilhelm's surgeons. Even the wounded managed to call Drew's name as he made his way across the crowded floor, waving to him and clasping his hand in thanks as he passed by.

Why do I deserve such adulation? It's you who've fought so valiantly for your homeland; your fallen brothers and sisters who have given the greatest sacrifice.

Drew smiled awkwardly, pausing at times to listen to what the survivors had to say. He crouched beside their beds, assisting surgeons as they administered medicines and changed dressings, keeping those with the gravest injuries occupied as the healers worked their magic.

To the rear of the throne, below the tall stained-glass windows, the wounded Werelords were being attended. Mia lay on a bed, three ladies-in-waiting nursing her, the girl's eyelids fluttering as she remained in a troubled sleep. The blow to her head she'd taken atop the Lady's Tower had caused Reinhardt's family much concern: Mia was the youngest of Duke Manfred's children and his only daughter, guaranteeing her a special place in the hearts and hopes of the people of Stormdale. Wilhelm had done all he could, tending her bruised temple and casting healing cantrips over her. As sweet-smelling herb candles burned low around her bedside, the child's future remained in the balance.

Brenn watch over her, Drew prayed silently. The girl had not even seen ten summers; he hoped she would live to see many more.

Two of the other Staglords, the sons of Hoffman, lay on pallets on the dais, awake and talking. Following their father they'd sallied forth, chasing the enemy beyond the walls of the keep, striking down the men of Vermire and Riven as they fought one another. The injuries the Staglords and Graycloaks had sustained had ensured that Wilhelm had been kept busy through the night. The brothers nodded to Drew as he stepped past them toward a wicker chair by the window.

Red Rufus sat upright, having refused Wilhelm's repeated offers of a bed; the grizzled Hawklord wasn't in the habit of turning others out of their cots for what he called "his feathered behind." The old Hawk's fight with the Crowlords had been epic, and his injuries had been sustained by falling through the castle roof in a shower of splintered tiles. Scree was the only surviving Crowlord, limping away through the sky, home to Riven.

One of Red Rufus's wings was broken, but the old Hawk would accept only the minimum of help from Wilhelm. He took healing drafts, chewed herbs, even tolerated the prayers of the priest of Brenn, but he wouldn't let the surgeons lay a finger on him.

Drew couldn't help but grin at the belligerent Hawk.

"So, how are you liking your father's sword, lad?" asked Rufus, wincing as he shifted uncomfortably. Drew's hand drifted over Moonbrand's white orb pommel.

"I might have said any blade was as good as the next before last night, but I'd have been mistaken." Drew pulled up a stool and sat down beside Red Rufus. "You knew it could do that?"

"The white flame? Aye, boy. I saw Wergar wield it during many a moonlit battle. When the heavens shine down on it, there's no deadlier sword in all the Seven Realms. That blade could cleave the mountain Tor Raptor in two."

Drew caught sight of Reinhardt embracing a gray-cloaked youth from across the courtroom. The hug was fierce, the boy's feet rising from the floor as the Staglord held him in his arms.

"I see he's recovered," said Red Rufus.

"Who?" said Drew, trying to see the hooded youth's face as Reinhardt held him close.

"The Stag's young brother," said the Hawklord.

Drew squinted, catching sight of the boy's face as the hood fell away. There was no mistaking him: he'd met Milo in Windfell, where the young Stag arrived, near death from Vermirian arrows, to plead for aid for besieged Stormdale. He was a brave boy, having ridden to find help against his brother's express command. It was good to see the boy well again; when

Drew and Red Rufus had left him in Windfell to rush to Stormdale's aid, he'd been in a bad way.

"How are you feeling?" asked Drew, returning his attention to the Hawklord.

"Like I've been in a fight with a Bearlord." Red Rufus winced. "Don't mind me; there are others 'ere who are in far greater need of old Wilhelm's attention."

At the mention of his name, the magister looked up from where he was tending one of Hoffman's sons.

"We've much to be thankful for," said Drew. "The Staglord and his healers have stitched up most of the wounded, and his cantrips and herb lore appear to be working wonders throughout the castle."

"He's no Stag," scoffed Red Rufus.

Drew looked perplexed, glancing back to Wilhelm as he helped the Staglord to settle.

"He's a Boarlord, ain't he?" added Rufus. "Like many of them magister folk throughout Lyssia. He was sent here many years ago once he'd learned his craft. Stayed in Stormdale ever since."

"He'll know my friend Hector, then."

"Huth's son? Aye, he will. He'd be his uncle—he was brother to the old baron."

Drew stared back at Wilhelm, suddenly recognizing the family resemblance between the old man and the young magister he'd left behind in Highcliff so long ago. Drew remembered what he'd heard about the Boarlords serving as court magisters throughout Lyssia, and Wilhelm's presence suddenly made more sense.

"Has he turned his back on Redmire, then?"

"They all do, once they take their positions within court. They're like monks, these magisters: married to their magicks. One of his cousins used to be magister to Griffyn in Windfell. Sorry old fool got the chop when Leopold hit us with his wrath. Fished his body out of the Steppen River the following spring."

Drew still struggled when confronted with the dead king's atrocities. Leopold's acts of violence against his subjects were a constant reminder of how *not* to rule, should Drew ever take his rightful seat on the throne.

"We've a lot to be thankful for," said Drew, thinking back to the night's events. "Brenn was certainly watching over us. Who knows what might have happened had that Vermirian archer not put an arrow in Croke."

Red Rufus patted Drew's knee with a gnarled hand. "Quite right." The Hawklord chuckled sarcastically. "Where would we have been, had Brenn not graced us with his attention?"

"I'd be mindful of what you say," said Drew uncomfortably. "Those'd be blasphemous words to the ears of Brenn-fearing folk, Red Rufus."

Red Rufus suddenly leaned forward. "It was I who plugged the old Crow with that rotten silver arrow," he hissed.

Drew's face drained of color. *"You killed Croke?"*

"Quiet, lad. There's no sense in letting 'em all know my handiwork. Let 'em think it was the Rats and Crows turning on 'emselves. It was as like to 'appen, anyway."

"You murdered him?" said Drew, Red Rufus's confession catching him unawares.

"Murder? This is *war*, boy. I've told you as much countless times. I asked what you might do, should the need arise, whether you were capable of taking a man's life for the greater good."

Drew sat on the stool, his mind flying back to the events on the wall. He'd spent the time since Croke's demise thanking the stars in the heavens that one of the Crow's own men had triggered the bloodbath between the Vermirians and the men of Riven.

"I thought that was divine intervention," he whispered.

"I did what had to be done, what you *couldn't* do. No shame in that, boy. Can't say I blame you. It's dirty work what sometimes needs doing to win a war."

"I said I wouldn't do it, and I meant it," said Drew.

"Right you did, and I spared you any more torment on that matter. You're the one who can sleep easy with a clear conscience. One dead Vermirian archer, me swiping his bow, cloak, and silver arrows; it was I who delivered the killing blow, and I alone who'll carry that deed to my grave. You can thank me later."

"Thank you? I don't know what to think," said Drew, shaking his head, caught between feelings of relief and dismay.

"The people want me to lead them into a bright new future, Red Rufus. A new age, with the Seven Realms united under the Wolf and not the Lion. Do the people not look to me to be more than just a sovereign? Should my actions not provide a moral and spiritual example to them? By sanctioning Croke's death, how am I any different from Leopold?"

"I'm a soldier, Drew, a man of action. I don't worry too much about what people may think of me, and you can be grateful for that fact when you count how many people still live in this sorry city when all could've died."

"That's where we're different, isn't it?" said Drew quietly. "I can see that your actions were for the greater good, but it still sits uneasy on my shoulders. Am I to thank you for what you did?"

"Let it go, lad," said Red Rufus, waving Drew away. "Plaudits have always been a poor fit on my scrawny shoulders. The battle's won, these people have escaped slaughter at the claws of the Rats and Crows. Surely you see that? If the truth of how the enemy turned on one another ever comes to light, I'll take that burden. And do you know what? I'd do it again, in the blink of an eye. I did the ugly thing without a second thought. The guilt's mine, Drew of the Dyrewood. I've *protected* you, boy."

There was no denying the truth in Red Rufus's words. He'd done all that Drew was incapable of, sparing him the burden of a dark deed. But he still wished Red Rufus had kept his secret to himself and let Drew live on in ignorance. Perhaps this was the sign Drew had sought, confirmation that he was no king, that he truly didn't understand what it meant to rule a nation and make the hard choices that were expected from a leader of men.

"This wasn't what I wanted." Drew sighed, his head slumping. He felt a hand on his shoulder, bony fingers gripping tight.

Magister Wilhelm leaned down from behind, his thin lips whispering in Drew's ear. "Do not be too hard on the Hawklord, Your Highness. He may have struck the killing blow, but the scheme wasn't of his own creation."

Drew looked up into Wilhelm's rheumy eyes. "This was *your* idea?"

Wilhelm's back creaked as he crouched between the two Werelords. "If I had not suggested such a grave course of action to Red Rufus, there would surely have been no one to heal. Look about you, Drew: these people live on account of Croke's death."

Drew nodded, the realization dawning on him that Red Rufus's actions, no matter how shocking, had been for the good of everyone.

The magister went on. "When the lives of so many depend upon your actions, you need the nerve to make those difficult, sometimes dreadful decisions. It doesn't sit comfortably with you; I understand that, truly I do. It doesn't seem noble, does it? But that's what it takes to be a leader. That's what it means to be a Werelord. It's what your father would have done."

Drew stood up, the wooden legs of the stool scraping against the gray stone floor. A grim smile creased his face, but his gray eyes showed no humor. "That's what scares me."

Drew's attention was drawn away from the Hawk and the Boar as he caught sight of a commotion at the far side of the throne room. An animated crowd of onlookers had gathered around Reinhardt and his young sibling. Making his way across the chamber, the Wolflord joined the gaggle of soldiers and courtiers who surrounded Milo. The sickly pale boy Drew had left in Windfell had been replaced by a bright, keen-eyed young therian lord. Reinhardt was now deep in conversation with his knights, a firm hand holding Milo protectively by the shoulder.

"Windfell's healers were able to work their magic on you then, Lord Milo?" asked Drew, bowing before the young Stag. The boy's brown eyes went as wide as dishes when he saw Drew.

"They said it was you," said Milo excitedly, dropping onto his knee reverently, his brother's hand falling into thin air. "When I awoke, the cleric said it was you who'd answered our call, Your Highness."

"*Your* call, as I understand it, Milo," said Drew, looking across at Reinhardt, who glowered shamefaced. The fact that his people's survival was due to a child's headstrong folly was one thing; the fact that the child was his brother just added to the Stag's embarrassment.

Drew reached down, offering a hand to help Milo up from the floor. "No need for airs and graces around me. Not until they stick that crown on my head in Highcliff, and that won't be happening any time soon. Drew will do just fine."

Reinhardt took over from Drew, helping his brother to his feet. The knights he'd spoken to had already departed the hall, others following them as word spread.

"Tell him what you saw, Milo," said Reinhardt, his jaw set grimly as he stared at the Wolflord.

"Fires, Your High—Drew," he corrected himself. "Fires from the forest."

"Forest?" asked Drew as Red Rufus limped up, keen to hear what the commotion was about.

"Which forest?" said the Hawklord.

"The Dyrewood, my lord," said Milo.

Drew was already running. He passed through the keep's huge double doors, feet kicking up the slush and snow that clogged the courtyard, barging between the men and women of Stormdale as he ran toward the ravaged walls. Bounding up the stairs three at a time, he nearly flew over the parapet when he hit the top, bouncing against the shoulders of the knights who looked out to the west.

There it was. Through the thin gray smoke that still drifted across Stormdale, far beyond the Staglords' lands, the telltale sign of fire on the horizon. As the first rays of morning light crept over the Barebones behind, the men on the shattered battlements stared toward the thick dark clouds that gathered far away above the ancient woodland; deathly black clouds, boiling like a storm-savaged sea over the Dyrewood.

Brackenholme was burning.

PART IV

PAINFUL PATHS

I

INTO THE WOODS

"THERE'S NO WAY through it," said Stirga, staring up at the giant palisade that encircled Brackenholme. Trent paced along the wall's edge, one hand feverishly running across each of the sturdy timber posts buried deep within the frozen earth, while the other held Gretchen slumped across his shoulder. *Trapped within the woodland city.* Trent could feel panic rising, his innards rolling with a sickly fire. He wiped a hand across his forehead, his palm coming away slick with sweat despite the freezing cold.

"There has to be another way out of here," said the young outrider, glancing back at the Romari through the pall of smoke and mist. Fires burned in the boughs overhead, though the Great Oak had so far been spared the Wyldermen's torches.

The heavens burned orange, tongues of red and yellow flames flickering and dancing against the dawn sky as the wild men unleashed their fury upon Brackenholme.

Trent looked to Stirga for a word of encouragement, searching for a means of escape. The fall from the Bearlord palace had been breakneck; the laundry basket plummeted to the ground barely hindered by winch and brakes. Miraculously, Trent and Gretchen had escaped unharmed by the impact as their makeshift lift had hit the ground. A giant drift of freshly fallen snow had cushioned their fall, no doubt saving the lives of all three of them. The Romari hadn't been so fortunate: Stirga's forearm had been crushed, snapping like a brittle branch as they'd landed, and he now held it close to his stomach. Gretchen remained heavily concussed; the blow from the Wereserpent and her flight through the window had knocked her senseless.

"There are three gates, lad," said the sword-swallower, wincing with discomfort as he cradled his broken arm. "The Dymling Road enters the city from the north and south; I believe our friends from the forest entered Brackenholme from the Southern Gate."

"They did," said Trent, thinking back to the screaming horde that had followed him into the city. "So we take the Northern Gate out, then?"

"The west side of the city's overrun. Do you want to head back into that chaos? I recommend we take the third gate, if possible." Stirga gestured through the gloom toward the east. "The Dyre Gate."

No noise came from that portion of the palisade wall; the sounds of battle emanated from the center of the city, where pockets of fighting still raged.

"Where does that lead?"

"The Dyre Road: cuts straight through the forest in the direction of the Barebones, right into the heart of Wylderman country."

"They're all here though, aren't they? The wild men?"

Stirga's lip turned up as he shook his head.

"There're a good number assembled for Vala's assault, but the Wyldermen number in the thousands. There are many more still in the Dyrewood, I don't doubt it, waiting to follow their brethren into Brackenholme. It's far from safe out there."

"So you're saying we *don't* take the Dyre Gate?" Trent felt exasperated. His strength was fading, ebbing with every passing moment, and yet Stirga spoke in riddles. The old man would suggest one thing and then throw an obstacle in their way.

"I never said that, Redcloak," the Romari sniped back. "We take the gate, but we get off the road. The Wyldermen will be using the Dyre Road as their remaining forces enter the city."

"Off the road? You mean we enter the haunted forest?" The words caught in the back of Trent's throat.

"I'd rather face whatever is within the Dyrewood than what we may find on the road. You've seen what the Wyldermen are capable of: they're monsters. But we need to be quick. Vala's army is preoccupied. We appear to have slipped through their net for the time being. The sooner we're out of Brackenholme the better."

Trent nodded. "We follow the perimeter wall, then. The Dyre Gate it is."

He was about to start walking when Gretchen began to murmur on his shoulder. The sounds were distressed, and her hands pawed at Trent's back.

"Let me look at her," said Stirga, indicating that Trent should lay her on the snow.

He was about to follow the Romari's instruction when a thundering sound approached fast from the darkness behind them.

The first of the horses appeared out of the smoke, running blind through the gloom in panic. More followed, shoulder to shoulder, following their instincts as they herded together in the chaos. Their eyes rolled in their heads as they stampeded past, snorting and whinnying, the screams of battle echoing behind them. Trent and Stirga staggered to one side for fear of being run over, Gretchen crying out as the two manhandled her clear.

Trent stood tall, catching sight of one particular horse that stood out from its companions, its saddled back marking it out as extraordinary. He put his fingers to his lips and whistled. The shrill noise rose above the sound of the horses' hooves as they charged by, slowing as they neared the palisade wall. Storm emerged from the throng; her ears pricked as she trotted toward the young outrider. Trent raised his hand as the chestnut-brown thoroughbred struck his face with her own. She let loose a brief snort of joy as he ran his fingers through her mane.

"Good girl," he whispered, smiling as he rested his sweating brow briefly against Storm's. He shifted Gretchen from his shoulder, hoisting her into the saddle. When he raised his arms, steadying her slumped form, he felt a sudden pain in his left shoulder as shockwaves raced through his body.

Stirga stared at Trent's back. "Your Redcloak appears that bit more scarlet," said the sword swallower, grimacing. "You've taken an arrow there that should be removed."

Trent remembered now what had happened up in the treetops when he'd tried to cut the rope bridge away. He reached back, finding the arrowhead still lodged in his shoulder blade.

"No time . . . later," he said as he handed Storm's reins to Stirga's good hand. He set off toward the herd of nervous horses. "We need another mount."

"You expect us just to ride out of here?" hissed Stirga as the mare stepped nervously at his side.

Trent barely paused to reply as he closed in on the nearest horse. "Something like that."

The Dyre Road passed between two tall timber doors, which yawned open in the jaws of Brackenholme's gatehouse. One enormous door was forced back against the wall, its surface splintered and misshapen. The other lay twisted beside the road, hanging broken from the enormous brackets that had once held it fixed to the guard tower. A tree trunk lay beyond the palisade walls, the ram having served its purpose as the Wyldermen coordinated their attack on the Dyre Gate.

Two dozen wild men now guarded the gatehouse, their eyes trained on the center of Brackenholme. Scarlet feathers adorned their scalps, woven into their hair like bloody blades. Their orders were clear: if any inhabitants of the Bears' woodland city tried to flee, they were to be cut down and shown no mercy. For too long, the Wyldermen had been forced into hiding by the Bear's clan. With Lyssia being torn apart in the bloody war that griped the western realms, Vala had chosen the perfect moment to strike back against the Bearlord. The Serpent Queen had returned from her exile in the Wyrmwood and all the tribes had come together, uniting behind their goddess in the face of a common foe. Brackenholme now belonged to the Wyldermen. Vala was triumphant.

The chieftain, known as Blacktooth, had been given the task of holding the Dyre Road. He sat on the timber slope of the broken gate, idly hacking at the splintered surface with his ax, eyeing the fires that burned deep inside the city. His red-feathered headdress hung around his throat, and dreadlocks of filthy hair matted into his beard. He ran his tongue across the sharp, discolored teeth that had given him his name. Blacktooth didn't want to be left guarding a pile of broken timbers. He wanted to be in the city, leading the fight against those who had lorded it over his forest for these long cruel years. While his brothers in the Blood Feathers lounged around the foot of the Great Oak, Blacktooth was left out on the fringe, a glorified sentry.

The goddess Vala had utterly fooled the people of Brackenholme. They'd carried her deep into the Bear city thinking she was one of their own, while her most faithful disciple, the warrior known as Darkheart, had spread the word, alerting the tribes and putting the attack into action. The tribes had gathered at the chosen time, rushing the wooden town once Darkheart had opened the gates. The handful of guards on the Dyre Gate had been woefully unprepared once their city was stormed. Blacktooth's men had already removed their bodies and were preparing to dine on their flesh tonight.

The beating of hooves made Blacktooth look up and squint through the gloom. The Blood Feathers readied themselves, shifting weapons in their hands while a couple leveled their bows from the wall. When the mists parted to reveal a herd of horses stampeding toward them, the Wyldermen split formation and fell away on either side of the road. Blacktooth jumped down from the broken gate, stepping into the middle of the road and hefting his ax in his hands.

"Get back, you mongrels," he shouted in the Wyld tongue.

"They're just horses! Bring 'em down; they're good to eat!"

As the first horse approached, the chieftain stood his ground. His heart raced; this was the closest he would get to battle this night. *I'll spill some blood, even if it's that of a horse.* His men whooped when they saw him in front of the charging herd, loosing their monstrous animal calls into the air. Blacktooth raised his ax and carved it into the first beast that rushed past, then swung it back the other way to catch another. The ground shook with their passing, and he let out a jubilant roar as the horses tumbled.

His men were relaxed now, clearly enjoying the spectacle. They lowered their weapons, all eyes focused on Blacktooth's revelry. He tugged his ax loose from the neck of the brown horse that he had just felled, and looked up as another brown horse leapt over it. Only this horse was different from the others. A pale rider sat astride it, a girl draped across the saddle before him. His cloak billowed like a crimson wave as he clutched the reins in one hand and a sword in the other. For the briefest moment a look of surprise passed over Blacktooth's face before the longsword slashed down and the steel bit his face, knocking him to the ground.

Through bloodied eyes he caught sight of another horse following the brown one, a wiry old man riding it bareback, gripping its mane in a gnarled hand. The horses continued to rush past, galloping up the road and disappearing into the forest.

As the last horse dashed by, Blacktooth rose from the floor and turned to the Blood Feathers, his face twisting with anger. The deep cut that had been carved into his face tore wider as he roared.

"After them!"

2

In Good Company

BERGAN SAT ON his haunches, looking back down the valley they had traversed that day, silently thanking Brenn for his favors. He and his small band were out of the awful catacombs deep beneath the earth, he'd enjoyed a meal of raw rabbit and the berries called black-hearts, he was reunited with his dear friend Hector, and the sun shone up above. All things considered, life was good.

The young magister stalked toward him up the trail, away from his resting Boarguard. The boy had gone through quite a transformation since the violence had begun. It had changed them all, though each in a different way. Could Drew have ever imagined what his emergence from the Dyrewood would lead to? While the Wolflord's claim to the throne had been the catalyst for the troubles, he hadn't been responsible for all that had followed. As the Werelords of Lyssia—and beyond—had chosen sides, the scope of the war that had engulfed the Seven Realms put even the bloody campaigns of Wergar to shame. Hector had been drawn into the very heart of the storm alongside Drew, the two once-inseparable friends torn apart by fate. Wergar's son was lost to them now, no doubt dead if Hector's news was to be believed, and the Boarlord had been left a shadow of his former self.

"Put your rump here, lad," said Bergan, patting a space on the large boulder that was his seat. Hector smiled, moving his traveling robes to one side so he could perch upon the rock alongside the Bearlord.

"How are you feeling, my lord?"

"Hector, drop the formalities. If you must call me anything, call me *uncle*, but *my lord* doesn't sit well, especially in light of your rescuing us from the Skirmishers."

Hector nodded, smiling. "How are you feeling, Uncle?"

"All the better for having something in my belly that doesn't resemble a grub. You'd shudder to imagine what we had to survive on in those catacombs. And the elixir you gave me, that's worked wonders, too. Thank you."

Hector and his medicine case—that was something else the group had to be thankful for. As a magister, he rarely went anywhere without it. Thank Brenn, thought Bergan, he'd had it with him when he'd been marooned on Moga by Vega. Within the leather bag he kept a variety of herbs and healing potions, salves, and ointments that could be applied to all manner of injuries. Bergan's chest had hurt terribly since half of Highcliff had collapsed upon him. Since then his condition had worsened; he'd developed a wheeze in the catacombs that continued to plague him when they returned to the light. The infections he'd suffered were alleviated by Hector's ministrations, improving almost overnight. It was good to have the Boarlord with them. Bergan reached out with his foot and gave the leather medicine case at Hector's feet a kick, causing its contents to jangle within.

"I don't know what you keep in that bag of tricks, but I'm grateful you brought it with you."

Hector smiled, carefully removing it from the duke's reach. "Best to keep it safe, Uncle," he said, by way of explaining his caution.

"Aye, don't want to be breaking its contents, eh?" said the old Bear, glancing back up the trail. "We'd best be moving soon while we still have daylight on our side. How long does your scout reckon until we're in Henrik's territory?"

"Well, these are just the foothills according to the Creep," said Hector. "My man says we should be in the heart of Sturmland by tomorrow if we keep up this pace. It would be a miracle if we don't run into some of the White Bear's scouts before then, mind you."

"Let us hope that he is in an assisting mood," said Bergan, scratching his threadbare beard.

"You're worried he won't be?"

"He and I go back a long way and our disagreements never have been resolved. He blames me for much of what came to pass, with the fall of Wergar and the rise of Leopold. The fact that the Wolf's Council sent many messages to him, seeking his aid, and not a single plea was answered causes me concern."

"I'm sure we'll find him in accommodating mood, Uncle. He was an ally of the Wolf once, a long time ago, and I'm sure he can be so again. Come, we should prepare to move."

Hector bent to take his case by the handles before standing and stretching. Bergan watched him, startled to see just how thin and drawn he'd become.

"You need to get some meat back onto those bones, Hector. It's simply not right, a Boarlord being so skinny!"

"You're one to talk, Uncle." The magister laughed as he slung the case across his shoulder.

"I've been living off worms and beetles, lad. What's your excuse?"

Hector smiled and walked back to his men without answering, as Bergan rose stiffly from the boulder. The tall one from Highcliff, Ringlin, drew the Baron of Redmire to one side to have words. Bergan didn't like the look of the rogue or his fat friend, Ibal, but he was unable to question their loyalty. Shifty though they appeared, they had stood shoulder to shoulder with their master when rescuing Bergan and his companions, and the Bearlord had gone out of his way to thank them on frequent occasions since.

"Keep themselves to themselves, don't they?"

Bergan turned, looking back up the trail to the man who had spoken. Bo Carver lay in the snow a short distance away, basking in the cold winter sun, his tattooed flesh scrunched up as he faced the bright heavens.

"Can you blame them? The Ugri hardly speak our language, and one of that pair is mute."

"The fat one isn't mute," said Carver, his eyes still closed, his hands folded neatly across his chest. It could have been summertime and the chilly slope a green meadow, so at peace appeared the Lord of Thieves.

"Ibal chooses not to speak?"

"I believe he speaks all right," said Carver. "He has Ringlin's ear when he needs it; the saying 'thick as thieves' could've been written with that pair in mind."

"You've a short memory, Carver," said Bergan as he trudged up the trail to where the man lay. "It wasn't so long ago that your name was dragged through the mud on account of your previous transgressions, and there weren't many who would speak in your defense as I recall. I'd have thought you'd be more understanding of your Thieves Guild brethren."

"Those two are no brothers of mine, Your Grace," said Carver, turning his hands to crack his knuckles. He sat upright, squinting at Bergan. "I never killed a man in cold blood. Not once on a single job. Same can't be said about those two. We are different breeds, and I wouldn't trust them as far as I could throw them."

Bergan looked back down the trail at the Boarguard, letting his eyes linger on the two longest-serving members of Hector's staff. He caught Ibal looking back at him. Bergan smiled and the short, round thief waved back.

"I doubt you could even lift him," muttered Bergan.

"My point precisely," said Carver, hopping to his feet and coming to stand beside the Bearlord. "They scare Pick. Remember, I was incarcerated for many years in Traitors' House. I've been removed from the goings-on of the Guild. Pick wasn't, though. She's seen a thing or two, and no doubt knows Ringlin and Ibal well enough. I trust what she tells me. She's a good kid, a cat burglar who might have had a great future ahead of her."

"A future," chuckled Bergan. "You make cat burgling sound like a profession."

"It's the only one available to some, my lord," said Carver. "Fancy opportunities to live in your world very rarely filter down to the gutter."

Bergan grunted by way of showing he understood, which was the closest Carver was going to get to an apology from the Lord of Brackenholme. He continued. "The girl sleeps by my side at night; I appear to have become some kind of surrogate father to the child. But one thing's for sure, Pick won't be left alone with them."

"So they were bad men—"

"They may *still* be bad men," said the Thief-lord swiftly.

"Regardless, we're not in a position to pick and choose our allies. They're loyal to Hector, and that's good enough for me."

"It is?" whispered Carver, standing beside the Bearlord, turning his face away from the Boarguard. "Then you're alone, it appears. I don't trust the company the baron keeps and neither does Fry."

Carver was right, of course: the Sturmlander, Fry, had serious reservations about the fact that Hector had Ugri warriors in his service. Between them, Carver and Fry had questions about the lot of them.

"Enough suspicion, Carver," snapped Bergan, loud enough to make Hector and his men look up from farther down the trail to see what the commotion was. Bergan smiled and waved nonchalantly before turning and taking Carver by the elbow. He led the man onward up the trail, away from the Boarguard and closer to where Fry and Pick waited for them ahead.

"They are with us," continued Bergan, "and you need to accept that, Bo. Let their actions prove their allegiance and start taking things at face value. Try to stop looking for ill in everyone."

Carver stopped walking when they'd passed a rock face on

the trail and were out of earshot of Hector and his men. He prodded Bergan in the chest with a thick finger, no airs and graces, social standing put aside. "As long as we travel with them, I keep one eye open."

"It must be awful to trust nobody, Carver."

The Lord of Thieves gave the Bearlord a brief sideways glance. "You think so? It's kept me alive all these years."

With that he turned and trudged onward toward the Sturmlander and child, leaving Bergan to wait for the magister and his Boarguard. The Lord of Brackenholme heard Ibal's sickly giggling well before the group finally appeared around the rocky corner.

3
THE DYRE ROAD

DREW TWISTED IN his saddle, glancing back down the snow-blanketed Dyre Road at his companion. Some people weren't born to ride, and the grumbling Hawklord was one of them. Red Rufus was locked in a constant battle of wills with his horse, and the gray mare reluctantly followed his instructions only when forced by both reins and boots. When the horse was in an especially belligerent mood, the old Hawk resorted to shouting a torrent of abuse, as he was presently doing. Drew turned Bravado around, biting his lip as he trotted back toward his comrade.

"Quiet!" he said. "You'll alert every Wylderman from here to Darke!"

"Not my fault I'm lumbered with a crotchety nag, is it?"

Rufus grumbled from the saddle of his motionless mount.

"I know how you feel," muttered Drew, but the Hawk didn't hear him.

"I swear this fool horse is mocking me!"

The mare snorted right on cue.

"A poor rider blames his horse," said Drew. "She's picking up on your anxiety. Try to relax."

"If you hadn't noticed, I'm a Hawklord. Don't have much need for anything other than my wings to get me around, do I?"

"But one of your wings is broken, remember?"

"Sprained." The Hawklord sniffed.

"However you dress this up, Red Rufus, flight is out of the question. So, for the time being, you need to be *kind* to your mount. If she bucks you off, you'll have more than a broken wing to worry about."

As if in response to Drew's words, the gray mare suddenly set off at a trot. Drew watched the glowering Red Rufus pass by, bouncing in his saddle with all the grace of a farmer on a donkey. Stifling a chuckle, Drew tapped his heels on Bravado's flanks, urging the white charger on until he reined in alongside the Hawklord.

The two of them were stuck together for the foreseeable future, traveling to Brackenholme to discover the cause of the fires. The Staglords had been unable to send any troops to accompany them and understandably so; Stormdale was wounded, her people and soldiers broken. The men of the Barebones were needed at home, to rebuild their defenses as best they could in case of any future attack from the Catlords.

Reinhardt's young brother, Milo, had wanted to accompany Drew to the Bearlord city, in an official capacity as envoy from Stormdale. Reinhardt had dismissed the request immediately, forbidding Manfred's son to leave the castle; the Dyrewood was a dangerous enough place during peacetime. With the Seven Realms at war, Reinhardt had declared that a journey through the haunted forest toward a burning city was entirely out of the question for the young Stag. Drew liked the boy: he saw something of himself in Milo, a willingness to act when the time demanded, and the confidence to challenge his elders. Reluctantly the boy had disappeared to his quarters but not before he'd given his older brother an earful.

"Is this your first time in the Dyrewood?" Drew asked Rufus now. The horses' hooves crunched along the Dyre Road, the snow untouched by anything bigger than a fox, tracks crisscrossing the ground where animals had traversed the ancient avenue. Overhead, bare black branches were intertwined, obscuring the pale winter sun from view.

"Aye, and hopefully my last; what a miserable hole it is! It's a dead place: who'd want to make a home here? The Wyldermen can keep it."

"The Wyldermen aren't the Dyrewood's sole inhabitants.

They share it with a whole host of dangers, both beast and plant."

"Dangerous plants?" said the Hawk. "Bad-tempered bracken? Hostile heather?"

"You're laughing, but you'd be a fool to ignore my warnings. The Dyrewood's very much alive. Whatever happens, stay on the road."

"Didn't have you down as the superstitious type, cub. You sound like some Romari baba who's had 'er palm crossed with coppers."

It was Drew's turn to laugh now. He'd tried to warn Red Rufus but suspected the old bird was a little long in the beak to be accepting the advice of others, especially someone as young as Drew. He looked over his shoulder, checking the road behind.

"Worrying, though, isn't it?" said Drew.

"What's that?" asked Red Rufus, binding the gnarled fingers of one hand round the reins.

"The Wyldermen: no sign of them at all. Reinhardt mentioned that we should expect to encounter them when we hit the forest. They have villages all around, within easy reach of the Dyre Road."

"Perhaps they're up to their scrawny chins in rituals, worshipping whatever monster passes for a god in these parts."

Drew felt his skin crawl, thinking back to the Wylderman shaman he'd encountered and the creature he and his people had worshipped: Vala, the Wereserpent.

"I know more than enough about the Wyldermen. I lived in the Dyrewood for a while."

"You?" said Red Rufus, his usual sarcastic tone missing for once.

"I spent an autumn and winter here, the two harshest seasons one could imagine. It was after I first discovered my . . . abilities. I'd fled my parents' farmstead, after the man I believed was my father stuck his Wolfshead blade clean through my gut, believing I'd killed the mother who raised me. He found me, half-transformed, with Ma dead in my arms and . . . Anyway, I ran, leaving my brother Trent and Pa behind, my old man blowing his hunting horn. The only sanctuary I could find was the Dyrewood."

Red Rufus scratched his grizzled chin, looking around them into the dark, gloomy forest. "This was your *sanctuary*? I'd hate to have seen what chased you."

"Every farmer up and down the Cold Coast must have answered my pa's hue and cry. They thought they were chasing a monster."

"They were, weren't they?"

Drew shot the Hawklord a withering look. "It was the Ratlord, Vanmorten, King Leopold's High Chancellor who killed her. Apparently Leopold saw Ma as a loose end, since she'd worked for Wergar and Amelie when Wergar was king. She'd seen the Lion butchering the Wolf's children, all but me, whom she'd managed to save. I'm sure it was as much a surprise to the Rat as it was to me when I transformed for the first time that night."

"Devils, them Rats," snarled Red Rufus, hawking up a glob of phlegm and spitting it to the ground. "Good company for Leopold, and no mistake. You get a claw into 'im, then?"

Drew's smile was forced, his mind's eye still lingering on the sight of Tilly Ferran lying dead in his arms.

"I tore half his face off."

Red Rufus clapped his thigh with his free hand. "You're all right by me, Wolf. Anyone who can maim a Ratlord and live to tell the tale's my kinda fellow."

Drew's mood was lightening as he watched the cantankerous old raptor relax. This was the first time the two of them had spent any time truly alone in each other's company. Their flight from Windfell had been a tense affair, with the Hawk resenting Drew's command to take him directly to Stormdale. Their time in the Staglord city had provided few opportunities for the two to get to know one another better, instead providing them with fresh reasons to irritate one another. Red Rufus might have been a throwback to another era, but he was slowly growing on Drew. The young Wolflord wasn't entirely sure he was happy with the notion.

"You know all about the Wyldermen, then?"

"I've had my run-ins. You could say we were neighbors for six months."

"Can't imagine they took too kindly to sharing their forest with the likes o' you."

"I spent the entire time hiding, avoiding them whenever I was away from my cave. I never knew whether each new day would be my last. I allowed the Wolf to take over. Entirely. I surrendered to it: if I hadn't, I'd have been dead. They knew I was out there, realized they were sharing their forest with another predator. They're brutal and fiercely territorial. I once saw a fight between two rival tribes. The victors dragged their fallen enemies back to their village. Back to the cooking pot . . ."

Red Rufus didn't have much to say about the last comment. Everyone had heard the stories about the Wyldermen. Drew had been told them himself when he'd been a wee boy, Pa taking great delight in scaring both Trent and him to sleep at night with his bogeyman tales. To the young Drew, those terrible wild men had been just that: bogeymen. The stories had served their purpose when he was a child, ensuring that he never wandered into the haunted forest. As he'd grown, he'd forgotten about them, and consigned them to childhood along with fairies and dragons. To his horror he'd discovered firsthand that the bad places and the bad people were all too real.

"So when Reinhardt said that we should expect to encounter them, I took him at his word," said Drew. "The Dyre Road isn't a safe place for any soul: there are Wyldermen villages throughout the forest, perhaps even larger settlements."

"Then it's our good fortune they're a primitive bunch, ain't it?" said Red Rufus. "Leave 'em to war with one another and bicker over their patches. We've got enough on our plates worryin' about them accursed Catlords."

With their thoughts drifting to their enemy, the two Werelords rode on in broken silence for the remainder of the day. Conversation was sparse, small exchanges of banter that were snuffed out as quickly as they began. They each knew that the greatest battles yet lay ahead of them. Whatever horrors awaited them in Brackenholme, they were a small part of a bigger picture: Prince Lucas and his Catlord brethren held Westland, the Longridings, and the Dalelands and, with a force already striking deep into Omir, were no doubt already assaulting Sturmland. Drew hoped that the enemy had stretched itself too thin, fighting on so many different fronts, but hope was a fool's gambit.

Night drew in early, the cruel chill of winter gripping both therians in their saddles. Drew could no longer feel his fingers, the thick glove that covered his right hand providing little protection from the constant cold. He glanced across at the Hawklord: he'd have smiled at sight of the icicle that had formed on the end of Red Rufus's nose if it hadn't hurt so much to smile, his lips chapped and cracked. Reluctant to stop in the afternoon, the two continued on their way until the gray mare and Bravado grew weary. The moon and stars were covered by a great swath of clouds, plunging the forest into a deeper gloom than before, the occasional owl's screech or wolf's howl causing the riders to start. The lupine wail sent shivers racing down Drew's spine, striking a chord deep within. When Red Rufus's horse stumbled over an unseen root beneath the snow, they knew it was time to rein in.

Wyldermen or not, there was no way the Werelords could go without a fire on such an inhospitable night. While Drew tethered the horses, Red Rufus set off into the forest in search of firewood.

"Won't be seeing any wild men tonight, I says," he muttered, stumbling into the darkness. "Any self-respectin' Wylderman'll be tucked up in his straw hut, prayin' to 'is demons that the cold don't get 'im. If I come across one, I'll snap 'is worthless bones into pieces and use 'em for kindling. . . ."

Drew threw blankets over the horses, shaking his head at the Hawklord's perpetually dark sense of humor. The falconthrope's actions in Stormdale had helped to tip the balance of battle in their favor, as Red Rufus and Magister Wilhelm had conspired to ensure that the enemy turned on itself. Drew still struggled with the idea of killing an unarmed man in cold blood, but he had to face the facts; the dark deed done when the Hawk sent an arrow into Croke's black heart had won them that fight. Many lived thanks to Red Rufus's actions.

Again, Duke Manfred's words returned to him: *There's a time and a place for underhandedness.* Shivering at the memory, Drew recalled how, mere moments later, the Ratlord Vankaskan had lured Manfred into an alley in Highcliff and stabbed him almost to death. Little could the noble Duke have imagined how far the Lions and their allies would go to seize Lyssia for their own. The time for chivalry now seemed a distant dream.

The young Werewolf needed to get his head straight, needed to accept that there were times when taking a life— even that of an unarmed victim—was vital if it meant saving many others. The boy who was once a shepherd from the Cold Coast, still so new to the world of war and the Werelords, was learning all the time.

"Funny," he whispered to Bravado as he stroked the charger's broad white nose. "A simple enough word: *death.* How a perspective can shift: I thought Croke's demise was murder yesterday and—"

The cry from Red Rufus made Drew's legs give way as he fell into a snow bank beside the road. The horses snorted as he struggled to his feet, scrambling through the drift and making for the Hawk's yell. Moonbrand was out, the glowing blade lighting the way ahead.

"Red Rufus!" he shouted, picking out the old falconthrope's tracks in the snow. Another cry, this one spluttering and high-pitched, signaled how close he was, and Drew sped up as he followed the footprints. The tracks stopped suddenly, and Drew looked up.

Red Rufus was suspended from branches ten feet overhead, a dark green vine noose tight around his neck. Drew recognized it straightaway: wych ivy. The Hawklord clawed at the emerald flesh of the vine, talons tearing from his fingertips and scratching welts into his own throat. His whole body shook and juddered, the animal within desperate to break out, but the man's mind winning; if he changed now, his whole body would grow—the noose would not. He'd be unconscious before his beak broke free and dead moments later. Another vine swung down, looping around a wrist and yanking it clear. Red Rufus's eyes bulged as he spied Drew, his face a ghoulish shade of purple as his tongue lolled from his mouth.

Drew welcomed the Wolf in, the beast's blood hot in his veins, coursing through his legs and arms. He crouched, his whole body creaking and cracking, the bones within elongating, thickening, transforming. His leg muscles ballooned, the thick, dark fur of the lycanthrope bristling beneath the taut leather. Holding Moonbrand at his back, he braced the stump of his muscular left arm in the packed ice, another point from which to launch himself from the earth. Arm and legs flexed for a moment before the Werewolf bounded skyward.

His leap was timed to perfection, his ascent slowing at the point where he was eye to bulging eye with Red Rufus. Moonbrand arced through the air, splitting the coils of the wych ivy into hissing, severed serpents above the Hawklord's head. Instantly Red Rufus was tumbling, his snared arm tearing the vines loose as he tumbled to the ground like a broken marionette.

Drew stood over him, still half-transformed, Moonbrand in hand. The wych ivy recoiled from the glowing white blade, like snakes backing away from a flame, slithering back into the branches high above. Drew's heartbeat was steady, the youth in total control, the Wolf mastered entirely in that moment. As his muscles relaxed and his human self returned, he looked down at the Hawklord on the frozen forest floor. Red Rufus tore the remnants of the ivy from his throat, poisonous sap drizzling onto the pristine white snow, his frantic eyes fixed on the young lycanthrope. Content that the awful weeds wouldn't reappear, Drew sheathed his sword and held his hand out.

"Come on," he said, hauling the Hawk to his feet. "We need to get a fire started before we freeze. We've a busy day ahead tomorrow," he said, strolling back toward the Dyre Road.

"Busy?" squawked the Hawklord.

Drew called back as the old therian raced after him. "We're doing battle with the bad-tempered bracken before breakfast."

4
Barbed

THE MENACE THAT pervaded the Dyrewood during daylight was amplified once the night drew in. Hours after the escape from Brackenholme, the occasional animal sounds that echoed through the forest had faded into the darkness, to be replaced by stranger, more sinister noises: the cries of the red-feathered Wyldermen. Trent was aware of their movements; his childhood growing up on the Cold Coast had left him with a fair knowledge of animal calls, and while the odd screeches and wails might have tricked a town dweller, there was no fooling the farmer's son. When one of the peculiar cries sounded and was echoed in another part of the forest, Trent was able to roughly place its point of origin. The Wyldermen had fanned out, coordinating their search to cover as wide an area as possible. But their strategy for communicating allowed the young outrider to stay one step ahead of those who hunted him.

The old Romari, Stirga, was out there somewhere, on his own. Trent prayed to Brenn that he was safe and had given their pursuers the slip: they had been separated when they'd ridden into the woods, immediately after escaping the Dyre Gate. While Trent had led Storm one way, Stirga had headed another, and had been gone from sight in seconds. With a broken sword arm and a pack of Wyldermen at his back, the Romari's chances of survival were slim at best.

Trent himself was relatively unscathed by the battle, though at times he was plagued by sweats, cold shivers wracking his body. The Werelady, Gretchen, had spent the day slumped in Storm's saddle, the reins held by Trent as he led his mount on foot beside her. The young outrider had been looking forward to Gretchen's awakening from her concussion, which would give him a chance to explain exactly who he was. The blow she'd taken in the Bearlord's hall had been tremendous. Vala had struck with all her fury and sent the girl hurtling through the window in a shower of glass and broken timber. She'd remained senseless since then, drifting in and out of consciousness. With the all too brief hours of daylight now stolen away, the Fox of Hedgemoor finally came around, her concussion lifting as she sat up in the saddle.

Trent looked up at her and managed a smile. "Do you feel better, my—?"

Trent never completed his sentence. Gretchen's boot connected with his jaw with an almighty crack, sending his head recoiling as if on a spring. The Werelady kicked the horse's flanks, and Storm's sudden gallop whipped the reins free from Trent's hand. He watched Storm hurdle a fallen tree, Gretchen struggling to steer the mount without the reins, before a low-hanging branch caught the girl cleanly across the temple. The branch switched one way and then the other as the rider tumbled from the saddle, spinning in the air before landing on her back with a thump.

As Storm came to a halt nearby, Trent walked slowly after them, stopping when he stood over the fallen noblewoman. She sat stunned, gingerly touching her forehead with trembling fingers, blinking with shock when the tips came away bloodied. The young soldier felt sick enough already as a result of the arrow wound in his shoulder: the kick from the therian lady didn't help matters. Nursing his jaw with one hand, he held his other out.

"Shall we try that again?" he asked, unable to hide his displeasure.

"I'd sooner take the hand of a Wylderman," she spat.

"That can be arranged," replied Trent, walking away to fetch Storm. Taking the reins, he ran his hands through her mane, leaning his forehead against the horse momentarily. He looked up as Gretchen rose to her feet, eyeing him warily as she mopped her torn brow with the back of her hand.

"What are you staring at, Redcloak?" she snarled.

"The great collection of bumps and lumps you're getting on that perfect head, my lady. First your dive through the window in Brackenholme Hall, then headbutting a tree; you'll be mistaken for a Staglord before long if you're not careful."

Gretchen shook her dress, and clods of mud and mulch spattered the forest floor around her. She held out her hand toward Trent, palm open.

"It's a bit late to be taking my hand now, my lady," said Trent, managing a grim smile. "The offer's gone."

"I don't want your filthy hand. Your horse; hand me the reins."

"No."

Gretchen walked closer, her lips curling as she bared her teeth at Trent. He caught a flicker of something; a growl, perhaps? He noticed her fingertips, the nails sharper than they were a moment ago; *the Fox shows itself?*

"You're not listening, Redcloak. With respect, I wasn't asking for the horse. I'm taking it from you, and you can count yourself fortunate that I'm sparing your life."

Trent winced as he wound the reins around his hand. "With rather less respect, *my lady*, you'll be doing no such thing.

The horse is mine, and if you know what's good for you, you'll remain in my company."

"Are you *threatening* me?" she gasped incredulously.

"No," said Trent, growling himself this time, annoyance thick in his voice. "I'm trying to *protect* you. These woods are alive with Wyldermen. They flank us, follow us, pursue us from all sides. As appalling as you must find the notion, you need to stay with me if you want to live. The wild men aren't discerning—human or therian, no doubt we all taste the same when it comes to the crunch."

Gretchen blanched, looking over her shoulder into the surrounding woodland. "And how do you intend to keep me alive? Why should I trust you, Redcloak?"

"I'm not with the Lion. My loyalty lies with the Wolf."

"I only have your word for that," she replied dismissively.

"And my actions," added Trent. "I worked alongside Stirga, Yuzhnik, and Captain Harker, trying to save the people of Brackenholme. I was trying to rescue you and Lady Whitley."

"*This* is a rescue?"

He'd had enough. Trent stepped closer to her, his blue eyes narrowing as he glared at the Lady of Hedgemoor. She refused to back away, but her petulance wilted under his fierce glare.

"I made a promise that I'd protect you," said the outrider, "and I intend to honor it, no matter how foolish that vow now appears. If you can look beyond the color of my cloak for a moment, you'll see that we're in this together. The Wyldermen are our enemy; if we're to survive this predicament, we need to work as one."

Right on cue, the hollering began once again in the forest. It was distant enough not to put them in immediate danger, but close enough to alarm the pair. Trent stood to one side and gestured to Storm with his free hand. "Please, my lady. Get back on the horse."

As the Werelady clambered back into Storm's saddle, it occurred to Trent that he'd never encountered a feistier, more headstrong girl in his life. He was having a hard time imagining what it was that had led his brother into friendship with the girl, when everything about her haughty manner left a rotten taste in his mouth.

He smacked his lips as he stumbled on, and the strange, sickly feeling that wracked his body returned. His clothes were soaked with sweat, his body oblivious to the icy chill of night. The pain in his left shoulder was now a dull throb, and the arrow head was still buried beneath the flesh. Any poisons the wild men might have added to the tip were working their dark magic.

He glanced up, catching the girl's gaze for an instant before she turned away.

"Don't worry, my lady." Trent coughed. "You won't catch anything from looking at me. The diseases we peasants carry require closer contact to spread."

"You're already quite close enough," she replied, her teeth chattering as she spoke.

"Therians," Trent muttered. His sight blurred as he walked, and tiny lights played across his field of vision like snowflakes hovering in the darkness. "You think you're better than us normal folk, don't you?"

"I may have once been guilty of that, but this has nothing to do with social standing. My dislike of you derives entirely from the color of the cloak you wear."

"I've told you already, I'm loyal to the Wolf."

"Loyalty? You wouldn't know its meaning," she said, trembling as the cold gripped her. Trent could see the gooseflesh on her bare arms, as her skin shone pale blue in the faint light. "You serve yourself, boy; you're a turncoat. I'd imagine neither side wants you in their rank."

Trent grimaced, staggering through the withered bracken. He snatched at the clasp around his throat, tearing the cloak free and throwing it up at the girl. His legs were failing, his clumsy walk now a series of stumbles.

"Take the wretched cloak. It would suit you well. Perhaps it'll stop your miserable jaws from rattling and alerting the Wyldermen to our presence."

Gretchen pulled the cloak from her face as if it were some monstrous cobweb, spluttering as she held it at arm's length.

She looked at it momentarily in disgust, torn between pride and practicality. The winter chill was bitter, and any clothing was better than none. Her eyes alighted on the large bloodstain on the shoulder, and the hole torn through the scarlet fabric. Gretchen was about to remark upon the damaged cloak when the outrider fell, the horse dragging his body through the snow by the reins.

Swinging down from the saddle, Gretchen quickly untangled the Lionguard's wrist from the reins. She tied Storm to a nearby tree before dropping to the frozen ground beside the youth. She could leave him here, of course. This would be the perfect opportunity: take his horse and filthy cloak and run. If she could pick her way north through the Dyrewood, there was a chance of finding the Dymling Road. Returning the way they'd come was out of the question. The Redcloak was right: the Wyldermen were on their trail, hunting them through the haunted forest. They certainly couldn't return to Brackenholme. She thought of the horror in the Bearlord's Hall, where Whitley and her mother faced the Wereserpent alone. She wiped her forearm across her eyes, tears rolling freely down her cheeks. They were lost: Gretchen had abandoned them.

She looked down at the Redcloak, chewing her lip as she decided what to do. His blond hair clung to his forehead, his blue eyes fluttering as he tried to focus. He was whispering for his mother, the word *Ma* wheezing from his cracked lips. *He looks half-dead; he'll only slow me down.* She recognized the voice in her head instantly, that of the self-centered princess she'd once been, re-emerging at this perilous time. Self-preservation was a powerful instinct, and her insecurities and fears were magnified tenfold when faced by this dilemma. *Can I leave him to die?* She rolled him over on his face, the decision made. The old Gretchen was silenced as the Werefox buried her terrors.

A splintered arrow protruded from the Redcloak's shoulder blade and was embedded in the leather jerkin. The armor was soaked with dark blood around the entry wound, and fresh rivulets rose and pooled around the shaft when she brushed the broken end with her fingertips. The young man cried out, the pain stirring him from his fevered state.

"Get it out," he whispered. "Please."

Gretchen shook her head, looking at her hands hopelessly. "How?"

"The armor," he murmured, vainly struggling with the clasps along his side that secured the breastplate. Gretchen reached down, unfastening them, pulling the buckles apart until the back was loose. She winced as she lifted the armor away from the skin, the leather scraping the shattered shaft and straining against it, twisting the arrowhead in the flesh. The youth bit his forearm, stifling a scream as the armor came away. Placing it gently to one side, Gretchen looked back at the wound.

The shirt on his back was stained with old blood and wet with fresh. She tore the material apart around the arrow exposing the flesh beneath. The head wasn't visible; it was buried within the shoulder, with only the thin snapped shaft standing proud.

"Take it out," he sobbed. Gretchen's hands trembled. The Redcloak's voice was barely audible, exhaustion taking its toll. The shirt was soaked. *How much blood has he lost?*

Gretchen gripped her fingers around the couple of inches of splintered wood and tugged. A fresh cry escaped the Redcloak's lips as his flesh rose with the shaft, showing no sign of relinquishing the arrowhead. He shook his head feebly as she loosened her grip on the arrow.

"No good," he said, his face turning as one blue eye settled on Gretchen. "Barbed . . . have to . . . cut it out . . ."

Gretchen shook her head furiously now.

"I can't, I don't know what I'm doing! I'll injure you further!"

The blond-haired youth closed his eyes.

"If you don't . . . I'll die. . . ."

A strange animal cry echoed in the forest, followed quickly by another more distant one. Gretchen looked up, her eyes wide with fear. She knew what the red-feathered Wyldermen were capable of. If the arrowhead was to be removed, it had to be done now. Gretchen reached down to the Lionguard's weapon belt, searching for a knife. She found his sword, the pommel twisting where he lay so that her eyes landed upon it. A snarling wolfshead stared back.

"Your sword," she gasped, recognizing it as the kind Drew had carried.

"My father's . . . " The youth sighed, his eyes still closed.

Her mind full of fresh questions, she moved the sword to one side, reaching round to his other hip.

"The Wolf," she said, still searching for a knife. "He has a blade such as this."

A smile creased the sickly, pale Redcloak's face. "This is that blade . . . " he mumbled. "The Wolf . . . is my brother."

Gretchen gasped, just as her hand closed on the leather-bound handle of a hunting knife. *This is Drew's brother? Impossible—the Redcloak has to be hallucinating. He is sick, his mind addled with fever.* With a yank, Gretchen tugged the knife free. The blade was dark, one edge serrated, the other smooth like a razor. Gretchen placed a hand over the Redcloak's back, and braced her palm against his cold flesh. *Drew's brother?* She whispered a brief prayer to Brenn. Then she started cutting.

5

FOLLOWED

DREW WOKE WITH a start as a rough hand closed over his mouth, stifling his cry. The grizzled face of Red Rufus stared down, his free hand open, a bony finger to his lips.

"Hush," whispered the Hawklord. "We're being followed."

Drew nodded, raising his hand to prize Red Rufus's dirty palm away. The falconthrope slid away, staying low to the ground as he scrambled back to his bedroll where his bow and quiver lay. Drew rolled onto his belly, following the old warrior across their tiny campsite and crawling up alongside him.

"How many?" he said quietly, his hand closing round Moonbrand's grip. He paused, deciding against withdrawing the blade from its scabbard. The enchanted weapon shone like a torch on even the darkest night: the last thing he wanted to do was alert their enemy to the fact that they were wise to their movements.

"Too soon to tell, but I heard 'em coming down the Dyre Road. Faint, but there's someone there all right."

The two Werelords had set up camp a short distance from the road, far enough away to remain concealed from anyone traveling the woodland avenue. Furthermore, they weren't so deep that Red Rufus need fear attack from any number of the Dyrewood's unholy denizens, be they beasts or even plants. The old bird's encounter with the wych ivy days earlier had left him shaken, jumping at shadows and starting every time a branch creaked. Sleep wasn't easy for the Hawklord, so he'd taken to sitting the night watch. Drew, on the other hand, had little difficulty sleeping within the Dyrewood. He felt strangely at home beneath the starlight in the forest. Invariably, Drew would have to secure Red Rufus into his saddle during the daylight hours, so the old Hawk could slumber as they rode, exhausted by the trials of the night.

"I'll take the woods," said Drew, pointing deeper into the forest.

"I'll hole up here. Minute I sees 'em . . ." Red Rufus pulled back on his bowstring, fingering the flight of his arrow. He winked. Drew nodded and was gone.

Hugging trees and staying low, Drew darted through the darkness, stalking back along the forest's edge. He allowed enough of the Wolf through to heighten his senses: his sight was instantly sharper, the world a canvas of sharp gray shapes as his night vision quickly acclimatized to the surroundings. His keen nose could pick out every smell on the wind, from the clean scent of freshly fallen snow to every animal trail that wound through the twisted undergrowth. He could pinpoint the enemy's odor now, the distinct tang of human sweat mixed with steel. *Armored?* That ruled out the Wyldermen, as the forest folk preferred hide and leather and weapons crafted from flint. Another smell, too: horses. *Riders? How many?*

Drew could see movement now, through the bare black trees and thick swathes of shadows. There he was: a lone figure on horseback, riding along the opposite bank of the road. He was traveling beneath the leafless canopy but avoiding the center of the avenue, staying close to the tree line, almost invisible but for Drew's night vision. The rider wore a dark hooded cloak, the cowl up about his face. *One of the Crow's men, perhaps? Or a straggler from the Vermirian Guard lost in the Dyrewood, trying to find his way home?* Drew's keen eyesight also spotted the rags the horse wore over its hooves, further dampening any noise the rider might make as he progressed along the Dyre Road. *Clever,* mused Drew, *but not clever enough to outwit the old Hawk.*

Crouching on all fours, Drew edged nearer, cutting his way through the briars and bracken as he stalked toward the road's edge. The route he took would allow the rider to get within bowshot of Red Rufus and afford him the chance to launch an attack at the same moment. Each footfall was silent, the

314

measured steps of the Wolf bringing him closer to his quarry. He dropped into a ditch that ran beside the ancient trail, the rider close now, a dozen yards or so away. Drew let his clawed hand slide around Moonbrand, dark flesh closing around the white leather grip. His jaws locked and broadened, lengthening into a muzzle, canines growing, gray hair peppering his face as his yellow eyes focused on the enemy. Drew tensed his body, leg muscles straining, ready to spring.

When the rider was parallel with him, Drew sprang forward, flying from the undergrowth directly toward him. Drew unsheathed Moonbrand at the height of his bound, the steel glowing with a pale blue light, illuminating both the Werewolf in all his monstrous glory and the foe he was about to strike. The rider half turned, his hood falling away to reveal the lean face of a boy—a boy Drew instantly recognized. The Werewolf halted the sword's blow, keeping Moonbrand trailing at his back as he raised the stump of his left arm defensively, crashing into the rider's mount. The horse reared up, almost bucking off the rider, as the twang of a bowstring sounded from the forest. Drew's reactions were lightning fast—he swung his disfigured arm up, striking the boy's chest and propelling him out of the saddle. The arrow whipped past, hitting a tree trunk behind and quivering where it struck. The boy landed with a crash, his steel breastplate ringing as the breath exploded from his lungs.

"Hold your fire, Red Rufus!" cried Drew as he knelt down

beside the boy, the Werewolf features slowly cracking back into place, dark hairs disappearing beneath his skin.

"What in Brenn's wide heaven are you doing here, Milo? You could have got yourself killed!" He put his arm around the young Staglord and helped him sit upright, the boy wincing with each movement. "Easy. You may have broken something."

The boy sat still for a moment, gathering his breath, as Red Rufus jogged toward them. The boy's eyes were wide, shock and fear still gripping his heart after his brief dance with death. Drew could now see the full plate armor Milo wore beneath his soot-gray cloak, the heraldic device of a leaping buck shining on his breastplate.

Red Rufus couldn't contain his anger.

"I swear by Tor Raptor I could've killed ya there, boy! You got this man to thank for things not goin' bad!"

Drew stifled a wry smile. He'd got used to hearing the Hawklord refer to *him* as a boy. Now in the presence of this youth, Drew had been elevated to the lofty title of "man." *I'll try to not let it go to my head*, he thought with amusement, helping Milo to his feet.

"You're a long way from home," said Drew, dusting snow from the boy's cloak. "You really shouldn't be here."

"I had to come," said the Staglord. "It wasn't right for none of us to aid you on your journey, after all you've done for Stormdale. I pledge my sword to you, Your Highness."

"You're here to aid us?" Red Rufus laughed. "You're a hin-

316

drance; it's as plain as the beak on my face! Turn around, boy, before my boot connects with your wee rump." Red Rufus took an intimidating step toward Milo, but the boy stood his ground, jutting his chin out at the falconthrope.

"You don't tell me what to do, my lord. Nobody does."

Red Rufus nodded, pretending to be impressed by the brave talk.

"You hear that, Wolf? Nobody tells this one what to do. I take it your brother Reinhardt didn't approve of your coming?"

"There was no point in consulting him."

"You might've been safer if you'd stayed in Stormdale, Milo," said Drew sympathetically. "Out here's as dangerous as it gets. It's no place for a boy."

"They said the same thing when I rode out to Windfell. They tried to stop me, but look what happened; I got a message to you, to both of you. You returned to Stormdale and helped us defeat Vorjavik's army."

Drew looked back at Red Rufus.

"He has an annoying way of throwing logic in our faces, doesn't he?"

"He's an idealistic wee grunt," said the Hawklord dismissively. "Send him packin', I say, back to his city where they might find some use for him."

"I can be of use to you here," implored the boy. "I'm not going back."

Red Rufus took a step forward, raising a hand to slap

him. Drew caught his wrist before he could strike, as the boy flinched.

"No, Red Rufus!" snarled Drew.

The Hawklord tugged his arm free, turning to Drew. "Just look at 'im! He filled his britches when he thought I was gonna backhand 'im! How in Brenn's name do ya think he'll cope when he's facing down a mob of Wyldermen?"

Drew looked back at Milo, who was straightening himself, trying to gather his composure. His steel gauntlets jangled as he hefted them onto his hips, trying to strike an intimidating pose of his own. He was failing.

"That plate mail you're wearing. Where's it from?"

"My father's armory," he said proudly. "This is the finest crafted Sturmish plate. The knights of Stormdale ride into battle in this very attire."

Drew glanced down at the cumbersome metal boots and greaves the boy wore. An elaborately plumed helmet hung from the rear of his horse's saddle.

"You'll have to lose it," Drew said simply. Both Red Rufus and Milo looked at him incredulously.

"You're *seriously considering* letting him join us?" squawked the old Hawk, his bushy eyebrows nearly flying off his forehead. The boy ignored Red Rufus, arguing a different point with the Wolflord.

"You would have me discard this armor, here by the

roadside? Out of the question: this armor has history, this very suit belonged to my father in his youth."

"In his youth, you say?" asked Drew. "I'd wager Duke Manfred was nearing manhood before he wore that plate, Milo. It's a man's suit of armor. You could break your neck if you fell over in it. You're lucky the fall from your horse didn't kill you!"

"This is the armor my father—"

"Yes, I understand, it was Manfred's, a man very dear to my heart, but the job at hand does not require a suit of field plate. It stays behind, Milo. Either it does, or you do."

Dark though the night was, Drew could sense the color rising in the boy's cheeks. He was well aware that his suggestion was an affront to anyone of noble stock, but no time was better than the present to drill the point home.

"You may join us, but these are my conditions. Lose the armor. We travel light and silently. You do *everything* Red Rufus and I tell you. You do not stray, and if you stay close at all times, you may just survive to see your family again."

Red Rufus watched, his temper simmering as the Wolf continued.

"Where we're going, we're likely to encounter terrible foes, witness horrific things. It's not the place for a boy, believe me. But I know how you feel: I *understand* your desire to help. And I'm grateful you've pledged your sword to our cause."

"Pah," muttered Red Rufus, turning and stalking back

toward their camp. Drew placed a hand on Milo's shoulder.

"Drop the armor, Milo. Don't dwell on this. They're just . . . things. We're not talking about life and death right now: they're still to come."

The boy nodded.

"Join us at the camp when you're ready," said Drew, following the Hawklord back to the bedrolls and leaving the boy to clamber out of his shining armor.

"You're a fool, Wolf," said the Hawk from where he sat. "You'll get that boy killed, letting him come with us."

"He's as likely to die if we send him back along the Dyre Road. You know what's out there. There're any number of things that might end his short life. I'm amazed he got this far without denting his fine armor."

"He's a boy."

"He's got guts."

"Again," said Red Rufus, quietly now, a hint of sincerity in his voice, and something else—concern? "He's a *boy*. This ain't no place for him."

Drew sat down, considering the other's words. He was correct, this was no place for Milo, but he was here now and there was little they could do about it.

"His best chance of survival's sticking with us. I know he's green, but you were too once, I'd guess."

Red Rufus rubbed at his jaw with his bony fingers, still clearly displeased. The clanging and grating of the plate mail cut through the night, causing the Hawklord to look back down the road.

"He might wake the dead, let alone the Wyldermen, with that rumpus!"

"If you're unhappy about keeping an eye on him, let him be *my* responsibility."

"You *know* I'll keep my eye on him, Wolf. Ain't in my nature to do otherwise. Just don't like the idea of havin' a kid in tow, is all. I've got a bad feeling about it."

"I wasn't that much older than him when I ended up in the Dyrewood, Red Rufus. A boy has to become a man sometime. I was forced into growing up, and growing up fast. Manfred's boy has made his own mind up on this, and you have to admire him for that."

"He's got some stones on 'im, I'll say that much," said the Hawk in reluctant agreement.

"He survived the ride to Windfell, didn't he? And he *did* succeed in acquiring our aid. He's resourceful. He may yet surprise us," Drew added as the boy walked up, leading his horse. The beast trampled across the foot of Red Rufus's bedroll, kicking it up and driving it into the dirty snow. The Hawk snarled, tugging the roll free and cursing.

"Sorry, my lord," said Milo, awkwardly leading his steed away to tie it alongside those of his newfound companions. Red Rufus straightened his blanket and turned on his side, grumbling with discontent while Milo made himself at home.

Drew watched the boy as he lifted a bedroll from his saddle, removing the plumed helmet at the same time. He looked at the fancy helm once before tossing it into the bushes.

"Your breastplate," Drew said, noticing that the boy still wore it, the tines of the rearing buck's antlers catching his eye beneath the folds of Milo's cloak.

"I figured I could keep this one thing," said Milo quietly. "It was my father's, Your Highness."

Drew was silent, the boy's words striking home resonantly. He thought back to the Wolfshead blade, the only thing he'd taken with him when he'd fled the Ferran farmhouse so many moons ago. *Where is it now? Still in that villain Sorin's hand?* He nodded, forcing a smile across his sad face.

"Unfurl your bedroll, Milo. Sit yourself down. And it's Drew. No cause for titles out here."

"He can keep calling me *my lord*," said Red Rufus from where he lay, not looking back. Drew smiled at the cantankerous old Hawk. "And tell 'im not to get comfy. We've got one fresh pair of eyes now: it's the boy's turn to watch."

Drew glanced across at Milo and saw that the boy recognized the note of reluctant acceptance in the Hawklord's miserable voice. Drew winked, and the boy smiled back.

6

RED SNOW

A LIFETIME OF hunting had not prepared Bergan for
this moment. Throughout his long years he'd enjoyed numerous
hunts, both through his own lands and those of his neighbors.
The Staglords of the Barebones had been famous for hosting
lavish events through their foothills, inviting Werelords from
across the Seven Realms to partake in the sport. One could
expect the hunt to last for weeks, with all the accompanying
festivities and feasting. Bergan's own hunts had often involved
the chasing of the notorious Dyrecat, an enormous feline that
was unique to the Woodland Realm. Therians would travel
from as far south as Cape Gala to join the chase, the beast
providing a match for any Werelord. When Leopold took the
throne, the king outlawed hunting the Dyrecat—a noble beast

to the felinthrope—leaving its numbers to grow throughout the Dyrewood. Now Bergan was the one being hunted, and he wasn't enjoying the experience.

The Bearlord's feet plowed up the snow as he traversed the slope, finding the fresh prints of those who ran ahead of him. Lean as he was after being starved beneath the earth, he was still a big man, and his heavy legs crumbled the packed ice with each step, causing him to stumble. His hands hit the snow, searching for extra purchase as he followed the girl ahead. Pick stopped, looking back and offering a hand.

"Keep going, child!" said the Bearlord, urging the girl to move. Pick obliged, following Captain Fry as the Sturmlander picked a path up the steep slope toward the summit. Bergan glanced at Carver, Hector and the Boarguard behind. Beyond the Ugri warriors he spied their enemy, spread out in a line, closing all the while. He gulped, his frostbitten lips cracking.

A hundred or so figures scurried up the slopes, close enough for Bergan to see where their loyalties lay. Many were foot soldiers from Muller's Skirmishers, keen to avenge the deaths of their comrades at the hands of Bergan and his allies. Among their number, he spied the black, scaled armor of the Vermirian Guard, the Rat King's best soldiers, pressing the Skirmishers on after their quarry. The Rat's warriors were a far more formidable foe than any of the cutthroats who wielded a club or ax in the name of Muller. These were battle-hardened veterans, no doubt armed with silver. At their back he spied

the unmistakable crooked figure of a Crowlord. Which one of
Count Croke's numerous sons this was, Bergan couldn't tell,
but the fact that a Werecrow was present made his heart sink.
What mischief was Croke involved in back in the Barebones?
He dreaded to imagine.

Farther down the white slopes, the foothills swarmed
with the men and tents of the Catlord army, a sea of tiny black
figures that bristled and shimmered with shining weapons.
Onyx was no fool: his elite Bastian forces were being kept out
of combat presently, which is why the men of Lyssia had been
sent after the ragtag band of refugees who scrambled through
the Whitepeaks. He'd hold back his best until last and throw
the Rats and Crows at the enemy to weaken their defenses
before letting his mightiest warriors off their leashes.

"The defenses!" shouted Fry, drawing Bergan's gaze to him.
The bowman had reached the top of the rise, revealing the heart
of the White Bear's realm ahead. There they were, jutting out
from the mountainside like a row of dark, jagged teeth across
the valley. Wooden stakes the length of tree trunks jutted out
from the tall, packed snow banks, driven in at angles that made
circumnavigating them almost impossible. Enormous ice walls
had been carved and crenellated, spears and pikes visible along
their length, hinting at the Sturmish numbers beyond. *You
have been a busy Bear, cousin*, thought Bergan, marveling at the
work Duke Henrik had done in the Whitepeaks.

"Hope at last!" said Bergan, finding strength in his aching

legs. "On! On!" The Bearlord began to follow his companions to the incline's top, his feet plunging through the packed snow. With a crunch, his right foot disappeared through the white powder, and he vanished up to the waist in snow as his whole frame rotated. The bank of ice the group had traversed suddenly sheared free, the Bearlord having broken its fragile grip on the mountainside. Fry threw out a hand, catching Pick before the girl followed Bergan, as the Lord of Brackenholme tumbled backward down the slope, engulfed in an avalanche of snow.

Bergan's world turned upside down, and the old Bear thundered down the slope on a torrent of white death. He could taste the fine, choking powder in his throat, blinding him. Its weight bent his limbs this way and that, threatening to break them at any moment. Gradually the roar of falling ice began to subside, as his momentum slowed and his descent became a slide, the Bearlord coming to a halt far below his companions, half buried, staring up at the cold heavens.

Fifty feet above he could see the last of the Ugri, Hector's Boarguard having brought up the rear as they'd tried to evade the enemy. There was Carver and the young magister, the two of them pushing past Hector's men and barking orders, clearly panicked by the turn of events. The Bearlord craned his head to see how close their pursuers were: the dull *thump* of an arrow disappearing into the snow nearby told him enough.

He twisted about, only his head, shoulders, and right arm free of the packed snow. To his horror he saw that the Catlords' soldiers were less than forty feet away and closing. The incline was negligible compared to that above, yet still their progress was slowed, the Skirmishers and Vermirians having to raise their legs high to step through the snow or kick their way through it, keen to reach the Bearlord. They shouted excitedly to one another, weapons ringing as they were drawn, sounding a grisly chorus across the white meadow.

Bergan roared with fury, calling upon the Bear, willing the beast into his weakened frame. The change was swift and painful, the therianthrope's body transforming beneath the snow. Those nearest the fallen Werelord might have caught sight of his flailing arm growing, the shaggy pelt of ruddy brown fur spreading across it, his hand widening into an enormous, black-clawed paw. Bergan snarled, his heart beating within his expanding chest as he neared freedom. He tried to drag himself from his white tomb: only to discover with dismay that he was still trapped, his greater mass having wedged him even tighter beneath the snow. The first of the Skirmishers was less than twenty feet away, closing fast. Bergan's roar wasn't the ferocious challenge of the Werebear but the scream of a snared beast.

The attacker was eight feet away, his spiked club raised high, ready to bury it in the Werebear's broad skull. Bergan raised his paw in a hopeless attempt at defense. The next moment the fighter's feet flew upward, his progress violently halted by a throwing knife in the chest. The snow crunched around the Bearlord as figures ran past him. Carver was at the front, his face and body covered in snow from his slide down the slope. Two of Hector's Boarguard were with him, shaking white powder from their shoulders, and the Ugri held their axes aloft as they rushed to meet the first Skirmishers.

Hector slid to the floor beside Bergan, and the Werebear instinctively growled as the youth came too close. The magister held up his gloved hands, pleading for restraint. His eyes constantly darted to the growing battle Carver and the Ugri had fallen into. The remainder of his Boarguard rushed past, including Ringlin and Ibal, preventing the enemy from reaching the Bearlord.

"Your Grace," said Hector, "you must relax! Send the beast away: push it back, deep inside!"

"Never!" rumbled Bergan, snapping his huge jaws. "To return to mortal state in battle? Without drawing the enemy's blood by tooth and claw?"

"What battle is it you're engaged in? You're buried, my lord! If you don't revert you'll be trapped here," said Hector, a note of irritation in his voice. "Shift back to human state and you'll loosen the packed ice: only *then* can we extricate you from your predicament!"

Humiliating as the idea was, Hector's plan made sense. *Smart lad.* Bergan tried to focus, the tempting sound of battle around him—ax against sword, spear against shield—making the change even more challenging. Gradually, he began to shift.

Hector ran on from where he'd left the duke in his icy trap. He had to act swiftly: more Skirmishers and the Vermirian Guard were joining the melee, and his Ugri warriors were wading in with Carver among them.

These men are supposed to be your allies, brother, yet you set your Boarguard upon them!

The Vincent-vile was correct: Hector had sworn an oath to Onyx and Lucas, siding with them, turning against those he'd once considered friends. But it was too soon to reveal his hand, too early to strike a blow against the Wolf's Council. He needed to get into Icegarden, high up in the mountains, beyond the barricades, and this over-zealous Crowlord's attack was in danger of scuppering his plans before they'd truly begun. Hector was resigned to the fact that blood would be spilled: he was only grateful that these were Muller's undisciplined rabble, plus a handful of Vermirians.

Carver held a knife in each hand, stolen from the corpses of Captain Stephan's men back in the gulch. The Lord of Thieves had his suspicions about Hector, the magister was in no doubt. In their more private moments, his right-hand man, Ringlin, had said that the two had known each other back in Highcliff. *We had dealings* was how his man had put it, which no doubt meant that Carver knew what Ringlin was capable of. That the Boarlord had taken men like this into his service wouldn't have been lost on the Thief-lord.

They could kill Carver now, Hector. A quick slip of the long knife or Ibal's sickle: who'd notice in the heat of battle?

Hector ignored the vile: he had more pressing need of his two oldest retainers.

"Ringlin! Ibal! With me!" called Hector as he withdrew his jeweled dagger. The two Boarguards ran to him, falling in behind him as he ran a short distance away from the melee.

"Where are you going, my lord?" said Ringlin, looking back to where the Ugri were engaged with their foes. "The fighting's that way!"

"Don't question me," said Hector, catching sight of Bergan, now in human form again, pulling himself from the snow. Half a dozen Skirmishers pulled away from the fight, following the magister, unaware the fact that their quarry was actually their ally.

"Come on," muttered Hector, looking through the massing crowd of the enemy, searching for sight of his target. "Show yourself. . . ."

As if in answer, a dark shape took flight from the rear of the small army, black wings fanning out and lifting it skyward in steady, powerful beats.

"Good," Hector said, ceasing running. "Here he comes."

Two of the Skirmishers carried crossbows, dropping to their knees to load and aim as their companions ran on. Hector didn't have to think twice.

Hector flung his left arm out, palm open, fingers twitching as he shot the vile invisibly across the snow. The first man dropped his weapon when he felt the ghostly noose around his throat. Hector yanked his arm back sharply: even from this distance, amid the sounds of battle, he heard the *crack* of the man's neck breaking. He drew his hand to the right, the vile moving on, at the limits of the magister's control. Shorter distances gave him absolute mastery over the phantom: the greater the distance, the more difficult it was to direct Vincent's movements. Yet the command got through. The second man unleashed one shot, the bolt whistling toward the magister and his men before he went down in the snow, clawing at his neck, kicking wildly as he tried to breathe.

Hector glanced at Ringlin to his right and saw that the rogue looked astonished. To his left, Ibal shared an equally disbelieving expression. *They've seen me do that before: why the wonderment?* Hector never got the chance to question his men: the four remaining Skirmishers ran at them, axes, clubs, and shortswords up and ready.

The Boarlord stepped back, leaving his men to contend with the four bandits, putting a little distance between them as the Werecrow circled overhead, swooping down. Hector ran farther away, seeking cover behind a tumbledown rock formation, away from prying eyes.

Lord Flint landed beside him, the earth exploding in a shower of white powder, his taloned feet splayed across the snow. The Werecrow couldn't resist a guttural *kaw* as he stepped forward on his monstrous legs, oily black wings arching, ruffling and rattling like a serpent's tail. Flint carried a scimitar in each hand, twirling them menacingly as Hector backed against the rocks.

"What in Brenn's name are you doing?" Hector asked Flint as the Vincent-vile suddenly rejoined him. The phantom was invisible to all but the magister, and it thrilled him to know it was there, ready to be unleashed should he desire it.

"You said you wanted an attack launched on your friends. This is that attack," said Flint, black beak snapping as his harsh voice hacked out the words.

"You already *did* that, back in the gulch! You could have left us to continue on to Icegarden with the duke's party. This attack is too much: my Ugri have put themselves in harm's way for this charade."

"What's a little blood between friends?" The Crow laughed, briefly glancing over his feathered shoulder to see if their rendezvous had been noticed.

Hector shuddered: these weren't his friends. None of them were. His recent audience with Lord Onyx had confirmed what he already knew: the Beast of Bast was aptly named, as terrifying as any creature he'd ever encountered. The Werepanther was to be feared. Hector was done with friends. He had only enemies now, to varying degrees, some hated more than others. Flint was quickly propelling himself to the top of that list.

"If any of my men die—"

"Quit worrying, Blackhand: this is war," Flint squawked, whipping a scimitar up to Hector's throat.

Release me, brother, said the vile. Yet Hector delayed, his eyes narrowing as the Werecrow continued.

"Men die all the while. That fool Onyx has my brothers fighting for War Marshal Vorjavik in the Barebones. Can you imagine that? The Crows having to serve a Rat? You think I care if any of those Vermirian scum should fall? They can all die as far as I care, so long as *my* people take Stormdale!"

Interesting, thought Hector, gently pushing the scimitar away with his dagger. Still the Vincent-vile waited to strike, anxious as a terrier on a short leash, gnashing its spectral teeth in the direction of the Crowlord.

"You'd betray your allies?" said Hector. "And you speak ill of the Beast of Bast? You're braver than I thought, Flint. I'm on a mission for Lord Onyx, if you recall."

"I know what you're capable of, Blackhand," said the Werecrow, leaning in close until his slate beak scratched Hector's chin. The black tongue flickered within like a dark flame, the large, avian eyes blinking.

"What of it?" said Hector, sneering at the Crow. "You'd

risk ruining my plan, all because of a falling out with the Rat King? Swallow your differences, Flint: work with Vorjavik. We all have our trials. I could *win* this war if I get into Icegarden. I can destroy the Wolf's Council in one fell swoop."

"I know what you're capable of," the Werecrow repeated. "And I want a part of it."

Hector was genuinely surprised.

"A part of what? The ancient art of magistry? I've studied my entire life to master these magicks and you expect me to teach you tricks?"

"You misunderstand me, Blackhand. You and I can work together. There are more twists and turns for all sides to endure before this war concludes. Take what you want from the Seven Realms: give my people the Barebones and the lands around it! The Boars and the Crows aren't so different—we've both lived too long in the shadow of Wolves and Lions. I can help you, Hector. Together, we may both triumph."

He bargains with you, brother. Might he be of use to us?

"The Whitepeaks," said Hector, looking anxiously at the mountains, the screams of battle still echoing around the valley. "Have you any news?"

"I've flown north of Icegarden, yes. All that you promised is coming to pass. They come."

"Excellent," said Hector, a note of nervous tension in his reply.

Lord Flint took a step back, glancing around the rocks.

"It appears your cavalry's arrived," he said, his beak clacking, eyes widening with surprise. Hector stepped forward to look.

A swirling white cloud rolled like a wave down the mountainside. More than fifty soldiers on horseback raced down the slope, snow cascading around them. Their steeds were heavyset horses, the kind Hector had once seen in the Barebones as a boy, favored by mountain men. The warriors' longswords were raised high as their crisp white cloaks billowed. Hector caught sight of an enormous white bear racing in the heart of the Sturmish knights, the ice splintering beneath each thundering footstep as it crashed into the battle, leading the charge: Duke Henrik, the Lord of Icegarden. The Vermirians and Skirmishers broke beneath the attack, either crumpled underfoot or fleeing down the slopes, away from the Sturmish horsemen and the ferocious Werebear. The knights gave chase, cutting down each one, showing no mercy.

"I'd best be going," said Flint with a sigh, turning back to Hector. "I'd do something about your accursed limb before rejoining the Bearlords, if I were you, Blackhand."

With that, Flint took off once more, limping through the sky back toward Onyx's camp, feigning injury with each weary wingbeat.

"My accursed limb?" said Hector to himself, just as Ringlin and Ibal arrived around the wall of rocks, searching for their liege. The two bloodied men looked relieved to see their master alive, but their concerned looks didn't go away; the two stared at Hector's left hand. His eyes followed theirs.

The second Skirmisher crossbowman had unleashed a shot just before Vincent had taken him down. Hector hadn't noticed where the loosed bolt had ended up. Now he saw it, a six-inch shaft sticking clean through the palm of his gloved hand. He cocked his head as he examined it, lifting it, turning the hand one way and then the next as he inspected the wound. He felt no pain, no discomfort. The hand was cold, numb. He gripped the bolt's head and pulled, drawing it out. Ringlin blanched. It came away with a sucking *pop*, and Hector tossed it into the snow. Again, he examined the hand, which had a perfectly neat hole punched clean through it. There was no blood, and he felt no distress. He felt nothing.

"You need a new pair of gloves, my lord," said Ringlin.

"I *need* to get into Icegarden," corrected Hector, moving the leather glove enough to hide the hole in his withered hand, his head full of questions. So odd that Lord Flint should make such an offer: did the Crow truly believe Hector was *that* powerful? Flint had watched him commune with the slain scout in Onyx's camp, but he was yet to witness the vile at work. Was Hector's command over the dead enough to change the Crow's disdain to grudging—or possibly fearful—respect? Or was this just another Werelord trying to feather his own nest, to ensure that whatever happened during the war he'd come out on the winning side? If Onyx's armies *were* turning on one another, what had driven them to such an act on the eve of their greatest victory, when they were so close to defeating the Wolf's Council? What other forces were at work?

You'll get your answers, brother, all in good time, whispered the vile. *Good things come to those who wait.*

"Come, gentlemen," the magister said, extending a hand before him. "We've the Lord of Sturmland to meet. Duke Henrik will want to shake hands with the heroes who saved the Bear of Brackenholme from an early grave."

7

Evening the Odds

THE HOLLERS OF the Wyldermen echoed through the forest, piercing the once-silent Dyrewood like a knife through the heart. The din had grown gradually, having been faint at first to Drew's ears, before rising in tempo and fervor as they neared. The wild men weren't coming for them; these warriors were hunting, closing in on their kill. He remembered the noise from his time in the wild, scared and alone, tracked all too frequently by the Wyldermen as they caught his scent on the wind. Only Drew's cunning and a lot of luck had prevented them from ever concluding their hunt. The Werewolf had always evaded them in the nick of time. No, they were hunting something else this cold gray afternoon.

"Do we leave 'em to it?" asked Red Rufus, squinting into the forest from atop his horse. Milo's mount sidled anxiously, the young rider equally ill at ease.

"Sounds like there's a great many of them," added the boy. "Maybe we just continue on our way?"

Drew looked to the others, managing a hard smile.

"The boy's right," said Red Rufus. "Whatever they're hunting, does it matter to us? Our task's to get to Brackenholme. Distraction like this could be the death of us."

Milo nodded, glad to hear his suggestion hadn't been dismissed by the Hawklord as so often was the case.

"I need to know what—or who—they're hunting," said Drew.

"I knew you were going to say that, lad," said the Hawk, rolling his eyes as he unslung his bow. He nodded toward the forest from where the cries were coming. "Lead on then, young Wolf."

The three jumped down from their horses, securing them to a tree before setting off into the forest. Drew glanced over his shoulder, relieved to see the Hawk and Stag following. He dipped his head, avoiding the branches and vines as he began to jog. The shouts of the wild men were close, maybe a hundred yards or so away through the forest. He could hear the undergrowth snapping as they forced their way through it, stealth abandoned now that the kill was close.

The Wyldermen might simply be hunting an animal, but Drew doubted it. His lupine senses told him this was almost certainly a hunt for a human. Be it one of their own or someone else, the Wolflord needed to discover the truth. He let the beast in as he ran, the transformation fluid with each step. His feet fell silently on the forest floor, the only sound that of his bones cracking within, reshaping beneath his shifting skin.

Dark shapes ran across his field of vision, two, then another, flitting between the trees as they pursued their target. Drew changed the angle of his run, hoping Red Rufus and Milo could follow but reluctant to wait. More of the wild men appeared, another pair farther away, a handful more behind the first three. None had noticed Drew shadowing them: their focus was entirely upon their prey. Drew loped along the floor, using his clawed right hand for extra purchase as he tore between the trees. His sword bounced in the scabbard on his hip, the gemstone pommel bouncing into his ribs with every stride. He'd overtaken the Wyldermen now but kept up his pace as he caught sight of their fleeing target. At first glance Drew thought him a boy, only realizing his mistake when the man glanced back, exhaustion etched on his leathery face, thin gray hair slick on his forehead.

Suddenly, the man came to a halt in a clearing, bending double to breathe in great gasps of air. *A man of Brackenholme perhaps?* Most of his clothes were torn from his body, and a tattered cloak hung from his shoulder. Drew slowed, now fully transformed, watching from less than ten yards away, completely hidden in the thick undergrowth. The wiry chap stood upright, staring at the forest back the way he'd come. *Keep running, old man! Don't give up!*

But the old man hadn't given up, Drew quickly realized. He winced, throwing his torn cloak back, reaching his left hand awkwardly to his hip where he took hold of the basket hilt of a rapier. Quick as a flash the blade was out. The man's right arm lay limp at his side, apparently broken. The torn clothes were more familiar to Drew now. He recognized them from his brief encounters with the man's people: Romari, a traveler. He carried a stringed musical instrument on his back, such as a minstrel might use. The man stood poised, legs apart, one behind the other, his chest turned sideways toward his advancing enemy, offering a smaller target for the wild men to hit. The rapier extended outward: *a gentleman's weapon*, Drew recalled, shocked by the absurdity of an old man surrounded by Wyldermen striking a fencing pose.

The tribesmen piled out from between the trees, ten in all, bumping into one another and spreading out. Red feathers adorned their heads and shoulders, bone necklaces jangling as they raised their axes and spears. Their skin was caked with oily mud, which covered them from head to toe. They hissed at the old Romari, who remained poised and elegant, as an assured calm settled over him. *If you're going to die, then die in style.* Drew had to admire the fellow, facing death so gracefully. *You've had a long life, old timer. Your days may be numbered, but this won't be your last.*

Before the Wyldermen could launch their attack, the undergrowth was ripped apart as the Werewolf leapt at them. Moonbrand was out, and the gloomy clearing glowed with a cold blue light. The tribesmen wailed, and even the old Romari looked fearful for a moment at the sight of the lycanthrope. The blade sliced down, cutting the first Wylderman across the belly before Drew ripped it out and slashed another. The Werewolf took hold of a wild man's arm in his jaws, snapping it instantly. Drew kicked out, his leg sending the next man flying, ribs crumpling with the impact. A pair of arrows whistled through the clearing in rapid succession, finding the exposed backs of two more and felling them on the spot. Suddenly the odds had swung against the men of the forest.

The Romari darted forward, jabbing his rapier awkwardly with his injured arm. One of the wild men went with him, trading blows, battering away at the old man with a heavy ax and sending him stumbling. Another red-feathered Wylderman jumped on Drew's back, his knife glancing off the side of the Werewolf's head, while the remaining two jabbed with their spears. Drew felt one of the flint-headed weapons cut into his chest, his thick, lycan ribs deflecting major injury though he still felt pain. He howled, snapping his head back, trying to reach the Wylderman who clung to him, an arm wrapped about his muscular throat. The knife went up again, and the blade bit into Drew's sword arm, so Moonbrand clattered to the icy ground.

Another lunge from the spearmen hit Drew's thigh, causing him to drop to one knee. His right hand was free now, while his left stump tried to parry the spears. He reached up, bloody gray fingers snatching at the fellow on his back. He grabbed him by the shoulder, his claws crunching through flesh, making the brute release his hold. As the first spearman came in, Drew spun where he crouched, whipping the Wylderman off his back and into the flint-headed weapon. The bone necklace rattled around the wild man's throat as the spear disappeared into his back. The second spearman took his chance at the distraction, his weapon speeding down toward the unguarded Werewolf.

Milo's sword slashed down, cutting the spear in two, splintering it in the Wylderman's hands before he could strike the Werewolf. This left the tip of the young Staglord's weapon buried in the hard earth. The Wylderman wasted no time, dropping the splintered spear to leap upon the fearful boy. Sharp, filed teeth snapped at Milo's face as he tried to hold the man back, but his opponent was too strong. The wild man's mouth yawned open as he brought his teeth down. The boy screamed, just as the man went limp. He landed lifelessly on top of Milo, an arrow protruding from his back. Red Rufus stepped out of the trees, nodding at the boy.

The last Wylderman stood facing the trio, his eyes flitting from Werewolf to boy to Hawklord. Drew noticed that the warrior's mouth was slick with blood, his sharp teeth coated with the red liquid as he grinned. The wild man let out a cry, hollering to the heavens as he raised his ax and charged at the lycanthrope. Drew brought Moonbrand back, about to run the man through, but before Drew could attack, the Wylderman's legs flew up as an arrow disappeared into his chest, sending him to the forest floor with a thump, his bloodied ax landing beside him.

Drew picked up the weapon, inspecting the gore on the flint head, his body slowly returning to human form. He looked back at his companions, expecting to see wounds but finding none. He brought his gaze back around, searching for the Romari in the clearing. They found him lying at the foot of a tree, his body resting in a cradle of exposed roots. His broken lute lay on the floor, his twisted, battered rapier cast aside. The old man's chest had been opened by an ax blow; his shirt was dark and wet, while his neck was torn, the flesh ripped from his throat. To Drew's amazement, the minstrel coughed, a splutter of bloody bubbles appearing on his lips.

"He lives," said Drew, crouching beside him.

The old Romari looked up, his jaw slack with wonderment as the lycanthrope's dark hair receded, his body shrinking in size as the Wolflord changed from beast to young man. Red Rufus and Milo joined Drew on either side of him.

"Drew Ferran?" gasped the old man, his voice a whisper.

"You know me?" said Drew, taking the old man's battered hand in his.

"I know *of* you: who doesn't?" he said, shifting awkwardly.

"Rest now," Drew said. "The Wyldermen are dead. You know my name, but I'm all the poorer for not knowing yours."

"Stirga," he spluttered. "But time is short. Brackenholme lies sacked. Your friends, Whitley and Gretchen; they're in grievous danger."

Drew's gray eyes burned with a sudden yellow fire as the Wolf threatened to return.

"You know Whitley and Gretchen? They're in Brackenholme?"

"They're dear to me. The Wolf is sacred to our people, my lord; a friend of the Wolf is a friend of ours."

Drew was sick with worry, the idea of Whitley and Gretchen being in danger making his head spin. So many questions to ask poor Stirga, but the old Romari's time was nearly up.

"How did the Wyldermen come to launch an attack on Brackenholme?" asked Red Rufus.

"The Wereserpent," said Stirga, his voice barely more than a sigh, his eyes struggling to focus on Drew. "Vala."

"Vala?" whispered Drew incredulously. He was transported briefly back to his encounter with the Wereserpent in the

Wyrmwood, when the monstrous therian had nearly killed him and his friends through coil, tooth, and poison.

"The city burns. The Wyldermen . . . it belongs to them now!"

Drew trembled with fear. "And my friends? What of Whitley and Gretchen?"

The Romari twitched his lips, his face draining of color. Milo dropped to his knees, fishing his waterskin from his backpack and pouring water between the old man's red lips. "Lady Whitley is a captive of Vala. Lady Gretchen . . . got out of there, with the aid of a Redcloak."

"A Redcloak?" said Drew.

"Said he was a Wolf's man," said Stirga, fading quickly now. Drew squeezed his hand, massaging his knuckles, willing the poor fellow to stay with them. "Played his part . . . got us out, and more," added the old man.

"These Wyldermen, Stirga," said Drew, staring at the slain warriors. "Were they all daubed this way, wearing clay and the like?"

"Some, my lord."

"It's Drew," he said. "Please, just Drew."

The Romari trembled, a cough rattling out of his savaged chest, his eyelids fluttering, threatening to close.

"Take the lute, Drew," Stirga whispered. "Was supposed . . . to write ballad . . . ballad of Yuzhnik . . . yet the long sleep comes. . . ."

Drew leaned close, his voice quiet as he brought his lips to the Romari's ears. "I shall see to it, Stirga, I swear to Brenn."

When he knelt upright, he looked back at the old minstrel. His eyes were closed, his head resting upon his shoulder as if asleep. Drew pulled his hand free from Stirga's death grip and swept his fingers across the old man's forehead, brushing the thin gray hair away from his brow.

"We'll bury him," Drew said. He didn't know the man, had exchanged just a few stolen words with him, yet he felt a pain in his heart as deep as a knife blow. He had lost a loved one, though he'd never known him.

"Aye," agreed Red Rufus as Milo simply stared at the slain Romari.

Drew glanced to one side at the nearest Wylderman body, reaching across and scraping a clump of clay from his flesh.

"I've an idea," he said, rolling the mud and feather in his hand. "And it may yet get us an audience with Vala."

8
THE CAMP OF
THE WHITE BEAR

THOUGH NOT THE palace of Icegarden, the Shepherds'
Hall was as welcome a sight for the travelers as any they might
have stumbled across on the frozen mountain slopes. Hall was
too grand a word to describe it, but it was a palace compared to
the cold outdoors. Ordinarily, the squat stone structure served
as a shelter for the brave folk who worked the Whitepeaks,
offering protection against storms when the wind and ice
became too much to endure. The cottage was crowded now,
with the White Bear's council joining him around the fire
pit as he welcomed his guests. Despite the fire's warmth, the
atmosphere remained chill.

"You've got some nerve, cousin," said Duke Henrik,
glowering across the flames at Bergan.

"We had nowhere else to go, nobody left to turn to," replied the Lord of Brackenholme curtly, the words catching in his throat. "Your kindness is greatly appreciated, Your Grace."

The two Bearlords were as different as chalk and cheese. Bergan's broad frame, though wasted by the trials he'd undergone, still marked him as a warrior among men. His thick red beard, thinning from malnourishment and peppered with gray, covered his entire jaw and throat, and his mouth was hidden beneath whiskers. Henrik was a good foot taller than his cousin, and lean with it. He was clean-shaven, his white hair cropped close to his scalp, a crown of plain Sturmish steel sitting tightly around his temples. His skin was smooth and unblemished as opposed to the craggy, weather-beaten flesh that puckered Bergan's face. The only feature they shared was the broad, flat nose that dominated their faces, and their eyes above locked intently upon one another.

"I can hardly turn you away under the circumstances now, can I?"

"So I'm not forgiven for whatever crimes you thought me guilty of so long ago?"

Henrik paused, considering his words, before raising a finger at Bergan.

"I hope your conscience gives you punishment enough for betraying Wergar. By letting the Lion into Westland, you might as well have opened the gates of Highcliff yourself for Leopold to take as his own. The poison that's spread across the

Seven Realms can be traced directly back to your cowardice, cousin."

"It wasn't cowardice!" said Bergan. "It was the only course of action! Wergar's warmongering in Omir had left his homeland near defenseless. Highcliff was Leopold's for the taking: I could have fought tooth and claw to hold back the Lion, but it would've been for naught."

"You could have at least tried. A valiant death might've been more honorable than a shamed existence."

Bergan growled, a rumbling sound that rattled through his expanding ribcage. When he spoke, his chunky white incisors were menacingly enlarged.

"Queen Amelie and her children were already Leopold's hostages. The Bastians *held* Highcliff. They offered me terms, which I passed on to Wergar. How was I to know that Leopold would renege on his word?"

"Those children were butchered by the Lion, just as Wergar was," said Henrik, the fire reflecting in his glaring eyes.

Bergan rose suddenly, feet stamping and sending up a shower of sparks from the fire pit. He towered over the flames, and Henrik leaned back as the Brown Bear of the Dyrewood threatened to explode in a therian rage. The White Bear's officers instantly unsheathed their weapons, ready to defend their liege, while Carver and Fry had their own blades ready. Hector and his Boarguard took a step away, eyes flitting between both groups, wary of what might happen. Duke Henrik raised his hand, palm out, calling his officers to halt.

"A day doesn't pass when I don't think of them! I loved Wergar as a brother, Amelie as a sister, and those children as my own!" Bergan roared, tears blinding him as he punched his chest. "Don't talk to me about the madness of Leopold and the crimes of yesterday, Henrik!"

He faltered where he stood, looking into the fire, his mind drifting to the past. The flames danced, sending him back to the throne room in Highcliff and the fire that had devoured the Wolf's children.

"I still see their faces," he whispered.

Henrik motioned with his hand, encouraging his cousin to be seated again, and the room grew calm once more as swords returned to sheaths and soldiers relaxed. Bergan collapsed, his gaze still locked on the flames, as Henrik spoke quietly.

"Please sit, cousin. It's clear the truth weighs heavy on your shoulders. The deeds of yesterday will haunt us all long into tomorrow."

The room descended into silence momentarily, the only sounds coming from outside as Sturmish troops went about their business. Bergan slowly regathered his senses, the doubts and denials that had haunted him fresh in his mind. He'd tried to convince himself that his actions had been just, for the good of the Seven Realms. He still didn't know whether he'd been fooling himself. Perhaps he *had* been a coward. Perhaps he *had* persuaded Wergar to surrender to Leopold simply to protect his people in Brackenholme against the Lion's rage. The more he thought about it, the more questions arose, as was always the case. There wasn't one particular reason for handing the Wolf over to the Lion: there had been many. But the horror that followed had been entirely unexpected. One thing was certain: Bergan would never trust a Catlord again.

"You've stepped in from the cold, then?" said the Lord of Brackenholme finally. "You fight by our side?"

"I fight for Sturmland," said Henrik, his mood less antagonistic after his cousin's show of remorse.

Bergan bit his lip. *Is that all he wanted? Did he need to see me weep for what I've done?*

"All the letters the Wolf Council sent you, and no reply? Couldn't you see we needed you to fight the Bastians?"

"I saw a group of Werelords building an empire. You, the Stags, and that loathsome Vega; how was I to know the threat from Bast was real?"

"We served the Wolf, Henrik; Drew was the only surviving son of Wergar, and we were duty-bound to protect him. He was the rightful king."

"You speak in the past tense, Bergan. Are we assuming this boy, true son of the Wolf or not, is dead?"

"We don't know, Your Grace," said Hector, causing all heads to turn. The Boarlord cleared his throat, coughing into his gloved left hand. Bergan noticed for the first time that there was a hole in the dark leather. Hector must have picked up a wound in the melee with the Skirmishers. "Lord Drew went missing when Cape Gala was seized by the Catlords; his whereabouts are unknown. Many fear our friend is dead."

"You're Huth's son," said Henrik, looking him up and down. "Hector, isn't it?"

Hector bowed. "Indeed, Your Grace. I'm at your service."

"Your father was a good and kind man," said Henrik. "You're a magister, I hear? A fine one at that, so they say."

"I am, though I'm still learning."

"You should speak with my sister, Lady Greta," said Henrik, glancing over his shoulder toward a tall, white-haired woman who stood at the rear of the chamber. The officers moved around her, allowing her to step forward. She carried in her hands a white metal gauntlet, fashioned in the style of a bear's paw. Her hand traced a line over the runes that covered its surface, strange symbols that hinted at magicks. Bergan recognized the gauntlet instantly: the White Fist of Icegarden, the enchanted weapon that Ragnor, Henrik's father, used to wear into battle.

Hector bowed once again. "You are a magister also, my lady?"

"Indeed," she replied, smiling warmly. She handed the gauntlet to her brother. "Alchemy's my discipline. The Daughters of Icegarden have always been married to the mountain, wedded to the steel that serves our people so well. We should speak, Baron Hector, once you've rested."

"She could teach you a thing or two, I daresay," added Henrik. He was silent for the briefest moment. "I never exchanged a cross word with the old baron, Hector. I'm sorry for your loss."

"It was the Lionguard's swords that took Huth from us," said Bergan, hoping that mention of the Catlords' vile actions might further strengthen their accord.

Henrik grunted, shaking his head. He put his left hand inside the White Fist, his fingers finding their way to the ends of the metal glove.

"Seems this young Lion's reach is long, and he now has the added muscle of the Werepanther."

After their rescue by the White Bear and his cavalry, Bergan's small troop had been escorted beyond the barricades, disappearing into the heart of Duke Henrik's war camp. While the White Bear had been silent as they'd trudged through the snow to the Shepherds' Hall, his officers had been happy to inform Bergan of their situation. The full might of the Sturmish army had assembled on the slopes. A skeleton crew remained in Icegarden itself, enough to man the walls and gates, but all eyes were on the mighty force that had gathered in the southern foothills. Onyx's army was a threat to Sturmland, and they were to meet them head-on. If the Beast of Bast wanted to take the Whitepeaks, he'd sorely underestimated Sturmish resolve. One cavalry officer had told Bergan that the mountains would be the undoing of the Bastians. The Bearlord prayed he was right.

"When did Onyx arrive in your foothills?" asked Bergan, keen to hear what had happened.

"They've worked their way up gradually. First the Dalelands, I'm afraid," he said, glancing at Hector. "Once Onyx had seized the Great West Road, he was free to move through the Badlands. Muller's rabble welcomed him and quickly fell in line. A considerable part of his army headed east, according to our scouts, with the Stags of the Barebones their likely target. I can't imagine Manfred's folk were able to put up much of a fight. More still joined the Doglords as they returned to Omir, to help take Azra from King Faisal. The Rats, Crows, and Skirmishers have bolstered Onyx's ranks enormously. So it looks grim all around for the Seven Realms."

"Your news leaves a bad taste," muttered Bergan, dismayed at the ill tidings.

"There is some good. Word has reached us that the Catlords' navy is in disarray. Piracy is afoot in the White Sea, and many Bastian ships have already been scuttled. Rumor has it that Baron Bosa, of all the salty old souls, is behind the attacks."

"Bosa?" exclaimed Hector, his voice cracking with surprise.

"Indeed," replied Henrik. "Much as I'd hoped my people might avoid the wrath of the Catlords, it seems the Werewhale of Moga had hoped for the same. Wishful thinking, eh? Still, it's good the old pirate has got off his fat behind and found his way back into the ocean. Brenn knows what stirred him into life, whether it was the Bastians landing on his doorstep or some other foul deed, but it's grand to know there's someone else on our side."

"You were there yourself, weren't you, Hector?" said Bergan. "Marooned up there by Vega. The Sharklord has Manfred and Queen Amelie aboard the *Maelstrom*, so our young friend informs me. I know you were never fond of Vega, Henrik, but try to put your concerns to the back of your mind. He's come to good in the end, as have many of us," he added.

Henrik arched an eyebrow.

"I'll never trust a Sharklord, less still one who proved to be such a turncoat. Vega will get what's coming to him one day, mark my word, cousin."

"As I said, he's changed. I can't say what the cause was: perhaps Drew."

"This Drew seems to have had a profound effect on all who've met him. I haven't found anyone who is indifferent to mention of his name. It seems the Bastians have an aversion to the young Wolf that borders on the psychotic, while you speak of him like a messiah."

"He's a rare breed, Henrik," said Bergan, his earnest voice thick with passion. "The Wolf is a noble beast, one of the first of Brenn's children; Drew's soul is as rich and pure as that of any of the Werelords who dined at the first Great Feast. Wergar's blood courses through his veins. Yet it is tempered. He was raised by humans, oblivious to his parentage. His understanding of the world is . . . different from our own. Wergar was stubborn, his world a tapestry of black and white, friends and enemies. This boy wants justice for all, equality between human and therian." Bergan smiled, thinking back fondly to the discussions he and Drew had often enjoyed, sometimes endured. "He sees all the shades of gray."

"A freethinker? Dangerous thing for a king to be." Henrik laughed. "Well, let's pray to Brenn the boy turns up and isn't lost to us." He raised the White Fist of Icegarden and clenched it, the shining steel claws disappearing into the paw's palm. "I'd like to shake that Wolf's paw!"

Henrik rose, as one of his men secured a long white cloak to the shoulders of his breastplate.

"I must take my leave, my lords. I need to inspect the lines before nightfall and hear the scouts' reports. You're most welcome to journey on to Icegarden; I can send a handful of outriders with you. You'll find little there—the old city's a bit of a ghost town at present. It's down here where all the fighting will happen."

"If you don't mind, cousin, we'll remain here with you," said Bergan. "This is our fight as well."

"You don't look fit to stand, let alone do battle, old Bear," said Henrik, grinning at last. It had been twenty years since the Lord of Icegarden had graced Bergan with his rare smile.

"You've food here?" said Bergan. "Feed me and let me sleep. I'll be fit to face anything those foul felinthropes dare throw our way. Besides, you look a bit low on numbers," he joked. "I reckon you could do with our help."

"Very well, stay on the front line and turn down my offer of a warm bath. I'll have my men find tents for you and yours. I couldn't help but notice," said Henrik, lowering his voice as he stepped closer to Bergan, "that you have Ugri warriors among your number. You do realize they have an unfortunate history with my people? Slotha and I have never seen eye to eye."

"Slotha's dead," said Hector, cutting into the conversation. "The Lion saw to that. Her people are being hunted by Lucas's forces as we speak. The men you saw outside have sought my stewardship, Your Grace; they're members of my Boarguard. They can be trusted."

"I hope you don't come to regret your choice of guard, then, Baron Hector," said Henrik, his brow knotted with concern. "They're brutal, the Ugri. The only language they understand is that of violence."

Hector smiled. "Then I'll endeavor to educate them, Your Grace."

Bergan stepped toward the Boarlord, taking his left wrist in his hand. "I see you picked up a war wound, my boy. You get that scratch in the fight back there?" he asked, nodding at the torn leather of his glove. Hector tugged his hand free, placing his right palm over it.

"Indeed," he replied, his voice strained. "If it's all the same with you, my lords, could I move straight on to Icegarden? I'm not sure there's a great deal I can add to the cause here. After all, I'm a mere magister."

"There's nothing trifling about a magister," said Lady Greta. "Your healing hands could do some good here."

"Then if I may, let me visit your wonderful city briefly, treat my injuries, then return."

Henrik and Bergan looked at one another, seeing no problem with Hector's suggestion.

"Very well," said the White Bear. "The outriders shall escort you. Return to us when you're recovered. There'll be little to entertain you in Icegarden."

Hector bowed to the three therians in turn before embracing Bergan.

"Take care, Hector," whispered Bergan. "A friend such as you is precious. I want to keep you close. Keep you safe."

Bergan kissed his cheek. Hector seemed taken aback.

"Yes . . . yes, Your Grace. I'll be careful." The young magister pulled away from Bergan and managed a smile before turning and walking out of the Shepherd's Hall, returning to the remainder of his Boarguard.

Henrik and Greta stepped away from Bergan and his companions, keen to speak with their officers regarding the day's business. Bergan spied a platter of cooked meats that had been prepared and brought through by a servant. The Bearlord took the metal tray from the surprised man, smiling as he stole it.

"I think we can take care of things from here," said Bergan, snatching up a charcoaled drumstick and tearing into it with his teeth. Captain Fry joined him, whipping a piece from the platter and setting to work as the two of them sat down once more. Only Carver didn't join them, instead staring at the door after Hector.

"You're not hungry, Carver?" said Bergan through a mouthful of chicken.

"I've an appetite, all right," replied the tattooed rogue. "But something irks me."

"Speak your mind."

"I don't trust your Boarlord."

"What's not to trust?" asked Bergan, wiping the juices from his beard with the back of his hand.

"This Boarguard he keeps. I know two of them from back in Highcliff: Ringlin and Ibal. Cutthroats, the pair of them. And as for the Ugri he travels with . . . Fry, you said yourself they can't be trusted."

The Sturmlander cleared his throat.

"Not in my eyes, no, but I wouldn't presume to know better than Baron Hector. They fought alongside us, remember?

They've put Skirmishers in the ground on a few occasions now, first in the ravine and then on the slopes. The baron's proved himself to us. Perhaps you could show a little more faith in him?"

Carver shook his head slowly.

"No. I don't like it. It was all rather convenient, him stumbling across us in that gulch as he did."

"You're a distrustful curmudgeon," grunted Bergan, biting into his fourth drumstick. "What would you have us do?"

"Let me head to the city. Keep an eye on him."

"You really feel this strongly about Hector?"

"Let's just say I'm a good judge of character. I've met enough rogues and seen enough treachery in my time. I've been responsible for a fair share, too, I might add."

"Treachery's a strong word," said Bergan, waving a fifth drumstick at the Thief-lord.

Carver snatched it from his fingertips. "Then let's hope I'm wrong, eh?"

He walked to the door, pausing to add, "There's a first time for everything."

With that, he departed, the snow swirling over the threshold before the door slammed shut at his back.

9

THE SERPENT REVEALED

WHILE THE SURVIVING members of Brackenholme court slept huddled around the Bearlord's throne, a solitary figure sat before them on the steps, keeping a lonely vigil. Three nights ago, the Wereserpent had come for one of their number, dragging the screaming boy away into the darkness. The group had fought back, trying to wrestle their companion free from the monster, but to no avail. The Wyldermen had closed ranks, striking the prisoners with spears and axes, forcing them back as their dark mistress disappeared with her meal. From that moment on, the survivors had agreed to keep watch: they wouldn't let Vala take one of them again so easily.

Whitley squinted, peering through the gloom that smothered the giant chamber. The fire pit in front of her father's dais had burned low, the wild men having allowed their prisoners the small luxury of a fragile flame. She could hear the Wyldermen moving and muttering beyond the giant pile of broken furniture that was heaped in the center of the room—chairs, heirlooms, curtains, paintings, beams, and floorboards. Initially the young Werelady had assumed they were building some kind of bonfire, that the wild men intended to burn Brackenholme's residents within their most revered hall. How wrong she had been. The Wyldermen now kept their distance from the ramshackle structure; only one of them was allowed anywhere near the pile, and Whitley recognized him well enough. He sat on top of the heap, faintly visible. As the Bearlady watched the room, so the wild man watched her.

A noise came from within the heart of the debris, causing Whitley's eyes to fix upon it. She rose to her feet, poised and prepared to call for her companions and alert them to forthcoming danger. The last thing she wanted to do was disturb her mother and the others: sleep had been difficult enough to come by, and any stolen moments of rest were precious. Up above, the Wylderman stood as the shadows parted below. Splintered planks groaned as something emerged from the twisted mass; torn drapes were pushed to one side as the occupant of the mountain of detritus appeared. The monster had slithered out of the heap frequently since making the hall its home, each time sending a wave of terror over the captive folk of Brackenholme, yet now it chose to leave its beast form behind. It was an old woman who clambered slowly out of the Wereserpent's nest.

"Gracious, my dear," said Vala. "Have they got you keeping watch again? Shouldn't it be someone else's turn? You must be exhausted!"

Whitley watched as the bent old woman came closer, stepping slowly through the darkness. The fire pit's glowing coals dimly illuminated her as she approached, a long, tattered shawl blanketing her, cowled about her face. This was the first occasion since they'd arrived in the woodland city that Vala had appeared as a human. The Serpent had cast aside her disguise of a Romari baba, reveling in the horror the sight of the Wyrm caused among her captives. For her to appear again as Korga no doubt meant more trickery, Whitley reasoned.

"You come to taunt me, Vala?" asked Whitley warily. "Tired so soon of slithering around on your belly?"

The twin sensations of fear and anger gripped her, the hairs on her arms tingling. She searched for the Bear in her heart, hoping the beast might come to her aid should she need it. She still lacked the control that the male therianthropes had mastered, that even Gretchen had some understanding of. She faced the monster alone.

"Oh, this?" the old woman cackled, passing a withered hand across her covered face in the gloom. "You were quite fond of dear old Korga, weren't you? I thought her reappearance would spark a warm glow in you, rekindling the fondness that we once held for each other."

Whitley managed a nervous laugh.

"Did the baba ever even exist?"

"Oh, she lived well enough. At least until Darkheart and I encountered her caravan on the edge of the Wyrmwood." She looked up briefly toward the Wylderman who stood on top of her nest, waving with a scrawny hand. "Your friends have a lot to answer for; his father was the shaman your Wolf killed, whose spirit your Piglord tortured. I'd ask him to join us, be Rolff for you again, for old times' sake, but he'd sooner sever his own throat with a blunt flint than play the filthy Romari again."

Whitley glowered at the wild man's silhouette, a statue in the dark. *I trusted them so much. This is all my fault. I brought them here.*

"You still blame yourself, don't you?" said Vala, as if reading the young Werelady's thoughts. "For my being here?"

The old woman settled on the floor on the other side of the fire pit, her movements awkward and ungainly. Whitley watched her, noticing that there was something different about Vala's body shape, even in the baba's guise.

"You shouldn't," the crone went on. "This would all have come to pass anyway. It is not just your misfortune that has brought me into the heart of your father's city, Bearchild. It's the misfortune of every Werelord who has made an enemy of me down the years. Now they fight and bicker with one another, providing me with the opportunity to strike at their homelands. And they shall all suffer in time, as my people grow in strength and number, as they rally to my call from across the Dyrewood and beyond. Your lords of Westland, the Woodland Realm, the Dalelands and farther afield: all are guilty of antagonizing the Wyldermen over my long lifetime."

"It is you and your people who are the monsters!" snapped Whitley. "Burning farmsteads, slaughtering families, butchering merchants on the Dyre Road; the Wyldermen are *cannibals*—they don't belong anywhere *near* civilized society!"

"They have lived in the forests as long as any human has walked this earth," hissed Vala, lurching forward over the fire pit, her gnarled hands holding her upright as the glowing coals lit her scarred face from below. Her right eye had been replaced by a puckered black socket, Gretchen having left an indelible, savage mark on the Wereserpent. "The Dyrewood was their realm once, and it shall be theirs again henceforth. The time of the Bearlords is over."

Whitley could see what was so unusual about the woman now. Vala was misshapen and malformed, her body rippling as she moved, her belly distended. It was as if her transformation had been unsuccessful, so that elements of the snake remained fused to her human form. Whitley recoiled at the sight, and Vala noticed her reaction.

"My stomach?" The old woman laughed, yanking the shawl to one side so the girl could better see it. The bile rose in Whitley's throat as she saw hard, irregular shapes jutting out of Vala's torso, like broken bones threatening to burst out of a bag of flesh. As the faux-baba moved, so the lumps and disfigurements shifted, grating against one another.

Vala continued. "It takes me a while to digest a meal . . . certainly a big one like that boy. This human form isn't ideal for my metabolism, which made dining terribly awkward for the last few months. I had to regurgitate one of the wretches one night when we rode through the Dyrewood. Thankfully my dear Darkheart was there to dispose of the child's body."

Whitley heaved now, her own stomach knotting as she realized the reason for Vala's bizarre shape. Her mind raced back to their journey toward Brackenholme, through the Longridings, as they made their way up the Dyre Road toward her home. Vala had spent the entire journey hiding in the back of her caravan, beneath a pile of blankets, her body out of sight. There had been so many abductions while the old baba had been in their company, so many unexplained disappearances.

"The children—" began Whitley, but Vala was ahead of her already.

"Even masquerading as a Romari witch, I had to eat. I can pick at a bowl of soup or stew like the rest of you, but it provides no sustenance. At the end of the day, it's *live* food a Serpent desires."

"You murderous monster," snarled Whitley, wiping tears from her eyes.

"This is not murder," corrected Vala, smoothing a hand over her deformed body. "I kill to eat, I eat to live; that is the nature of things, the hunter and her prey. I obey my instincts, and my instincts rightly tell me that humans are food."

"Is there even a shred of humanity inside you?" said Whitley, shaking her head sorrowfully.

"Beyond the boy in my belly?" The Wereserpent laughed. "None at all, and why should there be? I am pure therianthrope, Bearchild. To wish for human traits would be to pine for weakness. Perhaps that is where you Children of Brenn differ from my kind."

"Your kind?" asked Whitley wearily.

"The Old Therians, from a time before your Brenn and his Great Feasts. You and your Werelords would tremble before my kind. The Bears, the Wolves, the Lions, the Hawks; you think you *own* the earth, starting wars, making laws, believing that yours is the only kind of civilization the world has ever known. There was a time when your kind were ours to command, no better than humans in our eyes. In the Age of Dragonlords, it was we who ruled. And we may yet rule again. You bleat about humanity as if it's a gift," she scoffed. "It is as good as a curse. You are *all* weak in the eyes of an Old Therian such as I."

Whitley sat down finally, grief overwhelming her tired body. She dropped her head, trying to stifle her emotions.

"That's right, girl," said Vala, her voice quiet but animated. "Let it all out. Don't bottle it up any longer. Sob for your sorry situation. Your cause is lost. Hope? You have none."

Vala's poisonous words whispered across the fire pit, each one cutting into Whitley's soul, choking the life out of her resolve. She had endured so much while trying to get back home after losing her father and brother. And all for naught: she had brought a killer into her mother's welcoming arms.

"Know this, little ursanthrope; I shall make the end swift for you when it comes. Perhaps there is a semblance of humanity in me after all. I found you strangely enjoyable company while we traveled together, Bearchild; your wide-eyed innocence was quite entertaining. I might actually be sorry to see you dead when the time comes—it's too soon to tell for sure— but die you must as a friend to the Wolf."

"You wait for him to come, yet he could be dead!" Whitley sniffed, her head still in her hands. "He may *never* come, and then what? All this shall have been for nothing!"

"All for nothing? I have Brackenholme!" said the Wyrm. "No, he shall come. And once he arrives here, I promise I shall make it quick. I shall not make you suffer. Nor your mother."

Whitley was up and on her feet in a split second, her toes kicking the hot coals up from the fire so they showered the old woman. Vala struggled away from the pit's edge, brushing the embers from her shawl and flesh, hissing all the while, but the Bearlady of Brackenholme was still moving. Her hand closed around Vala's throat, and her fingertips had transformed into curving black blades.

"You will not *touch* my mother," Whitley growled, the words coming out low and bestial.

Vala looked up and grinned as Darkheart appeared at her side, knives in each hand, eyes fixed upon Whitley. "You think you can threaten me, Lady Whitley?"

Other Wyldermen began to appear, following their chieftain out of the shadows from around the Wereserpent's nest.

"You spare my mother's life, Vala," Whitley snarled, shaking the old snake by the throat. "Swear it!" she shouted.

Instantly the other captives on the dais awoke, rising around Duke Bergan's throne, blinking as their eyes adjusted to the horror in the darkness. Vala chuckled, a low, throaty rattle, as the wild men fanned out, stalking past Whitley and closer toward her fellow prisoners.

"Release me, Bearchild," hissed Vala, the menace and threat all too evident. Her one good eye stared past the young lady, following the movements of her men through the chamber.

Whitley glanced back, catching sight of her mother, Duchess Rainier, standing defensively in front of her courtiers as the Wyldermen circled them, weapons raised. Whitley released her grip on the old crone's throat, dashing back toward her companions and into her mother's arms. She glared at Vala as the old woman massaged her neck with a bony hand.

"So, little Bear." She chuckled. "You do have claws after all."

IO
COMMON GROUND

BIRDSONG DRIFTED THROUGH the swaying branches
that encircled the glade, sunlight fluttering through the canopy and
sending drops of gold dancing across the grass. Gretchen lay on her back,
staring skyward, her face fixed in a contented grin. This was her glade,
her secret refuge from court life in Hedgemoor. Many of her earliest
memories revolved around the clearing; her mother had brought her here
when she was little more than a babe in arms. She had missed the place,
had been away from home for far too long. She let the sun's warmth
wash over her, creeping through every fiber of her being. A shape passed
before it, casting her into shadow. Her disappointment instantly shifted
to a feeling of joy, when she recognized the face above as Drew's. Her
Drew. How had he found her? She couldn't remember having brought
him to Hedgemoor before. He stared down at her, the heat from the sun

fading fast around them, his shadow growing, as darkness spread across the clearing. With the shadow came the cold, bitter and biting. He wasn't smiling. This wasn't her Drew. She'd never taken him to Hedgemoor. His mouth opened slowly, revealing a row of jagged, serrated teeth as he moved to kiss her. . . .

Gretchen woke with a scream, a hand clamping over her mouth to cut it short. For the briefest moment she felt relief that it had been only a nightmare, until she realized she'd woken to one as well. The world was still grim, and their prospects bleak. The hand over her mouth was that of "Redcloak," as she'd come to call him; she knew his true name now well enough, but he'd responded to the other, so the nickname had stuck. Trent Ferran; human brother to Drew, the Wolflord who had stolen her heart.

The two of them lay among the bare roots of a fallen sycamore, their only shelter against the wind and snow. The tree had fallen into a shallow pit in the earth, which was the closest they'd come to a forest clearing for days. The only warmth was that of Redcloak's body up against her back, an arm round her waist holding her close. His scarlet cloak was draped over them, providing meager protection against the elements, but something nonetheless. Her breath steamed between his filthy fingers, drifting into the frosty air as his lips brushed her ear.

"Hush," whispered Redcloak, removing his hand from her mouth. "You were dreaming."

She felt her heart speeding, beating out of control. She had lost track of the days. The oppressive gloom of the Dyrewood was never ending, sapping their spirits. Constantly on the run from the Wyldermen, they rested only when exhausted, hoping that they had put enough distance between themselves and their hunters. It was difficult to tell where the terrors of the waking world ended and the nightmares began; her mind and spirit were under constant duress. Despite the continuing horror, she was thankful for one thing: Redcloak.

"Easy now, my lady," he said, shifting where he lay to allow her to roll back into the spot he'd vacated. It wasn't much, but there was a degree of warmth there, waiting for her, and she allowed him to put his arm back across her, straightening the ragged red cloak. "Another nightmare?"

Gretchen didn't answer, instead staring up at the cloudless sky, her breath steaming, lit by the stars.

"I'm sorry, my lady," he said awkwardly. "The hand . . . your mouth. It's just . . . your voice was rising. I was afraid if you screamed you might alert them."

Them: the Wyldermen. Their hopes of outrunning the chasing pack of wild men had come to nothing. On each occasion that the two had allowed themselves to relax, daring to believe they'd evaded the tribe of killers, their haunting calls would echo through the Dyrewood.

"No matter, Redcloak," she said, managing to smile. "I'd much prefer your filthy fingers across my face to a Wylderman's hands about my throat. Thank you."

He settled down once again beside her, tentatively moving closer to her, expelling the cold air that was gathering between their bodies. She felt his rough chin settle against the small of her neck, his hot breath behind her ear. At any other time, in any other place, she might have giggled or cringed at such a sensation, would have found his proximity intrusive. In some societies a commoner would be flogged or worse for behaving in this way with his betters. But this wasn't the place or time, and Redcloak was anything but common.

The initial frostiness between the two of them had thawed, although, as Brenn was her witness, Redcloak still had the ability to irritate Gretchen. Slowly, the two had lowered their guard in each other's company, the bickering growing less with the passing days. They found common ground to talk about: their childhoods—Gretchen's in Hedgemoor and Trent's on the Cold Coast, growing up on the farm with Drew. They could talk about their present situation, what their next step should be, what they might eat.

The one subject they avoided was the fate of Drew. Each feared the worst, rumors having reached them on their travels. Gretchen found herself guarded whenever Redcloak asked about Drew. She couldn't be sure why; she trusted him now, for sure. What was she afraid of? Did she fear she would jinx the small hope she had that Drew yet lived? Perhaps that's why she continued calling Trent "Redcloak." He was still a soldier, a virtual stranger. That name allowed her to keep a distance. To call him Trent would be an invitation for him to grow closer, and there was only room for one Ferran in her heart.

"It'll be dawn soon," he said. "I should probably get moving, check the traps and snares."

Redcloak was an ingenious youth, clearly with the same sharp mind as Drew. He'd fashioned snares from strips of saddle leather, which brought him mixed success in capturing small game: rabbits, rats, whatever the Dyrewood had to offer, which wasn't much. Thus far the sum total of their captured animals had consisted of two squirrels and a very large toad. There were other hunters snatching the lion's share of pickings: birds of prey, wolves, even the fabled Dyrecat, the forest's alpha predator. Redcloak and Gretchen had to make do with the leftovers, and even then only inedible ones or those foolish enough to have wandered into his crude traps.

"Can we not rest a little longer?" Gretchen sighed.

"Three things on that front, my lady," said Redcloak. "First, there's the small matter of the wild men. They'll be up and moving now, I guarantee it. Second, if I *don't* go and check my snares now, you can be sure they'll be picked clean. And last, and most important, you're a Werefox. How about helping by changing into a fox so you can catch us some breakfast?"

Gretchen laughed at this.

"I've told you," she scoffed. "The Fox only comes out when my safety depends upon it. Catching squirrels is hardly life and death!"

"You laugh, but a tasty squirrel could be that very thing. We may starve to death before the Wyldermen get their claws into us."

"How's your shoulder, Redcloak?"

"Hurts like sin. It throbs. It aches. The itch is incessant. I want to scratch it, tear the cursed scab from my shoulder. I can't sleep on it without feeling as if there's a knife twisting in my back. Every time I exert myself I fear the wound will tear open anew. But I'll live. Tell me if I start moaning, won't you?"

She sensed he was grinning.

"Thank you," said Redcloak.

"For what?"

"For seeing to the wound. I've heard mention of Wyldermen lacing their weapons with poison; looks like I was fortunate enough to be shot by a regular barbed arrow. Small mercies, eh?"

He sat upright, letting the crimson cloak fall away. Gretchen snatched at it, pulling it over herself as the cold leached into her skin.

"Come on, my lady," he said, hauling himself stiffly to his feet. "We need to think about making tracks."

"Making tracks? That's the last thing we need to do, surely, with Wyldermen following us?"

"A turn of phrase; blame my father."

Gretchen followed Redcloak's lead and sat upright as he stood over her, trying to stamp life into his frozen feet. He rubbed his hands together clumsily, willing warmth into his palms without success. His teeth chattered, and the young soldier grimaced as he tried to lock his jaws and prevent their traitorous rattling. The cold was bitter, and his extremities were suffering in these conditions. Gretchen's therian constitution stood her in good stead; her hardy animal side helped her to withstand extraordinary weather conditions. But Redcloak had no such luxury. Human blood coursed through his body, and with it human frailty. She watched him as he persevered, wincing with discomfort as he tried to flex his frigid fingers. For all the pain he was in, he wouldn't admit it to her.

"I suppose the winter also reminds you of the Cold Coast, then?"

"This?" said Redcloak, sniffing, stepping over to where they'd secured Storm to a nearby tree. "This is nothing. Bit of a chill is all. We'll be all right once the sun comes up."

She knew his words were bravado. The sun was a long way from showing its face, and they'd be lucky if any rays found their way through the tangle of trees to the forest floor. She allowed herself a moment to look at him as he brushed his horse's coat, his hands trembling. His fingers looked blue and bruised, surely not a good sign. *Had he even been under that cloak in the night?* His chivalry knew no bounds, and Gretchen couldn't help but feel ashamed.

"Here," she said, handing him the cloak. "Take a moment to get warm. I'll find the traps and check if Brenn has blessed us while we slept."

Redcloak grimaced, speaking through clenched teeth, struggling to stop their chatter. "Let me check the snares; I know where I left them, my lady."

"I might not be able to hunt like a Fox, but I do still have a keen sense of smell," she said, twitching her nose for him to see.

A distant cry stopped their banter instantly. It sounded like a capercaille to Gretchen, a bird familiar from her childhood that could be found on the moors in the Dalelands. She glanced at Redcloak, looking hopefully to him for a comforting nod, a wink to confirm her hopes that it was just a bird's cry. He stared back grimly, his jaw still set, but his blue eyes without humor.

"Take the cloak, my lady," he said, offering it back to her as she set off into the woods to check the traps.

"No," she called back as she hurried on her way, desperate that they should get moving once again, aware that every moment they delayed increased the chances that the outrider might freeze to death. "It's your cloak, Trent. Please wear it. For me."

PART V

THE GAME AND THE GAMBIT

I

THE WOLF IN WYLDERMAN'S CLOTHING

AT FIRST GLANCE the mist looked like any other, hanging over Brackenholme like a deathly gray shroud. The Great Trees, once visible to anyone approaching the city, were obscured by the impenetrable fog. The glow of occasional campfires caught the three travelers' attention out among the burned meadows that had once flourished beyond the palisade walls. The shouts and laughter of Wyldermen echoed all around, permeating the mist, adding to the sense of dread that followed their every step. It was only when they entered the fog bank that they realized this was no trick of the weather. They were surrounded by smoke: Brackenholme smoldered.

Drew led the way, Milo close behind, with Red Rufus bringing up the rear. They walked in single file, heads down but alert. They had already passed one group of wild men, their markings singling them out as a different clan from the ones who had hunted Stirga, blue woad circles painted over their torsos. No word had passed between them, nods sufficing as one tribe passed another. It was a blessing that the Wyldermen came from all over the Dyrewood, each with a variant of Wyld speech, none identical. While Drew and Red Rufus were almost naked, Milo wore two of the filthy animal-skin cloaks they'd pulled from the corpses, concealing his breastplate beneath. Along with the fallen Romari's lute, the rest of their equipment had been left with the horses, hidden off the Dyre Road a good distance away. The only item Drew had brought was Moonbrand, but the sword's handle and scabbard were swaddled in rags across his back.

He looked back at his companions, each caked in the foul dark clay that they'd scraped off the slain Wyldermen, their hair braided with the bright red feathers they'd scavenged. Their bare feet trudged through the churned-up snow, each painful step taking them deeper into the enemy camp. Light snow swirled around them, almost invisible through the mist, tiny white crystals that alighted on their mud-encrusted bodies. They were an odd-looking trio of wild men for sure, but Drew prayed that their ruse would get them through the Dyre Gate. If not, their rescue attempt would be over before it had begun. The whites of his friends' eyes glinted from their dark masks, and their attention was focused on him. They looked to him for direction, for decisions. Even Red Rufus had come around to the notion that the young Wolf was a capable leader, if a little young. The respect of the Hawklord had been hard-earned. Drew checked himself, his pink flesh obscured by the muddy paint. The stakes couldn't be higher, the trio risking everything with their plan. *Please, Brenn; let this work.*

The Dyre Gate materialized out of the mist ahead, its doors still hanging broken just as Stirga had described. Torches burned atop the towers on either side, the vague shapes of Wyldermen shifting behind the stake ramparts. A crowd of them had set up their camp within the heart of the battered gate, their makeshift settlement spilling across the Dyre Road between the towers. As they approached, the smell of cooking meat greeted them, the crackling glow of a bonfire spluttering behind the city walls. The smell was vaguely familiar, reminding Drew of hog roast. He swallowed back the bile, common sense battling with the hunger that gnawed in his belly. The Wolflord knew full well that the wild men's favored food walked on two legs, not four.

Drew glanced at his companions again. Milo's eyes were wide and white, the boy struggling to fight back the growing anxiety as it clawed its way up from the pit of his belly. Behind him, Red Rufus was showing no hint of the fear Drew felt, whether or not he shared it. His head may have been bowed, but his eyes were alert as they stepped over the city's threshold. His hand reached out, bony knuckles clenching briefly over Milo's shoulder in a reassuring squeeze of comfort. Drew gulped hard, his throat dry. *Stay calm, Milo, or you'll be the death of us all.*

Three Wyldermen emerged through the smoky mist, each carrying axes, blocking their path. Drew's stomach rolled: his overwhelming desire was to either run or fight. Neither would help them reach Whitley. He *had* to get past the guards and into the city. One of them muttered a harsh noise followed by a brief wave. *A greeting?* Drew did his best to mimic the wild man's utterance, raising his hand with the same gesticulation. The Wylderman nodded, stepping to one side, allowing the three to pass.

Drew stepped between them, the filthy snow stabbing at the soles of his feet and making him long for the comfort of his sturdy boots. They were back with Bravado, folded inside his cloak, hidden away with the rest of his clothes. He kept his gaze on the gate guards, sneering and lifting his jaw in a show of confidence. He knew enough about the Wyldermen to understand that their interactions revolved around posturing and confrontation. If they saw anything in his behavior that didn't match the demeanor of a Wylderman, the game would be up. Two of the wild men turned away, while the one who spoke kept his eyes on Drew. A look passed between them: two warriors showing respect. Drew was grateful the man kept his eyes on him and not the others—of all of them he was the one who could best pass for a wild man with his dark hair, tanned skin, and athletic body. The others sloped by, masked in mud and scabby animal skins, avoiding the lead Wylderman's challeng-ing glare. Finally, the man turned, following his companions as they sloped back toward the ruined gatehouse.

"Good thing you speak their language," whispered Milo as they left the Wyldermen behind.

"Good thing I can mimic animal sounds," said Drew. "How far to the Great Oak?"

"I thought you'd been here before?"

Drew sucked his teeth, trying to stop them from chattering. "On that occasion I was a guest in the cells of the Garrison Tree. No, I don't know the place, but I know the people well enough. Good men and women."

They marched on, deeper into Brackenholme's heart. Far-ther campfires shone dimly, dotting the land that surrounded the Great Trees and the city proper. Abandoned, blackened homesteads appeared through the smog, the fate of their oc-cupants too grim to imagine. No sooner had the burned struc-tures appeared than they vanished once more, like specters in the mist.

"Where are all the civilians?" said Milo.

Drew looked back as Red Rufus walked alongside the young Staglord. The Hawklord's eyebrows were arched over his crooked nose.

"I'm praying they've been spared," replied Drew, not wishing to elaborate and alarm the boy further. Clearly Milo was unaware of the Wylderman diet.

"Dear Brenn," said Red Rufus, his head craning up, the words attracting the attention of his two companions as the smoke began to thin. "The Great Trees."

The Hawk had visited the city once many years ago, but what greeted him on this occasion bore little resemblance to those distant memories. They came to a halt, Drew's legs threatening to fail him as he saw the devastation unleashed upon Brackenholme. Five enormous trunks rose from the ground, giant pillars that disappeared into the heavens. The silhouettes of smoking buildings huddled around their feet. High above, the boughs of one of the Great Trees were alight, the flames licking across its branches unchecked, roaring as they devoured it, the sound like that of an enraged beast. The nearest tree was instantly recognizable as the Great Oak, and the largest collection of campfires spluttered around its base.

"That's where Stirga said Lady Whitley was last seen," said Red Rufus, gesturing with a nod. "She was in the throne room when Vala and her people attacked."

Drew smacked his lips, still staring at the burning tree. He lowered his gaze to the Dyre Road. Screams intermittently pierced the shouts and laughter of the thousands of tribesmen who had taken Brackenholme for their own. Drew and his friends were deep within enemy territory, a handful of termites in a red ant nest, and somewhere within the Great Oak was the Red Queen, Vala.

"Don't mean to push you, lad," said Red Rufus, "but what's

the plan exactly? We can't stand around 'ere gawping; that's one way to attract these devils' attention. We need to move. We need to act."

Drew's knees felt weak, exhaustion and expectation suddenly catching up with him. He'd brought Red Rufus with him first from Windfell, then from Stormdale, and the old bird had stuck with him through thick and thin. They'd fought along the way, but the Hawklord now looked to him for orders, trusted his life to the young Wolf. Drew cast his eyes over Milo, the boy staring back with the same expression as Red Rufus. Drew balled his fist, trying to will his body into action. He checked himself, staring at the healed stump of his left arm, painfully aware there was only one hand left to clench. *Piece by piece, this world is killing me.* The Hawklord put a hand on Drew's shoulder, his voice unusually gentle as he pulled the youth's gaze back to his own.

"Drew," he whispered. "Every journey starts with a small step, every wave a ripple."

"I'm just one man."

"What you do now, today, affects every soul in Lyssia; don't underestimate the impact of your actions. Trust yourself, Drew. Take that step, let momentum do the rest. You are a great warrior, a leader of man and therian alike. There may be only two of us 'ere, an old fool and a boy, but *you're not alone.* The Wolf has friends and allies throughout the Seven Realms and beyond, and they will rally to your call. Stay true to your heart, ride this storm, face whatever these villains throw at you; we'll be there by your side. You're the son of Wergar, last of the Gray Wolves of Westland. You're our king."

Red Rufus gripped Drew's shoulders in each hand, squeezing hard and coaxing life into the youth's aching limbs, his words making the Wolflord's whole being course with a furious fire. Drew's gray eyes sparked with a newfound will. He gritted his teeth and nodded.

"Now," added Red Rufus. "What are we to do?"

"We need to get closer," said Drew, pointing at the Great Oak. "How does one get up into the tree, Red Rufus?"

"They have lifts that run on winches, counterbalanced against one another."

"Counterbalanced?"

"Two big wicker lifts are connected via a giant length of rope, running through a mechanism. The pulley's operated by a team of men. While one lift rises, the other drops, distributing the weight evenly and preventing undue strain on the winch."

"You're an observant old bird," said Drew.

"It pays to pay attention." Red Rufus smiled, his grin making the mud on his face crack.

"So," said Drew, "if the lifts are operated only from above, how do we get them moving?"

"I seem to remember they use a horn to signal," said the

Hawklord. "But I wouldn't hold out much hope for that with these wild men. They no doubt have their own way of getting messages to one another."

"I think we can rule out a climb." Drew sighed, waving his stump and glowering at their predicament.

"And my wing remains sprained, so you can forget about flight," said Red Rufus.

Drew suddenly noticed that while the two of them had been talking, the boy had disappeared. "Where's Milo?" he said, his head spinning as he looked around. Red Rufus joined him, equally alarmed at the situation.

"He was here a moment ago," said the Hawk, pounding a fist into his gnarly palm.

"He's there!" said Drew, pointing through the gloom as the boy ran to them.

"Fool, boy!" snarled Red Rufus. "What were you doing? You stay with *us*, remember? You'll get yourself—and us—killed!"

Milo stared at Drew, panting hard, his voice trembling with adrenaline.

"You said we needed a closer look," he gasped. "Well, I got one."

Drew placed his hand on Milo's back as the boy regained his breath.

"There's a corral," the Staglord wheezed, his speech clipped. "Close to the tree. Perhaps they kept horses. Don't know. But there are men."

"Men?" asked Drew.

"Townsfolk. Greencloaks. They've corralled them. Prisoners."

"Cattle," growled Red Rufus. Milo glanced at him, his panting ceasing instantly.

"If I head for the lift," said Drew, "I might be able to draw the wild men's attention my way, away from the prisoners. Provide the distraction that allows the Greencloaks to be freed. Increasing our numbers can only help our cause."

"Drawing a bunch of these monsters out into a fight? Sounds like a two-man job to me, Wolflord," grumbled Red Rufus.

Drew nodded, considering his next words carefully. "Milo, can you get back to the corral without being noticed by the Wyldermen?"

The boy's eyes lit up. "Of course."

Drew grabbed Milo's chin and lifted the boy's jaw until they faced one another. "You did good work back there, but there's more to do. Do you think you can help our captive friends? You'll need to be careful; this is no game. Your father's been good to me. I wouldn't want your death to spell the end of our friendship. If anything goes awry, you run, understand? You run and you don't stop!"

The boy nodded as Red Rufus glowered.

"Come on," said Drew, turning to the Hawklord. "We need to get moving, my feathered friend. There's a—"

His words were cut short by the appearance of a troop of Wyldermen, approaching through the falling snow from the Great Oak. Their discussions hadn't gone unnoticed, Drew realized to his horror, the conversation having raised suspicion among the more observant wild men. A stocky warrior led the ten tribesmen, a red deerskin draped across his torso, the animal's head still attached and lolling from his shoulder. His face bore a mask of white paint in the fashion of a skull, and his brothers shared similar ghoulish markings.

Drew spied Red Rufus's hand slipping to the knife on his belt. *If we fight now, we'll never reach the Great Oak!* He glanced beyond the Hawklord, seeing that Milo had again vanished. *Where's he gone now?* Drew prayed that the boy was already heading for the corral. His more pressing concern was Red Rufus. Stepping in front of the Hawklord, Drew hoped beyond reason that he might be able to prevent an altercation. The White Skulls fanned out around them, each of them snarling, their leader coming toe to toe with Drew.

Remembering what had worked previously, Drew stared the man down, raising his jaw until they were inches apart. The chieftain looked over his shoulder, inspecting the other scrawny Wylderman who acted so oddly. *If he looks hard enough, he'll see something's amiss,* thought Drew, butterflies scrabbling against his stomach wall. Wasting no time, Drew gave the chief a shove with his shoulder, snarling as the White Skull staggered back a step. The leader took offense, just as Drew had expected, immediately hunkering into an attack position and lifting his ax.

The Wolflord didn't panic, instead standing firm, glaring back. The chieftain stepped closer, peeling back his lips to reveal his rows of wicked, filed teeth. He gnashed them, teeth striking one another like flint against stone. His tongue trailed from between them, the warrior letting the tip trace along the tiny white blades, a ribbon of blood appearing across the purple flesh. His men whooped, clattering weapons at their chieftain's show of strength.

Drew let the Wolf in, just enough for his purpose. He felt his gums tear, his human teeth shifting, sharpening, reforming into deadly lycanthropic fangs. By the time he bared them at the chieftain, his mouth was slick with blood, dribbling from his lips and down his throat, revealing a set of razor teeth more impressive than any the Wyldermen had ever laid eyes on. Drew growled and stepped forward, snapping at the air.

The chieftain was beaten; Drew's show was clearly enough to not only make him doubt his chances in a fight but also dismiss any fears that he was an enemy. The White Skulls opened up, forming a guard of honor for Drew and his companion. The chieftain grinned, gesturing toward the Great Oak, apparently escorting the newcomers toward the main camp. Drew grinned back, hiding the fact that his innards were rolling against one another like a mass of snakes. He walked alongside the White Skull leader, both pleased by his performance and terrified by their predicament. He chanced a look at Red Rufus, and the old warrior drilled his eyes into him. *Please, Brenn; let Milo succeed!* There was no going back now.

Drew looked up as the trio and their honor guard approached the Great Oak, its outline shifting in and out of focus through the snowfall and smoke. He blinked, catching something in his eye. It wasn't a snowflake, the impact was different, yet still wet. Drops falling on the quagmire of mud, slush, and snow began to hammer, gently at first, the noise gradually rising in volume.

The snow had stopped. The rain had come.

2

In the Shadow of the Strakenberg

THE BROWN CLOAKS of the Boarguard whipped in the wind, snapping at the air as the gusts threatened to tear them from their shoulders. They walked with four at the front and four at the rear, with the Baron of Redmire in their middle. Three Sturmish outriders rode at the head of the procession, resplendent in steel armor, their horses stepping along the icy road with ease. At the rear of the group, Bo Carver trudged along, with Pick walking in silence beside him, the girl sticking close to the serpent-tattooed rogue. Carver felt very much like an outsider, and not for the first time. He'd spent a lifetime as a man people wouldn't dare to be seen associating with. But the Thief-lord had always proved a useful man to be called upon, whether by prince or pauper. His cold eyes were fixed on Baron

Hector, deep within his Boarguard. The magister's head was bowed as the company walked from the light into the darkness, the enormous shadows of Icegarden's white walls blotting the sun from the sky.

The walls were formed from giant blocks of ice, pieced together in a complex fashion. Each block was perhaps as tall as a man and twice as long, Brenn knew how deep. How the slabs had been hewn from the icy sides of the mountain, let alone transported into place, Carver could only imagine. They were fifty feet high, and there were no decorations along the ramparts; the occasional guard walked along its edge, precariously close to the sheer drop. The imposing metal gates that marked the entrance into the city opened silently, proving that the smiths of Icegarden were masters of mechanics as well as steelwork.

Carver looked up, a movement on the frozen slopes catching his eye. It was distant, up to the west of the city, but something caught the fading sunlight. He stopped in his tracks.

"What's the matter?" asked Pick, clasping her shivering hand in his grasp.

"Might be nothing," Carver lied, trying not to alarm the girl. He kept his gaze fixed on the bright white vista, searching for another telltale movement. *Who's up there?*

"Are you coming, my lord thief?"

It was Hector's voice, the young Boarlord having paused at the gates. His Boarguard were gathered, the outriders awaiting them within the walls, handing their horses over to the stablemen. Each of the Ugri stared at Carver impassively, showing no emotion. Ringlin was smiling, while the fat idiot Ibal giggled at his side. Hector gestured beyond the gate.

"Icegarden awaits."

Hector stared at the palm of his left hand. The hole left by the crossbow bolt was perfectly round; the missile had sailed through the dead flesh like a hot knife through butter. He dipped the forefinger of his right hand into the hole, forcing it through until it poked out the other side. He felt no sensation, no discomfort; nothing.

"Fascinating," he said, as much to himself as his companions.

Duke Henrik hadn't lied when he'd said that only a skeleton force remained within Icegarden. Once they were through the gates, it was clear that the city was mostly devoid of soldiers, bar those who manned the walls. Stone houses leaned against one another, reminding Hector of a herd of gray cattle huddling together against the elements. Townsfolk had looked out from their windows as they passed by, some showing alarm at the arrival of Ugri in their city. The White Bear's chamberlain had met them at the duke's palace, an ancient fellow named Janek whose spry step belied his advanced years. The palace dwarfed the city, a cathedral of white stone that flanked the Strakenberg. One dizzying tower reached to the heavens, its turret lost in the clouds—the Bone Tower, so called because it looked like an erect, skeletal finger, its summit promising a view across the Whitepeaks like no other.

The old chamberlain had led them through Henrik's palace, the interior of which was resplendent with symbols of the wealth Henrik had collected over the years. The walls glittered with gems and jewels of all shapes and sizes, embedded into the palace walls in intricate designs, reminding Hector of the runic devices he'd seen on the fabled gauntlet, the White Fist. The rumors were true: Henrik was a hoarder, a therian who'd spent his life guarding the wealth that lay buried within the mines of the Strakenberg.

The quarters Hector had been given were sumptuous, as befitted a visiting Werelord. Velvet drapes hung from the granite walls, tied back around tall arched windows that overlooked the city. The Ugri leader, Two Axes, stood by the curtains, leaning against the gray stone, watching the setting sun. The enormous four-poster bed was decked out in a mass of quilts, the fire beside it roaring hungrily in its hearth. Ringlin and Ibal lay on the bed, their sodden boots staining the covers while they stared up at the handsomely carved ceiling. A porcelain washstand stood on the other side of the bed, beside a dressing table and mirror that would please the vainest princess. Hector stood in front of the mirror, turning his hand, staring at his reflection as it gazed solemnly back.

Just imagine, brother, hissed the Vincent-vile, *if your entire body was devoured by the black mark! You'd be impervious to harm: you'd be immortal!*

The notion had crossed Hector's mind, and he wasn't keen. The darkness had crept up his forearm, where its progress had halted. If his research into dark magistry continued, who knew where the discoloration might stop? His torso? *His face?* He looked into the mirror, turning his head this way and that. His pale flesh shone in the firelight, hollow cheekbones giving his face an almost skeletal appearance, as if the skin was stretched thin against his skull. His tousled brown hair hung slick against his forehead, and his face was stricken with the appearance of perpetual illness. He bore little resemblance to the chubby young Boar who had once served Vankaskan.

You're looking more like a Rat each day, Hector!

"Don't like what you see, my lord?" said Ringlin, catching the Boarlord inspecting himself in the mirror.

"I don't recognize myself, Ringlin. What happened to the Hector you first met, the boy you thought you could intimidate?"

The thief sat upright, swinging his legs off the bed. His wet boots hit the floorboards with a slap.

"That boy's dead. I see a man before me now, and a powerful one at that."

Hector stared at the gaunt face in the polished glass. How did he get here? Did everything stem from that dead shaman in the Wylderman village so long ago? In a misplaced step, the brimstone had been disturbed and the darkness had got into him. What might have happened if he'd carried out the communing ceremony successfully? The risen corpse would never have grappled with him. Perhaps he could have gone on his way, a happy soul with only a fleeting interest in necromancy. How different might his life have been if he'd never carried out that first incantation?

Don't doubt yourself now, brother, whispered Vincent in his ear, the vile all too aware of Hector's thoughts. *Clumsy you may have been, but look at the world that blessed mishap has opened up to you! You're on the verge of greatness, Hector; you could be the most powerful magister Lyssia's ever seen!*

Hector raised his hand again, clenching the gnarled black fingers into a fist. The skin creaked like old dry leather. He could command the limb to move, was in complete control of it, but felt nothing. Despite his brother's words, he was still racked by doubt.

"Is this what my future holds? Bit by bit, eaten away by the darkness?"

Ringlin rose from the bed and joined him by the mirror.

"May I speak openly, my lord?"

Hector looked at the man for a moment, a man he'd once feared might kill him in the blink of an eye. He was now one of the few men Hector could depend on. There was little he couldn't trust Ringlin with.

"Speak freely."

"Hector's dead, Blackhand." There was a light in the rogue's eyes that the magister had never seen before, the tall thin soldier speaking earnestly and from the heart.

Does he truly believe in me?

"Sure, you have to keep up the pretense for the Bearlord and others," Ringlin went on, "play the part as long as you must, but that existence is over now. What life did you truly have before? I remember the sniveling scared child back in Bevan's Tower, filling his britches at the sight of his own shadow. Your talent has taken you in a new direction. You're losing nothing and gaining everything."

"How can you say I'm losing nothing?" snapped Hector, waving his blackened limb. "Have you not seen my hand?"

"I know little about necromancy, Blackhand. But I recognize power. You've a gift, and I don't doubt you can master whatever ailment corrupts your flesh." He grabbed Hector's withered wrist. "This hand is a badge of *honor.* It'll strike fear into your enemies' hearts. All shall know your name and fear it, even your allies!"

"And what of those I once loved? What of Duke Bergan? He's not the same as Vega or Manfred. He still cares for me."

"The old Bear will tell you what he thinks you need to hear. He sees you're changed. He's never trusted you since you betrayed the Wolf's Council. You can't think he has a place in your life now, surely?"

"But I've known him since I was a child. He was my father's

best friend, an uncle to me. He's always looked out for me. Did you not see the emotion he showed when we saved him from the Skirmishers in that canyon?"

"Skirmishers *you* sent there: a ruse, a ploy to win him over and regain his trust. How do you think he'll react when he discovers your duplicity, the game you've played? Do you *honestly* think you'll have a place in his heart when he finds out? Because he will, Blackhand, soon enough."

"Soon enough," echoed Two Axes from the window. The giant Ugri didn't turn to them, his eyes still fixed on the white world beyond and the setting sun in the west.

Hector shook his head. Now, so close to his greatest triumph, he was faltering.

Listen to the man, brother. He speaks sense.

"Your old life's *dead*, Blackhand. Your old friends are dead to you. Show that single-mindedness that won over Ibal and me and your Ugri friend over there. Stay true to your path!"

One name returned to Hector's mind, again and again, fighting to the surface each time he buried his feelings for those he'd once loved. Vega and Manfred were lost to him, as was the girl he'd loved, Bethwyn. Queen Amelie, too, was blinded by the Wolf's Council, and even poor Bergan would have to answer for his allegiance to that sorry group. He could deal with the loss of Gretchen and Whitley, the childhood friends he'd shared happiness with; they were already fading from his mind, their voices silent, the memories growing hazy. But one other soul kept gasping for air, fighting to live, poking at his dark heart and crying out his name.

"And what of Drew?"

Ringlin sighed.

"The Wolf's dead, Blackhand. If not, where is he? It's been months since he was last sighted in the carnage of High Stable. If he lived, surely he'd have returned by now, or at the very least been heard from? If he truly is the man you believe him to be—"

"He was a great man."

"*Was* is true. He's gone. Stop thinking he's going to come back from the dead. Put these doubts away for one final time. You need to be focused when you act. The game draws to a close, my lord; your finest hour approaches. Such distractions don't befit the Baron of Redmire, the King of Tuskun. . . ."

"And the future Lord of Icegarden," added Two Axes from where he stood.

Hector and Ringlin both turned to the Ugri, as he strode over to stand beside them. Even Ibal leapt up from where he lounged on the quilts, his fat body rolling off the bed.

"Can you see them?" said Hector, his voice trembling with anticipation.

"They're in place, as you commanded. They've likely been there for days, biding their time, waiting for your arrival."

"They'll be half-dead if that's the case," said Ringlin. "These mountains are cruel. The cold alone's caused the death of many Bastians."

Two Axes turned and grinned. "Bastians' flesh is weak. Ugri are strong, little man. The cold holds no fear."

Hector shivered, trying to imagine how grim a night on the mountains might be. He and Bergan's party had endured the fierce weather in the foothills, the frost and wind biting at their flesh and freezing their extremities. Icegarden was even higher, straddling the mighty Strakenberg. He struggled to imagine *anyone* surviving a night in the wilds. He smiled: anyone except for the ice warriors of Tuskun.

"They know the signal?" asked Ringlin.

"A blast from my horn and they'll come," replied Two Axes, returning his gaze to the mountain slopes beyond the walls. Even with the night closing in, the snowfields still shone, the moon throwing her light over the Whitepeaks.

"The remainder of the Boarguard," said Hector, a nervous energy in his voice. "Where are they?"

"They're in the common room down the hall, my lord," said Ringlin, returning to his more formal manner. "Say the word and we can have them in position."

"What of Carver? Where's he?"

"Next door in a room of his own," said Ringlin. "It seems that old chamberlain, Janek, actually believes the Thief-lord to be some kind of noble."

"He can't be trusted, of course," said Hector. "He's a spy. The only reason he accompanied us to Icegarden was so he could keep an eye on me. A friend of Vega's is an enemy of mine."

"What would you have us do with him?"

Hector stepped around his men toward the door, pausing to grab his thick winter cloak from where he'd flung it on a chair.

"Kill him."

"And the girl?"

Hector's face blanched in horror as he secured his cloak. "Of course not, Ringlin; we're not monsters! Have her tied up and kept out of the way. There'll be plenty of room in the cells once our friends arrive."

Ringlin and Ibal sidled past the Boarlord, opening the door and stepping into the corridor. This had to be quick, and preferably silent. The two rogues were the perfect men for the job. Hector craned his neck, glancing up and down the deserted corridor as the duo readied themselves at Carver's door. Ibal's sickle was out, glinting in his pudgy hand, while Ringlin weighed a long knife in each of his. Ibal reached out and turned the handle of the guest room, finding it locked. He looked toward Hector, seeking direction. Hector walked closer, nodding, urging them on, Two Axes looming at his shoulder. Ibal braced himself against the wall opposite, then charged, striking the wooden door and splintering it at the lock. The timbers twisted as the door gave way with a groan. Ibal and Ringlin shoved at the door, forcing it back, finding to their surprise furniture stacked against it. Hector's eyes widened with alarm.

He knew you were coming for him, brother!

"Get in there!" the Boarlord squealed, glancing furtively up and down the corridor, worried that the noise might alert Henrik's household staff.

The pair of thieves kicked the door farther open, snatching at the furniture that Carver had stacked against the entrance, shoving it clear. A chest, a cupboard, a coat stand all clattered to the floor as the Boarguard desperately pushed them clear, forcing the door open. Once the gap was wide enough, Ringlin was first through, long knives ready for the waiting Thief-lord. Ibal followed quickly after, then Two Axes, and finally Hector.

The room was empty, the windows wide open, tiny clouds of snowflakes swirling into the chamber. The end of a bed sheet had been knotted around the stone arch that split the frame in two, and the windows creaked on their hinges. Ringlin raced over to the window and looked out, Hector close behind. A trail of knotted sheets flapped in the wind, whipping against the wall all the way to the icy ground below. Hector turned his head, back toward the light of his own room. A trail of small prints was visible in the snow along the thin ledge that ran between each room: a child's footsteps.

"They heard everything," he whispered, staggering back into the room.

"Quickly," said Ringlin, wasting no more time. "Two Axes, head to the Strakenberg Gate with your warriors. You know what to do!"

The Ugri stared at Hector, waiting for the command to come from his liege.

"You heard the man!" cried Hector. "To the northern gate!"

The giant moved fast, hurdling over the broken furniture around the doorway as he sprinted from the room. Hector grabbed hold of Ringlin and Ibal, black hand on the tall one, pink on the short.

"Find Carver and the child," he spat, froth on his lips, his eyes narrow with rage. "Kill them both!"

3

AN END TO RUNNING

GRETCHEN LOOKED OUT across the frozen river, her eyes fixed on the opposite bank. There was the opening in the tree line, where the stream they'd followed flowed into the larger body of water. Her companion had suggested taking the brook in the hope that it might throw their pursuers off the scent, but Gretchen's hopes weren't high. The Wyldermen had tracked them for days now, their calls echoing through the forest, horribly close, whenever they'd prayed they were rid of them. Their calls were silent at present, and the pair had heard nothing for the last few hours.

"Do you think we've lost them?" she said quietly.

Trent didn't reply, his back resting against a hollow tree

trunk on the forest floor behind her. "If the previous week's anything to go by, I'd prepare for disappointment."

Gretchen remained where she stood, staring across the ice.

"Sit down. You must be exhausted, my lady."

"As must you," she snipped, irritated by his patronizing remark.

"Which is why I rest beside this bug-infested log." He brushed a hand against the trunk, chasing away a beetle that had burrowed out of the bark to investigate the Redcloak.

She ignored him, eyes still watching the stream that emerged from the dark forest, searching for signs of the wild men.

"Please, Gretchen," said Trent. "Sit and rest."

She turned to him. He appeared as different from Drew as she was from Whitley, which was not surprising when one considered that he and Drew weren't blood relatives. Drew was the child of noble stock, the last son of the Gray Wolves of Westland, whereas Trent was the son of ordinary humans, as uncomplicated in lineage as one could imagine. For all that, the brothers had a great deal in common, not least their ability to infuriate her. Trent's honest manner and way of straight talking also reminded her of Drew. Gretchen guessed that Mack and Tilly Ferran, the boys' parents, had instilled the same strong moral code into each of them. Regardless of having different bloodlines and looking utterly dissimilar, the Ferran brothers were cut from the same cloth, each equally fascinating to the Werefox.

Gretchen walked back toward where the outrider lay, pausing to run her hand over Storm's head. The horse snorted contentedly, nudging her nose against the Lady of Hedgemoor's palm. She joined Trent on the forest floor, sitting beside him. The log rocked back as she leaned against it, startling the two with the sudden movement.

"Go easy," said Trent. "The only thing that's holding it together is beetle dung."

The therian girl gave a brief, unladylike snort of laughter, rousing a string of chuckles from the young outrider.

"Do all Wereladies grunt like piglets? Is that something they teach you in court?"

"No, there's a special class we take in the Dalelands, hosted by the Boarlords. The late Earl Huth taught me everything there is to know about snorting."

"Boars? I heard that my brother had fallen in with one of them. Is that right?"

Gretchen nodded. "Hector. He's the Baron of Redmire now. A good man, and a great friend to Drew. They're as close as . . ."

She let the words trail away, suddenly realizing where her comment was heading.

"It's all right, my lady. You can say it. I won't take offense. Drew's no doubt got more in common with the Boarlord than me anyway," he said. "I doubt your Lord Hector tried to have him killed, to start with."

Gretchen didn't know what to say. Since she had discovered the outrider's true identity some days earlier, he had confided in her. Trent had revealed the terrible guilt he carried with him. He'd taken sides against his brother, believing that Drew had killed their mother, and helped King Leopold in his campaign against the Wolf. She hadn't pressed him on the tasks he'd carried out for the Lions, but judging by the shame he felt, she could imagine what they might have been. She didn't doubt for a moment that Trent had killed in the name of the Lion, and that was something the young man would carry to his grave.

"What's going to happen to us?" she whispered, breaking the awkward silence. Gretchen made no attempt to hide her fear. Neither of them did: they'd been running for so long, the pretense only added to their exhaustion.

"I couldn't say," Trent replied wearily, "but we can't go on as we are."

"We can keep riding. We're wasting time sitting here talking. Come," said Gretchen, rising and striding over to Storm, taking the tattered reins in her hand. "Let's go."

Trent stood, following and taking the leather straps from her. He smoothed his hand over the horse's mane affectionately.

"We won't get far. I didn't tell you earlier, but Storm went over on an ankle back there. If we push her now, through the night, she might break the leg."

A sickening sensation clawed at Gretchen's throat as she realized what he proposed. "What would you suggest? We wait for the Wyldermen to catch up with us?"

"Why not? Better to face them and be done with this hunt one way or the other."

"There are but two of us, though. You saw how many guarded the Dyre Gate!"

"Let's hope Stirga managed to draw a few away when we were separated then."

"This is madness, Trent. We need to keep moving. Let's walk and lead Storm along behind if we must, but we cannot remain here."

"We don't even know where we're heading anymore," said Trent. "North's my best guess, but this forest has a way of throwing one's sense of direction. We're lost, Gretchen. If we can stop the Wyldermen, we may stand a chance of getting our bearings, but flight such as ours hardly allows us to stop and think, let alone catch something that could pass for a proper meal. I'm sorry, my lady, but I see no other way."

He was right, of course. They'd been fleeing from the Wyldermen for over a week and had had no luck in shaking them loose. The two had survived on whatever they could find, mushrooms and edible mosses, or even insects when they'd come across them. No doubt the bugs in the rotten log would be harvested before they left camp. Without a bow, they'd been unable to hunt, but one of Trent's makeshift snares had caught a young hare the previous morning. Only scraps of leveret meat remained, and the fugitives faced starvation unless something changed soon. Drew had survived the two harshest seasons alone in the Dyrewood, while she and Trent had struggled to manage for a week. Not for the first time, Gretchen wished she could better control her therianthropy so she could hunt.

Reaching up into the tree beside Storm, Gretchen let her hands play over the vines that hung down, parting them like an emerald curtain. She took hold of one and gave it a firm tug, but the vine remained fixed in the darkness above. Placing both hands on the length of greenery, she hoisted her legs off the ground, allowing herself to swing momentarily, as the vine took her weight.

"This is hardly the time for playing swing," said Trent, but the girl was moving again, walking across to the log the outrider had been leaning against. Placing both hands on it, she rolled it forward, as a handful of bugs scurried out from beneath it. She lifted her eyes to the frozen river.

"How would you like a fire tonight?" she asked, without looking at Trent.

"It's out of the question." They'd spent so many nights in the Dyrewood and had not once resorted to lighting a campfire. That was just the kind of signal the Wyldermen would be looking for, something to pinpoint the pair's location.

"Maybe not," said Gretchen, looking back at him.

"You may as well hoot and holler as light a fire if you want to catch the wild men's attention."

"I think we're resigned to the fact that they're coming. As you said only moments ago, let's face them on *our* terms. If that means with a bit of warmth in our flesh, then all the better for us. If tonight's to be our last, let's indulge ourselves a bit."

Trent frowned.

"If this is your plan, it doesn't seem terribly grand."

Gretchen allowed herself to smile, watching the Redcloak as he struggled to follow her thinking. Maybe Trent and Drew weren't as alike as she'd imagined.

"Tell me the idea of a flame under your hands doesn't sound like heaven, Ferran."

Trent nodded reluctantly. "I can even cook the remainder of that hare. How's that for a last supper?"

Gretchen shivered, looking back across the frozen river. The ice had creaked and groaned as they'd passed across it, objecting to their passage, especially at the heart of the waterway. She glanced up into the treetops that arced out from their bank, hanging over the river like skeletal black fingers.

"We could always hope their whole damn tribe turns up, and they break the ice beneath their feet," she said quietly.

"Now that would be a blessing from Brenn," said Trent, already foraging beneath the vines around the trees, away from where the snow had fallen. "Make yourself useful, my lady. Help me search for firewood. Hares don't cook themselves, you know."

Gretchen glowered at the young man from the Cold Coast, irritated by his impertinence.

"You're just like your brother," she said, bending her back as she picked up a damp stick from the forest floor.

"Thank you, my lady," replied Trent, grinning, white teeth shining in the gloom. His blue eyes twinkled mischievously. This was the first time she'd seen him smile, and she prayed it wouldn't be the last.

"It wasn't meant to be a compliment."

4
DOWNPOUR

THE SHOWER HAD become a downpour. Campfires hissed and spluttered around the base of the Great Oak, the rain trying in vain to douse them. The more heavily it fell, the more violently the flames reacted, devouring the dry timber that had been stripped from the townhouses, belching smoke and steam back into the sky. The rain provided no hindrance to the Wyldermen; these woodland warriors were all too used to the elements. Each tribe had its own plot of earth, its own stake of land around the ancient tree roots. They vied with one another for prominence, jostling for position and proximity to the giant oak. High above, their Serpent goddess had made her nest, the wild men worshipping from far below. They gathered around the blazing piles of wood, turning the meat on their spits, bright tongues of fire licking at the bodies of their enemies.

Drew strode between the campfires, the White Skull chieftain at his side and Red Rufus behind. The constant *rat-tat-tat* of the rain provided a staccato accompaniment, each drop reminding Drew of the danger they were in. Most of the White Skull warriors had broken away from the group now, disappearing into the encampment, with only three now following at their backs. Of Milo there was still no sign; Drew prayed he was safe. He was depending upon the boy, and the young Staglord's task was onerous and fraught with peril.

Even surrounded by a cannibal horde, Drew couldn't help but marvel at the Great Oak. As they approached the huge tree, it grew ever larger and more impressive, its enormous trunk thrusting skyward like a terrible, dark spear. The rutted bark reminded him of the volcanic rock of Scoria's Black Staircase, fissures breaking its surface in sharp, jagged fault lines. The vague shape of the access lift was visible ahead, sitting close to the oak's base, a thick length of rope disappearing into the gloom overhead. The chieftain continued apace, leading them deep into the Wylderman camp.

Drew turned to Red Rufus, who stared back, eyes wide with alarm. Drew could see the thin trickles of water running down the Hawklord's cheeks, tracing lines through the caked mud. Red Rufus's gaze went down Drew's body, and the young lycanthrope's own eyes followed.

He looked at his forearms. They were being spattered by the rain, and the dry mud was changing in consistency to slick, dripping mud. He watched in horror as rivulets of brown water raced across his flesh. Still, the White Skull men marched forward, escorting the badly disguised duo on their way. *The tree*, thought Drew. *They're leading us straight to the Great Oak! But why?*

Drew checked his arms once again, as the rainwater ran clear from hand and stump, and his skin was washed clean. If the White Skull chieftain were to look at them now, even in the dim light of dusk, the chances were that he'd recognize them for who they truly were. Drew looked back at the Hawk, walking with his head bowed, arms close to his chest, the slushy snow stained brown with each footstep as the camouflage ran freely from his flesh.

The Wolflord slowed, letting the White Skulls walk on, enough to chance a few whispered words to his friend.

"Straight to the lift; stay close."

"This is madness," muttered Red Rufus, the mud falling in clumps from his soaking scalp and beard, revealing the bright ginger locks that had earned him his name.

"Hush," said Drew as they approached the bamboo cage.

A dozen Wyldermen sat in the filthy puddles around the lift's base, some leaning on the bars while others had their backs to the bark of the giant tree. They wore red feathers in their hair, the same as the ones that adorned Drew and his companion. *The White Skulls think we're with* them! *He's returned us to our tribe!* Many were eating, ripping into the charred meat they'd torn from the roasting spits. Drew blanched as he caught sight of recognizable body parts.

A handful of the red-feathered warriors glanced up as the group approached. Drew nodded at Red Rufus, his hand reaching for the swaddled handle of Moonbrand on his back. The White Skull leader barked words at the Red Feathers, who jumped to their feet. One approached, squinting through the downpour at the two stragglers from his tribe. He saw the red-haired old man and the snarling youth with eyes that glowed yellow. The mud ran in rivers from their pale pink flesh. Before he could shout a warning, Red Rufus's long dagger shot forward, jabbing the man's throat and sending him into the mud.

The rest reached for their weapons, including the White Skull chieftain and his men, but they were surprised by two Werelords materializing in their midst. The rain and smoke obscured their changing bodies, but their therian forms were unmistakable. Drew was the first forward. The Werewolf came at the Wyldermen, red feathers fluttering free from his pelt as his glowing white blade and teeth tore into the tribesmen. Wings erupted from Red Rufus's back, rattling as the rain pounded on them, flexing as he leapt forward on monstrous avian feet. With the downpour and dusk cloaking them, the therianthropes had the elements on their side, but the Wyldermen's ferocity was overwhelming. Those with weapons threw themselves into Drew's path, fearless in the face of the Werewolf and intent upon preventing him from reaching the lift. Those without blades attacked like wild animals, hands clawing and teeth snapping as they surged onto Wolf and Hawk. Drew felt flint and canine teeth stabbing at him and pushed the pain to one side as he struggled to dispatch his enemies. Moonbrand sailed through the rain, opening up wild men and sending their limbs spinning through the air.

More of the wild men joined the melee, leaving their camps to investigate the commotion. Within moments a mob surrounded the Werelords, the Wyldermen eager to engage in battle. Close combat wasn't Red Rufus's preferred style of fighting—he was an archer—but beggars couldn't be choosers. His shortsword flashed and stabbed, his clawed feet kicked out, and his hooked beak ripped strips from the enemies' exposed flesh.

Drew had felled a dozen of the wild men, but as one dropped another replaced him. The Werewolf crashed into the bamboo bars of the lift, two Wyldermen on his broad back, and he scrabbled for purchase. He felt a knife jab into his ribs, while an ax glanced off his skull. His vision blurred as a club struck his right leg, dropping him to his knees. More of the wild men rushed him, dragging him to the ground, stamping and slashing. The lift was no longer visible, and the possibility of reaching it looked increasingly slim. Drew caught sight of an ax hurtling toward his head and lifted his left arm up at the last moment. The stone blade caught the stump, ringing off the bone and sending shockwaves coursing through the Werewolf's body.

A foot came down, submerging Drew's shortened limb in the freezing mud. The Wyldermen tried to tear Moonbrand free from his hand, but Drew kept hold, death being the only thing that would part him from Wergar's ancient blade. He tried to rise, but his progress was halted as a club smashed him across the face and sent his head back with a crunch. Hands swarmed over him, closing around his throat, gripping his muzzle, forcing his jaw to one side and submerging his face in the mud and melting snow. Bubbles rushed from his mouth and nose as the brackish meltwater rushed down his throat. He could feel the sharpened teeth of the tribesmen all over his body. The irony wasn't lost on Drew: a Werewolf, most savage of all Lyssia's therianthropes, was being torn apart by a pack of humans. *What fate has befallen Red Rufus? Milo?*

"For Brackenholme!"

Even over the snarls of the Wyldermen, Drew recognized the man's voice. Captain Harker's cry was a rage-filled roar that screamed for vengeance. Many of the wild men who covered Drew were suddenly pushed clear as they faced new opponents. The tattered cloaks of green swirled overhead as Drew saw the men of the Woodland Watch throw themselves at the Wyldermen, tearing them off the besieged Wolflord. The Greencloaks carried makeshift weapons—sticks, rocks, lengths of rope—whatever they'd managed to gather from the corral.

Many used their bare hands as they pushed and pulled the Wyldermen away, freeing the Werewolf from his foes. A thin hand helped him up, the familiar face of Milo smiling grimly.

"You freed them!" gasped the Werewolf, shaking his head as his senses returned.

"For what good, I don't know," said the young Staglord over the din of battle. A pair of short twisting horns had torn from his forehead, and a sword was raised in his other shaking hand. "I fear I've only sped them to Brenn's arms!" He disappeared once more into the melee.

"For Duke Bergan!" cried Harker, a welcome face amid the fracas at the base of the Great Oak. The captain was at the heart of the fight, meeting a Wylderman's ax blows with his bare fists. Having regained his footing, Drew joined the scrum of Greencloaks who struggled against the overwhelming odds. There were hundreds of Wyldermen, thousands in the city, no doubt. Milo was right: this would be a bloodbath. There were maybe fifty Greencloaks and a handful of townsfolk, beaten and exhausted, making a valiant last stand.

Red Rufus pushed through the crowd toward Drew, pulling Milo along in a taloned hand, the boy's head lolling; he was clearly concussed.

"The tree, Drew!" screeched the Hawklord. "You came to save your friends and stop the Serpent! Go now!"

The old Hawk gave the Wolf a shove, urging him into the bamboo cage.

"The mechanism!" Drew shouted. "It's at the top?"

The Hawk nodded, about to answer when an arrow caught him, sending him flying into Drew's arms. The Werewolf slipped and staggered through the cold mud, as the black-feathered flight of the missile trembled in Red Rufus's hip. The grizzled avianthrope struggled to stay upright, reaching back to snap the arrow shaft in half.

"You heard me, Drew," said Red Rufus, his eyes blinking as he tossed away the broken arrow. He gave the youth another push toward the cage. "The tree; go to your friends."

Before Drew could reply, the Hawk was engaged once again, standing over the dazed figure of Milo, the boy's chin resting on his breastplate as he knelt in the mud, oblivious to the battle around him.

This is a massacre. Vala must be stopped, even if it kills me.

With new resolve he crouched and leapt, landing on the roof grille of the lift. The thick rope was twined through the bars, securely attached to the bamboo cage. Drew looked around frantically, trying to work out how he could reach the Great Oak's boughs. *If the mechanism's at the top, then I'm stuck down here!* He looked at his missing left hand. *It must be hundreds of feet to the treetop!* He could try to climb the rope, using his clawed feet perhaps? It was dangerous, but his only hope.

He was about to act when he felt a hand snatch at his ankle, his lycan foot tugged away, sending him face-first onto the lift roof. He glanced over his shoulder and caught sight of a pale, skeletal face appearing over the cage's edge: The chieftain had sought him out. Drew kicked out but the White Skull leader was fast, dipping his head, dodging the blow. The warrior was on the roof quickly, swinging his ax down. Moonbrand came up, deflecting the blow, and sending sparks showering off the flint ax head.

The White Skull punched the Werewolf in the muzzle twice in quick succession, and Drew's head recoiled with each blow. The Wylderman was fearless, his face set in a terrible grin as he brought down another punch. His eyes were wild, the chieftain relishing the chance to fight the therianthrope. The Wolf's mouth opened, catching the fist in his jaws. Drew snapped them shut, but before he could grind his teeth he felt the ax shaft strike his nose, the pain instant and dreadful, making him release his jaws. The ax flew down again, and a blind parry from Moonbrand sent it away.

The two wrestled across the bars, rolling and bucking, each trying to overpower the other. Below, Drew spied four Wyldermen who had split away from the Greencloaks to get into the lift. They jabbed upward with their spears, careful to avoid the White Skull but keen to find the Werewolf. The chieftain grinned, letting his ax go with a clatter to take hold of the lycanthrope by the shoulders. With his only hand holding Moonbrand, Drew was helpless to prevent the White Skull from rolling him over. As the two turned, the chieftain slowly got the upper hand, and Drew reached out with his legs, his transformed feet taking firm hold of the lift rope that disappeared into the dark sky overhead.

The Wyldermen below saw the White Skull chieftain turning the Werewolf. Finally he was on top, his bare back exposed above, dark fur bristling between the bars. As they readied to strike, Drew lashed out with Moonbrand, every ounce of his strength focused on the sword. The glowing blade swung around, and the chieftain was relieved that the blow missed him. But the White Skull was not aware of the Werewolf's target.

Moonbrand scythed through the rope as the Wyldermen in the cage decided to strike. The sword tore through the thick hemp that was bound around the bars. Instantly, Drew was catapulted skyward, his powerful clawed feet clenched tightly around the rope's end. The White Skull chieftain spun and crashed back onto the cage roof, the four spearheads striking through the grille, entering his body and emerging from his back.

Drew watched the dead Wylderman and the battle disappear from view as he raced into the heavens, another lift hurtling by in the opposite direction, empty and earthbound. He looked up, holding onto the rope for dear life, as the dark branches of the Great Oak rushed to meet him.

5

SNOWSTORM

THE LORD OF Thieves ran. In his arms, Bo Carver carried Pick, her head buried in the crook of his neck as fresh winds picked up the snow. He glanced back toward the palace nervously, expecting the Boarguard to emerge from the ornate doors at any moment. Icegarden's townhouses lit the way, and he plowed on, his feet struggling for purchase on the icy street. The building he aimed for was the one he'd spied earlier that day: the garrison. The huge gray building covered the length of the northern quarter, buttressing the enormous wall of ice that protected the capital from invasion. The entrance to the building was beside the Strakenberg Gate, hidden in shadows, its great doors closed against the elements. He skidded to a

426

halt and searched for a handle. Finding none he balled his fist, hammering on the wooden door.

"Hold your horses," came the reply from within, briefly followed by laughter. Carver bit his lip, looking back to the palace once more: still no sign of movement. A wooden slat slammed to one side, revealing a long-faced guardsman who peered out of the spyhole.

"What the devil's got into you?"

"The city," said Carver. "It's in danger."

The guard dipped his head one way and the other, looking past the Thief-lord into the darkness beyond.

"Who would you be, anyway?" asked the man suspiciously.

"A guest of Duke Henrik's. You need to *listen*: there are men in the palace who mean to attack Icegarden."

"What men?"

"Who is it?" called another guard.

The man turned. "Says he's a guest of His Grace. Don't look like a nobleman, mind."

"You're wasting time!" said Carver, looking back to the palace once more. The double doors were wide open, but there was no sign of anyone in the street. He reached through the spyhole and caught the man by the collar.

"They're coming," he snarled. "Raise the alarm, do whatever it is you're supposed to do, but ready your weapons. How many man your walls?"

The man was struggling, trying to free himself from Carver's iron grip, while his companions could be heard rushing to his aid. Carver shook him and pulled him close, dragging the man's shirt collar through the opening until his ear was flush to the hole.

"How many men on the wall?"

"Three dozen!" said the man, panicked.

"And in there?"

"The same number!"

"Wake them, move them!" He released his grip, and the startled watchman fell into his companions' arms. "Do it *now!*" shouted Carver. To the Thief-lord's relief, the command in his voice was enough to spur the guards into action without further questions. Carver wasted no time, rushing up to the Strakenberg Gate, where he found another locked door. The stone structure of the gatehouse framed the giant steel doors to the city, the wall's polished blocks of ice sitting flush to its edge. He hammered on the guards' door, looking back nervously.

"What's going to happen?" asked Pick, icy tears streaming down her face.

"Hush, child," said Carver with an unconvincing smile. He tugged her cloak around her chin and smoothed the hood against her head.

"Who goes there?" The call came from above. Carver looked up and saw three helmed heads peering over the frozen battlements.

"Bo Carver. I'm lodging in the castle as a guest of your duke. You have to listen: the city's in danger. You saw the Ugri warriors who arrived today from the front line?"

The men above nodded, as the door to the garrison finally opened. A procession of soldiers made their way out, some half-dressed, clearly having been asleep while they rested from watch. Many were still buckling on their armor, one man stopping to stretch and yawn.

"I saw them come, aye. I was on the South Gate this afternoon when you arrived. You're with them, no?"

"Thank Brenn," said Carver, relieved to have found someone he could get some sense out of. "I was indeed. We thought they were allies. That's not the case."

"This fool's woken the barracks, Harlan!" shouted the the man Carver had accosted.

"They're planning something!" continued Carver, addressing the man on the wall named Harlan. "They're going to attack!"

Right on cue, the arrows whistled, six flights finding targets in the men who had shambled out of the garrison building. The soldiers went down, felled in seconds, those still standing either looking around frantically or dashing back toward their barracks. Fresh arrows flew from the darkness, leaving many of the fleeing men dead in their tracks.

"Let me in!" yelled Carver, pounding the gate door with renewed fury. "I have a child here!"

"Open the door!" Harlan shouted into the guardhouse.

A handful of fully armed guards who had emerged from the garrison took cover in the street, ducking behind the walls of homes and outhouses, but the confusion in their ranks was clear. They called for crossbows, cried for reinforcements, begged to know where the arrows had come from, but in each case found no answer. Carver's eyes, already accustomed to the dark, flitted across the road, searching the shadows for movement. Here and there he caught sight of a figure passing in and out of the darkness of the buildings opposite, drawing ever closer. An arrow bounced off the wall beside his head.

Carver dropped to his knees, curling his body around Pick, his back to the street. He looked over his shoulder as he saw the first of the Ugri lope out of the shadows, quickly followed by five more. Their bows were put away now, and the warriors had resorted to their formidable array of melee weapons—axes, war mattocks, maces, and morning stars—all sure to do a great deal of damage to an unarmored man like Carver. Three ran straight toward the garrison, one of them carrying a burning oil flask in his hand, while the other three came straight for the gatehouse.

The first Ugri kicked at the garrison door just as the guards within were trying to close it, the wooden barrier twisting on its hinges as his companion with the flaming oil pulled back his arm to throw. A flurry of bolts sailed down from the Strakenberg Gate, one of them hitting the clay flask in the Ugri's hand. The oil pot exploded, its contents spilling over the warrior's head and torso, the oily pelts he wore adding fuel to the fire. Any ordinary man might have dropped to the floor and tried to douse the flames by rolling in the snow, but not the Ugri. He rushed over the broken threshold of the garrison, his body alive with flames, the screams from the Sturmlanders within suddenly rising a notch. His two brothers followed him into the building, seeking out their enemies.

The final three closed on Carver, the lead warrior recognizable to the Thief-lord as Two Axes. *Where are the others? Where are Ringlin and Ibal? Where's Hector?* Two Axes covered the distance fast, his arms trailing behind him as he charged, leaning into the wind, feet dancing over the ice with well-practiced grace. Crossbows sang overhead, bows twanging, bolts and arrows bouncing off the ice and skittering harmlessly away as the Ugri dodged them. In each fist the Ugri chieftain carried an ax, dark blades shining menacingly. The door suddenly opened in front of Carver, and gauntleted hands reached out to grab hold and haul him in.

The Thief-lord shoved Pick into the guards' arms, pushing the girl up the stairs as two more guards forced the door shut behind him. Carver looked back as he ran up the steps. The guards had hold of the deadbolt, about to slam it in place, when the door crashed open, crushing one of the Sturmlanders instantly behind it. The foot of the stairwell was littered with splintered timbers as Two Axes stepped through the broken door frame. The second guard raised his sword against the Ugri, but one blow from an ax at close quarters sent the sword ricocheting into the man's face, a second ax striking him in the guts below his breastplate.

Carver raced on, following on another Sturmlander's heels as the soldiers hurried Pick up the stairs. Behind, Carver could hear the Ugri clambering over the wood and bodies as they came after him. The torchlight at the top of the staircase lit up a small guardroom, machinery and cogs lining one wall, the door from which opened onto the battlements. Pick and the two remaining soldiers from the tower disappeared out onto the ice wall, and Carver recognized the figure of Harlan at the door, beckoning him frantically.

"Hurry!" he cried, snatching at Carver's hand and dragging him onto the ice wall. The door was slammed shut and more bolts rammed into place, sealing it behind him. Instantly the sound of axes striking the wood could be heard; the door trembled with each blow as the Ugri within set to work on the timber.

"How many of them are there?" asked Harlan, readying his broadsword. About a dozen armed men had gathered round the top of the Strakenberg Gate, prepared to cut down the Ugri should they break through the barrier. Carver could tell from Harlan's uniform that he was a captain, clearly the officer charged with manning the walls in the absence of the army.

"Six Ugri, and the Boarlord Hector has a couple of others in his service, of whom I've seen no sign."

"A Boarlord?" said the captain. "An enemy of the Free People? It's unheard of!"

"Yet it's a fact," said Carver, gasping for air. "The fool in the garrison said you had around thirty men on the wall?"

"Indeed. We also have the duke's household guard within the palace, as well as a few hundred townsfolk who can be called upon. I'll send word along the wall, have the militia roused. That's more than enough to deal with eight men, nine at a push if you throw in the traitorous Boar."

The axes stopped striking the door, the sudden silence taking Carver and the Sturmlanders by surprise. Harlan and the Thief-lord looked at one another, while Pick stared up at them fearfully.

"Have they given in?"

Before Carver could answer, the deep boom of a hunting horn reverberated from behind the door, making them all jump with alarm. Three loud blasts were sounded, each one chilling the defenders' blood.

"They'll hear that in the Strakenberg mines," said a soldier, shifting his domed helm nervously with his gauntlet.

After the last blow on the horn, the axes began their work again, striking the door, the pace quickening.

"What was that about?" asked another guard, as Harlan watched Carver step gingerly to the wall's edge, looking out into the great white landscape beyond. The captain followed, Pick standing between them.

Carver's eyes scanned the white slopes beyond the walls, as the moonlight made the snowfields sparkle like a sea of glittering gems.

"By the dead . . ." whispered Carver as Captain Harlan made the sign of Brenn. Pick's hand tightened around the Thief-lord's as they watched the snow come to life.

The slopes shuddered as if a tremor had passed beneath them, disturbed by a wave of movement. Snow tumbled as figures rose from the ground, the fine white powder falling from their bodies as they climbed from their hiding places. More and more Ugri appeared, icy golems standing to silent attention as far as the eye could see, surrounding the frozen walls of Icegarden. Carver cursed under his breath. *What are they waiting for?*

"There are hundreds," said Harlan with a gasp, swinging his broadsword anxiously at his side.

A horrifying notion hit Carver like a hammer blow. He turned to the captain suddenly, snatching at his shoulder.

"The mechanism for the gates, Harlan; where is it?"

Harlan didn't need to answer. The gates were already stirring to life, as Two Axes's companions worked the wheels within the guardroom. The soldiers glanced down from the walls in horror as the gates opened silently outward, the army beyond the city suddenly surging to life. Hundreds of Ugri dashed through the snow, weapons raised above their heads, a silent horde of death rolling down the mountainside toward them.

"Close the gates!" roared Harlan, pushing through his men to the guardhouse door. A trio of soldiers stood ready, shields and swords raised. Taking hold of the deadbolts, the captain cranked them back into their brackets as the door cracked open, another ax blow sending it flying on its hinges. Two Axes stood there, his skin coated in sweat, a weapon in each hand as he leapt through the opening. The first ax smashed into a Sturmlander's shield, launching the man into his companions, while one of the soldiers lunged, catching the Ugri in the armpit. The other ax scythed around, shattering the jaw of the soldier who'd hit him, and Two Axes's booted foot caught the third in the chest.

Carver looked beyond the warrior into the guardhouse: the remaining two Ugri stood at their chieftain's back, ready to defend the wheel mechanism with their lives. A glance down the icy incline revealed the first of the Ugri soldiers flooding through the huge opening. The Strakenberg Gate had fallen; Icegarden was breached.

The Thief-lord snatched up Pick, shouting for Harlan's attention, the captain mesmerized by the ferocity of Two Axes's assault.

"Is there another way down from the walls, Captain?"

"The South Gate!" replied Harlan, his eyes never straying

435

from the Tuskun warrior. His men's blades were connecting with their enemy, but the chieftain was berserk, ignoring the blows and giving many in return. "Hurry—it may be your only chance of getting the child to safety!"

Carver was running, skidding along the wall top, grateful for the flags the Sturmlanders had embedded along the parapet. He looked down to his left, catching sight of the barracks on fire, flames gorging hungrily on the structure's wooden roof. The Ugri were working their terrible magic within, spreading chaos and death wherever they went. Pockets of the Tuskun warriors could be seen running through the city, kicking in the doors of townhouses, the screams of the occupants growing into a crescendo.

The Thief-lord turned the northwest corner of the wall, heading south, passing the occasional guard running in the opposite direction, toward the Strakenberg Gate. No words passed between them: the looks on their horrified faces told their tale. Reaching the end of the western wall, Carver sprinted the final length of the frozen parapet toward the South Gate. The door to the guardhouse was wide open, the men having abandoned their positions to rush into the city and repel the invaders. The cause was lost, any fight in vain. Icegarden had been taken by the Ugri, stolen from them by the Boarlord's duplicity. Carver had been right all along.

He put Pick down gingerly and set to work on the gate mechanism in the guardhouse, straining hard on a handle that was designed to be turned by three men. Gradually the wheel moved, the cogs turning painfully slowly as Carver's muscles burned with the effort. He gave it three revolutions and left it, praying to Brenn that the huge steel doors had opened enough to let the two of them out. There was nothing he could do in the city: he had to get word back to the front line, to the two Bearlords, let them know the fate that had befallen the Sturmish city behind them. Lifting Pick up once again he set off down the stairwell, her teeth clacking against one another with each pounding step, her body lying limp in his arms. Reaching the ground he found the door at street level swinging on its hinges, a trail of guards' footsteps disappearing through the snow into the city. Carver stepped into the street.

The gates were open a crack, big enough for Pick to slip through, but a squeeze for Carver. He pushed her on, gently enough not to hurt, but firmly enough to propel her out of the city. The girl looked back, eyes wide and tearful.

"One moment," he whispered. The Thief-lord shifted his weapon belt around his hip, breathing in as he tried to slip through the narrow opening. He cursed aloud as he felt a sharp pain in his side. One of his daggers, perhaps? With a sickening realization, Carver knew it wasn't one of *his* blades at all, the cut too deep and purposeful to be a mere accident. He looked back, coming face to face with Ringlin; it was the rogue's long knife buried in his flank.

Ringlin yanked Carver back, the Thief-lord dropping to

his knees, blood flowing freely from the injury, pooling in the snow around him.

"Run, child!" he shouted, as Ringlin dashed to the gap in the gates, trying to squeeze through, his hand reaching out and snatching at Pick. The girl stumbled out of reach, falling into the snow, as the villain began to work his way through the opening.

"Run to Bergan, Pick!" cried Carver, his vision fading as a coldness raced through his aching body. "Run for your—"

His last cry was cut short as Ibal's sickle came down with a sickening crunch.

6

TERROR IN THE TREETOPS

THE WYLDERMEN IN the tree gathered around the lift hatch, half expecting to see the other cage arrive after the first had departed so suddenly. Instead, the severed end of the rope flew into sight, whipping against the enormous wheel that spun above them. The three wild men stared at the rope as its lashing motion snared it within the mechanism, the wheel screeching to a halt as it bit into the hemp. Each warrior stepped forward to the platform's edge, curiosity getting the better of them as they looked down through the rain.

Drew was already moving, his lupine form leaping across the thick branches that supported the wooden landing, the footsteps of the Wyldermen echoing overhead. He hopped through the shadows, clawed feet and hand gripping the bark,

Moonbrand strapped into his back scabbard again. On the far side of the platform, the wooden planks were stacked on top of one another. Straining, Drew reached up, his clawed hand taking a firm hold of the uppermost board, claws burrowing into the timber for the strongest purchase. The Werewolf took a couple of deep breaths before swinging out and around, throwing his body into the night in a fluid motion. He released his hold once his legs had passed beyond the horizontal, allowing his momentum to carry him onto the landing. He rolled, coming up growling as the three guards turned in surprise.

Drew kicked out, snapping the first wild man's leg and propelling him into the open hatch. The remaining two came straight at him, one jabbing with a spear while the other swung his club. Drew dodged, caught the end of the spear and yanked, pulling the Wylderman in the direction the Werewolf had come from. The man sailed off the landing, following his companion into the night. The third's club cracked into Drew's back; his shoulder blade hummed from the impact and the blow propelled him toward the edge. His claws dug into the floorboards, tracking scored lines through the aged timber.

The club came down again, striking the Werewolf's temple and sending him crashing to the deck. Drew lashed out with his leg, sweeping the Wylderman's feet from under him until he toppled beside him. The club went up one more time, but Drew's hand was quicker, closing around the man's throat and tearing it from his body. He hopped to his feet, crouching and panting as he surveyed the Great Oak's walkways through the rain.

There was little sign of more Wyldermen, Vala having apparently kept the treetop to herself, with the wild men left to gather far below. Interconnecting bridges ran between the Great Oak's boughs, disappearing into the gloom, the occasional torch guttering in its bracket to throw light onto a platform or building. The greatest number burned around the edge of an enormous structure that sat in the heart of the tree's giant branches: Brackenholme Hall, the Bearlord's palace. Drew loped toward it, his feet bouncing off planks as he sped across the walkways through the drizzle.

The hall dominated the central section of the tree, a series of bridges spanning out and linking it to the surrounding structures. A platform ran around its exterior, while a flight of wide wooden steps led up to an enormous opening, where the torchlight sent shadows dancing across the splintered timbers that had once been double doors. Deep within the hall, Drew could see the glow of a fire at the rear of the great chamber. Arched windows dominated the walls on either side of the entrance, their panes of stained glass shattered, jagged shards littering the walkway alongside the debris from the doors.

Treading carefully, the Werewolf made his way up the wooden flight, stepping over the pieces of twisted glass and broken timber. His gaze fell upon the hall's exterior, the wooden posts distorted as if great pressure had been applied to them. A piece of glass, obscured by the shadows, crunched beneath the thick skin of his foot, making Drew wince. It was sure to alert those within of his presence, though it hardly seemed to matter. *If they don't know there's a battle on below, then they never will.*

He clambered over a broken beam that had fallen from above the door, now reduced to kindling. A few hundred feet ahead, black smoke clogged the vaulted ceiling, the fire itself obscured from view by great piles of twisted furniture. The occasional tapestry or painting remained in place on the walls, dimly visible, ripped and defaced by the hall's new occupant. Others had been torn down, and discolored woodwork revealed where they'd once hung proudly.

Of Vala, there was no sign. Drew tiptoed through the clutter, eyes searching the shadows for any sudden movement. A huge circular stone hearth housed the fire, and a great black pot straddled it, the contents steaming in the flames' caress. As Drew passed the pile of wreckage, he spied bodies laid out on the floor. Instantly his heart jumped to his mouth: *Whitley?* He dashed forward, throwing caution to the wind, glancing at the eleven still forms arranged in a line. In some cases, telltale fang marks were visible on their flesh, across their torsos or necks. Whether they were dead or merely unconscious, Drew couldn't tell at a glance, but his eyes raced over them, searching for his friend. Three Greencapes were shoulder to shoulder, two old men beside them, then a boy, little older than Milo. Two serving girls lay motionless beside the boy, followed by two noblewomen, their arms crossed over their chests. The last in the row was an old lady, her withered face as still as a corpse, one eye missing, her puckered lips shriveled in a death mask.

Whitley wasn't there. Drew jumped over the bodies, his lycanthrope feet landing silently as he looked frantically for the Bearlady. *Dear Brenn, no*, he thought. *Don't let her be gone. Please no!* Beyond the dim noise of battle far below, a new sound captured Drew's attention. He looked up.

Suspended from the rafters at the back of the hall, bound in ropes and securely gagged, spun Whitley. Her body twisted on the rope as she bucked, clearly alive, her eyes wide as she saw Drew below. Drew bounded across the hall until he stood beneath her. She was at least twenty feet above his head, out of the reach of even a leaping therian. His eyes followed the path of the rope as it wound around the rafters and then straight down the wall at the rear of the throne room. The Werewolf sprinted to the rope's end, twined and knotted around the base of Duke Bergan's huge chair. He worked at the hemp, putting his teeth to the knot and worrying it loose, his eyes looking up at his friend all the while. Finally, the rope went slack, Drew snatching it in a clawed hand and let it run through his grip. His palm burned as the rope passed through it, taking the weight of the Bearlady as she descended from the ceiling, turning all the while. Eventually the girl landed on the floor, where she lay in a cocoon of rope. He ran across.

All the worry and fear that he'd bottled up in the past months came to the surface as he tore at her ropes. Drew's hand was shifting back to its human state, tears flowing down his cheeks as the Wolf retreated, his joy at being reunited with his friend overwhelming. Whitley kicked at the ropes, trying to worry them loose from her feet, her eyes fixed on the bodies on the floor. Drew yanked at the bonds around her wrists, ripping them away, as Whitley's freed hands went straight for her gag.

"I thought I'd lost you forever," Drew exclaimed, laughing through the tears, delirious with relief as he ran his hand through her hair.

Whitley tugged the gag loose, spluttering, her eyes still fixed on the bodies. Drew turned, following her gaze. There they were: ten of them. One was missing. Drew rose to his feet, the hairs standing up on his neck, the Wolf's growl rising in his throat. The old woman was gone.

Whitley coughed, her voice reed thin. "Vala," she said.

Drew stepped in front of her, lowering his shortened arm to help her climb from the floor to his side.

"Show yourself, Vala," shouted Drew, his face wet with tears but now set with grim determination.

"Ssssilly Wolf." Her voice echoed around the room, but the Wereserpent remained hidden in the darkness. "I have waited sssso long for thissss. What'ssss the hurry, sssson of Wergar? Let ussss ssssavor our reunion."

Drew squinted, as the flames from the fire pit hampered his vision. The hearth was directly before him, below the dais, and the rest of the room was shrouded in shadows. Still the sound of battle could be heard, faint and far below. He turned to Whitley.

"Stay behind me," he whispered. "Don't put yourself in harm's way. If you can get out, run for it."

"I'm going nowhere: my mother's down there," she croaked, pointing toward the lifeless bodies.

"Don't you know it'ssss rude to whissssper, boy?"

Drew raised his voice again.

"It's rude to eavesdrop, my lady!"

"Poor little pup. What hassss happened to hissss paw?"

Drew glanced at the stump of his left arm as Vala continued.

"*The one-handed man sssshall fall:* that'ssss what they ssssay, issssn't it?"

"That's what who says?" asked Drew, thrown by her riddling talk. "If you've something to tell me, my lady, pray spit it out!"

"Propheciessss, child," she hissed cryptically. "I have missssed our little chatssss."

"I've missed you, too, my lady. I never truly got to say good-bye, our parting was so hurried. Did my flight offend you that much? It seems you hold a grudge for a surprisingly long time."

Something large and dark raced through the shadows beyond the giant pile of ruined furniture, vanishing again in an instant.

"Don't talk to me about time, Wolf. I am agelessss, I have lived for centuriessss in the woodssss of Lyssssia. Now, after all thessss years, I claim the home of the Bearlordssss asss my own! You couldn't imagine the depth of vengeance that runssss through my blood."

Drew focused his exhausted body, embracing the beast for one last time. The Wereserpent had talked enough; she had to answer for her crimes. He felt the hairs coursing over his skin, chest and ribs expanding as his skull shifted. He grimaced as his teeth tore through his widening, lengthening gums, the lips of his muzzle peeling back with a growl.

"Let's see that proud blood you boast of then, Vala. Do your worst!"

Drew unleashed a howl, the noise thundering through the hall like a gale and rushing out of the shattered doors. The noise was primal, erupting from his core, a rallying cry to his brethren and allies. All below in the city and beyond the walls heard the Wolf's call, and those who yet lived and fought in his name found renewed strength and purpose in their weary hearts and limbs.

The Werewolf took two steps, growling, watching the

shadows. He saw the Wereserpent's tail whip out from behind the stack of broken trappings, making him leap back up the dais. But the strike wasn't aimed at the Wolf. The tail connected with the black cauldron, the pot ringing like a bell as it tipped, spilling its contents over the fire. The flames were instantly doused by the boiling water, and a great cloud of choking steam and smoke billowed from the hearth, filling the hall.

The Wolf was blind in the steaming fog, his mind racing back to his first terrifying encounter with Vala so long ago. His heart thundered, his fear of the Wyrm all too real and fresh in his memory. One long, malevolent hiss broke the silence. Hurriedly, Drew unsheathed Moonbrand, whipping the glowing blade from the leather loop on his back, illuminating the hot smoke that surrounded him. The pale light of the longsword pierced the gloom as the Wereserpent rushed toward him.

7
BENEATH THE ICE

A WOLF'S DISTANT howl made all but one of the seven Wyldermen look up from the banks of the frozen stream. Their leader ignored the beast's cry, his eyes settling on the ice before him. Blacktooth stared down the watercourse and smiled, his sharp, filthy teeth breaking into a crooked grin. *Stupid, soft townsfolk. Try to outwit him by taking the streambed? When it was frozen? His laugh was guttural. Thought they could lose Blacktooth and his Blood Feathers by that old trick, did they?*

He stepped down the incline, following the hoofprints of his prey. He'd left ten of his warriors to go after the old man, but the young ones would be Blacktooth's. He didn't care about what happened in Brackenholme now. He wasn't going to sit around on a gate watching Wyldermen come and go. He was born to hunt, and the hunting was good. He traced a finger along the scar the boy's sword had left down the side of his face, the tip running over the gnarled scab. The boy in the red cloak would suffer most of all.

The warrior said nothing to his men, but a glance told them to follow him. Blacktooth clambered down onto the frozen water and stepped forward, his tribe falling in behind, following the brook's course. It began to widen, the stream gradually running into a river, one of the many that wound their way through the Dyrewood. He raised a hand, signaling his men to stop, as he looked out over the larger body of water.

A sheet of ice spread out before him, winter having transformed the water into a shining blue road in each direction. The canopy arched over the river, tree branches twining against one another from either bank, casting a crazed pattern of shadows across the ice below. Blacktooth's breath caught in his throat. On the opposite bank a fire burned low, and a brown horse was tethered to a tree. Two figures lay together beside the dying flames, the unmistakable red cloak of the boy clearly visible, shrouding them. The warrior made a motion with his hand, ordering the Blood Feathers to fan out, three flanking him as he stepped out onto the frozen river.

The Wyldermen unhitched their weapons, axes, clubs, spears, and knives shifting in their hands, eyes fixed on the figures ahead. The horse snorted, stopping their progress for a moment. It threw up its head, giving a gentle whinny. *Had it seen them?* When the sleeping figures didn't stir, Blacktooth advanced once more, his men following in a V-shaped formation on either side of him.

Reaching the center of the river, the warrior could feel his heart racing, so close to the kill. They would eat tonight, feast on the flesh of these pale fools! The ice groaned beneath him, a crack appearing suddenly and snaking out from beneath his bare toes. Blacktooth slid his feet forward, pointing to the ice with his ax, the Blood Feathers following his lead. Each of the Wyldermen kept both feet on the ice's fragile surface, edging on slowly, tentatively. It slowed their progress but prevented them from ending up in the water below.

A snapping sound from the opposite bank made the wild men look up from the river; it was followed by a cracking noise in the canopy overhead. Branches splintered as a large dark shape descended at great speed. Blacktooth dived forward, throwing caution to the wind, as a gnarled section of tree trunk crashed into the frozen river among his Blood Feather brethren. The river exploded, huge sheets of ice splintering up, tipping the Wyldermen off their feet. Some dived for the ice as it fractured into a hundred pieces; others disappeared below the surface. The cracks spread, the sheets of ice disintegrating beneath the bodies of the panicked wild men. Only Blacktooth and two others avoided the swift, deadly pull of the river's current. The warrior looked up, his scarred face contorting with rage as two figures emerged from the trees on either side of the campsite.

Trent stepped onto the river, Wolfshead blade trailing at his side, tattered leather boots testing the ice's strength. It was still firm by the bank, although the cracks from the trunk's impact had sent shockwaves and fault lines running right to the river's edge. He glanced back at Gretchen, who held a hunting dagger before her in both hands, one foot stepping toward the frozen river.

"Get back," Trent said. "Stay on the bank—it's not safe!"

"There are *three* of them, Ferran," she said sharply, her eyes never leaving the Wyldermen as they scrambled forward over the shattered ice floes.

She's not wrong, thought Trent. At first he'd thought Gretchen had gone mad, suggesting they should start a fire that evening. If they were to face the Wyldermen, stealth should have been the key, a surprise attack that the wild men weren't expecting. But the Werefox was far craftier than he'd expected. The rotten trunk, the vines, and the ice; Gretchen had seen it all, piecing together a plan while Trent still wondered where they should set up their ambush.

It had taken their combined strength to haul the trunk into the canopy, and Trent had fashioned a makeshift rope out of vines to raise it into position. So much had gone right, yet still three Wyldermen remained standing.

"Stay where you are!" he shouted to Gretchen, who had taken another step forward.

The Werelady growled, not used to taking orders, especially from a human. He didn't care. He'd let Drew down in a stupendous manner, believing the lies of Prince Lucas, Lord Frost, and the others. He would never doubt Drew again, and he would die before letting Gretchen come to any harm.

Trent watched the Wyldermen fan out. The lead warrior swung his ax through the air in front of Trent as his two companions moved to flank the Redcloak. Trent faced him, backing away and changing position, aware that they were trying to surround him. He kept the shore to his right and the river's center to his left. Trent held the black-toothed leader's attention, inviting one of the Wyldermen to move closer to the bank as the last of them was drawn back toward the broken ice. Gretchen backed away, wary of the one nearest the shore, but the wild man's eyes were fixed on the Redcloak, the warrior having already dismissed any idea of a threat from the girl.

As the group rotated about Trent, the last of them was finally directly to his left. Trent wasted no time, lunging at him with the sword. The wild man was out of reach, but the sudden attack caused him to back away a couple of paces, where the weakened ice creaked and groaned under his weight. His arms went out, spear wobbling as he tried to balance. Trent took one more step, ignoring the advancing leader and the one man at his back, and with both hands drove the Wolfshead blade into the ice before him. The shining surface shattered like glass, sending a ravine through the ice floe that ran straight to the Wylderman's feet. The fragile crystal platform collapsed beneath him, and the wild man sank with a scream and a splash, his body swiftly carried away beneath the ice.

Trent tugged at the sword as the lead warrior's ax came down, but it was stuck fast, leaving him for a split second between life and death. He rolled back, tumbling clear, as the ax sent powdered ice into the air where he'd stood. The black-toothed warrior swung again, as Trent scrambled aside, feeling the ice groan beneath his frantic retreat. The ax blows came thick and fast, scything and slashing and only narrowly missing him. He cried out as he struggled desperately to evade the warrior, the arrow wound in his shoulder tearing open through the exertion, his blood rushing out anew.

The other Wylderman was circling, dashing along the river's frozen edge, trying to get behind Trent, intent upon a rear attack. He didn't see Gretchen leap from the bank, and she landed on the wild man's back. Her blade came down toward his neck, but the power of the impact sent them both rolling onto the ice, the knife lunge going wide as the warrior's club flew from his grasp. Skidding to a halt, Gretchen was up on her feet again as he struggled to rise. She kicked out, her heel catching him across the jaw and sending his head flying back. As he fell she pounced, the knife clutched in her hands, arcing down.

The Wylderman's knees rose, catching her in the stomach, knocking the air from her lungs. The knife bounced ineffectually onto the ice beside him, and the warrior hauled

Gretchen over his head as she came crashing down on her back. The Wylderman's club having skittered from his grasp, he now attacked with his bare hands, filthy fingers closing around Gretchen's throat. She moved to stab him, but his bony knee landed on her forearm, pinning it in place. He ground it down, forcing the hunting knife from her grip.

Trent was also in trouble. The ice was splintering beneath him, and the surface ran red with his blood as the black-toothed warrior forced him ever nearer the surging water. He kicked out, and the old wild man leapt clear, giving Trent just enough time to scramble back along the crumbling ice in the direction of his sword. But the Wylderman blocked the move, bringing the ax back down when the youth was only a yard from the blade. Trent turned his face as the flint head caught him a glancing blow and propelled him toward the water. He threw out a desperate hand, finding the Wolfshead blade. His fingers closed around the shining steel edge, provoking a scream of agony from the Redcloak but halting his slide. The two smallest fingers of his left hand lay severed beside the sword where it was buried in the ice, perfect red pools round each of them.

Gretchen spluttered, her eyes bulging as the wild man throttled her, striking her head against the ice. He opened his mouth, sharp teeth slimy with spittle as he brought them down to her face. But by the time his jaws were close to biting point, he faced a very different foe. Russet red hairs had sprouted around her jaw, her hairline closing in around her features as they distorted, shifting into those of the Fox. Her muzzle snapped, catching hold of the Wylderman's lower lip and tearing it from his face. The wild man instantly released his grip, sitting upright on top of Gretchen, his jaw awash with blood as the Werefox lashed out. A succession of blows pounded the Wylderman's face, crumpling his features as she spent her rage upon him. Her clawed hands tore across his unprotected body, striking home and rending the flesh. The warrior looked down, eyes widening, as twin sets of red ribbons appeared in his belly, the claws gouging deep and deadly slashes through his torso. A final shove from Gretchen sent the man tumbling lifelessly away, his body slipping through the broken ice and into the freezing river.

The Wyldermen's leader raised his ax one last time, standing over the young Redcloak who lay helpless on the ice. With a loud cracking noise, the ice floe tilted suddenly, and a jagged platform appeared around the two combatants. Trent held on to the blade for dear life as his feet dipped into the freezing water. The warrior fell, ax flying and landing on the floe as it separated from the ice that adjoined the shore. The platform bobbed back the other way, and the wild man began to slide back as Trent now rose up out of the water. The warrior lashed out with both hands, also grabbing the blade above Trent's grip. The two remained there for a moment before the Wylderman's greater weight began to tilt the ice back his way. Slowly his feet were submerged, followed by his legs, as Trent was able to right himself above him. He stamped down on the warrior's hand as his body came around, and the black-toothed monster let out a fleeting cry as he released his hold on the Wolfshead blade and disappeared beneath the river, carried away by the voracious current.

With the Wylderman gone, the ice floe crashed back down into the water, Trent its sole passenger as it spun into the heart of the river. He snatched at the handle of the Wolfshead blade, looking to the shore as Gretchen, part-transformed, edged across the fragile ice toward him, her arms outstretched.

"Jump, Trent! Leap to me, quick, and I'll catch you!"

He looked at the sword in his hands. His father's sword: the weapon of the Wolfguard. *I can't leave it behind, Pa. I can't. . . .*

Trent pulled with all his might, his bloodied palms trembling as he ripped it free. As the blade emerged from the ice, the twirling platform crumbled beneath his feet, plunging him down into the dark and deadly water. He held his breath, clutching the sword as the current buffeted him, hauling him into the darkness. He kicked for the surface, finding only a sheet of crystalline ice waiting for him, the stars dim in the night sky beyond. Bubbles raced from his mouth and nose as his remaining fingers clawed at the ice, his sword bouncing ineffectually off the translucent coffin lid.

As Trent's last breaths escaped his lungs in a fountain of bubbles, he felt hands grabbing him, snatching at his breastplate from above. Claws connected with the leather, halting his passage, while the water still tugged at him, trying to wrestle him from his rescuer's grasp. But his savior wouldn't be beaten by the current. The hands didn't relinquish their grip, holding firm, inching him slowly up to the shattered hole above. His head emerged from the water as Gretchen dragged him higher, one set of claws over the other as she freed him from the river's dark embrace.

Hauling him clear, Gretchen stumbled as she went, coming closer to the shore with each faltering footfall. She collapsed, rolling Trent over as he let the Wolfshead blade clatter to the ice, coughing up lungsful of foul water, his battered body exhausted. Gretchen cradled him in her lap, steam billowing from their bodies into the frigid night air, nursing his face with broken knuckles. He held her clawed hands in his, examining the cracked and shattered fingers she'd used to pound the ice and break him free. She kissed him on the forehead tenderly. He raised his head, catching her lips with his own.

The Lady of Hedgemoor and the youth from the Cold Coast held one another as the howling of wolves echoed distantly in the Dyrewood.

8

THE CALL OF THE WOLF

THE WYLDERMEN CIRCLED like a pack of wild dogs closing in for the kill. Of the freed people of Brackenholme only twenty remained, the bodies of their brethren littering the floor around the Great Oak alongside a multitude of slain wild men. Harker, Red Rufus, and Milo stood their ground in front of the weary soldiers, awaiting the onslaught. The avianthrope looked down at the wound in his hip, the broken arrow shaft jutting from his bloody flank. Harker breathed heavily while the Werehawk flexed his battered wings. Hundreds of Wyldermen surrounded them. They had withdrawn to regroup and waited to deal the killing blows. The assembled horde carried the markings of over more than thirty different tribes, each keen to participate in the slaughter. The lull in battle allowed

Harker and Red Rufus to inspect each other's wounds.

"Hell of a way to crash to earth, Hawklord," said Harker through bloodied teeth. He held a flint ax, his free hand clutching a leg wound that ran red.

"Was heading for Windfell; must have been blown off-course," said the Werehawk, his wings hacked and tattered by the enemies' blows. Milo, the boy Staglord, snarled beside him, his shortsword raised and ready.

"I'd blame the winter winds," said Harker, his gallows humor provoking no laughter from his exhausted comrade. He shifted the ax in his battered grip. Rank upon rank of Wyldermen lined up, ready for the final attack. The whispered prayers of the surviving Greencloaks echoed like a ghostly chorus around the Great Oak.

Red Rufus was well aware that the end was nigh: once the wild men came at them, he and the Greencloaks would be crushed beneath a wave of weapons. He looked down at Milo, and the lad glanced up at him.

"It's been a pleasure to fight by your side, Staglord," said the Werehawk. The boy's fierce expression softened, as if realizing this was Red Rufus's way of saying good-bye. Milo said nothing, nodding his understanding to the old Hawk and turning back to the Wyldermen.

"What are you waiting for?" bellowed Red Rufus, clawing at the muddy earth with his huge taloned feet.

The line of Wyldermen rippled, some stumbling back

warily as the Hawklord let loose a bloodcurdling cry. The twang of a bow preceded the whistle of an arrow as a deadly missile sailed from the horde toward the screaming Werehawk. It never hit its target. Milo was fast, leaping up in front of the old Hawk, the arrow striking home and dropping him to the cold, bloody mud.

Red Rufus looked down at Milo's body. When the Hawk's head came up, his huge eyes were black as pitch and he was bent upon vengeance. He screeched and bounded over the boy, long knife raised, Harker and the Greencloaks following. Before they could meet, the Wyldermen's ranks broke as a new enemy assaulted them from behind. The Hawklord caught the snarls and growls, not from the wild men, but from the beasts that tore into them. As his knife cut into the first Wylderman, he saw flashes of gray fur, the color of dark steel.

The wolves had come.

Whitley rose from the floor beside the dais, a hand to her forehead. She blinked as warm liquid pooled in the corner of her eye, the deep gash along her brow bleeding profusely. It had all happened so fast. The fire had been doused by Vala, plunging the room into an impenetrable fog, and no sooner had Drew unsheathed his sword than the Wereserpent had struck.

Vala went straight for Drew, her attack entirely focused on the young Wolflord, Whitley having served her purpose. She was the bait in the Serpent's trap, the lure that had brought her the Werewolf. Whitley had bounded forward, trying to draw the charge away from her friend, but the tail end of the giant snake had lashed out like a bullwhip, striking her in the chest and catapulting her back up the steps, into her father's throne. She had lain there for a moment, concussed, staring into the hot smoke as it rolled overhead.

The sounds of battle gradually attracted her attention, pulling her from her stupor as she caught sight of Drew's pale blue sword cutting through the smog. Occasionally the glowing blade flashed away, swallowed by the shadows, the Wereserpent's coils swirling around the Wolflord like a monstrous vortex. Drew lashed out, deflecting blows from the creature, battered this way and that by her relentless barrage. Another snap from the tail sent the sword flying from the Wolf's hand, and it clattered to the floor in the darkness.

Whitley staggered down the steps, gathering her senses. The steam and smoke boiled around her, choking and blinding her in equal measure. She stumbled, tripping over something large and heavy at her feet. She dropped to her knees, feeling the lifeless form of one of Vala's bound prisoners, laid out across the floor like the dead on a battlefield. She craned her neck, lifting the limp body until she could make out its face. It was one of the serving girls from the hall's kitchens, her skin icy to the touch. Her death had been anything but peaceful. The duchess lay somewhere else in the gloom, beside her lady-in-waiting, Vala having struck each survivor in turn before laying them down in a neat row. Was the duchess also dead; had the poison worked its foul magic on her? Whitley gently lowered the girl's head to the floor as Drew's pained roars pulled her to her feet. Her immediate concern was her friend, and the danger he was in. As she rose, she felt a growl emanating from the center of her torso, her ribs reverberating. Hot tears raced down her face as she grimaced, her teeth aching, thrumming, threatening to tear free. She advanced through the darkness toward the two battling therianthropes, each growing more distinct with every footstep.

Vala had Drew wrapped tightly in her enormous black coils, her bright purple underbelly pulsing as she constricted her victim. Whitley snarled, and the Bear's fangs burst through her straining gums with a rush of blood. Black claws emerged from her fingertips, her delicate hands shifting in size from those of a girl to the broader, heavier paw of the beast. She leapt forward, arms raised, slashing down to cut mighty gashes through the snake's tight skin. White flesh bulged from the wounds, dark blood arcing as the Wereserpent released her grip. The beast unwound itself from the young Werewolf, striking Whitley hard and sending her tumbling into the fire pit. She rolled away, covered in nuggets of smoking coal.

Wolf and Bearlady were briefly reunited, Drew dashing to Whitley's aid as she hauled herself to her feet. Before Drew could speak, the Serpent's rattling tail whipped out of the smoke again, snaring Whitley around the ankle and hurling her into the ramshackle nest.

"Sssstay out of thissss, little urssssanthrope! Your time sssshall come sssssoon enough!"

Whitley felt as if Brackenholme Hall had collapsed on top of her, timber, rubble, and broken furniture striking her. Chairs, desks, beams from the ceiling; all manner of splintering, shattering objects landed on top of her as the Wereserpent's lair threatened to bury her. The tail disengaged from her leg, slithering away, leaving the Bearlady for dead.

Whitley lay motionless as the rubble continued to fall, buried in the wreckage of her father's throne room. Her mouth and lips were coated with dust and blood, her eyes refusing to focus as her limbs failed to respond. She wanted to move, to free herself from the mass of twisted timber, but all strength had fled her weary body. *Am I to lie here, broken and beaten, while Drew faces Vala alone? He's traveled from Brenn knows where to come to our aid. He's lost a hand, his loved ones, and friends—faced so many horrors—and still risks everything to save me. How can I possibly help him?*

Nearby, she could hear the Wereserpent preparing for the killing blow, Vala's laughter cutting through the dark like a dagger, while the Werewolf was helpless in her coils, utterly at her mercy. With lightning-quick strikes her head battered Drew, smashing him repeatedly, each blow like that of a warhammer. Whitley turned her head to one side in the rubble, her every movement agony, and her eyes were drawn to a pale blue light nearby. The object was solid, substantial, and the thin band of illumination stood out starkly against the dark, the gloom ripped open by an azure flash. Stretching and straining, she reached out, fingers trembling as her claws snagged the white gemstone at one end. Whitley tugged, drawing the object closer, and the blue light moved across the floor.

She felt the handle of Drew's sword in her palm, her fingers tightening around its white leather binding. She thought about her father, her brother, her mother, and family. She thought about Brackenholme and the atrocities the Wyldermen had carried out in Vala's name. She thought about Drew, close to death in the Wereserpent's grasp. And just when she thought all hope was gone, her courage and strength began to build, a catching, flickering flame like the glow of the pale blue sword.

"Thesssse are your lasssst breathssss, Wolflord," said Vala. "Your people die below ussss; my Wyldermen sssslaughter them assss I sssspeak. We sssshall have a banquet thissss night, with your flessssh the greatessssst offering to the Wyrm Goddessss!"

Drew clawed in vain with his one good hand, but Vala tightened her grip, working her coils over his body, drawing him in, his arms disappearing beneath her squeezing flesh. Her head swayed above him, one emerald eye fixed on him, the other missing, a weeping wound in its place.

"Who spoiled your pretty features, Vala?" Drew choked out. "You had two eyes the last time we met!"

"Your red-haired lady friend did thisssss!" she spat, rage coursing through her and rattling Drew's bones. "There will be a reckoning. I sssshall dine on Fox after I've had my fill of Wolf and Bear!"

Drew saw Moonbrand rise in the air behind Vala, levitating in the gloom as if by magic; his eyes widened, unable to hide his surprise. The Serpent noticed and turned suddenly, whipping her head around as the sword cut through the steam and smoke.

Whitley unleashed a roar as she plunged the blade home, Moonbrand disappearing into the Wereserpent's good eye. Vala rolled and spun, lashing out with her tail, but the Werebear held on tight, the sword stuck fast, embedded in the monster's huge skull. With each thrash and judder, the coils slackened, until Drew was able to pull his arms free. Into the black flesh went the clawed hand, down into the skin went his teeth, as lycanthrope joined ursanthrope against their foe.

The Werebear held on tightly to the Serpent, as Vala heaved her head one way and then the other. One clawed paw remained buried in the Wyrm's scales while the other kept a tight grip on the sword handle, refusing to relinquish her hold. Vala's head came back down, snapping inches away from Drew, her wound lit up in grisly detail by Moonbrand's pale blue light. She was striking blind, her fangs ripping into her own skin as she tried to find the Wolf in her coils and to throw the Bear from her head.

Vala trembled suddenly, as the Werebear shifted on top of

her enormous, hooded head. Whitley reached down with her free hand into the gap between Vala's fangs. Her claws sank into the soft flesh of the Wyrm's upper palate, taking a firm grip. She tugged hard, yanking the Serpent's head back. As the Werebear pulled at the top of Vala's huge skull, the Werewolf threw all his strength onto the bottom of it, his claws digging deep into the pink muscle of her jaw.

Wolf and Bear roared as one as they tore the Wereserpent's jaws apart with a sickening *snap*, the monster's head and body going instantly limp, leaving the two therianthropes to tumble to the floor. Drew pushed the rolls of Vala's flesh away, crawling over the beast until he could take Whitley in his arms.

Standing over the slain Wereserpent, the two held one another, no words needing to be spoken. Their human selves were fast reappearing, dark fur shifting beneath their skin as warm flesh touched. In a moment, they were just a young man and woman, alone in a sea of smoke.

9

THE BONE AND THE BARGAIN

STEP A LITTLE closer, dear brother. It can't hurt. . . .

Hector edged closer toward the parapet edge, goaded on by his dead brother's words as the wind raced around him. The vile flitted across his shoulders, whispering in his ears, its excitement building as the magister neared the precipice. A tumbledown wall, barely a foot high, was the only barrier, and great pieces of masonry were missing where time and the elements had worked their magic. The Boarlord stopped suddenly, a squall of snow battering the tower top and blinding him momentarily. He raised his blackened hand across his face, covering his eyes until the blizzard cleared. The wind dropped, the snowstorm lessening, allowing him to look out over

Sturmland once more, standing atop the giant tower known to all as the Bone.

A few hundred feet directly below was the great arched roof of the White Bear's palace, a complex spine of white stone and bleached timber hulking over Icegarden. With intricate flying buttresses supporting its great weight from the north and south, it reminded Hector of a monstrous spider whose enormous stone limbs straddled the city. Farther below, house lights shone on the snow in the street, the city's inhabitants clustered around the base of Henrik's grand palace. Beyond the great ice walls the slopes of the Whitepeaks shone blue under the moon and stars, the vast frozen meadows rolling south toward the Badlands.

The wind tugged at Hector, snatching at his cloak and making him wobble where he stood.

So very high, brother, and to think . . . you used to suffer from vertigo as a child!

The Vincent-vile was correct, of course. In addition to the many physical ailments Hector had endured in his early years, he'd had many phobias, and one of his greatest had been of high places, yet here he was, conquering the fear. Even a visit to Bevan's Tower in Highcliff would have brought on the jitters when he was a boy. Now the Boarlord's residence in Westland had very different and dark connotations, having been the scene of Vincent's death at Hector's hand.

"Bevan's Tower; my world turned upside down that day," he whispered. "It's yet to right itself."

I'd say you got the better part of the deal, brother, hissed Vincent bitterly.

The campfires of Duke Henrik's army could be clearly seen several leagues away, dotting the length of the palisade wall the Sturmlanders had constructed across the mountains. The battlement wound up and down, an undulating black ridge on the horizon, like a monstrous serpent cresting a sea of snow. Farther south were the Badlands proper, the bandit lands dotted with their own glowing campfires as the Lion's army gathered for battle. Hector brought his eyes back to his eyrie, the Bone Tower rising high into the heavens, dwarfed only by the magnificent Strakenberg at his back. He still couldn't quite believe that he'd seized the city, that his plan had worked.

Everything had happened so fast he'd hardly had time to stop and breathe. Carver and the child had nearly caused chaos, eavesdropping on his plans, but that little fiasco had been nipped in the bud. The Thief-lord had been subdued by Hector's most faithful Boarguard, Ringlin and Ibal making short work of the old rogue. The girl had given them the slip, but Hector didn't much fancy her chances in the wild. The temperature had dropped below freezing with nightfall, and the mountains were sure to claim her scrawny life. And now he stood atop Icegarden—his city—pondering his next step.

Your next step? asked Vincent, none of Hector's thoughts sacred or secret. There was nothing the magister could think that wasn't open to comment from the vile. *That's a giddy thought, brother, so high up. So close to the edge. Just imagine. One step . . .*

Hector shook his head, blinking, his vision blurring as the vile's words washed over him. He found himself leaning farther forward, looking down the entire length of the Bone Tower, the white masonry fading into the darkness below. Hector's stomach lurched as he took a nervous step backward, away from the drop. Vincent had fallen silent, for now. Although Hector had mastered the vile, the phantom's powers of suggestion could never be underestimated, its words both poisonous and intoxicating depending upon its mood.

A shadow flitted over the tower top, causing Hector to turn and look up. A dark shape passed over the moon above, circling sharply as it drew swiftly nearer. Hector glanced to the open stairwell a few feet away, tempted to call for Ringlin or Ibal, but realizing that even if they heard him it would take them too long to reach him. He tugged the jewel-encrusted dagger from his belt and glared at the approaching avianthrope.

With a few heavy beats of his wings, the Crowlord alighted on the Bone Tower beside Hector, his black taloned feet gripping the icy flags. Lord Flint shook his head, the frill of black feathers rattling as he blinked at Hector with a glassy, dark eye.

"You can put the knife away, Blackhand," Flint cawed, his

470

voice rough as a saw as his features began to shift. Gradually the wings retreated, the feathers and beak disappearing beneath the skin. "I'm no Hawklord, magister. You and I are allies, remember?"

"Indeed," said Hector warily, smiling as he resheathed the blade. The dagger was, of course, for show; the real damage, should it need to be dealt out, would be delivered by the vile. "What brings you to Icegarden, Lord Flint?"

"Matters most urgent, Blackhand. My fears about the Vermirians were well founded. The Rats turned on my men at the gates of Stormdale, betraying us when we were about to seize the city. One of their archers killed my father, leading to a battle within our ranks."

"Grave news indeed," said Hector, studying the Crow. "I fail to see how this affects me, though, my lord?"

Flint sneered, his twisting features contorting once more as they settled back into place. "The Catlords have their favorites, Boarlord. Do you really think—and I mean this with respect—a humble Werelord of the Dalelands can ever rise to a position of power at Lucas's table? Even now Onyx calls for reinforcements from Bast, Werelords from his own continent to surround him and set to work in the Seven Realms. He will discard you, just as he intends to be rid of me and my brethren."

"You talk of ifs and maybes, Flint. I am Lord Magister to Prince Lucas, an important member of the King's Council. My position is not under threat."

"Oh, really?" said the Crow, stroking his crooked jaw as he stepped alongside the Boar. He straightened the uneven waxy hairs over his black eyebrows as he peered over the edge to the city below.

He is bluffing, brother; do not listen to him, Hector!

"What have you heard?" asked the magister, unable to refuse the bait.

Flint shrugged sheepishly. "I suppose I shouldn't say anything, but as the Catlords show their true colors I see no reason to hold my tongue. We all know that Lucas hates you. And now Onyx distrusts you—you're a loose blade, too powerful and unpredictable. That little show with the dead scout back in the camp spooked the big cat properly. Well, the Beast of Bast would see you carry out your mission and then have me carry out mine. . . ."

Hector backed away a step, his retreat inadvertently bringing him closer to the edge.

"What do you mean?" he hissed, flexing his left hand, ready to unleash the vile at any moment.

"You've served your purpose in Onyx's eyes. You've got the city, and Henrik's out on a limb and likely to be cut down. The Werepanther wants the keys to Icegarden, Blackhand. And if that means peeling them out of your cold, dead hands, then so be it."

Hector brought his emaciated limb up suddenly, the black palm open, fingers splayed.

"Whoa!" exclaimed Flint, backing up a step. "Steady, Blackhand. We're allies, remember? Whatever task Onyx would have me do, rest assured I've no intention of seeing it through."

Hector glared at the Crow, a heartbeat away from unleashing the vile.

Let me have him, brother. This would be so sweet . . . a therianthrope kill . . .

"You would lose everything by turning against Lucas and Onyx, regardless of the atrocities in Stormdale," said Hector. "You'll be just another enemy to add to the Lion's long list, someone else to crush as the Cats subjugate Lyssia. Can you not reconcile your differences with the Rat King?"

Flint shook his head, grinning grimly. "Lucas is fond of his Rats. I am not. This is the opportunity I spoke to you about, Blackhand. This is the chance for you and me to forge a new power in Lyssia. My army moves this way, waiting for our direction. It was but a fraction that worked under War Marshal Vorjavik in Stormdale. My men of Riven, joined with your warriors of Tuskun: was there ever a more savage army?"

He makes a convincing case, Hector.

"You say your army is already on its way? Have you not considered the conditions, the dangers?"

"A bit of snow is nothing for the men of Riven to fear. We're a mountain breed, not like these soft folk of the south. They will be here in a matter of days, under the command of Lord Scree. Onyx is oblivious to our movements, and we've kept a constant eye from the sky to ensure that remains the case. The armies of the Lion and the Wolf can throw whatever forces they have left at these walls once they've beaten each other to death. Only the long sleep awaits them at our feet, Blackhand."

Flint held his hand out to the magister, awaiting the other's. Hector could find no more words, no counter to the Crowlord's argument. If Flint was to be believed—and his view was convincing—then it appeared the magister had no option. A union with the Werelords of Riven was the only way forward. Hector reached out, allowing the Crow to grasp his wizened hand. Flint squeezed tight, pulling the Boarlord into an embrace. Some of the avianthrope's oily black feathers had yet to recede from his chest, and the young magister spluttered as they brushed his face, the sensation at once tickling and revolting him.

"We keep this between ourselves for now," said the Crow, clapping Hector's back. "We mustn't alert Onyx to our plans. Let him think you and I still serve him; let him believe we're his lackeys and unaware of his machinations. We will strike when he least expects it."

Flint craned his neck, whispering into Hector's ear as he held the magister's head to his dark bosom. "We have to keep our enemies close. . . ."

10

BETTER LATE THAN NEVER

IF THE WOLF'S Council that had governed Westland had seemed a peculiar crowd, it paled in comparison to the motley group who had gathered in its name in Brackenholme. The throne room was still in disarray, Vala's occupation having taken its toll on the Great Hall, but in time, like the city, it would be returned to former glory. *It'll be an age before my mother can chase Vala's stench away*, thought Whitley as she sat in her father's seat, looking across the chamber. Her first act as Lady of Brackenholme was to promote Captain Harker, a long overdue honor. The newly titled general stood a few steps down the dais, his face unreadable. He was black and blue with wounds and bruises but had refused to be tended to. His place was beside his lord or lady.

The boy from Stormdale stood beside the throne, keen to remain close to Whitley. Milo was a shadow of his former self after the battle he'd endured at the foot of the Great Oak. His eyes were lidded but unblinking, staring into nothingness. The young Stag had shown great bravery, leaping in front of an arrow destined for Red Rufus's heart, and only his father's shining breastplate had saved him from being gored with it himself.

A dozen assorted Greencloak and Greencape officers stood on either side of the hall, heroes of the battle of Brackenholme to a man and woman. It warmed Whitley's heart to see some familiar faces among their number, including Tristam and Quist, survivors of the escape from Cape Gala. Another of those soldiers, Machin, had been less lucky, killed during the initial attack on the Great Oaks. The events in the Horselord city seemed so very long ago now, although it was only a matter of months. *So very much has happened, so many lives lost.*

A handful of Romari zadkas had also gathered, the male elders of the traveling people who had rushed to the aid of Brackenholme in the final hour arriving in great numbers along the Dymling Road. Baba Soba, leader of the Romari, stood before them, her sightless gaze fixed on Whitley. The giant, Yuzhnik, stood beside her, Whitley catching a wink from him as her gaze passed by. The wound Darkheart had dealt him during Gretchen's escape had been left untreated, festering and causing the surrounding flesh to go bad. He was a shadow of his former self, his imprisonment in the corral at the foot of the Great Oak having left him close to death's door. The healers in the White Tree had since seen to the injury, but it would be some time until Yuzhnik would be truly mobile again, if ever.

The blind old woman had been escorted straight to the Great Oak as her people entered the city, choosing Yuzhnik to be her eyes, the fire-eater having been so deeply involved in all that had occurred that Soba could think of no better companion. He was another whom Whitley could trust with her life, as the vagabond player had supported her through thick and thin. Yuzhnik had helped Gretchen escape from the Great Oak when the Wyldermen had struck. The Werelady had escaped with Stirga and the Redcloak, as they were currently discussing.

It was Baba Soba who spoke. "The boy's name was Trent Ferran. He was the brother of the Wolf."

"He was a Redcloak, though," said Quist, her voice fiery. "You saw it with your own eyes, did you not?" She bit her lip as the words came out, instantly regretting her turn of phrase.

"Not quite"—the blind soothsayer laughed, tapping her temple with a bony finger—"but I saw into his heart. The young man had nothing but love for Drew Ferran, surrounded by layers of grief and regret. He will not do wrong by the Lady of Hedgemoor. Do not doubt his loyalty."

"I fought alongside him myself," said General Harker. "Try not to worry, Quist."

The tall woodlander grimaced. "I can't help it, sir. Any man who dons the Red . . . well, that speaks volumes to me."

She remembers the ambush in Cape Gala by Redcloaks, thought Whitley. The Bearlady had been there herself, watching in horror as the soldiers of the Woodland Watch were cut down by the Lion's men.

"Try not to worry, friends," said Yuzhnik, speaking up at last. "My old friend Stirga is with them. Should this Ferran boy prove unfaithful—and the baba says he won't—then the minstrel's rapier will find his heart."

The fire-eater's words suddenly stirred Milo from his trance, and the boy left Whitley's side to retreat down the steps to where his saddlebags still lay. As the hall was uninhabitable, every soul carried their belongings with them. The clean-up was already under way, and the sound of people working echoed through the treetop beyond the broken walls and windows.

"Are you all right, Lord Milo?" asked Whitley, alarmed by the boy's strange behavior. He had insisted on following Drew and Red Rufus from Stormdale as the Werelords had ridden for Brackenholme. The adventure he'd so desperately sought had proved far more damaging to his spirit than he could ever have imagined.

The young Staglord returned from his kit bag, cradling something in his arms. He stepped gingerly past Whitley, down the steps of the dais, and toward the Romari. Yuzhnik saw what he carried, his arm falling away from the baba's grip

478

as he limped forward to meet the boy in the center of the throne room. The boy gently handed the item over: a broken lute, its neck splintered, its strings snapped. The big man looked at the musical instrument, tiny in his huge hands. He nodded to the boy, no words passing between them. Whitley wanted to cry, wanted to sob for the loss of another of her friends, but she couldn't, not now; the time for mourning would come. For now, she had to be strong, for Brackenholme.

"What of the wolves?" she asked, leaving the lame Romari and the boy from Stormdale in one another's grief-laden company.

"They remain within the city, my lady," answered Baba Soba. "They're gathered below the White Oak presently."

Duchess Rainier was convalescing in the White Oak, where the healers cared for her and others who had been injured during the Wyldermen's reign of terror.

"I know they're kin to Lord Drew, but they give me the shivers," said Tristam.

"You've nothing to fear from the wolves," said Baba Soba. "They're proud, noble animals. They answered his call."

Hundreds of wolves had poured into the city after Drew's howl had shaken Brackenholme and the surrounding forest. It was the wolves that had turned the tide in the battle, drawing the Wyldermen away from the Greencloaks as they tore into the wild men in packs. The Romari had surged through the Dymling Gate next, having ridden north from the Longridings to the aid of the Wereladies, breaking the ranks of panicked wild men. *Better late than never*, mused Whitley, thankful for the presence of their saviors.

"I must ask the question," said Baba Soba. "What is to be done next?"

"We must secure Brackenholme," replied Whitley. "Repair the defenses, reinforce the palisades. The Wyldermen may yet return."

"The Wereserpent may no longer lead them," said Harker, "but there are others who may try and step into her void. Darkheart is still at large, unaccounted for among the fallen Wyldermen."

Whitley sneered at the mention of Vala's right-hand man, the monster who had posed as Rolff.

"But you're correct," continued Harker. "The walls do need our immediate attention, the gates especially. Those people unscathed who were holed up in the Garrison Tree can be put to work immediately. I suspect we'll have to argue with the injured to keep them in their beds, such is the desire of Brackenholme's people to repair their spoiled city."

To Whitley's relief, the Wyldermen hadn't slain all the inhabitants of her city, although not a single family survived untouched by their murderous rampage. Many hundreds had fled to the Garrison Tree, making their stand against the enemy from within its blackened trunk. The wild men had laid siege to the enormous oak, trying to burn its wizened bark and hacking at it with axes, but the ancient tree had withstood attack by flame and flint, impervious to harm. When the wolves and Romari had arrived, the defenders had sallied forth, joining the battle, finally meeting their foe in the streets of Brackenholme.

"The rebuilding won't be accomplished fast," added Harker. "It will take years for us to return Brackenholme to its former glory, but thanks to your aid in our time of need, my lords, we can begin today."

"And the remaining force of the Catlords?" said Whitley. "They've taken the Dalelands and Westland for their own. The Longridings is lost, with only the Bull, Duke Brand, and Lord Conrad's surviving Horselords providing resistance in Calico."

"Many Romari still fight in the Longridings," interjected the old Romari woman. "All is *not* lost."

"I thank you once more for coming to the aid of Brackenholme, Baba Soba," said Whitley.

The baba smiled and nodded. "The Wolf's allies are everywhere," she replied.

One of the Romari zadkas spoke up. "Lord Drew's friends may indeed number many, but they're fractured and far-flung. Word reached us that Prince Lucas's greatest army has gathered in the Whitepeaks, under the command of Onyx, the Beast of Bast. Icegarden's their goal," said the man. "If Duke Henrik falls, that truly leaves no one to stand in the prince's way. He could crown himself king tomorrow if he likes: this is no longer about gathering a majority decision from each of the Seven Realms."

"It's conquest that Prince Lucas seeks," said Baba Soba quietly. "Total subjugation of the free people of Lyssia."

"This is all well and good, discussing what the next course of action is," said Harker, looking around the room at the assembled counselors. "But we're missing a vital voice in any decision making."

"I shall speak with him," said Whitley, walking down from the dais and striding from the throne room.

Drew sat on the stool beside the bed as the magister stepped away. The Wolflord said nothing, his eyes fixed on the bed. Patting his shoulder once, the healer turned to the open door, finding the Lady of Brackenholme at the threshold. Standing to one side, Whitley smiled awkwardly as the magister left the chamber, the door swinging shut behind him. The air in the room was thick with incense, smoking herbs having alleviated the falconthrope's suffering. Whitley walked over to Drew, coming to a halt beside him and crouching by his side. His sword was propped against the wall beside his backpack, his weapon belt hanging from the scabbard, trailing to the floor. She placed her arm around his shoulder and followed his gaze to the deathbed.

Drew held the bony hand of Red Rufus in his, the Hawklord's

scarred and bloody knuckles broken from battle. A thin white sheet was draped over the old bird, folded back beneath his chin, and she had the impression of a man sleeping peacefully. His eyes were closed, never to reopen. Candles burned on either side of the bed, their perfume masking the grim smell of the injured body. A wooden pail stood in the corner of the room, full to the brim with blood-soaked bandages.

"The injuries were too severe," Drew whispered, biting his lip.

"Were you here? When he passed?"

Drew nodded mournfully.

"We spoke." Drew sniffed, a brief laugh catching in his throat. "He called me a wet fool for crying: he was a curmudgeon to his last breath."

"I never knew him," said Whitley, resting her head on Drew's shoulder. "It sounds as though you grew quite close to each other."

Drew smiled.

"In a strange way we did. We may not have agreed with one another very often, but Red Rufus was as brave a man as I ever met. I'll miss him, and his foul temper."

The Hawklord had taken the fatal blow at the base of the Great Oak, the wolves and Romari arriving a moment too late to prevent a Wylderman's spear from being driven clean through him. His heart had stood in the blade's path, and the wild man hadn't missed.

Whitley patted her friend's back. "They're waiting for you in Brackenholme Hall. They won't make any decisions without you."

"Makes a change from your father's style, Whitley; I was the last person he'd consult when deciding what the Wolf's Council would do."

"Maybe they've learned from his mistakes," she said, only half joking. It was well known that Drew and Bergan hadn't often seen eye to eye, with the Bearlord having the final say in all decisions.

"Perhaps they see me as a man, a boy no more?"

"I wouldn't go that far," said Whitley. "You still have an astounding ability to get yourself into trouble." She placed her hands over the stump of his left wrist, Drew twitching at her touch before allowing her palms to settle over it. "Does it still hurt?"

Drew's eyes remained on Red Rufus. "It's nothing, in the grand scheme of things," he said, rising from the stool.

"And talking of grand schemes, what do you intend to do?"

Drew turned to her, startled for a moment. *If I'm a boy no more, then what's Whitley?* She bore little resemblance to the scared tomboy scout he'd met in the Dyrewood so long ago. Her hair was braided, piled on top of her head in the fashion of a noblewoman of the Bearlord's court. She wore a long ivory dress, laced with tiny flowers along the cuffs and throat. Her big brown eyes stared into his intently, searching for an answer.

"All roads seem to lead to Icegarden. If that's where Lucas has headed with his army, would it be rude if I didn't join him? We are family, after all," he added grimly.

"And Gretchen?" asked Whitley, her eyes still fixed on his.

"She disappeared into the Dyrewood, a Redcloak in her company. Not my choice of bodyguard, but if he can keep her safe, he may be able to buy a pardon. Whoever he is, if he harms her—"

"Hush," said Whitley, placing a finger to his lips. "You haven't heard. The Redcloak who's with her—it's your brother, Trent."

"What?" Drew rocked on the stool, the news hitting him like a body blow. His vision blurred momentarily, a light-headedness washing over him, threatening to send him to the floor. "How can that be? Trent a Lionguard?"

"I don't know, Drew. But he's your brother, all right, according to the Romari."

Drew suddenly felt torn as never before. To hear that Trent lived was joyous news, tempered by the knowledge that he'd taken the Red with the Lion. That Gretchen was out in the wilds with his brother as her companion provided solace, but in the Dyrewood with a Lionguard? Drew felt fresh nausea rise. Pinching the bridge of his nose between thumb and forefinger, he tried to chase away the building headache. When he closed his eyes he saw two faces: Trent and Gretchen. *Are you still my brother, Trent? Or my enemy?* The more he thought about it, the more the pain intensified. Lyssia: that was his priority. A battle awaited him, greater and more terrible than any other he'd faced, the lives of all in the Seven Realms depending upon his actions. He could let nothing stand in the way of his destiny.

"So Lucas marches on Icegarden, his army led by Onyx? Duke Henrik awaits the Catlord forces in the field alone?"

"Who could come to his assistance?" replied Whitley. "His neighbors are overrun. Westland and the Dalelands belong to Lucas. My father, if he lived, would ride to Henrik's aid, I don't doubt it, even with a depleted Woodland Watch."

"There are other Bearlords in the forest, are there not? You need to regroup, rebuild the Greencloak army as best you can. Prepare for the worst; Lucas is not done with the Woodland Realm, Whitley. Brackenholme is still a target for our enemies, and you need reinforcements. Your uncle, Baron Redfern— if word hasn't yet been sent to Darke-in-the-Dyrewood, you should do so."

"I'll speak to Harker, see that it's done."

"And still no news from Azra," added Drew.

"Nothing," said Whitley bitterly.

Drew had hoped that the war in the east might have ended favorably, with the Hawklords having flown to King Faisal's side. A vast army had marched upon the Jackal's lands, bolstered by ranks of Doglords. With no news having reached them of their allies' fortunes, he feared the worst.

"And Calico is besieged," said Whitley. "The Horselords

486

remain trapped within Duke Brand's city, unable to take to the field. The Bastians have blockaded the city by land and sea. The war spreads in every direction, and the balance swings in the felinthropes' favor."

Sturmland in the north, Omir in the east, the Longridings in the south; wars being lost on every front, but there was one point of the compass where hope yet remained. A fledgling idea began to take shape in Drew's head.

"Our answer lies to the west."

"Westland has fallen, Drew. The people may still love you, but the army wears the Red once more. You have no allies there."

"Farther west," said Drew, remembering what he'd heard. "Some brave souls have taken the fight to the Catlords. The White Sea, Whitley; if we find who has been attacking the Catlords' fleet, maybe we find that elusive ally."

"And then?"

"Who knows, but it's a start." Drew looked to the bed, staring at the covered body of his departed friend. He thought of the Hawklord's words and smiled bitterly. "Every journey starts with a small step, every wave a ripple."

Drew reached down and grabbed his weapon belt, swinging it about his waist as he tugged the tongue of leather through the steel buckle. The belt snapped into place, Moonbrand swinging weightlessly on his hip. He turned to his friend, catching her looking at Red Rufus's body. "I need to prepare for the road, Whitley. Is Bravado ready?"

"Our horses are in the stables by the Garrison Tree," she said, pulling her gaze back to the young Wolflord. "They're ready when we are."

"We?" said Drew incredulously. "You're mistaken if you think you're joining me. You need to stay here. Your people need you. Brackenholme needs you."

"My mother's recovering. It's the duchess the people need, not her daughter."

Drew snarled, unimpressed by her remarks.

"I forbid you to come, Whitley. I couldn't abide it if my actions were to put you in further danger."

Whitley growled back, the Wolf's intimidation having no effect on her. "You don't understand, Drew Ferran. It's up to *me* if I want to put myself in harm's way. You don't have a say in this, be you king or shepherd boy."

Beyond the House of Healing, at the base of the White Oak, the wolves began to howl, a haunting song for their brother high above. Drew turned his head to the door, hearing their call.

"Besides . . . " said Whitley, kissing him on the cheek before striding toward the door. Drew's hand went to his face, his color rising. The Bearlady of Brackenholme turned back just once, adding her final words on the matter.

"You still need a scout."

Epilogue
The Dymling Bridge

THE REDWINE RIVER carved a mighty path across Lyssia, cutting through four of the Seven Realms, from the Barebones at its source to Westland, where it emptied into the White Sea. The Dymling Bridge straddled the fast-flowing waters at its halfway point, carrying the road of the same name north into the Dalelands from the dark depths of the Dyrewood. In times long gone, settlements had existed on both sides of the bridge, with its ownership a source of constant dispute. These towns and their inhabitants had long since turned to dust, the stone thoroughfare's proximity to the Woodland Realm attracting the wilderness's more nefarious denizens. The Wyldermen of the Wyrmwood had ensured that the lands around the Dymling Bridge could never again be settled.

The small wooden tower was a new addition to the southern bank, at the point where the bridge met the riverbank. Having taken the Dalelands with little resistance, the Lionguard had built the guard post initially as a temporary structure, their intention being to construct one out of stone once the war in the north finally drew to a close. A larger camp was stationed on the north bank, housing fifty men and a team of fast horses, ready to send for reinforcements should the need arise. The horses remained in their stables, growing idle, the need never having arisen. Who would attack the Lion's forces so deep in their occupied territory?

Six men manned the watchtower, the most onerous shift always that which passed through the witching hour. It was in the dead of night when the tales were told, myths rekindled of the monsters that had once wandered the riverbanks and nearby forest: giants, ghouls, rabid river-hags, and trolls that would snap a man's bones to slurp out the marrow. One such tale was now being recounted by an old Redcloak, newly conscripted from the Kinmoors.

"I swear," said the old soldier, "this whole river is cursed. The river men won't work it at night from here to beyond the Bott Marshes. Haunted, it is."

"By what?" asked his officer, a far younger man, scratching his jaw as he yawned. "The ghosts of other yokels you've bored to death down the years?"

Three more soldiers chuckled as they sat nearby playing

cards, while the last of their number stood atop the wooden structure, enduring the cold winter weather alone. The men could hear the wind howling beyond the walls, snarling at the tower top overhead.

"Mock me all you like," said the old guard. "I grew up around these parts. There's more to fear than them wild men in the Wyrmwood. There's things in the river what ought to be avoided. The Marshmen, they call 'em down my way."

"I've heard enough," said the young officer, rising and stretching. Picking up a lantern, he set off toward the door just as the sound of footsteps could be heard hurrying down the tower from above. He slammed the deadbolts back in their brackets. "I'm off to stretch my legs, if anyone wants to join me. See if I can find one of your bog-trotting Marshmen and shake him by his webbed hand."

He grabbed the door handle just as the duty guard rushed down the staircase, his face white with worry.

"Captain!" he exclaimed. "Don't—"

It was too late. The handle had already turned, and the door swung outward, caught by the wind so it clattered on its hinges. The captain squinted into the white world beyond the tower, the snow and sleet driving across the road and finding its way into the guard room. He could see them now, working their way toward the tower, a band of spectral silhouettes materializing through the gloom. There were maybe twenty of them, their spears and axes carried menacingly at their sides, shaggy hair whipped about by the blizzard. The captain gasped, instinct telling him to shut the door instantly as the Redcloaks at his back began to panic. He reached for the handle, only for a spear to strike the timber, causing him to recoil. He staggered back, drawing his longsword as the first of the figures approached, the whites of its eyes, woad-smeared cheeks, and sharpened teeth catching his lantern light.

The other Lionguard rallied around their captain, all except for the old man who newly wore the Red. As his companions snatched their swords, the veteran storyteller backed away, clawing at the walls, his face pale with horror.

"It's the Marshmen! They've come for us! They'll take us all!"

"The horn!" the captain screamed. "Signal the camp!"

The old man reached for the horn hanging chained to the wall beside him. By the time he'd brought it to his lips, their foes were in the room and a flint spearhead was at his throat. The Wyldermen spread quickly through the guard room, the long reach of their weapons forcing the cramped Lionguard back. The captain made a brief stand, striking out with his longsword, knocking the first spears to one side before one shaft found its way through, striking his breastplate and pushing him back. His knees buckled as the weapon made him tumble, not breaking through his armor, but strong enough to drive him to the floor. The Wylderman held him there, poised to run him through as the other wild men overpowered the

Redcloaks, snatching their weapons from them. The one atop the captain snarled, his razor-sharp teeth bared.

The Wyldermen wore different kinds of battle paints and outfits: blue woad, white skulls, red feathers, black clay. Some wore animal skins; others were barely dressed at all. This wasn't one tribe, the captain realized, as the leader of the wild men finally entered the room, his companions standing to one side. These represented clans from across the Woodland Realm.

The leader of the warriors was tall, his long black hair plastered against his lean, weather-beaten face. He carried a wickedly serrated knife in each hand, the gray flint gleaming as he kept his dark eyes fixed on the captain. He crouched down beside the Redcloak officer, the young man wincing as the spearman who pinned him applied more pressure.

"What do you want?" the captain gasped, his voice breaking with fear.

"You are the Lion's men, no?" asked the Wylderman leader. The Redcloak nodded, tears streaking his cheeks. "You fight the Wolf, then?" the wild man went on, the officer nodding again. "As do we."

"That's good then, isn't it?" squealed the captain, his eyes flitting among the Wyldermen, his men moaning all around him. None of the warriors relinquished the grip on their weapons, still holding the Lionguard at spear-, ax-, and knife-point. "Well, isn't it?"

"I would stop at nothing to see the Wolf killed," said

the warrior, baring his terrible teeth. "Not even death. What lengths would you go to in order to see the Wolf slaughtered, you soft-fleshed town dweller?"

The Redcloak captain licked his lips, words failing him as the Wylderman glared down.

"I am a shaman, as my father was before me, and my blood burns with the old Wyrm magicks. My mistress may be dead, but her fight is not yet done. My name is Darkheart; take me to your chieftain."

STORM OF SHARKS

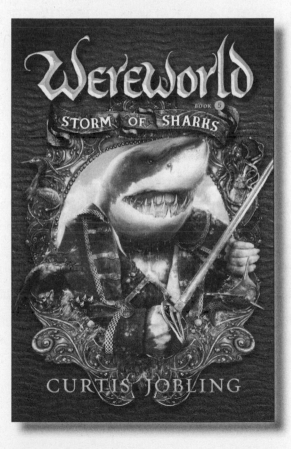

I

LACKEYS AND LICKSPITTLES

WITH WINTER FINALLY relinquishing her cruel hold over the Cold Coast, All Hallows Bay had gradually returned to life. The piers and jetties, home to only the hardiest vessels weeks earlier, were now crowded with boats of all sizes, weatherworn fishing skiffs bumping up against the barnacle-encrusted hulls of their huge, oceangoing cousins. The taverns and inns, so quiet during the harshest months, now thronged with life, sea captains and merchants haggling for bargains while less fortunate souls drowned their sorrows. The streets thrummed with activity, spring bringing hope to the people of the bustling port. All Hallows Bay was alive once more, but it came at a cost.

A Lion once more ruled Westland. The newly crowned

King Lucas had reclaimed his father's stolen throne from the young Werewolf Drew Ferran. The Catlords of Bast had sailed to Lucas's aid, strengthening his hold over the Seven Realms and helping to put the Werelords of the Wolf's Council to the sword. The Lion's ranks had swelled, warriors from across the vast continent of Bast heeding his rallying roar and landing on Lyssian soil. Shape-shifting Werelords of all color and size had marched to support Lucas, their enslaved homelands ensuring allegiance. Lucas ruled with an iron paw, squeezing every copper from his people's pockets and pressing them into his army of Redcloaks. He turned wives into widows as he sought to destroy the last of the Gray Wolves and all who supported Drew.

The Lionguard's presence had never been more apparent in All Hallows Bay. Many of the locals kept a wary distance, the violent reputation of the king's soldiers well-known to all. As with every land under Lucas's control, the Lionguard raised a force from the indigenous population. Though many people were reluctant to "take the red," some were happy to swear fealty to King Lucas. The Redcloaks of All Hallows Bay had a large proportion of the latter, made up of rogues and ruffians. The odd Bastian captain or Lyssian from more noble stock broke up their numbers, but for the most part the Lionguard were a cruel bunch. Rarely a day went by without brutality, ensuring the locals remained fearful of their so-called guardians.

Whitley sat in a booth at the back of the smoke-choked bar,

the hood of her traveling cloak raised around her face. Though she kept her head dipped, her eyes missed nothing, passing over the inn's clientele. There were few present whose homeland she could name. Olive-skinned sailors from the south rubbed shoulders with the pale-fleshed men of the north, granting the Drowning Man a cosmopolitan feel. One fellow strode past her booth, his face wrapped in an Omiri kash, the favored head-dress of the Desert Realm. His eyes narrowed as they caught hers before he joined his companions in the recesses of the bar. Whitley stared into her half-empty mug, avoiding further eye contact. Here she was, one of the most wanted therianthropes in all of Lyssia, right under the Lionguard's noses but lost in a sea of strangers.

She and her companions had witnessed Redcloak justice as they'd made their way down the steep, cobbled streets toward the harbor. The grisly remains of King Lucas's enemies hung from gibbets beside the road as a warning for all. Whether they were guilty of genuine crimes or not, Whitley would never know, but none deserved such a fate. Her father, the Werebear Duke Bergan, had executed men in the past. Such ceremonies were not for public consumption: they were a means to an end, the punishment for crimes committed, and were carried out behind closed doors. The torment ended with the ax blow—that was the law back in Brackenholme. Whitley couldn't imagine the pain the families of the gibbeted criminals were now feeling, their loved ones swinging in the cages, crows and gulls pecking at their corpses. The king's justice was a cruel business, and judging by the number of gallows that lined the streets of All Hallows Bay, business had been good.

"A crowd gathers."

Whitley glanced up, the imposing figure of Yuzhnik materializing beside her table. The Romari strongman squinted through the dirty glass windowpanes to the street outside. Whitley followed his gaze, lifting her head to observe the commotion. Sure enough, a boisterous mob had assembled in the darkness, the blurred red cloaks of the Lionguard faintly visible by torchlight as they led a prisoner through the street.

"Another hanging? Another murder?"

"It's none of our business," replied Yuzhnik, coldly cutting the chat short before their anger could rise.

He was correct, of course, figured Whitley. They weren't in All Hallows Bay to attract attention. The fishing port was a stepping-stone that would take her out to the White Sea, where the true destination lay. Sighing, she pulled her attention away from the window and back to her giant companion.

"Did you find him?"

"I found *her*," said Yuzhnik, scratching his jaw ruefully. "I spoke to her first mate, Mister Ramzi. You'll find Captain Violca aboard her ship, the *Lucky Shot*."